Traditional Lov3 Book 1:
Three Souls Found

Robert L. Cauley

I0675987

Q.E.S.

Quantum Eccentric Studios

Author: Robert L. Cauley

Editor: Carlo DeCarlo

First edition

ISBN 979-8-9919904-0-0

To my beloved wife, Elizabeth,
you have always been my muse

Contents

Opening: Tri-Union

I lay in bed feeling like the luckiest man alive. Filled with an enthusiasm for the future that I cannot seem to contain. Through the labyrinth of life, I had found something... something so rare that it felt like I had entered a state of Elysian. This thing was love. Love in its purest form. Filling the void in the souls of those who possess it. Removing all appetence, ceasing the dire longing to be united. A love that would burn throughout eternity.

My left arm wrapped tightly around Victoria. Her shoulder-length raven hair feathered on my chest. Her face nuzzled in with a caring look even while she slept. Her arm was around my waist. Her leg kicked over my left knee. Her breaths a lyrical sound.

I looked to my right. Sarah cuddled me just as deeply as my other arm held her close. Her face had an angelic glow. Her long legs pinned my right calf to the bed. Her hand clasped across my chest. That long fiery hair that went down to the middle of her cute back smelled so good.

The warmth of their naked bodies filled me with contentment. Their breasts perched at my sides, nipples tenderly jabbing into my ribs. The warmth of their love altars rested on my thighs, a reminder of their passion for me. My body interlocked neatly between them, a testament to how we fit together in tendresse.

Reverie reigned upon me. What luck to be wed to them both. My wives, my beauties. They had become my salvation, my home. Legally, we three cannot be married but that doesn't stop us from being happily united in love.

My mind wandered to the day I met them. The day that changed our three lives forever.

Chapter 1: Gathering of Soulmates

I was napping on the couch. I had spent far too much time in the Texas sun. The muggy heat reflected off the hot pavement of the Dallas streets, making it unbearable. It was only June, the start of the busy season, yet I felt that I needed a vacation. I had been back from Afghanistan for almost half a year, but my body didn't feel like it had fully acclimated from those cold mountains.

I barely got home from a ten-hour shift before exhaustion immediately set in. I'd stripped down to my boxers and crashed hard. The hot sun had beat me into nothing. I lazily dived into the couch and fell asleep. I was too tired to care about the sweat and grime that covered me.

I awoke to a knock at the door. Stumbling off the couch, I answered it in a haze. As I cracked the door, I saw two gorgeous women, their eyes wide once I grudgingly swung the door completely open. Laughter spilled from their lips.

One had lusciously long red hair, like a fiery blaze on her head that hid most of her face. Her breasts perked up; her long legs slightly bent. She towered over me like a winged Valkyrie amid a glorious battle. The other beauty was short, like a diminutive but cute succubus, ready to attack, ready to devour my soul. Her black hair, a darkened veil on her shoulders, cascaded into a cloak of mystique. She was as curvy as the first.

"Sa— sa— sir, um..." The redhead's soft voice stumbled over her words, her eyes fixed below my waist.

"Sir, your pizza," the brunette said with a raspy voice through her giggling.

"Pizza? I didn't order pizza." I looked at them, puzzled, as I tried to figure out why they were giddy.

"This is apartment two-nineteen?" Red questioned, her eyes still fixed below.

"No, ma'am, this is two-seventeen," I huffed, trying to wrap my mind around these two airheads.

"Well, you are an impressive man, I have to say." The dark-haired one chuckled as she looked me up and down. "I'm Vicky; this is Sarah."

1

"Oooh-kay. Hello. So, do you two always laugh and giggle when you deliver pizza?" My eyes started to focus through the sleepiness.

"Only when we see such a massive man like you." Sarah's eyes didn't break from my legs.

I am of average stature, I thought. Toned, yes, but mostly an average physique. "Well, two-nineteen is just one door over. You girls have a good night," I said as I started to close the door.

Vicky held her hand flat against the door, keeping it open. Hot. So damn hot. Her power tugged at my desire to break a woman like her. To make her feel the dominance that I wished I could enact. But not now, Sergeant. Calm your desires. Pizza, let them deliver it.

"Maybe you should call us sometime. Sarah and I get off work in a while." She looked below my belt again and made sure I noticed her looking down.

I finally glanced at what was drawing her attention and realized why they were giggly. Damn, my boner had been full mast this whole time. Straining at the seams, my boxers were about to be torn apart by my manhood. I'm surprised it hadn't already emerged through the fly opening. I must have answered the door with my little guy saluting them. Embarrassed, I held my hands over myself.

"Um... sure." My cheeks flushed with heat.

"Don't be shy now." Sarah giggled, trying to hide her smile.

Flashing like a lightning bolt, I quickly removed Vicky's hand from the door, and she backed away. I took that as my chance to close it, saving myself from further embarrassment. I rested my back on the hard wooden door as I let out a sigh.

They were so stunning. So enticing. Morsels that permeated sensuality, a prowess of sexuality. Unique to each. But I embarrassed myself. There was no way they would go for a geek like me. Especially a perverted one that met them at the door with an erection. My ear listened for a moment to see if they had moved on. I heard rustling and a knock on the neighbor's door. Their sweet voices told the elderly woman that her pizza had arrived.

Mrs. Helderman was a kind lady. We'd talk often even though I'd only moved in a few months earlier. And she was the only person I could speak to without stumbling over myself. She had been widowed some years back and often ate by herself. Dining alone, the same as I did. But sometimes, we would share a meal, and that was when we had our chats.

I eased away from the door and paced back to the living room, seating my shame on the couch. My body ached with such embarrassment. It had been hard to embarrass me since the Army. I was sure I wouldn't get any sleep without properly unwinding from the day and from that mortifying episode. So, I turned the TV on to find something to distract myself from my shame.

The news was roaring over the presidential election. This one said that; that one did this, etc. Always the same, sending my brothers-in-arms to some sad-sack foreign country to fight psychopaths. I didn't care much about who gave the orders, just whose fingers were on the trigger. That's what mattered in the moment. I had my fill of deployments and got out after six years. Two tours were enough. The killing, watching my soldiers die... I'd had enough. My fingers stroked the remote-control buttons, trying to remove those thoughts. I had to find something not so disheartening.

I found solace in my new career as an HVAC technician. Just a few more months, then I could take my contractor's test. Then—boom!—my own business. Goodbye, tiny apartment. Hello, big, beautiful house. And that beater that I was driving would become a nice work truck. Just three more months and a wakeup.

Hoo-ah. I felt that in my bones. To be successful. To be a self-made man. Then maybe find a nice woman with traditional values. Soft and nurturing. A woman that I won't mind having kids with. And we could have fun together as we created our legacy. Maybe she'd be up for my kinkier desires. I always yearned to be successful and find a woman to submit to my every desire. To be mine completely. No desire too great, no wish too taxing. Just the softness of her submission.

I never really fit in anywhere. Even in the Army, I felt like an outcast. But I was good at the job. That 50-caliber machine gun made me unstoppable. That M-4 rifle made me sing the freedoms of my people. But I wished I could fit in with my own tribe. Build a family of my own, with her, whoever *she* was. I just had to find her first.

I turned on Prime. I saw that they had *Secretary*. I loved that movie. Some might find it strange that a movie about a young woman entering an S&M relationship with her boss could be romantic. Mmm… but to me, it felt very romantic. I hit *"Play"* to watch this classic.

The main character, Lee, was almost exactly what I fantasized my bride to be like. Coy and shy to the world, but completely open to me. All her thoughts, all her desires: mine. Subservient yet competitive. She would acquiesce to my every command yet challenge me.

I watched the opening as my feelings of embarrassment started to fade. My mind followed along with the story, dreaming of that woman. How she would be with me. How we would live together in a world of our own. Love each other in a way that we chose. Play together in a way that no one on the outside could understand. Sharing things together that only we knew.

I was near the end of the movie when I heard another knock. I quickly threw my pants on. I wasn't going to get caught off guard again. Pulling my belt closed, I walked toward the door. As my hand turned the knob, the door flew open. Vicky had pushed it open on me. She stormed into my apartment with Sarah following close behind, neither one speaking a word. Their uniforms pulled against their bodies, capturing every curve. My eyes were drawn to their grace and beauty. My mind wondered what treasures those uniforms hid underneath.

Nope. Stop. Think.

"Hello again, sir," Vicky said, her lips tugged at the corners showing the dimples in her cheeks.

"Uh… hello. What the hell are you doing busting into my home," I demanded.

"We didn't 'bust in.' You invited us." Sarah snickered.

"The hell I did." Confusion formed on my face.

Vicky giggled as she pointed at my crotch. "More like *that* did."

"Um… I'm sure you two are lovely ladies, but this is inappropriate." I sighed. "Aren't you two working?"

"Just got off. Now we want to see if you can get *us* off." Sarah smirked with a devilish grin as both ladies brushed past me. Their shoulders rubbed against me as they walked by.

I gave in since they had already made their way to the couch. "Come in, why don't you," I said, the sarcasm dripping from each word. I slowly closed the door, my mind reeling to understand what was happening. To understand why they were here. "Are you going

4

to tell me why two crazy, strange women forced their way into my home?" I couldn't withhold the snark as I moved into the living room.

"Like we said, you sort of invited us. Besides, this place can't be a home," Vicky said condescendingly. "It's just you here. A home is filled with the people you care about the most."

Her tone started to piss me off. What the hell? Just run up and push their way into my own home, then take an arrogant tone with me. Who did these women think they were?

"Oh, okay," I spat out. "Let me be blunt. What the hell are you crazy bitches doing in my apartment?" My frustration boomed through my voice. The non-commissioned officer, NCO, in me, ached to dole out some discipline. But I resisted.

"Feisty," Sarah said with a smirk. "You were right, Vicky. He is a very aggressive type." She looked to Vicky, pleased with my aggressive tone. Her eyes twinkled with excitement.

I sat down in the La-Z-Boy next to the couch, trying to calm myself. I shook my head; this must be a dream. Two beautiful women forced their way into my place, all to...

Huh. Those sexy eyes gazed upon me as I collected myself. Vicky's eyes were crystal blue, like an ocean of deep desire. Sarah's a gilded green, begging tenderly with a longing for something she hasn't found. No way. No way they were here for me. Not women this gorgeous. Maybe this was a prank. Some kind of sorority thing. Or a hidden camera show.

"Is this a prank?" I asked, not really directing my question at either one.

"Prank?" Vicky eyed me with a grim smirk.

"Not a prank." Sarah averted her eyes to the carpet. "We think you would make a great boyfriend. Only one problem."

"What's that?" My eyebrow arched up.

"We can't figure out which of us you would date," Vicky answered quickly.

My mind felt dizzy. I was a nerdy guy. Sure, I was tight and fit. But I was also a nerd. They could clearly see my D&D figures on display in the living room. My kitchen table still had my Magic cards scattered out from the last deck I built. Maybe things had changed since I got back from overseas. Or had I changed? Or were these two

5

bat-shit crazy? I smirked. If we were going to play this game, fine. I would up the stakes.

"Both," I announced. "I'll date you both at the same time."

The world halted. The room was eerily quiet, like the seconds before the gunfire started in a battle. I looked back and forth between them. Sarah's eyes were confused but seemed excited. Vicky had a stern and imposing look. I couldn't read the room. Did I just rid myself of these crazy broads? I fortified myself, ready for the insults and possible crying.

Sarah sighed as she looked at Vicky. "Fine."

YES! Finally, they'd leave. This situation was too bizarre for me to handle. I just wanted to hurry them off so I could get some rest for my long workday tomorrow.

"Okay, both," Vicky said, nodding at Sarah. Sarah nodded her head back in agreement.

WHAT! Both? How the— who— what— My mind stumbled to understand what I'd just done. No freaking way these women agreed to me dating them both. I'd only blurted it out to get them riled up and out of my apartment. I didn't expect them to agree. I figured they would run out of here calling me a pig or an asshole. But they agreed. Fine. They don't know anything about me. That was my chance to get them gone. Convince them that I was a player, or some crazy guy, or a drunk... or something.

"Neither one of you even knows my name. How can you date someone you don't know?"

"Your name is Kyle Forester," Vicky announced with a tinge of coolness in her words. "You're twenty-four. Just got out of the Army. And now you are working on owning your own air-conditioning business."

"Oh, and you're single," Sarah spouted with glee.

How did they know any of that? Aah, Mrs. Helderman. They must have spoken with her. She knew all of that and more. The fact that my parents are dead. My sister, who married a drunk douche bag. All of it. How much did she tell them? It's only been a couple of hours since they were here earlier. Dammit, even just a few minutes of them talking with her, and I was never going to convince them of anything wild. Anything that would send them running for the hills they hadn't already learned.

"Did you know you are excellent boyfriend real estate?" Sarah beamed as she folded her hands together, bringing them to her face. "Government-approved prime meat."

Fine. These insane girls want to play? Okay. I can play games too.

"Show me what I now own," I demanded, trying to screw with their minds. My voice was low and stern. The way I always fantasized about being with women. The way I desired a woman to let me be with her. Dominant and commanding.

"Okay. What would you like to see, sir?" Vicky perked up, excited at the idea.

"First of all, it's Master to you. You both will call me Master. Is that understood?" My voice was cold with that strict NCO command presence. I wanted to see how long it would take before they turned tail and ran.

Sarah smiled. "Of course, you can be our Master."

"Yes, Master, instruct us. What sight would please you?" Vicky peered deep into my eyes.

Damn, that was so hot. Being called Master. These women just gave in to my commands. Submitting. I felt something awakening inside me. No way this was real. No way.

"All of it. Undress. I want to see what I now own." My voice got determined, like I was back on the battlefield.

They sprung up from the couch and wasted no time disrobing. Those uniforms were now just crumpled pieces of cloth on the floor. Panties and bras were thrown down with haste. Every stitch was discarded as if the command was a dire action. As if what I had asked was a direct and imminent salvation to their lives. Even on the battlefield, I had not seen such compliance. Such devotion. I was getting strangely aroused by my power over them. I felt my member pulsate against my pants. They stood in front of me, fully nude. My eyes drank in their beauty.

Both had neatly trimmed bushes in the shape of a triangle. Sarah's a fire-engine red, flaming to be tenderly tamed. Vicky's a dark patch that challenged you to enter if you dared. Sarah's skin was milky white, contrasted by Vicky's darker, tanned skin.

Sarah's breasts hung low with large areolas and tiny nipples. Her body was long but curvy. Her plump figure was glowing with a need to be touched softly.

7

Vicky's breasts perked up at attention with quarter-sized areolas that fostered thumb-sized nipples. She was stout and toned. Her body was sculpted to be caressed with a harsh, dangerous touch. Each was beautiful in her own way.

I had to pick my jaw up from the ground. There was no way that two bountiful women had just rushed into my apartment and then, out of nowhere, started submitting to my commands. Not even in my wildest dreams could this happen.

"Spin," I said, twirling my finger in a circling motion.

They complied without hesitation. Was I in the twilight zone? Did the Army give me some kind of sex-powered booster shot? This was my fantasy—on steroids. They simply complied without protest. Without shaming me. Did they really want this? Did they like this? I shook my dazed state.

The sight of their backsides was something that invoked a coital hunger. I wanted to lean down, to bite each one of them on the butt cheek. Vicky had a toned but bulbous rump. The kind that you could bounce a coin off. Sarah had a plump rear that jiggled as she turned. Her cheeks rested in a nice crease above her thighs. My mouth watered; my hands wanted to touch them... to caress them. To feel those ample bottoms. My palms ached to slap the curves of their derrières.

"Good girls. You can get dressed now." I didn't break my sternness.

They both looked at me with a sense of love in their eyes. It was as if calling them "good girls" were the words they had waited their entire lives to hear. They dressed slowly to make sure that I saw everything that I wanted to.

I started commanding them as a joke and a way to scare them out of my apartment, but now they seemed to enjoy it. I enjoyed it as well, maybe too much. What did I know about them? I had to slow this down before it went too far. Halt it before I had sex with two strangers.

"Is there anything else you need, Master?" Vicky asked as she pouted. Sarah looked up at me with sad eyes as well.

I didn't want to take advantage of these ladies—at least not yet. I am a perv, but not a bastard. I sat in the recliner for a moment, collecting myself.

"I think we are done for the night," I said as I looked at the clock. It was barely 22:30 hours. I didn't feel like sleeping, not yet. But I knew I had to get them out of here before the night had gone too far.

"We can't leave yet... um... Master. What about a date?" Sarah looked at me with a pout in her eyes.

"Yeah, aren't boyfriends supposed to offer a date?" Vicky smirked as she tilted her head.

What do I do with them now? They weren't going to leave... not until I agreed to a date. A date is what they want. My eyes flicked around the room for a moment. I was trying to find something that would be "date" material.

The movie was still paused on the TV. Good. Watching *Secretary* together would tell me a lot about them. Either they would run away in disgust or be more intrigued. Since I barely knew anything about them, it would be a great way to express what I wanted in a relationship without those long explanations.

The movie was about an hour and a half long. We would finish around midnight. Then, we could have a quick Q&A. That way, I could understand whether they were serious about this—if they make it that far into the movie before becoming disgusted and running for the door.

I moved from the recliner and positioned myself in front of the couch. I sat on the middle seat, patting the cushions on either side of me. They moved to each side and sat next to me. I felt virile at that moment. Something had awoken inside of me. Something that I never had. Or had it been there all along, but I'd never had a chance to release it?

"Well, since tonight is sort of our first date. Why don't we watch a movie? I can start this one over again. It has a great story." My voice softened back to normal.

"Um, didn't you just finish watching this, Kyle?" Sarah caught her error as her hand slid up my left thigh. "I mean 'Master.'"

"Yes, you had just finished it before we came in, Master." Vicky said with a hint of a coquettish tone; she seemed to have something else in mind. But for now, I just wanted to get to know them.

I started the movie from the beginning. They offered no further protests. Sarah laid her head in my lap as she watched. Vicky

9

cuddled around my arm. It felt so wonderful to have the admiration of a woman—two women, damn! They watched the movie intently.

"We have never seen this before, Master," Vicky softly whispered into my ear as the opening scene started.

Her warm breath on my earlobe sent shivers down my spine. And being called "Master"... oh God. Every inch of my manhood felt that. My little soldier bounced up quickly, pushing against Sarah's face. She giggled a bit as her cheek felt my member straining to be freed. Calm down. Just relax. I need to be a gentleman. I won't take advantage of them. I won't. I can't. But Sarah's head was right there. Right freaking there on my crotch.

On the TV screen, the main character, Lee, had arm shackles around her wrists while performing various office tasks. The movie proceeded through its run time.

The first time Mr. Grey spanked Lee was the scene where Vicky sighed in a swoon. Was she getting excited by this? Sarah chuckled at the saddle and carrot scene. These women are what I have needed for a long time. But I never thought about two. How was I going to deal with that?

The movie came to its finale. Lee was sitting in the office chair, hands planted on the table, feet on the floor, not moving an inch as he had commanded. That scene was always my favorite. She proved her love through her obedience. Her devotion was so strong.

I had always wanted a woman with that much love for me. My affections to be a mix of hard and soft only for her. Then he took her to wash every inch of her body, carefully caressing her. He cherished every part of her. The quiet marriage with just the two of them. She was his, and he was hers. Then that playful and funny final scene before the credits started to roll.

I ran my hand through Sarah's hair; her head remained in my lap. Vicky was still squeezing my arm. They had made it to the end.

"So, what did you think?" I looked between them to catch a glimpse of their facial expressions.

Sarah looked up, smiling at me. "Cute. It's a cute movie, Master. But three days of not moving from a chair seemed a bit harsh. However, the part after was my favorite. When he tenderly washed her. Cherishing her like she was his goddess."

"I thought it was extremely romantic, Master. That first spanking scene was the most entertaining. And her surprised yet relieved look after the first strike was priceless." Vicky gripped my arm tighter.

"What about the relationship?" I inquired. This question would surely be the nail in the coffin for whatever was happening here.

"I'm not going to lie, Master. The fact that he was her boss was creepy." Sarah sat up. Her green eyes sparkled with a deep, innocent sexiness. "But I loved the way he empowered her. Helping her to get control over her life. She was spiraling into oblivion, yet with his dominant guidance, she became far more than she ever was alone."

"Two orders of spankings for me. Please, Master." Vicky laughed as she released my arm. She continued with a more serious tone in her voice. "But I think it was a beautiful romance. I agree with Sarah; how he empowered her was an inspiring aspiration for any relationship. And that thing she said in the newspaper report. About finding someone to love and play with in a way that only they understood. So romantic."

I was beside myself. They enjoyed the movie. And they both liked the dynamic. Interesting. I felt the blood start to rush to my member once more. Nope, stay calm, Sergeant. I looked at the clock. It was almost 00:30 hours. I had about five or so hours left before I had to get up for work. And my body was too tired to fight back my desires any longer. I had to sleep. If they didn't leave, I would have to call in tomorrow. I yawned a purposefully exaggerated yawn.

"I'm tired, girls. I've work in the morning." I stood, motioning them toward the door.

They stumbled almost in protest. They stood there for a minute, a confused look on their faces. They turned to each other. Mouthing something that I couldn't hear.

Those luscious, plump lips on their gorgeous faces asked—no, begged—to be kissed. Their sultry eyes periodically darted at me, stealing glances as they conversed. The sexiness of their posture was what my mind had focused on, a crisp picture scoped in my sights. Sarah had cocked her hips to the left; her breasts shook as she was whispering to Vicky. Vicky leaned forward into Sarah; her butt poked out, almost inviting me to bite it.

Oh God, go. Please leave. The limits of my sexual desires have been reached more than once tonight. Please leave before I am no longer the gentleman. Hurry, before I can no longer cage the beastly side of my sex drive. Save yourselves before I ravage your bodies. Before I take everything that I crave from you two. Leave. Go. Go!

"Okay," both said in unison. "Good night, Master." It was creepy how they stayed in a cadence in their farewell—creepy yet strangely arousing. They left without further protest.

I closed the door, locking it. Was I locking them out to protect myself? Or was I locking myself in to protect them from the carnal beast within?

Chapter 2: The Lingering Tease

My alarm blasted me awake. I trudged to the shower and jumped in, turning the knob to steaming hot. The water cascaded over my body, but the soothing feeling of the shower couldn't stop my mind from reeling over the night before. Was it real? Who were those women? Did I dream it? I had to have dreamed it. That's it! I must have fallen asleep watching *Secretary*, then dreamed of being sexually dominant, desired by courtesans. Adored by them. Man, even in my dreams, I am such a nerd. My wet dreams throw themselves at me, and still, I don't act.

I finished my shower and dried off. My manhood grew just thinking about those sultry looks they gave me, those tantalizing bodies. Their muffs beckoned me to be inside them. God, stop it, Kyle. It was just a dream, a very hot dream. Stop it. You have to get to work. Get your ass in gear.

I put my uniform on in a flash. I begrudgingly trudged through the apartment. As I briskly passed the kitchen, I looked at the mess on the dining table. Damn, nerd! I will get my Magic cards picked up tonight, I promised myself. As I rushed out the door, my heart felt the deep emptiness that my hollow apartment held. Down the hall, Mrs. Helderman smiled at me with a knowing look. But she didn't say a word to me as I passed. I nodded back. Her grin grew wider. Odd.

I glanced at my phone. Damn! Traffic would be bad at this time. There was no way I could get to work on time now. I took too much time in the shower thinking about that dream. I hurried to my car, pumped the accelerator, and was off. I cleared my head of everything. I had to get to work. I was on a mission. The streets went by without a thought. My crappy car pulled into the lot. I parked and rushed to the time clock. I was cutting it close. There would be hell to pay if—boom! Punched in just in the nick of time.

"Kyle, you okay?" Mr. McKellen asked. My body stiffened at the sound of his voice.

"Sure, boss. Why do you ask?" I felt concerned that he had suspected I was late. Or the van—shit! I hadn't cleaned it. I was sure that I would be in trouble for something.

"You look pale. Are you coming down with something?" His eyes studied me for a moment.

"No, I'm fine. Just had some wild dreams last night. I'm ready to go. After getting my day's call list, I'll jump in the work van." I said, relieved. My body relaxed because he hadn't noticed me rushing in to punch the clock. His policy was to be fifteen minutes early to work.

Myra, one of the work dispatchers, looked at me knowingly as Mr. McKellen left the punch-in area. Her desk was beside the time clock, so there was no escaping the fact that she knew I had rushed through the door, barely clocking in on time.

"You're lucky he didn't bust you for being late." She glared at me with a strange look. I couldn't tell if she would use this as blackmail over me or keep it a secret.

Her blonde pixie-cut hair shimmered in the light. The sheen made it look as if she had a glowing aura around her, almost like an angelic halo that christened her from above.

"But I doubt he would have done anything anyway. In the past few months, you have proven to be one of the best journeymen we have ever had. You put most to shame with how efficient you are. I can barely keep up with your invoices." Myra's words seemed sincere as she tilted her head a bit, continuing to look at me with that strange stare.

My mind snapped to her words. That was the most she had ever spoken to me. And it was a compliment. We barely spoke a word to each other in the few months I had worked here. When she did say something to me, often it was some off-putting or awkward comment. I could never understand her intentions. I couldn't tell if she attempted to joke with a strange sense of humor or if her remarks were meant to insult. But today, she clearly complimented me on my work ethic.

"Thank you," I graciously said. I forced an awkward smile. Her eyes roamed over me.

"If there is anything you need, don't hesitate to call me," she said before staring at me with that strange look again. She bit her lower lip, almost like she wanted to say something more. But not a word came out. The awkward silence felt weird.

After briefly standing still in that peculiar quiet, I felt uneasy and walked on. I went to the briefing room and got my assignments for the day. Then, I headed out to my van.

The van was a mess. I was so tired yesterday that I didn't bother to straighten it up. I was also relieved that Mr. McKellen hadn't inspected my van. I jumped in and drove off the lot. I pulled in when I got to the convenience store down the street. I spent a few minutes composing the van for the day's workload. A sense of accomplishment washed over me as I quickly tidied the van. I was off to my first call without further incident.

The day was long and exhausting, as always. For most of it, I had simple repair calls. A capacitor here, a contactor there—nothing too complex or complicated. However, I had thirteen calls in total— twice as many as the other technicians. Maybe what Myra had said about my efficiency held some merit. But now, the end of the day had finally come, and I was ready to leave.

I made my way home much earlier than yesterday. It was only sixteen hundred hours. Maybe I could visit the hobby gaming store and get some new figures.

I had been thinking about starting a Warhammer 40K army but couldn't decide on Necrons or Eldars. However, the price made me leery of the purchase.

As I climbed the stairs, I saw Mrs. Helderman. She stood perched on the landing near the second floor. That frail seventy-two-year-old body stood with an adeptness of experience. She wore the dress that she usually preferred when visiting the cemetery. Her face seemed to be worried, possibly in pain. I wondered what happened. Had her son visited again? Had she gotten into an argument with his wife again? I approached her with concern.

"Good evening, Mrs. Helderman."

"Oh, hi, Kyle. You look so handsome. Almost thought you were my Jimmy for a minute." Her mouth had a slight twinkle. That was the third time she mentioned her husband in four months.

"Did you visit him today?" I asked, trying to probe into her expression.

15

"Yes, those pigeons had their way with his headstone again. I spent most of the afternoon cleaning it for him." She seemed a bit frustrated but relieved at the same time.

"I bet he is all shined up now." I hoped my words were a soothing encouragement to her.

"I had a long talk with him today about you. I wished he could still answer me. I guess he does in his way." The pain of being a widow had shown through for a moment.

"Oh, about what?" I asked.

"Those young ladies, they seemed nice." Her voice had a sincere tone.

My heart sank. I thought it was a dream. At least I had convinced myself it was a dream, but they were real. They truly existed. I felt at a loss. Strangled with excitement, anxiety, and a bit of shame. Did she know that I was bursting to have them but stilled myself? Did they tell her their plans to seduce me? That I didn't... that I couldn't... She must've thought me a dirty, horny young guy.

"Yeah, I hope the movie wasn't too loud and kept you up too late." I tried to regain my composure.

"No, dear, you didn't keep me up. But I had a long two-hour conversation with them." Her words held a mischievous tone. Then, a wicked smirk grew across her face.

Mrs. Helderman put those two onto me. That smirk told me that she knew what they had planned. She was much more than an elderly woman, that was for sure. You can't judge a book by its cover; it may hide kinky content.

"Oh, what did you tell them?" I questioned with unease.

"Not much. Just that you are a kind young man fresh from the Army." She paused as she tilted her head. Her hands tugged at the sides of her dress before continuing. "And some other girl talk. I didn't think you had it in you, but boy, you have something they both desire." Her arm nudged mine with an odd sort of approval.

"Mrs. Helderman, those girls came back to visit me last night." I watched her intently, trying to read her expressions.

"Of course they did. They told me they were going back to your apartment after leaving mine." She sighed with a playful, inward chuckle. "I figured they had properly broken you back into civilian life last night, huh." She winked at me with an approving nod.

Damn, she was a grandma and still had a sense of sexual liberation. If only I had released my sexual frustrations with them, but I was a coward. I didn't want to take advantage of them. I wanted to be the gallant man that I was raised to be.

"Menage a trois is nothing to be ashamed of, my boy. I remember when Jimmy got back from Vietnam. Hmm... such a fun time..." She trailed off into her memories.

I used her remembrance to escape the awkward turn I figured this conversation was on course for. "Have a good night, Mrs. Helderman." I moved on while she was caught in her memories.

Menage a trois, huh. Would it be possible? They said I could have both. Was it an impulse to agree? Or could it work? I just said it as a way to mess with them. To scare them away. But instead, I may have started something that I was unsure if I was equipped to handle.

As I strolled down the hall, I noticed distinct silhouettes in front of my apartment door. It was them. Vicky and Sarah. They sat in front of my apartment. No freaking way. Go. Go away. I didn't think I could handle another round of their seductive ways without becoming primitive, only being driven by my need to have them. To be inside them. To own them completely. Please go.

I waited for a moment at the end of the hall. They hadn't spotted me yet. They were giggling again. The way they smiled was beatific in a very heavenly way. Smiles so bright that any hellish creature would be soothed, calmed by their feminine might. And those laughs, a sound that filled my heart with joy. Like sirens calling to the sailor on a dark night at sea, beckoning him to draw near. To follow them into the depths. I eavesdropped to see what they were talking about.

"Come on, Vicky, I know you loved it when he called us good girls. I did, too." Sarah giggled; her chest bounced as she sat cross-legged.

Vicky's eyes shot up with appreciation. She gazed briefly at my apartment door before turning back to Sarah. "Yes, it felt so good to be called that. And oh, he is so damn hot. I would give him a hundred babies if he asked," she said in a smitten voice.

Damn, a hundred babies. I'll need a bigger wallet.

17

"Do you remember when we kissed in the tenth grade?" Sarah coyishly asked, glancing at my door. Then she looked at Vicky intently.

"Yeah, I also remember when we fingered each other at that sleepover," Vicky said in a sultry voice.

Both women broke into sexy laughter. As they tenderly caressed each other's faces, I stood there in amazement. Their eyes locked onto each other for a moment, as if they were silently remembering each other's touch, much like lovers that had long been apart.

They wanted me and weren't afraid to play together. This could be interesting. Desires that I never knew had washed over me. One woman on top of me, the other touching me. A mesh of flesh rolling all over the bed, not knowing what body part belonged to whom. Just the feeling that we all fit together in some form of a sexually feral puzzle. I listened harder. But my ears were not the only thing focusing harder. Down boy. Down.

"If we are both his girlfriend, do you think he will want us to... you know... together?" Sarah asked shyly as she removed her hand from Vicky's cheek.

"We can only hope. It would be fun. Right?" Beguiled by the thought, Vicky also placed her hand back in her lap.

I couldn't hide from my own apartment all night. Screw it. I walked up to the door. My focus was solely on the door. Stay focused, Sergeant. Door. Open it. I stepped over the top of them, pretending I didn't notice their presence.

"Master!" Sarah yelled excitedly. I looked around to ensure none of my neighbors heard her, especially Mrs. Helderman. If Her Kinkiness heard them say that, I don't think I could ever look her in the eyes again.

"Hello, Master," Vicky said as she sat with pride.

"Ladies." I modestly acknowledged them.

My keys fumbled in my hands. Hurry, open the door, Kyle. Go. Get inside before this becomes one of those porno scenes right in the hallway.

I felt a hand tug at my pants. Sarah had reached up from her seated position. She pulled herself up with my waistline. Vicky was nuzzling my thigh. What the hell? Are they in heat? I can't have my neighbors see this. I opened the door, almost stumbling inside. Vicky held my leg tightly as I tried to move forward.

"Ladies," I said, "we can't do it this way. We need to—" I fell into the apartment face-first.

They giggled as I started to pick myself up. Vicky released my leg. My mind was about to break, a thimble of sanity still intact. I was not hurt or angered by the fall, just embarrassed. But I was nowhere near as embarrassed as I was last night.

"We know, Master, that's why we are coming in to talk." Vicky picked herself up off the floor.

I stood up. Talk... huh... yeah... talk... just talk. Keep it together, Sergeant. Talk, you can do that, right? It's just words, nothing more. Move your mouth, and words will come out. That's it. You can keep yourself from being a sex-starved monster for just a few minutes. Yes, I can do this.

"Come in, ladies," I said, motioning to them invitingly.

I sat on the floor in front of the couch, grabbing a pillow to put in my lap. The pillow was a precaution. I was sure they would do or say something that would have my mini-me barking to be free from my fly.

They lounged on the couch. Sarah had on tight jeans and a tank top. Vicky was in yoga pants and a halter. Why, goddammit, why did they have to look so enticing? I wanted to rip those clothes to shreds. I wanted to take from their bodies all the pleasures I could. I wanted them. No, I needed them. Focus, dammit.

"Okay, you two wanted to talk. So..." I watched their movements.

"Sarah and I have been friends since before pre-school. We have shared almost everything. And we are willing to try this." Vicky's voice had a soft quality.

"Okay, so you want to share me as a boyfriend. Got it." My lips pursed as I nodded. I tried to keep up but was infatuated with how their eyes sparkled in the light.

"Well, maybe more. But that depends on how it works out," Sarah added as she bit her lower lip seductively.

God, please don't bite your lip like that. I am trying to be a gentleman. It's so hard to be good when they do things like that. What they do to me. How they make me feel. How they make my manhood feel. Snap out of it and talk. Remember. Only talking.

"More? I'm listening." I tried to fight off my desire.

19

What a chump. Two stunning women sitting on my couch, and I try to be the "nice" guy. NERD! Thoughts of making them moan in pleasure. Thoughts of hearing that word "Master" spoken to me while I catapulted my phallus deep into their chalices. Then, for no reason, it crept in. The thought that they may be younger, like way younger, entered my mind.

"First off, how old are you two? I am not going down any pedo roads am I?" My mind raced with doubt and shame. My body tensed; my heart raced like a dragster. God, I had made them undress in front of me last night. I am going to jail. Worse, I am going to Hell. Pervert! I will be branded a nasty pervert for sure.

Vicky and Sarah laughed as they could see my anxiety rise. Neither spoke for a moment. They simply laughed. This was dialing my anxiety to almost max volume. I just knew that I was a goner. Then Vicky broke the laughter.

"No, Master, you are not going down that road. I am twenty-three, twenty-four in a month. Sarah just turned twenty-four three months ago."

My body and mind relaxed as I exhaled a huge sigh. Okay. Chill, Sgt. Forester, pull yourself together. You have fought in the sands of Iraq and the mountains of Afghanistan. You got this. You can handle these two. If you can be dropped in a hot zone and beat the odds, you can do this. Stay on mission.

In high school, no girl would look at my pimply face. No girl gave me the time of day. Then, after graduation, I went straight into the Army. I didn't even lose my virginity until I was twenty. And that wasn't a great experience. Some "dependa" who wanted my basic allowance for housing while I was deployed. A couple of rolls in the hay but nothing before or since. Just good old Rosy Palm and her five daughters. If these ladies knew how inexperienced I was, they would see the man I was last night as nothing more than a ruse, a fluke. It was who I wished I could be but not who I put forward to others.

"You seem tense, Master. Here, let me help." Vicky started rubbing my shoulders.

I was so caught up in my thoughts that I hadn't noticed they had moved. Vicky was behind me; her hands felt so good, rubbing the tension out of my shoulders. Sarah had crawled down on her hands and knees, her elbows cocked up. Her face rested in her palms as she looked up at me. Her ass was high in the air, purposefully. Damn tease.

Ah... Okay. I can do this. Snap back, Sergeant. You got this. Don't give in. Not yet. Remember, keep the conversation flowing. Talk... just talk.

"What about this 'more' you mentioned?" I relaxed into Vicky's massage.

"Husband, of course," Sarah said nonchalantly.

I about choked. Husband? To both? That's not even legal. Could I handle that? Could my wallet handle that?

Twenty-four years of being overlooked by every girl. Now two—TWO—want marriage. TWO! And Vicky had mentioned a hundred babies. Babies? As in plural? As in, both of them knocked up? Impregnating them both? Kids? How many?

Do I have the stamina for that? I have only had sex twice, with only one partner. Could I pleasure two women at once? However, it would be nice to have two submissive wives. Yeah. So wonderful. My every desire would be met completely. My needs would always be met.

"Master, are you okay?" Sarah's concern shot her to her feet.

She ran her fingers through my hair. Then her nails massaged my scalp to soothe me. Oh, all the worry was fading... but husband? Really?

"Um... husband? As in married to both of you? Hold up. Wait a minute. Let's slow down," I stammered, trying to get my courage back to continue the conversation.

Vicky leaned into my ear. "Not right away, of course. We just want to date at first. Experiment and see if this arrangement can work for us."

"Okay, but I have a certain type. How do either of you know what I want in a woman?" I smirked, trying to be facetious.

Vicky whispered in my ear. "Mrs. Helderman said that you want a traditional woman. Subservient and elegant. Yet she must be nasty and playful in bed." God, her voice was so sexy when she whispered. I pushed the pillow down hard. Stay down, boy.

"Yeah, she can hear the type of porn you watch," Sarah roared aloud, breaking from her soft voice. "She said you like the submissive ones that you can do anything with. That lets you have them however your dirty desires decided."

My face felt like it turned a deep crimson. That old widow heard my porn. And she didn't judge me? She approved and sent these horny women my way. I have been watching porn in the living room since I moved in. That means that she has known what I desired the entire time. And she never mentioned it. Never confronted me about my dominant desires.

The thought of spraying a hot load on both of their sweet faces assaulted my thoughts. Hearing them praise me for doing so. Hearing the "thank you, Master" that would come from their lips as they licked it off of each other. Nope. Stop. Talk. Talk.

"What about your jobs at the pizza joint?" I tried to move the conversation away from my porn selection.

Sarah halted the scalp massage for a moment to explain. "I'm between jobs. My career is actually in HR. Vicky got me the job as a delivery driver after my pig of a boss tried to seduce me and failed. Then he held my job over my head unless I gave in. So, I quickly resigned."

He seemed like such a vulgar man; I wanted to pelt him in his jaw for such a cowardly dick move. Maybe that was why she felt the relationship in *Secretary* was creepy. And damn, I felt so protective of them already. I was surprised by my own desire to protect them.

"And I'm just there until I get my masseuse license. Then outty three thousand," Vicky said as her hand started working lower on my back. It felt so good.

Well, at least they seemed to be put together. They were crazy but had seemingly stable financial plans. My empty wallet had started looking like less of an issue, which was good because all my money was being saved to start my business. I barely kept enough to live off of and buy a few things here and there. Okay, keep the conversation flowing...

"How would your parents feel about this three-way marriage?"

Both of them eyed me for a moment with an inkling of happiness. They seemed to be interested in exploring the topic of marriage and families.

"My parents retired to Florida about a year ago. And I don't think they would care so long as I am happy." Sarah tilted my head up to look at her. "Besides, I am not a kid anymore; my life is mine to do with as I please. And for now, I want to please my Master." Her grin was so bright.

"My dad died when I was sixteen; my mom would just be ecstatic to see me happy with the man I chose in the way I chose to love him." Vicky worked her hands even lower. Close to my lower back. "And your parents, Master?"

I thought about the crash that had taken them from Elle and me. It was painful to think about, but they had to know, especially if we would pursue this in any capacity.

"Both died in a car accident about four years ago. It's just my older sister and me now. She is a bit protective of me, so I have no clue how she will react if I show up with two women swinging on my arms."

I frowned, thinking about how Elle would react. It could go either way. But she had no room to judge me. She stayed with Stephen even though he was a drunk. Even after he beat her.

I can't be in the same room with Stephen without wanting to smash his face in. I only put up with it on holidays to see my big sis and my goofy niece. Jenny was such a cute kid. She was five years old and had a feistiness about her. The thoughts of Jenny reminded me of Vicky's words in the hallway.

"In the hall, I heard something about babies." My words almost faltered as they came out.

"Yes, babies. If we get that far, it shouldn't be a problem to impregnate your wives, Master," Vicky whispered, her words oozing with a dark sexiness that I'd only heard in pornos. She continued to work my back with her fingers, her hands kneading the knots out.

"Breeding us should be the top priority once we are married," Sarah said, smiling down at me with an innocent mischief.

Breed them. That sounded so hot. Impregnating my wanton wives. Damn, my manhood was jumping with joy. Thinking about my hot sticky goo rushing deep inside them, making babies. The way it would look dripping down their thighs. Chill. Cool it. Sarah reached down and snatched my pillow from me. My erection pressed against my work pants.

"Ahem, Master, you don't have to hide it. You don't have to be ashamed. We know what we do to you." Sarah's words were playfully sexual as she smirked devilishly.

Vicky leaned over gazing upon my manhood. "It will be ours soon anyway. So, please don't be scared to show us how you feel.

23

Your cock sure isn't shy. It seems to love our attention," Her tone playfully teased with that sexiness.

"What about you two? How will this work? What will it do to your friendship?" I tried to divert the conversation away from my soldier standing tall in my pants.

"We have had an on-and-off playful friendship," Vicky announced, she seemed flustered in remembrance.

"It would be the first time we shared a guy," Sarah assured me. "We had our own boyfriends, but this is not the first time that we have been more than friends, even sort of lovers together."

"If you give us your attention equally, it should work out fine," Vicky said, her words holding an air of affection. Her fingers dug deeper into the knots in my back.

"And communicate to each other always. No secrets. Just the truth spoken between all three of us," Sarah added as she pulled her nails from my scalp.

Okay, so now what? I have exhausted all topics that could turn them away. And thanks to Mrs. Helderman's nosiness, they know about some of my kinks. They know my fantasy. My big fantasy. To be granted the gift of submission.

Sarah sniffed me. "You need a shower, Master. You stink and are so dirty." She ruffled my hair before stepping back, licking her lips seductively.

Vicky leaned down; her cheek rubbed against mine. "I agree. Please, Master, take a shower. Or a bath? We can bathe you. We will scrub every inch of you clean if you so wish." Her hands slid teasingly along the side of my ribs.

"Shower, yes, yes!" I was losing control. Dammit. You got this. Be firm... but with whom? Them? Or yourself?

I scurried up. Before they could react, I ran to the bathroom, locking the door. Aahhh! Just do it, you idiot. They are right there. Right freaking there. Take them. Use their bodies. Stop being a coward. No! You are a soldier, a man with honor. You are a gentleman. You will not take advantage of them. You will make yourself wait.

I turned the shower on—cold. I let the freezing water cool down my flaming desires. Okay... think... think. You can make a condition. Yes, a condition before sex. God, how hot the sex would be with them. The "yes Master" treatment. The filthy commands I could give them. The wanton looks they would give me. Their warm sweaty skin on mine.

No, focus. Conditions, conditions... I got it. Three dates. We have to go on three real dates as a throuple, then—and only then—we can negotiate sex. Yes, three dates should give me enough time to learn about them. To get to know them. And if they back out in the meantime, no big loss. If only one drops out, I still get a win. But if they both stay, it's a big win. Or big trouble.

I reached for the towel. I dried off, satisfied that I had figured out how to keep them at bay, at least until I could garner a real connection. I looked around the room. Did I... I did. I forgot my clothes. SHIT! I was so rushed that I didn't even think about clothes. And my work clothes are full of mud and grime.

I took a deep breath and wrapped the towel around my waist. I could barely keep them away from my dick when I had pants on. How am I going to do this? Whatever. Time to go. My hand opened the doorknob. I poked my head out, scanning the living room. Nothing. They were gone. Okay. Cool. I strutted to the bedroom. I would get some clothes on, then see if I could catch up with them.

I opened my bedroom door to a heavenly sight, so delightful that I almost died. Vicky kneeled carnally beside the bed. Her perky bosom exposed; her red panties curved so neatly around her butt. Those blue eyes gazed at me in covetous lust. Sarah sat on the bed. Her large breasts out, they lay to the sides as she bent slightly backward. Her legs spread wide, showing her blue panties where her fingers moved slowly and meticulously in tender circles inside them. Her eyes closed as she was working herself into an animalistic urge. This scene was so inviting... so tempting... DAMN!

Before I could contain myself, Vicky had pulled the towel down. There was no hiding my manhood at this point. They hadn't actually seen it completely yet. They had just seen the silhouette of my manhood straining through clothes. But now he was giving them both a standing ovation. And there was nothing I could do. Their eyes stared in admiration and burned with desire.

"Beautiful... what a beautiful cock." Vicky licked her lips, entranced by my shaft.

"The biggest one I've ever seen in real life." Sarah gulped hard as she tried to adjust her legs, most likely to accommodate my member.

My hands slammed over myself to cover it. I turned to my dresser, grabbing the first pair of boxers I could. Spider-Man. Ugh! The freaking Spider-Man boxers Elle got me as a gag gift. I quickly pulled them on.

They gaped at me in confusion. They had finally gotten a sight, a peek of what they desired. But I had stolen the hope of having it from them. I felt wrong not to let them have what they wanted. But it also felt wrong to let this continue down its intended course without getting to know them. I breathed deeply. Conditions. Do it. I had time to collect myself since they were in a confused daze.

"Okay, okay, look. I would love to plow the both of you until my dick falls off, but..." GOD! do I need the "but"?

Yes, you do, Kyle. Stand strong. We both know that your manhood is raring to... just don't give in. "Deal is three dates," I blurted out.

"Three dates?" Sarah tilted her head sideways as she tried to pin down my intentions.

Vicky smirked wickedly. "Then what, after these dates, huh, Master?" Her words flowed with that raspy sexiness. She had me. She knew... And the way she said Master only shook my fortitude more.

Focus. "Then, we can negotiate sexual relations." I stood strong on my conviction. "Deal?"

"As you wish, Master." They said eerily in unison. But for some reason, that eeriness turned me on.

"Saturday night, dinner, and..." What else can I do? This was honestly the first actual date I had ever had. "Miss Dependa" just wanted to hang out at her place off post. No actual dates. No movies, no dinners. Nothing. Just went there to listen to her sob about the other three soldiers she had been with before. I was an ear for her sorrows. And a dummy that gave her a year and a half of my housing allowance while I was deployed for the first time.

"Then we can cruise around town," Sarah gleefully blurted. "Find a backroad... or somewhere private?"

"Slow down. This is date number one," I reminded them both.

"No, watching *Secretary* was date number one, Master," Vicky crossed her arms as she tried to get her way quicker.

"Wrong. Date numbers start tonight." My NCO voice chilled them both.

"But, Master, you said that watching *Secretary* was a date. You can't go back on that now." Sarah whimpered, seemingly hurt by my chilly tone.

Sarah gave me the saddest puppy eyes I had ever seen. It was so cute, so sexy. Her innocence had a sensual flavor to it. I looked over to Vicky, her face more of an angry pout. Much like a bratty and sultry vixen that knew what she wanted. Both were so hot. Plus, she had a point. What good was a Master if your submissives can't trust your word.

"Fine, Saturday will be date two. But don't push it."

"Yes, Master." Their voices were like a rehearsed choir: creepy but sexy.

With my eyes filled by those curvaceous bodies, Spider-Man down below was about to sling his gooey web. I had to get them out of here.

"Get dressed, my beauties, time for you to go home. On Saturday, don't be late. And wear something..." Yes, do it! My inner dominant side was in full swing.

My voice cooled and smoothed into that NCO tone. "Something tight and sexy."

They dressed very slowly. Their eyes were a sad pout but so cute. They complied with my command without protesting. They, again, fully submitted like last night. Was it the voice? That NCO voice. Even their compliance to dress was stirring the desire in me.

I could only handle so much. Before long—just a few more moments—the beast of a man inside me would be here, emerging from the depths of my raging desires, taking from them all the pleasures that he could. He was held within the cage of his temptations, which I had built.

"Good night, Master," Sarah said, kissing my cheek as if she had been defeated.

"Sweet dreams, Master. Dream of us." Vicky, a little more aggressive, pressed into me with her lips puckered. Her kiss hit the intended target as her tongue probed my mouth momentarily. I passionately kissed her back. Her hand slid up my thigh, rubbing my member. It was throbbing.

Instinctively, my hand reached out, grappling Sarah by the wrist. I broke my kiss with Vicky, a thread of saliva trailing out. I pulled Sarah close as I re-emerged, kissing her with just as much passion. Damn, calm it, soldier, before it was too la—

Vicky slid her hand into my boxers, grabbing my hilt tightly before I could finish my thought. My kiss deepened into Sarah as Vicky started stroking me slowly and steadily. Vicky nibbled at my ear. Oh hell, this was it. No holding back anymore.

"Just a portion, Master. Of what you do to us." Vicky whispered that sexy vixen voice into my ear.

Sarah broke away from our kiss. Their eyes locked into each other's for a moment; they gave each other a knowing look. Without a word, they both kneeled before me. They eyed my boxers as if it were a present on Christmas day that they had been denied for so long but now could open. The ache of desire had washed over them as they pulled my boxers to the floor. My rod was extended to its fullest.

With grace, both of their tongues lashed out at me. They moved up and down my shaft, twirling those soft tongues around every inch. Oh shit! The spectacle of being worshipped by two sultry vixens was intoxicating. The power dynamic was on full display. I was the Master, yet they led the dance of affection with power over my desire. The heat of their warm saliva greasing my stem made me whimper in pleasure.

They both smirked as my reactions empowered their delight. I had lost all my strength, but from their feminine power, I had gained something else. A sense of controlled chaos. My hands moved down to their scalps. My fingers played through their locks. I closed my eyes as I gave into their reverence of my masculinity. I felt one of them move away. Cracking my eyes, I peeped down. Sarah had moved back as Vicky was right in front of me, her mouth open.

Vicky took me completely into her mouth. She had consumed every inch. Wincing, my body tensed as I felt the heat... the wetness of her throat wrapped around me. I let out a stunted howl as I felt the rapture of her service. Her head bobbed slowly as moans slipped from my lips into the air.

My head rolled backward at the sensation. My sac twiddled between Sarah's fingers. I was in the throes of passion, in the fires of this... feeling. They both lovingly looked up at me. Vicky's blue sapphires and Sarah's green emeralds showed an admiration that I always yearned to be the recipient of.

Sarah lightly tugged Vicky backward. Vicky freed me from her mouth as Sarah replaced her. She took over the dance as she took me even deeper into her moist mouth. Vicky assisted Sarah with her hand on her head, shoving her further upon me. She gagged as I hit the back of her throat. Her head moved faster.

Without thinking, my hands grabbed the sides of her face. I shoved in as far as I could, and she choked for a moment. I looked down. Sarah's face was dripping with drool. Her eyes twinkled with slight tears as she looked up at me with an amorous look. This sight made all my wants, all my needs, come to reality. I was close. They were milking me to the edge of no return.

Then, without warning, they stopped. Sarah pulled away from my soaked organ. Each took my boxers and secured them back into place. Damn, teasing bitches. Goddammit. My balls ached; I was ready to give in to their desires, yet they stopped.

They nodded to each other and then stood. Not a word said. Just wicked grins on both of their faces. They walked to the door in a victory strut as if they had won this round. Teases!

I wanted to stop them. I wanted to continue. I wanted to throw them both to the floor, taking what I felt—no, what I knew—was mine. But the coward in me was letting them exit the front door without intervention.

"Saturday, Master. Your girlfriends will see you Saturday. For date two," Vicky said as she closed the door behind them.

After they left, the apartment became lonely again. It was time to get some sleep. I lay in bed, falling into my thoughts. Even though I had only known them for two days, I was oddly fond of them. And there he was, standing up. Those damn women worked him up. He was about to burst through my good old Spider-Man boxers. Thanks, sis; you managed to emphasize my nerdiness without even being present. Was that why they stopped? Damn! I tried to ignore the erection, ignore the fact that my balls were ready to blow. But I was too worked up for no as an answer.

Miss Rosy Palm had to pay a visit to my little soldier. He had been denied too many times in the past couple of days. Then those bratty women worked him up. I pounded my soldier with vigor, thinking of being sandwiched between Vicky and Sarah.

29

Commanding them. Fantasizing about hearing the phrases "Yes, Master," "Please, Master," and "As you wish, Master." Those bodies crawling all over me. Hot and sweaty. Remembering the feeling of their soft, warm mouths around me. In no time, I was spent. I slapped the goo on the sheets, I was too lazy to clean it up. What a waste. This could have been inside of one of them—inside them both. Go to bed, you nerd.

But still, the idea of a relationship, the promise of it, that was intriguing. A loving relationship with both...

Chapter 3: Unexpected Friendships

The next few days were boring, for the most part. I didn't see Vicky and Sarah the entire time. Had I scared them off? As my awkwardness scared off most people, it was possible. I hoped not. I loved the feeling of being with them. At first, they seemed annoying, but after that second meeting, they became something else to me. Girlfriends, maybe?

Mrs. Helderman was much more open with me after our last conversation. At first, our friendship was nothing more than an elder to youngling, like a grandmother to a grandson. But now, our conversations felt more like we were peers. We shared something that neither of us spoke a word about to anyone else.

She had confessed that she and Jimmy had a mistress together. That their third had died long ago in a car accident. That was one reason why she took a shine to me, my parents having died in a car crash. And Jimmy had served in the Army, like I had. I reminded her of Jimmy in many ways. She had told me that I had some of the same qualities: his kindness, his courage, his honor... and yes, even his carnal desires. When she first met me, she thought I was Jimmy's spirit in a new body.

I questioned her about how a three-way relationship worked. She explained that the love had to be shared evenly among all three involved. I confessed to her the possibility of this happening with Sarah and Vicky. She was more than excited about the idea. She encouraged me, saying she would act as my advisor on this matter. She counseled me to keep clear and honest communication among all of us—no secrets, ever. We had many conversations throughout the week on this subject.

She shared an interesting fact with me about the term "ménage a trois." In American culture, the phrase refers to a three-way sexual fling. However, the actual French translation was "household of three," which was often used for a three-way romantic relationship.

Work had lost all flavor for me. I went through the motions of the job, but my passion and mind were elsewhere. Of course, it was because of them—my girlies. I could call them that, right? That was where my head seemed to be instead of my work. My head swelled, both of my heads thinking about them.

Friday night had finally come; I made it home quickly. I flung the work clothes off and changed into civies. I'd already spent the nights this week tirelessly cleaning my apartment. What guy doesn't clean up his home for his girlfriend... I mean girlfriends.

But for now, the night was mine, free of this sexual escapade. I could finally get to the hobby gaming shop, Ground Zero.

I tried to rehearse a few different greetings as I drove across town. Even in the nerd community, I was an outcast. I could barely relate to them. I loved the games. I was good with games that required strategic and tactical planning. But as for people, I was never good with them. I could never seem to say the right things at the right time.

Other than Sarah and Vicky, I had never really had a decent conversation with people my own age outside of the Army. Mrs. Helderman was older and understood my personality. Even Elle was six years older than me.

The closest I came to being a social butterfly was on my first deployment with my battle buddies Gordon, Weir, and young Donovan. Those goofy guys made the sands of Iraq bearable. However, that didn't end well and is now a painful scar. I quickly pushed the images of that horrifying event from my mind. There was no need to open old wounds.

When I arrived, the place seemed almost deserted. I had been to graveyards with more activity. But the bar next door seemed bustling. If I couldn't connect with any neckbeards, then there was no way I could hang with a rowdier crowd. I left the car and walked inside. There were seven people inside, including the guy behind the counter.

I strolled through the shelves and studied the 40K figures. Damn, why was it so freaking expensive? I wanted to start on Warhammer 40K, hoping to make a friend. Most of the guys that come here play Magic or 40K. I just wanted to belong. Magic was okay, but I disliked the fact that they would print these awesome cards only to ban them from play. Warhammer looked fun but too expensive. All my savings were earmarked to start my business.

There was no way I would throw away my financial freedom for some figurines and a friend or two. I worked too hard for this. I literally killed for that money. I stayed in the barracks on post. I ate only at the chow hall. I saved every penny. And my beater car was the same one my parents co-signed with me when I was fifteen. That was when I started working with Mr. Roger. He was an HVAC contractor; he started me down the HVAC path. But then the call to war filled my soul before I could settle into something peaceful.

I couldn't find anything of interest in the store, at least not anything that wouldn't break my piggy bank. I went to the gaming area, where a few guys were playing 40K, and two were playing Magic. One guy was reading the Third Edition of Ravenloft by himself. I walked over and sat across from him.

Ravenloft was a dark campaign in D&D. In that setting players could be vampires or death knights. I played it briefly as a kid with Elle and her friends before she left for college.

"Ravenloft was always a great campaign. My sister used to make me a vampire in that setting," I awkwardly mumbled in an attempt to start up a conversation.

"Cool," he said, annoyed that I had disturbed him.

"How many players are you planning for? Do you have room for one more?" I asked as I tried to get invited by interjecting myself into his vision.

"Nah, man. We are all full up. I'm already setting up the campaign, and those guys are waiting for me to get it going," he snarled, pointing to the other guys in the gaming area.

It must have been nice to be able to point to five of your friends. This reminded me of my loneliness and my awkwardness. I can only point to Mrs. Helderman, my only friend.

"Okay, sorry to bother you. I hope your campaign goes well." I nodded at him, smiling briefly before I took my leave.

I perused the store one last time. Then I saw it. There was a Harley Quinn bust sitting on a high shelf. This thing was so cute. And it would look so cool next to the TV. It wasn't too expensive either. When I took it to the register, the guy seemed to barely notice me. However, once he saw I was buying something, he was all too happy to take my money.

As I walked out of the shop, I held the figure in front of me, admiring my new purchase.

"What kinda sicko gets a plastic girlfriend in a geek store?" a slurred voice said from my right side.

I looked over; a muscled man in a red tank top with a black leather jacket overture stood there. He must have come from the bar next door. He smelled of cigarettes and booze.

"Dude, I don't want any trouble. I was just leaving." My heart turned to that coldness that I knew all too well. I could feel my emotions shutting off. Don't do it, guy; I am not your typical nerd.

"Fucken punk ass bitch. What gives ya the right to whack off to some cartoon character?"

His words were starting to push me back to Afghanistan. Calm yourself. Stay calm. He is just drunk. "I'm leaving now. Have a great night." I turned toward my car and started to walk away.

I felt something grab at my arm. He spun me around. His sleight of hand was quick as he took Harley from me. He smashed her to the ground into countless pieces.

Standfast, Sergeant. "Good night, sir." I gritted, holding back my rage.

"Fuck dat!" Those were the last words I heard before his knuckles cracked into my jaw.

I didn't think. My body reacted on its own, and muscle memory took over. After his punch, I struck him in the face a few times, and I kicked my leg behind him. I pushed his shoulder as I swept him down. I followed through and took him to the ground. My training had emerged. My emotions were gone. I was the soldier, once again. I pinned him to the ground. My legs swung over his hips as I got into the mount position. My hands instinctively started to strangle him with a blood choke. He was out in no time. I regained myself. Did I kill him? Shit. Did I? Over a stupid plastic toy?

He coughed loudly. He was okay. Good. I hadn't killed him.

"Man, ya got that nerd strength, huh, borderin' on retard strength." He playfully snorted from the ground. "Mind lettin' me up." His hand motioned upward.

"Sure, sorry. I lost control for a moment." I said, ashamed that the soldier in me had surfaced again. I moved off of him. My hand held out to help him up.

"No shit." His voice was hoarse as he smirked. He took my hand, and I helped him to his feet.

"I'm Kyle, and you owe me. That thing was a hundred and fifty bucks," I said, trying to soften my tone.

"Well, that's far less than I've paid for some rub and tugs," he said with a chuckle. "Name's Howard." His hand extended out into a handshake.

I shook his hand. Did I just make a friend? After kicking his ass? "Dude you gotta be careful who you pick fights with." I laughed.

"Apparently. Where did ya learn to do that?" He eyed me, sizing me up.

"The Army. Spent a bit of time overseas." I said. Sighing deeply, I was glad that the beast in me hadn't murdered him.

"The Army, huh. Didn't know they let nerds in these days." His words started pushing my buttons again. But I brushed it off.

"Nerds and... sometimes even drunk idiots." I joked, hoping it would lighten the conversation.

"Fair enough. Wanna get a drink? I'm buying," he offered.

"Sure, one drink won't hurt." I shrugged in acceptance. He turned, moving toward the bar. I followed him with caution.

We sat in a booth away from almost everyone. The barmaid was a cute thing. Not much of a body, but still cute. I ordered rum and coke, my go-to after deployment. He had whiskey and a beer chaser. The waitress flirted a bit, and I was sure that this was her way to get better tips. I just shrugged it off. Besides, she wasn't "them." She could not give me what Vicky and Sarah had offered. Not the treatment that I had desired, that I longed for.

We sat talking for a few hours. For some reason, he reminded me of the guys on my first deployment. I felt an immediate connection and was comfortable talking with him. Which allowed me to lower my guard.

He inquired about my military service, so I obliged him. I told him about my rank and military occupation. About my time at basic and other training. I carried on with some of my war stories, the funny ones, and some gorier ones too.

I asked him about his rowdiness. He told me about his rough upbringing. Howard drunkenly confessed that he didn't have any friends either. He also explained that he had been coming to the bar for a couple of years, trying to make friends. Or to find a girlfriend. But he had no luck. It was odd that he was an outcast like me.

"So, ya got a girl?" he probed.

Damn, what do I say? Yes, but no. Two. But would that make him hit me again? Then, another fight would ensue.

"Sort of." I tried to dodge the question in a noncommittal way.

"How do ya sort of have a girl? Ya either do or ya don't." His eyes saw through my attempted dodge.

"Well…" I began explaining the situation I found myself in with Vicky and Sarah. I excluded the incomplete head that had left me sexually frustrated. That was far too embarrassing to admit to. He listened with awe. I watched his expressions go from jealousy to amazement and back again.

"So, lemme get this straight. Two hot women are throwing themselves at ya feet and ya brushed them off? I would've fucked them both." As he spoke, his hands gestured like we were in a business meeting.

"Yeah, eventually. But I don't feel right about it. At least until I get to know them." I grinned awkwardly. "I want it to stick this time, ya know. To be in a real relationship."

"I can see ya point. But damn, that would've been too fucken hard for me. I don't think I could've had that kinda discipline. Are ya sure ya not gay?" His words started to slur again.

"Nope, not gay. Just really inexperienced, I guess." I looked at the empty glass in pity.

"It's cool, man. I've never really had a girl other than the ones I pay every now and then," he confessed. "But in ya shoes, I would've blown their backs out."

He nursed his beer for a while longer as we sat in silence.

"Man, it was nice meeting ya. Here, take my number. Let's hang out again. Next time, buy me a drink before ya straddle my hips," he joked as he stood up. He stumbled toward the door.

"Dude, let me take you home. I can drive," I said, concerned that he might kill himself.

"Sure, bro." He gave in.

I drove him to his house. On the ride, he told me he had been working from home. Some kind of remote work. I couldn't determine exactly what it was due to his slurred, drunken words. I explained that I was working in the air-conditioning industry, and soon, I would own my own business. He congratulated me and said that we would need to celebrate once I was up and running.

As we pulled down the road, the streetlights started to have an aura around them. He directed me to a really nice neighborhood. He motioned to a house. It was a large two-story brick house. The kind that you see in movies or one of those fancy magazines. There was no way he owned this. I pulled into the driveway, amazed at the size of the house. It was big... like mansion-sized big.

I helped Howard out of the car. I carried him to the door as I had done for my battle buddies in the field. The porch light was on. There was movement next to the door. An elderly man sat on the porch with a disappointed face. I assumed he was Howard's father, but he didn't say a word, he just watched us with disappointment. I carried Howard into the house, past the foyer, and into the living room. Aiding him to the couch, I eased him down.

"Thanks, brah. I got it now." He motioned me off.

"Okay, just be safe. And if you can't be safe, be deadly," I said as I helped him lay on his side.

"Be deadly. I like dat." His last words before he passed out.

I placed the blanket that was draped over the back of the couch on him. For some reason, I felt at ease with him. Yes, he was a bit rowdy... well, rough, really—but actually, he was a good guy. I was glad that we met.

I exited the house. His father watched me with suspicion. I left and drove carefully home. I was pretty toasted but didn't want to let him drive. He was in a much worse shape than I was.

Once at my complex, I stumbled up the stairs. Man, drinking was never my thing. After a few shots, I was almost completely wasted. I made it into the apartment, then flopped onto the couch. I looked up at the clock. It was almost zero one hundred hours. Damn, I spent more time with Howard than I had thought. I was too tired and too drunk to care at the moment. I kicked my shoes off and rolled onto my side before I crashed hard.

The sun broke into the window, hitting me in the face. Those ungodly rays beamed down upon me. Go back to bed, Sun. I felt hazy but got up. I looked around the apartment. I had done a great job cleaning up over the week. Getting things ready for whatever these ladies would throw at me.

My laptop was on the end table. I opened it and logged in. I rummaged through my emails. Nothing good. A few bills and a ton of spam. I closed the screen in frustration. Damn, this apartment had seemed so lively when they were here. Now, it felt empty. What was I going to do?

I stood up, stretched, and thought about having kids with the girls. I had always wanted to be a father. When I was in high school, I volunteered as a camp counselor. I had been great at that. And anytime I babysat my niece, she would cling to me like white on rice. Father: a title that seemed to fit me well. For that matter, the title husband also made me feel good.

Breed them. I could do that. Put babies inside them both. I could go to work, come home, play with the kids, eat dinner, and watch something on TV. Then, when the house was settled, the night would be mine... to have them.

Shut up, you horny bastard.

I turned on YouTube to step out of my mind. I danced around to nineties dance music. My feet moved gracefully from room to room. I was excited. Today was the day. My date... wait!

I hadn't given them a time. I didn't even know their numbers to call them. Was this really the first time I had thought about that? I had been so involved in the sexual tension that I forgot to get basic information. Last names. Phone numbers. Addresses. Facebook. Twitter. Nothing. I had nothing on them. Shit!

I sat on the couch. Had I lost them? It had been days since they were here. Was I being too prudish? Damn it, Sarge. Relax. Take a shower. I'd feel better after I washed away this fear.

I cranked the shower to hot. My body ached but not with pain. What was this feeling? I felt it deep in my gut. The water hammered my body, soothing my muscles but not my soul. I lathered the soap, trying to scrub away this feeling. But that didn't work either.

Dammit! How could I have been so stupid? What I wanted—desired—I let slip through my fingers. Submissive women that worshipped me. All I could do was wait. I had told them the day. But not the time. The ball was completely in their court.

I dried myself off. Leaning down, I smelled my clothes. The raw smell of a bar and an ashtray filled my nostrils. Nope. Not putting that back on. I scooped up the bundle and carried my dirty clothes out of the bathroom. My flaccid penis slapped my naked legs as I sauntered to the bedroom. I just needed to relax. They would show up at some point. Most likely in the evening. Besides, that's when they had sexually accosted me before. Evening. Yeah, so just wait, Sergeant, your lovelies will be here soon enough.

Chapter 4: Honey for Breakfast

I pushed the bedroom door open. My eyes were blinded by a wonderful surprise that ravished my senses. Sarah and Vicky lay naked on my bed. When did they get here? Wait, how did they get in? I dropped my clothes on the floor. My mind took in the beauty of what was mine. I was angry but happy. They came into my apartment without me knowing. Without permission. Fine. I will get the explanation for this. Nothing that I can't forgive.

Then, the spite of them leaving me high and dry the other night filled me. No explanation would quell the sexual frustrations that wanted to punish them for leaving me like that. Oh, you bratty women are going to pay.

"Attention!" My command voice was so loud that I was sure all my neighbors in the apartment complex heard it—and maybe some down the street, as well.

Sarah jumped up, startled. Vicky just rolled over, eyeing me with a pissed look.

"Hello, Master." Sarah retracted her tension and softened with her sweet voice.

Vicky begrudgingly hurled out with a harsh and irritated rasp. "Fuck. Master, couldn't you wake us up with something nice? Like breakfast in bed?" Her arms angrily crossed at her chest, as she huffed a bratty sigh.

"Breakfast in bed, huh? Only good girls get that kind of treatment. Right now, I want to bend you both over my knee and spank your asses until they are fucking purple." My command voice lowered but was still harsh.

"Why, Master?" Sarah asked, her eyes started to water a bit. Vicky just kept her pissed composure.

"Why? You really have to ask why?" My command voice was now soft and low.

Vicky breathed heavily before scolding. "Spit it out. We can't read your mind; not after being startled awake by your yelling." Her words were talons of challenge.

"Master, remember?" I said, trying to politely yet sternly remind Vicky.

"Master," Vicky said mockingly as she eyed me with that annoyed look.

My little soldier started to stiffen up. Was it the way Sarah seemed so innocent? Or the way Vicky was challenging my authority?

It was both. Sarah's innocence and Vicky's brattiness.

"You are not as angry with us as your voice makes it seem... Master." Vicky eyed my groin as a wicked smirk broke across her face.

"We are sorry, Master. You texted me last night. We were worried because it was a jumble of letters." Sarah sobbed out as she held back her tears.

What? I texted her? How? I don't even have their numbers.

"We both rushed over, fearing something had happened to you," Sarah continued. "Mrs. Helderman, let us in with the spare key you keep stashed at her place."

"We found your drunk ass passed out on the couch... Master," Vicky interjected, still with a bratty tone.

"How did I text either of you? I don't have your numbers," I said, crossing my arms.

"Yes, you do, Master." Sarah sniffled as she sat up in bed. "The other night, when you were in the shower, we both put our numbers in your phone. We even added you to our Facebook accounts."

The hell... I had their contact information this whole time? I worried myself sick, literally sick, this morning for nothing. I could have been texting all those cute things I thought about this week. So much for being a smart geek.

"I was shocked to see you two here, but I really wasn't angry about that. That is not why I am upset with you two." I reinitiated my strictness.

Vicky broke into a roaring cackle. She motioned to Sarah with her hand in a fist, moving it in front of her face and bobbing her head. Sarah grinned and then looked back at me, batting her eyelashes with a coyness. Was I that obvious?

"Why didn't you finish what you had started? I went to bed with my balls about to explode. I had to beat the motherfucker like it owed me money." I almost laughed at my own comment. Did I really just say that?

"Speaking of beating. What happened to your chin?" Vicky and Sarah both got out of bed to inspect my face. They both reached out and rubbed the area where Howard had popped me a good one the night before.

"I got into a fight, but it's all good now." I tried to comfort them. "He bought me drinks afterward, and we talked for a bit."

"Master? What do you mean he bought you drinks?" Sarah inquired.

"You got into a fight, then afterward drank with the guy you got into it with?" Vicky was surprised.

I wasn't sure if they were shocked by hearing about me scrapping. Could it be they were surprised at the fact that I hung out with Howard after the tussle?

"Like I said, he bought me drinks. We hung out for a bit. Then I drove him home." I was confused. How was this hard to grasp?

"You what? Master, you were in no shape to drive when we got here." Sarah's concern soothed me.

Vicky glanced at Sarah. "Looks like we aren't the ones that need the spanking, huh." Then she eyed me up and down.

I calmed down, elated by their concerned and nurturing natures. Each were unique in their own way. Sarah was a distraught, worried mess. And Vicky was a harsh worry, almost motherly. The way they left me the other night was not completely forgiven. But this... this concern of theirs had tugged at my softer side.

"Breakfast? I'll cook you two eggs. But as for the blowjob, that business is not finished. Just parlayed for now." My voice tried to regain its sternness, but I couldn't mask my ecstatic feelings.

I walked toward the kitchen; they followed behind me without a word. They sat at the dining table as I gathered the ingredients and supplies. I was determined to cook for them. I worked to give them a treat since they had shown up with concern. My cooking was okay, but not the best, so I hoped they would like it.

I could feel their eyes on me as they sat at the table, both, of course, still nude. Never letting up from me, their eyes trained on my every action. They whispered back and forth to each other.

Scrambled eggs, sausage, toast, and bacon were done in no time. I set the table and served the food.

41

"I hope you enjoy your breakfast," I said as I sat to eat with them.

"We already are just watching you, Master." Vicky's tone was more endearing than earlier as she started making her plate.

"It's nice to sit together like this." Sarah gestured her hands up and down her naked body. I looked down; I was still nude as well. I felt so comfortable around them that I had forgotten I had no clothes on.

"What's new since Tuesday?" I asked, trying to start up a conversation about something other than nudity and sex.

"Well, I have less than a week before I take my massage and bodywork exam." Vicky sighed with anxiety.

"I'm sure you'll do great. That massage you gave me the other night worked out some kinks in my back." I said, trying to encourage her. And it was true; the pain in my lower back had not been there since that night.

"Hope so, Master. But it's a written exam, not a skills exam. Around a hundred questions." Vicky shrugged as she corrected me.

"With all the studying you've been doing lately, you should ace it," Sarah said in a comforting tone.

"I believe in you. I think you can accomplish anything you want," I said as I attempted to encourage her.

"It's nice to know that you believe in me. Both of you," Vicky said with a sound of relief. Her breasts jiggled a bit as she took a deep breath.

Seeing Vicky in a vulnerable way made me think that she needed something more from me. I wasn't sure what. All I knew was that I wanted to be there for her... and Sarah. I felt that I needed to be more for them, but I was at a loss for what "more" meant.

"What's new with you?" I turned the conversation to Sarah.

"I applied for a few jobs—two HR ones and a payroll position at another company. But my hope is I get the one at the publishing company downtown." Sarah smirked for a moment; she seemed to be fantasizing about the job.

"Sweet. But why is the publishing company your top pick?" I looked at her as I took a bite of eggs.

"Sometimes, you can volunteer to beta read the new books. That seems like an enjoyable perk of the job, reading a book before it's released. To be one of the first to see it," Sarah excitedly said.

42

"She loves to read. Nose in a book all the time. So that one may be the best fit for her." Vicky said nodding with an approving grin.

"That would be a pretty cool perk of a job. To be the first to see something before the world gets it." It was strange that talking with them felt so comfortable. And I was doing it in the nude. They were nude, too. Yet I was more intrigued by what they had to say rather than thinking about sex in this moment.

"My mother called me. I explained our new relationship to her. She was excited about it," Vicky informed me.

"Mama Naomi is so freaking awesome!" Sarah bounced in her seat with excitement. Her arm plopped down on the table in a crash. I thought she had knocked something off, but she hadn't.

She told her mother! Damn. I hoped that I didn't have to meet her anytime soon. If I did, what would I say? How would I explain that I was with both of them? Oh, hi, Naomi, I'm dating your daughter and her best friend. Real smooth. I'll sound like such a dope, like some horny, perverted dude. A player or something.

"Yeah. She is somewhere abroad right now. Not sure where. But she said she was meeting with a client or something." Vicky gave a dismissive wave.

I felt relieved. I could put off meeting their parents and avoid explaining all this to them for a while. Besides, I barely understood it myself.

"I started reading this book, a real dirty one." Sarah giggled before sipping her orange juice.

"You always read dirty books." Vicky rolled her eyes.

"So, what? They have great stories. And well... get my juices flowing," Sarah said, her lips curled up coquettishly.

"What did your imaginary book boyfriend do in this one?" Vicky asked mockingly. I stayed quiet during their exchange, intrigued by their interaction.

"More interesting stuff than the imaginary places you paint." Sarah briefly stuck out her tongue.

"Vicky, you paint?" I had to know.

"Occasionally. I'm not too good. Mostly, I paint landscapes. The ones I have in my mind. Places that I dream of." Vicky looked at me with a bit of embarrassment on her face.

"Cool. I would love to see them sometime."

"Really?" Vicky eased from her embarrassment.

"Yeah. I want to see where your mind lives." The smoothness of the NCO's voice oozed from my lips.

The table was silent as we finished our plates. I stood, picked up the dishes, and placed them in the sink. I would get to cleaning later. But for now, I wanted to continue talking with them.

"So, should I be jealous of this book guy?" I smiled at Sarah.

"Um... maybe." Sarah giggled as her cheeks flushed crimson.

"Just watch out; the pages might come alive, sweeping us off our feet." Vicky exaggerated. She put her hand on her forehead as she feigned swooning.

"Oh, yeah. I would give him the old one-two. But fair warning, I am prone to paper cuts." I chuckled as I took my place back at the table. However, after sitting down, I quickly realized that joking might be insensitive to Sarah's hobby.

"Don't make me call up all my story boyfriends. Paper cuts all around." Sarah laughed. She seemed to take the banter well.

I felt at ease that I hadn't screwed up. My awkward joke was taken in stride. I relaxed in the chair.

"So, how was your week?" Vicky asked, turning the conversation to me.

"Yeah, Master, anything new with you?" Sarah aided Vicky in turning the focus to me.

"Nothing, really, most of my week was boring." My response was subtle and abrupt.

There really wasn't much that happened. I worked, saved money, and slept. There was nothing exciting to report. My life was honestly dull in comparison to theirs.

"Come on, last night was not nothing," Vicky said, frustrated by my answer.

"I agree; he owes us an explanation."

"Fine. I went to the gaming store downtown. You know, Ground Zero. I thought I might buy something. Maybe make a friend." I looked at them. They both stared at me with anticipation.

"Is that where you got into a fight, a gaming store?" Vicky asked, trying to get more details.

"No... well, sort of. In the parking lot."

"Someone didn't agree with how you played or something?" Sarah looked at me, confused.

"The guys in the shop really didn't talk to me. I had found this charming figurine; I figured it would look good sitting on the entertainment center." I pointed toward the living room.

"So... how did you get in a fight, Master?" Sarah squinted at me like she was trying to see through me.

"Howard, the guy, was standing outside. I guess he had stumbled over from the bar next door. He took the figure and smashed it." My voice fell dark for a moment.

"Did you beat his ass?" Vicky said excitedly. She seemed to be getting turned on by her own question.

"Yeah. I guess. Then, after, he offered to buy me a drink. So, we sat for a few hours talking. The rest you already know."

"Why did he smash the figurine?" Sarah asked.

"It was a Harley Quinn bust, an adorable and sexy one. So, he had commented about beating off to it or something."

"Harley Quinn, that sexy Batman villain?" Vicky giggled.

"Oh no, Vicky. He was trying to replace us." Sarah laughed with her.

"I think that guy was right: Master bought it to choke the chicken to." Vicky started roaring with laughter as she motioned her hand up and down.

I started to laugh along with them. It was pretty silly that I bought it. And maybe they were half-right. I had just been sexually aroused by them for two days, so most of my thoughts were on sex.

Sarah laughed. "We aren't enough for you, Master?"

"Guess not. He had to get something synthetic to replace us." Vicky jokingly added.

"At least she would have finished the job." I chuckled, jokingly jabbing at them.

"You think we aren't up to the task, Master?" Vicky's tone went from laughter to seductive as she scooted over to me. She planted a hand on my thigh, motioning to Sarah with the other.

Sarah grinned wickedly as her laughter changed to a devilish giggle. She crawled under the table. I felt her breath on my pole; that was all it took. My flag was flying high in a nanosecond. She didn't retreat; her mouth engulfed me whole. Vicky looked down at Sarah seductively, then leaned into my ear.

"About that blowjob, I hope you can accept our apology, Master," Vicky softly whispered in my ear. Her words pushed me back into that sexually frenzied state of mind. The one they had ignited in me the last two times they were here.

The slurping and gagging sounds from under the table were so rhythmic. It sounded like a beautifully composed orchestra. I gazed under the table. That red hair flowed into a dancing flame. Her face repeatedly slid down, then back up the entire length of my erection. The warmth of her mouth around me made me squirm in the chair. I huffed out cursory whines of pleasure. As those green jewels eyed me, they expressed love and demand. She was demanding to have my hot ooze. She was drawing me near. I let her take complete control over me as she worked the entire length of my shaft.

Vicky kissed me deeply as Sarah did her work. I felt her soft breasts against my chest as she deepened the kiss. It wasn't long before I shot my seed into the depths of Sarah's mouth. She emerged from under the table. Her jaw closed; her cheeks puffed out. She opened her mouth, showing me that my love juice was still inside. She then swallowed it with one gulp. Sarah stood stiff for a moment, her eyes fixed forward. Then, just as quickly as she had stiffened, she shook loose and regained her playful composure.

"Every drop, Master," Sarah said as she smiled, her teeth still stained with seminal fluids.

"Master, your precious seed will never be wasted again. It will always be in our holes. We promise, Master," Vicky said as she started to stroke my shaft. "Even if it leaks out, even if it's on the filthy floor, we will lap it up. Every drop."

That's so hot.

"You think that's hot, Master?" Sarah said wide-eyed with glee.

Shit, did I say that out loud?

"What else do you think is hot... Master?" Vicky's voice had a sexy tone in my ear as her hand hastened. "We have tasted your sweetness, but you haven't tasted us."

Vicky stopped stroking, and an inkling of disappointment washed over me. She stood up and jumped onto the table, her legs spread wide before me. Her hands were on either side of her thighs, opening herself to me.

"You made us breakfast, Master. Now it's time for you to eat the meal we have for you," Sarah said as she leaned down, pointing to Vicky's open and exposed flower.

I moved forward, my face near her moist opening. Her sweet aroma filled me with a delight I had never known before. I nuzzled into the soft pinkness of her box. The heat on my face aroused my desire to taste her.

My nose rubbed along her bud as my tongue traced her folds. I felt her hands wrap around the back of my head as she pushed me deeper into her. Her dark bush grazed my face like a velvet fabric.

I lightly nibbled her bud before my tongue flicked it. I suckled the tender flesh of her clit with my tongue twisting into her warm vulva. I lapped at the inside of her.

The taste was so... mmm... so delicious. Her moans encouraged me to continue. I moved my head up and down. I compelled her body—no, commanded her body—to bend to my will. My hands gripped her outer thighs. I ate her sweetness like the last pumpkin pie piece on Thanksgiving Day. I felt Sarah's breasts on my back; she must have been watching me go to town on Vicky.
"She tastes great, doesn't she, Master?" Sarah's low tone made me want to get Vicky to the edge and taste her next.

I hastened my pace, my tongue building her to release. Her hands pulled rougher and strained to hold my head in place. Her hips rocked as she was nearing. There was no escaping; her thighs wrenched around my face. Then a loud moan as she flooded me with her honey. The way her body held me in place, I felt like I would drown in her warm fluids. I drank down all that I could. She laid back on the table as her body released my head. Her legs went limp. Her breaths were shallow and rapid. Her head laid back.

This was the first time I had pleasured a woman like this. I felt accomplished that she had orgasmed.

I sat straight in my chair, her warm juices dripping from my chin. My eyes studied the beautiful mess that I had just made of Vicky before they darted to Sarah. Sarah stood there in lusty amazement. Her hand between her legs rubbed vigorously; she had just witnessed the rawness of my power. The power of bringing Vicky to delight. A power that I didn't even know I had.

"Oh, fuck, Master. That was incredible." Vicky sighed weakly as she struggled to get to her elbows. Her eyes beamed upon me in a religious awakening. I could see that she saw me as her god, a sexual deity to be worshipped.

I stood up confidently and scooped Vicky into my arms with one fluid motion. I carried her to the couch. Sarah followed behind us. I gently laid Vicky down to rest on the sofa. As I pulled my arms away, I leaned over her. My lips locked into hers with a fiery caress. We kissed for a moment before I pulled away. I turned to Sarah. My eyes roamed up and down her—mm-mm... so gorgeous. I looked into her eyes and motioned her to the La-Z-Boy.

"Put your knees in the chair, rest your arms on the back. Grip the headrest tight. And bend that big, beautiful ass outward toward me." My voice was so smooth and confident.

"Yes, Master." Sarah's tone was surprised yet endearing. She complied as I had instructed.

The way her body bent over the chair was a sight that would humble the most powerful of kings. The roundness of her derrière was like two succulent globes smashed together. I kneeled behind her; her sweet aroma was just as intoxicating as Vicky's. My hands spread open her cheeks, exposing both her holes to me.

A sharp and sly grin grew across my face as I looked over to Vicky one last time. She had regained her strength, her hand beating a hard rhythm into the mess I had made of her.

I turned my focus back to Sarah, my face plunged in. My tongue whipped across her rectum first. She let out a loud whimper, surprised by my attack. I swirled around her forbidden cave for a moment before exploring further down.

I licked deep inside her labia; she was already soaked. I probed inward, deep into her moist pink snatch. The taste was different than Vicky's but just as delectable. I lashed out, striking her love button. My nose rubbed against her anal opening. Her fiery pubic hair brushed against my chin. I suckled her button deeply; she cried out in pleasure.

My assault on her became rougher. My tongue thrashed at her. Her butt cheeks squeezed around my face as I quickened my attack. I lapped into her, more wildly as I became greedy. I needed to taste her sweetness, for her torrent to flow like a tsunami onto me. I could hear Vicky huffing on the couch, and I knew she was about there again. But this was my time with Sarah.

"Taste her, Master. Mm-mm. Eat her dirty ass," Vicky encouraged me as she began her second orgasm.

Those words were all I needed to finish Sarah. My head moved side to side, deep into her cheeks. My tongue flogged her with passion. I pressed my face deeper into her. She cried out with a wail of pleasure.

It wasn't long before Sarah became a waterfall. Her body twitched and tensed as she flowed all her warm juices upon me. I was showered, both literally and metaphorically, with her affections.

Her body pressed forward on the chair as she fell limp. However, that was not a good move. The chair fell backward. Oh shit, Sarah. No!

Sarah screamed as the chair hit the ground. I was afraid that she would be hurt. That she was injured due to some dumb kinky idea of mine. But she quickly began laughing. She didn't move, but she was laughing.

"Master, can we do that—oh fuck—can we do that again?" Sarah looked up at me, her eyes pulsed with a form of admiration I had never seen before.

I felt relieved as I helped her up. I pushed the chair into place. She sat, weak from our sexual passions. I could tell she was spent. Vicky and Sarah gave each other knowing looks. They both relaxed with a sense of ease. I sat on the floor admiring my beauties in their expelled state. That was me. I did that. I made their bodies roar with fierce orgasms. I couldn't help but grin wide, knowing I had that much power over them. That much power over their bodies.

"How was your meal, Master?" Vicky moved up on the couch as she peered down at me.

"Five stars. Best meal I have ever had the pleasure of eating." My grin couldn't get any wider. "Does it come with seconds?"

"Seconds? Damn, please let us catch our breath first, Master," Sarah said as her eyes beat upon me with a sultry glare.

I chuckled at her comment. But I was honestly surprised. That was the first time I had gone down on a woman, let alone two. And to get that reaction twice. Was it a fluke? Or was I really that good?

"Not a fluke, Master. You are really that good." Vicky growled with a sexy tone as she crawled off the couch toward me.

My eyes scoped in... Had I confessed that out loud? Did they know I was inexperienced?

"I don't think he realizes how sexy he is when he talks to himself," Sarah said seductively as she joined Vicky in a crawl toward me.

All the color from my face flushed away as I felt deeply embarrassed once more. Shit! How much of my private thoughts had I let out during all of our exchanges?

"It's okay, Master. There is no need to be ashamed. We are yours, and you are ours," they said together in an eerie but sexy way.

They approached me at the same time. They kneeled and slung their arms around me and each other. We all three embraced. Vicky leaned in to kiss me first, then Sarah. I kissed them both with a ferocity that removed my embarrassment. They pulled back and locked a kiss into each other. I was surprised but happy to see this. Then they broke from each other, their tongues out, and turned to me. All three of our tongues collided into a kiss so passionately that I felt it in my core. I felt a sense of pride as I knew they were mine.

After our kiss, they pulled off of me. But I was ready for more. My eyes shot up at them as they stood after our kiss. They were peering down at me with playful yet sensual stares.

Their bodies were so arousing as the sweat beads rolled down them. I gazed upon those dripping roses; my eyes studied them. God, I needed more. I needed to be inside them. I plotted the vector of approach for each one. Vicky, I would turn her around, shoving her into the wall. Her rear at my hips, I would thrust in with a sexual rage. Sarah, more tenderly, I would lay her down on the bed, her legs spread wide. Ease into her with a slow pace, gently building her up into orgasm. I had to have them, but they got up, left me sitting here. Now... now I was so... *without.*

I must have had a saddened expression. They both seemed to express a bit of pity. But that was soon replaced with giggles.

"We didn't break your rule, Master." Sarah giggled as her hands moved to her mouth to hide her laughter.

"No penetration, so no sex happened. See, we were good girls, Master," Vicky said with her sly grin.

"What rule?" I questioned as my throbbing instrument hungered for more.

They held up three fingers. This reminded me of my three-date rule. YOU IDIOT! Now I sat on the floor, my little soldier standing at attention. Blocked by my own rule. Okay, well played, ladies.

I watched as those gorgeous bodies went to the bedroom. Their hips swayed in such a seductive way it made the beast inside me roar. If only I could take them back into the moments of ecstasy that we were just at. Then those warm morsels I had tasted would be mine, all mine. I started to follow them. But as I got to the door, Sarah closed it before I arrived. I turned the knob, but it was locked. Dammit. I guess they took my command seriously.

I didn't enjoy being locked out of my own bedroom, but I really had no one to blame. I moved to the living room, waiting for them to come out. My mind was a fray of those juicy flowers that were just on my lips. How I wanted, no, I needed to be inside them. To feel them sink down upon me completely. They were beautiful in that exhausted state. Their bodies were covered in sweat; it sent my lust into overdrive. Those dripping, soaked caves of pleasure, I had done that. Oh God, the way their faces looked at me after I had brought them to the edge. Brought them to delight.

I moved back to the living room. My eyes looked over at the clock. It was only eleven-thirty. The day was still young. The ruckus this morning had lasted over two and a half hours between breakfast and the morning delights. My jaw ached a bit. Had I really done that for almost an hour on each?

I slumped into the La-Z-Boy. I noticed that the armrest was cantered outward, barely hanging on. I laughed to myself thinking of Sarah's fall. I guess I will have to fix that at some point.

I reviewed the events of the morning, attempting to quell my sexual desires. Sarah was a bookworm. Smutty romance books were her forte. Nope, not going there! Sex is off the table for now.

Painting. Vicky liked to paint landscapes. I knew of a few places that could inspire her works. Maybe, in the future, I could take them to those spots. We could go camping with a romantic fire warming the night, easing into the tent to cuddle. Take in the howls of nature while I made them howl in pleasure. Stop it. Just stop, Sergeant.

Sarah liked jobs that required her to think—office work, which seemed to suit her librarian sexiness. Vicky liked working with her hands, caressing bodies. Dammit, can't I think about anything other than sex right now?

I gave in, all my thoughts were currently clouded in a sensual haze. I recounted what they had said at the kitchen table.

Every drop. That was interesting. Interesting and hot. They would make sure that every drop of my seed was inside them. My hot loads inside their holes: mouths, cunts, asses. All holes? Did that mean they now claimed ownership of all of my semen? Was it theirs now?

"Of course, Master, all of it belongs to us now." Vicky spooked me as she emerged from behind the chair, fully clothed.

"Here, Master, we picked you out something to wear." Sarah's joy was bursting as she threw some clothes on my lap.

I looked down. A white button-up shirt, the only one that I owned, black cargo pants, socks, and my tactical belt. I didn't have many clothes really. Mostly practical wear. I didn't need that many clothes; I was used to being in one uniform or the other. I guess this was their way of dressing me up. But I noticed that they had forgotten boxers.

"What about underwear?" I questioned, puzzled as to how they could have made such an oversight.

"We think Spider-Man can take the day off, Master," Vicky said in a slightly sarcastic tone, reminding me that they had seen Elle's birth control present.

I reluctantly stood and put on my clothes. My member had finally subsided, for now. I looked at the clock; it was about twelve-fifteen. They had been in my room for almost an hour. What had they been doing in there?

Eyeing them, I scanned what they had on. Sarah's large cleavage was revealed in a blue V-cut spaghetti strap shirt. Her nipples poked through the fabric. Blue jean shorts hugged her hips tightly. Vicky was in a red T-shirt that showed her belly and a short black skirt; obviously, she didn't have a bra either. Again, why did they wear such things? To entice me? To instigate my desires? I cinched my belt down and slid into my boots. Not a word was spoken. They just stood there watching me dress.

Sarah's red hair was brushed out neatly; it cascaded over her shoulders. Vicky's darkened mane was pulled back into a ponytail.

"Can date two be a lunch instead of dinner, Master?" Sarah coyishly asked.

Crap! I hadn't thought about the cost of taking a woman out. Let alone two. And I had spent a stupid amount on that Harley Quinn, which I had for all of three minutes. Embarrassment crept up inside of me. I was ashamed that I couldn't take them somewhere nice. Somewhere that they deserved.

"Yes, but I am afraid that I don't have money for anywhere expensive." I walked toward the door, feeling defeated by my small wallet.

"Master, we did not agree to be yours for what you can provide." I felt Vicky's hand on my shoulder as she assured me. "We are yours because of who you are."

"You are a good man, Master. Our good man. That is what matters to us." Sarah's eyes gazed upon me in admiration.

Their words shoved the shame and embarrassment aside. They both kissed my cheek before we all stepped out of the apartment.

Chapter 5: Majestic Romance

Vicky locked her arm into mine on my right, and Sarah mirrored her on my left. We moved down the hallway toward our first actual date. This was the first time I walked beside a real woman, well, two, and the first time I did so as an appreciated boyfriend. I walked much higher than I ever had; a sense of pride that I had never known swept over me. The only experience I could compare to the feeling they gave me was the Blue Steel Ceremony at the end of basic training.

The ceremony happened after the last field training exercise. The tradition made each of us young soldiers shed a tear. It consisted of an anvil, a hammer, a fire, and a piece of straight rebar. The First Sergeant spoke throughout the entire process. He gave a speech about what each item was and what it represented.

The unit commander placed the rebar into the fire. He then pulled it out to hammer it on the anvil. The rebar represented us when we first arrived at Basic. Out of shape and not ready for battle. The commander pulled out a more defined piece of steel and repeated the process of the fire and hammering.

Then, finally, the commander drew a beautifully crafted ornate sword. This sword represented what we had become. That was the first time I had ever felt like a man. I knew that I was no longer a boy. I felt powerful knowing that I was the sword. That I was the protector I always wanted to be.

That feeling had now been shadowed by how my girlfriends made me feel. I felt even more powerful, as if the world was mine. I was their protector and their lover. I just needed to take the final step of being their provider. With them by my side, I knew that I could conquer that. And so much more. As we made our way to the end of the hall, we saw Mrs. Helderman.

"Kyle. Ladies." She nodded as the age lines on her face smoothed into a grin. She seemed pleased to acknowledge her own happiness with the situation. Her eyes sparkled with a sense that she had done her part.

"Good afternoon, Mrs. Helderman. Sorry we can't stay and chat, but I promised them a date." My words were saturated with my apology as I nodded back at her.

"Young love is so wonderful. Have fun, you three." Those wise eyes winked at us as she passed us with a pep in her step.

We made our way to my beater. Neither of them seemed to mind that my car was banged up and barely road-worthy. Their grins never broke.

I opened the doors for them. Vicky jumped in the front passenger seat, Sarah in the back on the driver's side. I eased in, seating myself proudly. Gracefully, my hand turned the ignition. With ease, my foot pressed down on the pedal. We pulled out, heading toward our first real date. They wanted to drive around for a while before we went to the restaurant. I complied with their wishes.

"Honda Civic, not bad. But, when you get your company going, you will need a big double-cabbed truck." Vicky's hand fell on my thigh as she looked over at me.

"That was the plan. A utility work truck with toolboxes on the sides." I explained. I was happy that she knew what I needed for my business.

Sarah chimed in jokingly from the back seat. "But, Master, no cute women in the office. We can't have you straying from us. If you do, we might have to chop the little guy off."

We all laughed at Sarah's joke. I felt so at ease with them. They had never judged me. They were just happy to be with me.

As we drove, they both probed me about my business aspirations. I admitted that I wanted to start small, just me and an apprentice at first. I explained that all the tools in my current work van were all mine. I was less than three months away from starting. I shared all the plans I had for the HVAC business. They encouraged me throughout the conversation. I felt so inspired to begin, so motivated. The topic of my current finances came up. The number that was in my little nest egg was brought to light.

"Wow, Master. That must have taken some real discipline to save up that much," Sarah shouted with glee. Her hand moved to the front seat, tenderly placing it over my chest.

"Your business should have a great start with all that." Vicky expressed her admiration with an encouraging tone.

"So, what about you? Sticking to human resource representative? Or are there other plans?" I asked Sarah.

"I would like to go back to school to be a teacher. I love working with children." I could tell the excitement in Sarah's voice over the idea. She seemed like she would be great with kids.

Vicky turned in her seat and looked at Sarah with a supporting gaze. "You would make a great teacher."

"That sounds awesome. Maybe when you settle in with a new job, we might look at finding ways for you to get your degree. Or forego the job and just focus on the degree," I said, trying to find a way to aid her.

"I don't want to burden Vicky if I go to college." Sarah's voice was low and full of defeat.

"Hey, we can figure it out. Besides, you have me now. I can pick up the slack. If you want to go back to school full-time, I will help." I tried to fill my words with deep encouragement.

"Yeah, see, even Kyle is willing to help. And you are never a burden to me," Vicky assured Sarah before turning back to face the front of the car.

"Thank you both. But for now, I want to see if I get that job with the publishing company. And Vicky... he is Master, not Kyle." Sarah's voice seemed filled with thought.

"Sorry, Master. It sometimes feels weird to call him that, but most of the time, it feels right," Vicky said as she turned to look out the window.

"I know what you mean. But as you said, it feels comforting most of the time." Sarah sat back in her seat.

"And you?" I asked, turning the conversation toward Vicky.

"What?" Vicky asked, she turned from the window to look at me.

"So, masseuse, anything planned there?" I asked as my eyes briefly left the road to glance at her.

"Don't know, really," Vicky bleated, her words fading into a depressive mood. "Maybe one day, open a spa or something." It was obvious that she really wanted to open a spa. But something was holding her back.

"A spa would be so cool. Just don't put seaweed up my butt or anything like that." I attempted to make a joke to pull Vicky out of her seemingly depressed thoughts.

"Yeah. Seaweed, yeah. The spa is a dumb idea." Vicky pulled back further.

I guess joking was not the right idea. I screwed up like I always did with people. But she wasn't "people." She was my girlfriend, which made my miscalculation feel much more devastating. I wanted to encourage her. "I think a spa is an awesome idea. And we can work together to find a way to start it up."

"I always thought it was a great business idea. Hire more masseuses, some beauty experts, and a chiropractor. Would be perfect." Sarah tried to help uplift Vicky's suddenly sullen mood.

"You guys think so?" Vicky's voice sounded hopeful.

"Yeah. That would be a great business venture." The NCO tone slipped softly from my lips.

"Thank you," Vicky said softly with resilience as she turned back to the window.

"Maybe we should get something on the go; I want to drive around more, please, Master," Sarah said in a cute and innocent baby voice.

"Burger King? But instead of driving around more, I have a place that I'd like to show you two," I replied as I thought about my favorite spot. I went there to escape people and not be in an empty apartment. And Vicky liked painting landscapes, so I was sure this place would inspire her.

"Okay, Master." Sarah jumped around ecstatically in the back.

"Show us some place, huh, Master? If I didn't know better, I would think you were trying to take us somewhere to have your way with us." Vicky's tone had that sexy undertone she excelled at.

We pulled into the drive-through. I got a double cheeseburger, Sarah a chicken sandwich, and Vicky a burger. Once I had paid and got our food, we were off again. The conversation started back up as we headed for my spot. This time, the topic of choice was siblings.

"Do either of you have brothers or sisters?" I questioned.

"No," they said in unison.

"I was an only child. After I was born, my parents had just moved next door to the Scheins, Vicky's family." Sarah had a soft quality to her voice.

"I was an only child as well," Vicky added.

"Our families became really close. They even removed the fence that divided our backyards, so Vicky and I had this giant backyard between the two houses to play in. From then on, we shared everything." Sarah fondly reminisced.

"Until my dad died. Mom couldn't afford to pay the mortgage anymore." Vicky pressed on somberly. "We had to move into a low-rent apartment across town."

I wanted to pull over. To hug her. But I left it alone.

"Yeah, but we stayed sisters." Sarah tried to pull Vicky out of the mood she was getting back into.

"We will always be sisters, Sarah Jones," Vicky announced, perking up a bit.

"Till the day we die, we will always be by each other's side, sharing our lives together," Sarah excitedly said, reaching up to rub Vicky's shoulder.

As the conversation turned to different antics they got up to in their youth, I began to understand why this arrangement didn't bother them. I could see a unique connection. From what I could tell, they, in an odd sort of way, had a connection very much like twins sometimes share. Maybe that was why, at times, they would say the same thing at the same time the other did. And through all the ups and downs, their sisterhood had stayed intact.

"What about your sister, Master? Is she your only sibling?" Vicky asked, her voice more cheerful.

"Yeah, at least on the days she claims me," I joked as I turned off the smooth pavement onto the rough dirt road.

"Oh, days she would claim you, huh," Sarah said in a low voice from the back seat. Her remark felt more rhetorical, as if she was trying to understand.

"Since Elle is six years older than me, she sort of was always highly protective over me. She always came to my rescue as a kid," I continued.

"What did you need rescuing from?" Vicky asked with intrigue in her voice.

"It should come as no surprise, but I was always bullied. I guess I was the quiet, weird, creepy kid in the back of class. Something like that," I reluctantly admitted.

"You are not creepy, Master. Different, maybe weird. But not creepy." Sarah leaned forward, her hand rubbing my shoulder.

"So, what brought you to Dallas?" Vicky tried to change the subject.

"After I got out of the Army five months ago, I had nowhere to go. I basically followed Elle here. She and Stephen had moved to Dallas a few years back for his job. So, here I am." I shrugged.

"How are things with your sister, Master?" Sarah asked.

"Okay, I guess. She's been different since I moved here. And I don't know how she would take it if she heard you two call me Master. She has been strange, so I just don't know..." Elle hadn't really wanted to hang out with me, almost like she had avoided me.

"But Jenny, my niece. I have a much better relationship with her these days. She is a funny little thing. Five years old and would tell the world off if she had to. Always dragging around her favorite doll everywhere." My eyes watched the road as I spoke.

The car was silent for a moment after I brought up Jenny. It was almost as if they were both thinking about children or something. My mind drifted off into thought.

I remembered last week that Vicky said her birthday was in a month. I wanted to know the exact date and maybe figure out what she wanted to do for her birthday. She had said Sarah's had been three months ago, so I assumed sometime in March. It was too bad that I didn't know them when I moved here. I could have celebrated both their birthdays with something special. But what would they both want to do for their birthdays?

I broke the awkward silence. "So, birthdays? Vicky, you mentioned yours was in a month and Sarah's a few months back."

"Cake and ice cream day for me is March seventeenth," Sarah roared with that cute child-like tone she often took.

"Mine is July thirteenth," Vicky said semi-excitedly.

"I'm too late for Sarah's this year. But any plans for yours, Vicky?" I was trying to figure out if anything was already in the works. If not, I wanted to do something special. I just didn't know what.

"Eat cake... I guess." Vicky let out a sarcastic huff.

"We can try something better than just eating cake. Sarah, do you want to help me with setting it up?" I glanced in the rearview mirror at Sarah as my words came out frantically. I beamed brightly before quickly focusing back on the road. I was happy I could now do something special for one of them.

"Yes! We can plan something fun, Master." Sarah was giddy at the idea of making Vicky's birthday a special event.

"We can't do anything too big. Our apartment is tiny, and so is Masters'," Vicky stated with a cool but intrigued voice. She seemed happy that I wanted to celebrate her birthday.

"Sarah and I will figure it out. Just leave it to us." My words bubbled with excitement. I could now plan a birthday party for one of my girlfriends. I had always wanted to do something like that. I hoped to get many opportunities to plan things for them. Christmas presents would also be a fun one.

"It's about time we upgraded apartments anyway. We have lived together in ours since we graduated high school." Sarah's tone suggested she was hinting at something.

"Hmm... we could go house hunting once Master's business is going well." Vicky's excitement started to highlight her playful tone.

"Four bedrooms. That should be enough to expand our family," Sarah expressed with excitement in her voice.

"Better make it six bedrooms; he is a horny little toad." Vicky laughed, poking at my sexual desires.

I chuckled. "Hey, that's y'all's fault."

"Nuh-uh. We're good girls. Said so yourself, Master." Sarah started to giggle.

"Only one person in this car with a perverted mind. And it's not us girls, Master." Vicky laughed.

"Sure." I snickered sarcastically.

They stopped picking on me and went back to the house talk. They filled the time with details on their dream house.

"We need a library for all my books," Sarah pointed out.

"And a studio room for me to paint. Get some nice brushes," Vicky said as she stared at the dashboard.

"A kids' playroom. Somewhere we can put all the toys, and the kids can play on rainy days." Sarah jumped around with joy.

"What about the kitchen? We will need a big stove and oven. A huge fridge. And lots of space to feed all our children." Vicky turned around in her seat again. Her hands mapped the dining table as they plotted the seating arrangements.

As they described this place further, a sense of love rained upon me. I could imagine living with them happily in our three-way marital bliss. And the talk of children made me think about the act of making them.

I drove around the curvy dirt road to the lake. The rough roads made them bounce around the car. I was having a hard time keeping my eyes on the road. If my eyes weren't glancing over at Vicky's breasts, they were staring at Sarah's in the rearview mirror. Vicky's bounced like two basketballs colliding into each other. Sarah's jiggled like two waterbeds. I could feel my member growing. Stay focused, Sergeant. The road. Focus on the road.

"Our favorite little soldier is standing up," Vicky told Sarah as her hand slid up, groping the bulge on my thigh.

"Naughty, naughty. This is only the second date, Master." Sarah leaned into the front seat, whispering in my ear.

What they do to me. How they make me feel. My mind had flashes of taking them both right here in the car. Just pull over and use their bodies. Slam them over the hood or pound them in the back seat—

No! Focus on the road.

Sarah started nibbling my ear. Vicky rubbed me through my cargo pants. I groaned out in pleasure. It was all I could do to keep us on the narrow road. I tried to focus, but they were making it impossible to concentrate. We arrived at the spot. As I parked the car, they pulled back. Vicky moved her hand away, and Sarah sat back in the back seat. Damn, I was ready again, but they had cooled off just as quickly as they had heated me up. Teases. Real goddamn teasing bitches.

The overlook was secluded, and there was seldom anyone there. The place was deserted as usual.

Taking a moment to collect myself and calm down my little soldier, I breathed deeply. When I looked over the dashboard out the window, my eyes were met with a majestic sight.

The way the rocks meshed into the sand, the trees on all sides, the grass so green and lush. The sun beamed down across the lake at a perfect angle, making those small sparkles, as if the light was dancing over the water. The sky was a deep blue, and small puffs of clouds slowly moved across it.

I opened my door and walked to the front of the car. I sat on the hood and peered out at the beauty of this scenery. This was my home away from home. I smirked; I had never brought anyone here before, and I was happy to share it with them.

Vicky and Sarah soon followed with the food and drinks. Vicky placed mine beside me on the hood. They sat cross-legged on the ground below me, their backs against the car. In silence for a moment, we all admired the area's beauty.

"This is gorgeous. Thank you, Master," Vicky said, her eyes peeking up to me.

"Beautiful, Master. How did you find this place? It didn't seem easy to get here." Sarah looked at the lake as she took a bite from her chicken sandwich.

I looked down at them. I admired how they looked when they were eating. It was so cute. Watching them consume their nourishment was a gratifying and delightful sight—sensual even. As they took small bites, I felt like a voyeur—a feeling of happiness that I couldn't explain. Just that I liked watching them eat.

"I found it driving around a few days after I had moved here." My voice was low, almost a whisper.

Jumping down from the hood, I sat on the ground between my girlfriends. We ate in silence as we drank in the beauty of this place. All we could hear was leaves rustling as the wind pressed against the trees. This felt so right. The beauty of nature around the beauty of my beloveds. There was nowhere else I would rather be than here. In this moment, with them. My mind wondered what else I could learn about them.

"What kind of music do you each like?" I asked as we peered over the serenity of the lake.

"Country is my main jam. But really, anything with songs that have a longing for love," Sarah said as she shook a fry around.

"Rock... punk rock. Raw tasty riffs with lyrics that are the stuff of rebellion." Vicky's hands air-guitared as her face briefly scrunched into a mean look.

Their musical tastes mirrored their personalities. I guess I shouldn't be surprised. Long trips were going to be interesting. Hank Williams, followed by The Clash. Throw in my dance music, and an eclectic soundtrack will be born.

Vicky turned to me. "What music gets you going?"

"Toe tappers. I don't care about the genre, really. I just want music that inspires me to dance," I explained as I looked over at Vicky. Those blue ovals ripped into my core as she winked at me.

"Dancing, hmm. Someday, you will have to dance with us, Master." Sarah slapped her hand on my knee.

"Deal." I turned to look at Sarah. Her green eyes sparkled with excitement.

We continued eating in silence for a moment as we enjoyed the scenery. After we were done, I stood up and discarded the trash into a bag I had in the backseat. Then, I held my hands out to help them to their feet.

"Let's take a walk," I suggested. They both took my hands, and I helped them up.

"But Master, it's so beautiful here." Sarah didn't seem to want to leave this spot.

"Trust me, I have somewhere you will love even more," I assured her as a soft NCO tone slid from my lips.

"Hmm..." That was all that Vicky said. She eyed me with a bit of suspicion.

We started walking toward the trees. I walked ahead of them into the woods, knowing exactly where I was going. A beautiful waterfall area was just on the other side of the wood line. I often went there to hear the water splashing against the rocks. It was a very peaceful place.

We walked for several minutes in silence. I glanced back. They were still following close behind me. Due to the thick brush, we had to walk single file. You could tell the path was barely used. There were grass patches every so often along the trail. Tones of running water filled the air as we neared the clearing.

"Where are we going?" Sarah asked.

"This is the part in the movie where the unassuming boyfriend turns out to be a serial killer." Vicky laughed at her own joke.

"Maybe." I shrugged nonchalantly. "We are almost there."

The clearing came up, and the waterfall roared at full volume. I sat on the edge of the bank, looking at the waterfall.

Sarah and Vicky sat on either side of me. I put my arms around them. They both leaned into me, their heads tilted into my shoulders. A fiery red patch to my left, and a darkened veil to my right. I felt joyous as the sun's warmth bathed us in its glow. My hands snuggled tightly as I gripped their waists.

We sat in silence as the three of us admired the waterfall. The light played along the rapids in a beautiful spectrum of colors. At the bottom, the water pounded against the rocks, foaming into a creamy white cloud. The air was filled with the soft scent of nature. It was a majestic sight. The only thing I could think of that was more beautiful was the two women beside me.

All these years I had been a prisoner of my loneliness, starved of affection. Now, the key to my cell was in the hands of these two maidens. Two damsels rescued the fearless knight. Saved from his sorrow. Life anew.

I cuddled them closer without a word. We stayed like this, in silence, for almost an hour, enchanted by the beauty of nature that surrounded us. I beamed; this was the perfect date.

"You're a surprising man, Master." Sarah sighed, smitten.

"A romantic horndog, so valiant and honorable. Yet so damned dirty. No wonder we have fallen in love with him," Vicky whispered to herself, biting her lower lip.

I kissed them one by one. Sarah, first. I tasted the innocence of her affections. Our tongues gently caressed each other's. Soft whimpers from her vibrated inside my mouth. The tenderness was a sweetness of refreshing love. Her softness tugged at my heart.

Vicky second, my lips into hers as I sipped in the soul of her beauty. Our mouths were a fierce melee. A battle ensued between our tongues as we combated each other's desires. She was the harshness that pulled the beast in me to the forefront.

Not long after our kiss, a crowd rushed into the area. They started jumping into the water and screaming. One guy splashed so hard that we were almost soaked. The romance of my spot had now become a muddle of loud music and obnoxious chatter.

It was time to go. I stood up, helping them to their feet. We made our way back to the car.

"That was fun and so romantic," Sarah said as we walked back up the path.

"Very beautiful. Thank you for showing us that, Master," Vicky said as we reached the parking spot.

"Yes, today was wonderful. Thank you, Master." Sarah's bubbly voice was ecstatic. She blew a kiss at me before she and Vicky walked to the car's back doors.

"You are welcome. I knew that you two would love this place." I said with soft affection. I walked to the car with a big goofy grin pinned on my face.

64

Jumping into the car, we started back down the long road home. Vicky and Sarah had got in the back seat together. I didn't mind much. I figured that they had some girl talk they wanted to do about the date. I felt happy that they had a great time.

On the way home, they sat whispering to each other. There was no way I could figure out what they were talking about. I could only make out a word or two here and there. But mostly, they were giggling. It warmed me, knowing that they were most likely conversing about me. In the rearview mirror, I would catch glimpses of their happy faces.

The drive back took almost an hour and a half with traffic. I had fun just peaking at them through the mirror. As we got close to the apartment, their behavior got strange. I could only make out bits of it as my eyes bounced between the road and the rearview mirror.

They both suddenly sat up straight. They seemed to be in a kind of trance. It was unnerving how silent and still they were. My eyes rapidly rushed between the lines of the road and the mirror. Was something wrong?

"Hey, y'all okay?" They didn't respond; they just stayed in that weird state.

After a few moments, they whispered in unison: "Warning, accessing permanent and irreversible configuration settings. Server settings accessed. Server Disconnected. Connection permanently severed."

I was naturally confused by the words. What did they mean by connection permanently severed? Was that code for something? I wasn't sure what that meant. But I didn't want to spoil the mood. We all enjoyed ourselves at the lake. Still, I had to ask.

"What was that all about?" I questioned, looking back in the mirror. They seemed to be animated again.

"Nothing, we were just goofing off, Master." Sarah giggled as she turned to look out the window.

"Maybe you'll find out later, Master." Vicky leaned forward, blowing a kiss to the rearview mirror.

As we pulled into the apartment complex, I pushed the odd behavior aside in my mind. Maybe it was some kind of weird inside joke or game... or something. Once parked, I opened their doors. They exited the car with an allure of happiness. It was almost as if the weird behavior had not happened. I shook it off. It was a joke; it had to be some sort of inside joke.

They walked ahead of me as we returned to the apartment. I didn't mind much as it gave me a great view. Sarah's rear wiggled in those jean shorts as her thighs hit the pavement. I was reminded of how she looked bent over in the chair. And Vicky's skirt flowed slightly upward with each stride. I watched to see if it would expose those panties, if she was wearing any. Mm-mm... those asses begged me to bite them. To plunge myself deep into them.

They periodically looked back at me with sultry and inviting gazes. As we walked up the stairs, I saw Vicky's red panties under her skirt. The creases of Sarah's butt looked so hot from this angle. Damn, just a few more steps. Then again, why wait. I could take them here on the stairs. Bend them over and take what was mine. Those sweet moans would ring in my ears as I folded their bodies over the stairs as if they were origami dolls. The interesting poses and positions that I could place them in... I could even bend them over the railing, then rail the hell out of them. I was beyond ready to take them as we got to the second floor.

"Soon, Master." They both turned and whispered in unison to me as we got to the hall.

We started down the hall. But to all our surprise, Elle and Jenny stood in front of my door. An expression of dread on Elle's face. Jenny was holding her doll in her left hand. Jenny started spinning in circles before she stopped and suddenly turned. That was when she saw us. Her eyes sparkled with happiness as she darted toward us.

"Uncle Kyle!" Jenny yelled as she ran down the hall to me. I instinctively leaned down, hugged her tight, and picked her up.

"Hey, Bootyhead." I beamed at Jenny.

Vicky and Sarah watched me with Jenny in silence. Their eyes sparkled with approbation and admiration.

I shuffled Jenny to my right side, then carried her to my door. Vicky and Sarah followed close behind us. I walked up to Elle. Her face still weary with concern. She didn't have to say a word. I knew. Stephen was drunk again, a bad drunk. Violently drunk. My nostrils flared with anger, but I tried to hide it.

"Want to come in, Sis?"

"We don't want to disturb you." Elle's eyes glanced behind me. I turned my head to look. Vicky and Sarah stood less than a step behind Jenny and me.

"Don't be silly, you aren't disturbing us," Sarah blurted out. "Your little girl is so cute."

"Elle, I presume." Vicky's voice assumed a motherly tone as she tried to comfort Elle. "You are more than welcome to come in. I will make some coffee, if he has any."

Elle's eyes widened in surprise. Obviously, she didn't know what to make of the situation that she had stumbled upon. She eyed me with a bit of confusion for a moment. I just grinned the awkward grin I had when we were kids. She knew it too well. The one I had when I was caught doing something I shouldn't be doing. I unlocked the apartment and opened the door.

"These are my girlfriends, Vicky and Sarah." My words almost didn't come out at all.

"Girlfriends..." Elle eyed me with a ghastly shock.

"Yes, we are Mas— Kyle's girlfriends." Sarah jumped with joy.

I was glad Sarah caught herself. Elle hearing them call me Master would have made her head explode.

"I'll get the coffee started immediately," Vicky said without missing a beat.

"Aunt Sarah and Aunt Vicky. I get two aunts!" Jenny's excitement could barely be contained as we all piled into my apartment.

Jenny jumped down from my arms and ran into the living room. Sarah followed behind Jenny, almost skipping to catch up. Vicky walked into the kitchen, her movements full of a grace I had yet to see from her, as if she were a ballerina.

Elle... looked shaken, like the world had been nuked, and we were in the aftermath of an apocalypse. I watched as she reluctantly walked in, and I closed the door behind us.

Chapter 6: Abrasive Disapproval

Vicky wasted no time starting a pot of coffee. She stayed in the kitchen, cleaning up after the breakfast mess we had all neglected. Sarah sat on the living room floor playing with Jenny.

I stood between the living room and the kitchen, trying to gather myself. Elle was here. Why? For her to leave, Stephen must have done something rough. She had always been scared of him, that was for sure. But she seemed more shaken this time.

I glanced at Vicky, who was washing the dishes, her back to us. Then I watched Sarah playing with Jenny on the floor, the doll set between them as they giggled and conversed about tea. This may have been odd, but it was my first time seeing them in a domestic role. Not as some sexual vixens vying for my lust. "Wives" seemed to be the word that fit this situation. It was bizarre that it took Elle to show up shaken for me to realize they were more than sexual beings. Showing me that they meant more to me than that.

Elle, skittish, fidgeted in the La-Z-Boy. Her body was tense, in a state of nervous anxiety. Her face revealed a deep longing to be safe. She had a cautious posture. She couldn't seem to quell her agitation. I decided it would be best to let her speak first.

As she looked around the room, I saw the bruise on her cheek. I recognized immediately that it was a knuckle imprint. I had seen many of those before.

Elle tried to distract herself. She pushed the chair arm back and forth, trying to figure out what had happened to it. Frustrated, she finally left it alone. Then her head turned to me.

"He was violent... more violent than I've ever seen him. I got Jenny out of there before he did something really bad this time." Elle looked at me, her eyes full of sadness.

"He destroyed mom's china cabinet that I inherited. He hit me again." She sobbed as she showed me her bruised cheek. It was starting to swell. "He went after Jenny, but I snatched her up and got in the car."

Elle paused for a moment. Tears flowed down her face, but she stayed silent. I didn't want to interrupt her. But I could feel my heart pounding in my chest. The blood coursing through my veins felt like battery acid. Flashes of combat filled my mind. I was being

68

brought back to the war, back to being a monster. But Elle began to speak again.

"We rushed over here; we waited outside your apartment for a while." She continued as her voice began to crack. She held back her tears once again as she paused to gather herself.

"I can't go back. I can't... I can't do that to Jenny. I can't let him hurt her." Her voice was a wail as she cried out. My heart shattered.

I leaned down, hugging Elle tightly. Stephen's actions had me on the edge. My emotions were shutting down. That coldness bathed me in its bloodthirsty chill. I could feel the soldier emerging. That feeling you get just as the firefight starts. The feeling of killing. Killing them before they could hurt... destroy... kill everything good in this world. I held Elle for a while, then released her.

Without a word, I moved to the door. My arms were at my sides. My hands tensed into fists. Murder was on my mind. I was going to rip his face off. I was going to tear his guts out with my bare hands. He was going to suffer. He wasn't worthy of a good death. He would leave this world in the most horrific way I could inflict upon him. Vicky stepped in front of me as I moved to the door.

"Stay, Master." Her whisper was somber as she held her hand flat on my shoulder.

I felt two soft bulbs press into my back; arms wrapped around my chest from behind.

"Calm yourself, Master," Sarah whispered in my ear.

That coldness of killing that was inside me had started to warm again. I felt my emotions slowly returning. Sarah and Vicky's affections had begun to flood my soul. I could feel their femininity that reigned over my masculinity. A power play over my hardness as their softness pulled me back.

I was me again. They had soothed away the bloodthirsty monster that was under the surface. I hung limp between them for a few seconds, at ease in the feeling that they were mine. No one had ever been able to tame the monster. No one. But they did it almost immediately. My beauties.

"Aunt Sarah, come back. Princess Lulu wants to finish our tea party." Jenny had tugged at Sarah's shirt.

All three of us looked down at Jenny. Her eyes were so big with joy. Sarah moved away and returned to the spot on the floor where they were playing. Vicky stayed for a moment. Her hand was still flat on my shoulder as she looked deep into my soul with those ocean-blue eyes.

"You don't have to be a soldier anymore. Stay here with us. Console your sister. We can help. Let us help." Vicky leaned into me; her lips kissed my cheek.

She pulled away, whispering, "Please, Master."

Moving away from the door, I sat on the couch. I glanced over at Elle. The dazed look on her face told me that she had no idea what had just unfolded in front of her eyes. She must have been too far into her own thoughts to acknowledge... or care.

I silently sat there for a while, watching Sarah and Jenny play. Sarah pretended to drink tea from an imaginary cup; her pinky extended out. Jenny was talking about how handsome the prince was and that he was hosting a ball to find a wife. I chuckled at the idea of marriage. It has been a hot topic lately.

"Here, honey, drink some coffee. It will make you feel better," Vicky said as she handed Elle the mug.

Elle looked up at her as she took the cup. She sipped in the hot coffee with a sense of reassurance. Her tension lessened as she relaxed back into the chair.

"Thank you," Elle softly spoke as she nodded to Vicky.

"You are most welcome," Vicky said in her motherly tone. She sat next to me on the couch, holding her own mug of coffee.

Elle sipped her coffee for a few moments as she collected herself. Once calm, she turned to Vicky and met her eyes. "So, care to explain what my pervy brother has gotten himself into?"

"Well, as he said in the hallway, we are his girlfriends." Vicky nodded toward Sarah as she pulled her mug up to take another sip.

"Girlfriends... or friends that are girls?" Elle eyed Vicky, who noticed Elle's bruised cheek shining in the light.

"Yes, girlfriends. As in, we are both in love with your brother." Vicky took another sip.

I sat back, easing myself into the couch. I again admired how they fit nicely into the domestic role. Sarah made Jenny laugh as they played, bonding with her as an aunt. Vicky consoled Elle, chatting girl talk like a sister-in-law would. I could easily see myself married to them. Very easily. Maybe I was that handsome prince that Jenny had mentioned. One could only hope...

"How did my goofy brother land two hotties?" Elle asked Vicky as she poked me in the ribs.

"It wasn't too hard, really. All he had to do was be himself." Vicky glanced at me as she held her mug out.

Be myself? I was a nerdy mess. I was barely able to talk to anyone. It was them. They were the Rosetta stone to my power.

"I don't know what to say about two women. That is a shock. Are you two okay with that?" Elle looked concerned. "I mean, is there any jealousy? How does it work?"

"So far, no jealousy. He seems to give both of us his attention equally," Vicky said, thinking back and smiling. "So, about your husband?"

"Right now, I don't know what to do. But I know that I have to protect Jenny." Elle sank back into her sorrow.

"Do you have somewhere to stay?" Vicky asked, concerned.

I interrupted without thinking. "No, she doesn't. That's why she's here."

"I am sure Mast— I mean Kyle wouldn't mind you staying here with Jenny," Vicky said as she took control of the conversation back.

"That's the second time I have heard you two call him Mass. Is that some kind of pet name?"

"Something like that," Vicky said with an awkward tone, acknowledging her slip-up.

"The couch has a pullout bed, sis. Or you and Jenny can take my room if you want," I said, trying to get back on the topic of helping Elle and Jenny.

Before Elle could answer, there was a knock at the door. I scurried up to answer it. I was afraid it would be Stephen. Seeing him standing in the doorway, I didn't know if I could restrain myself. I might have beaten him to a bloody pulp. Ground his face into the pavement, turning it into hamburger meat before my girlfriends could pull me off of him. As I opened the door, to my surprise, a pizza delivery guy was standing in front of me.

"Two large pizzas for... Vicky?" the delivery driver asked.

"Yep, I'm coming." Vicky got off the couch and gently pushed me to the side. She reached into her wallet and paid him.

He grinned at her like he was trying to flirt. I watched her give him an evil "go to hell" look. She then shook her head in disappointment and closed the door.

She really didn't like him flirting with her, almost as if it disgusted her. Was that because I was there? Or was it that she felt his flirting was disrespectful? She never really minded me coyishly flirting. Was it a sign, a testament of her loyalty to me?

"I ordered pizza. I figured everyone would be starving," she explained as she took the pizzas into the kitchen.

"Pizza! Did you get a cheese one, Aunt Vicky?" Jenny ran into the kitchen with glee.

"Of course! And the biggest piece is yours." Vicky beamed down at Jenny.

Sarah got up and walked over beside me. Her hand was on my shoulder, and she looked down at me. I peered into her forest-green eyes; they held great happiness deep inside them. She was almost frantic. I could tell that children were her biggest goal in life. Mother was a role she was more than fit to have.

"Jenny is so smart, Master," Sarah said, elated. There was no way that Elle didn't hear that one. She passed by me, joining the others in the kitchen.

I watched as everyone grabbed a slice, all but Elle. She hadn't moved from the chair. I made my way to her. I kneeled; my hand took her cheek with care. I looked her in the eyes.

"Sis, you need to eat. We can figure all this out later. Just stay the night. And get something in your stomach." My words were soft. I had calmed down, thanks to my girlfriends. I could now be the ear, the caring brother Elle needed at this moment.

She didn't say anything; she simply gave me a defeated look. She frowned, her eyes watering as she held back tears. I could tell anger and fear were building inside her. I just knew. This was the look I saw in young soldiers during their first firefight. I tried to think of something to pull her back. To get her calm.

"Besides, this is the first time I have had girlfriends. Imagine all the embarrassing things you can tell them," I joked. Her frown turned to a grin as she huffed inward with a slight laugh.

Elle got up, joining everyone else around the table. I just stood there for a moment in amazement.

My girlfriends—my beauties—had shown me something today. Something that made me want to propose right here and now. Slow down, Sergeant. You have only known them for a week. Besides, you are only on date two, and Elle and Jenny need you. After I get Elle back on her feet, there will be time for all of that.

I decided that I needed to grab a slice before all the womenfolk gobbled them down. I moved into the kitchen, joining the others around the dining table.

"Master, can we stay over too? Jenny and I haven't finished playing," Sarah asked as she patted Jenny's head.

"Sure. Just make sure she is asleep by nine." My mind didn't even register her slip-up.

"Master? I thought I heard them call you that disgusting, perverted word." Elle scowled at me, her eyes filled with all the rage she should have directed at Stephen.

"It's not what you think, Elle. We want to call him that. It was our choice," Vicky said. "He is a good man. You know your brother."

"No, I don't. Not anymore. He was gone for six years doing God knows what." Elle spat her misplaced anger onto me.

"He was doing what good men do," Vicky said. "Serving his country and protecting what he cared about. Now settle down. *He* is not your husband. He is your brother, Kyle."

"No, he is a disgusting pig," Elle shouted. "He is a dirty pervert. *All men are!* He is no different than Stephen." With the outburst, Jenny started crying loudly.

"Calm down, Sis. You're upsetting Jenny." I tried to hug Elle, but she winced backward.

"Don't fucking touch me! Don't you dare! You sick fuck!" Elle screamed in my face. "He *makes* you call him Master! I bet he beats on you two dumb bitches all the time!"

I flinched at her remark. "Elle, don't call them that."

"No, he would never, ever do that to us." Sarah's voice cracked with emotion.

"Fucking liar. All of you are liars!" Elle grabbed Jenny's hand and started toward the door.

"Elle, Kyle is not like that." Vicky tried again to use a soothing voice to de-escalate the tensions.

"Master! Only an abusive fuck would make you call him that!" Elle's words cut through me.

"Kyle's not abusive. Where is this coming from?" Sarah asked, puzzled as to what was upsetting Elle.

"Kyle, you're a fucking disgusting piece of shit! I never want to see you again! Don't you dare come near Jenny, you abusive fuck!" Elle rushed herself and Jenny through the door, slamming it closed. We heard Jenny crying as they went down the hall.

What the Hell? What was that? I felt dizzy and walked toward the living room.

I sat on the couch. I felt shame. I felt anger. I felt... I couldn't explain all the feelings. Betrayal? How could Elle lump me in with scum like Stephen? Tears started to cloud my eyes. My sister stormed out, acting like I was the enemy. Like I were this disgusting creature. Was I scum? Was I a dirty pervert for wanting what I did?

"No, Master. You are not scum." Vicky kneeled down before me, taking my hands in hers.

"You are a good man, Master. That is why we chose you." Sarah kneeled next to me on the couch, her arms around my neck in a strong hug.

They both leaned in, kissing my cheeks. I felt comforted by their affection. But my heart ached. Why was Elle so angered because they called me Master? It wasn't like I had done something that was wrong. It was just a word. A single word. Master.

Sarah sat down properly on the couch, and Vicky slid next to me. They both embraced me tightly, but my mind was in disarray. My heart was broken into pieces. Elle. Jenny. I may never see them again. I sat on the couch, deep in thought.

Chapter 7: Trifecta of Awakenings

My eyes struggled to open through a groggy haze. My arms tingled, probably from reduced circulation, as I sensed weight on them. I looked around. I was sitting on the couch.

Sarah's head nestled into my right shoulder. Her red hair draped into a pauldron of fire. Vicky leaned over me on my left side, her head in my lap. Those dark locks a veil of protection on me. My arms cradled them both.

They were both lightly snoring. I enjoyed the musical way their snuffles filled the air—a gentle sound that calmed the spirit. We must have fallen asleep on the couch. My eyes darted to the clock. Zero seven-thirty: it was early Sunday morning.

I had finally fallen asleep beside them. I smirked to myself. This was something I had always wished to wake up to. Two beauties lying beside me in the morning.

It felt so right—so good—to be so admired that they would stay beside me while I slept, to be greeted in the morning by those gorgeous faces. Their bodies were a peaceful amnesty to caress upon waking. I had been summoned from my dreams to find myself next to something even more... alluring. My beauties. I could feel my heart swell. My soul was soothed by their presence...

Until last night's feelings... Elle's words... started to disrupt my happiness. She never wanted to see me again. Was my love life that revolting? She called me a disgusting piece of shit and said that she didn't know me anymore. Had I changed that much in the war? Had I become something sinister? Why would she think I'd ever raise my hand to Vicky and Sarah? Why would she think I was abusive at all?

The last thing I remembered from last night was them comforting me. Reassuring me that this relationship was not bad. That they saw me as a good man. Was I a good man? What made a man good? How could I tell if I was a good man?

In war, I was a monster. We all were. That was the job. Be the bigger monster to stop—to end—the other monsters. Take their lives before they can inflict their hatred and violence upon someone weaker.

Elle didn't know that part of me. No one really did. Only the men I was deployed with knew what kind of creature I was. But I have never let that monster out on innocent people. I don't think that I ever would. I would never want to be that monster unless I had to be. Unless I needed to be.

"Mmm, Master, good morning." Vicky turned her head in my lap and gazed up at me lovingly.

"Morning? How is it morning?" Sarah nestled deeper into my shoulder as she started to wake up. "Vicky, just five more minutes. It feels so nice cuddling Master like this."

"I see you're not feeling much better, Master." Vicky turned her voice into that gentle motherly tone she used with Elle last night.

I didn't say anything. I tried to push away the feelings of dread to enjoy having them with me. Their warmth was more of a loving feeling this morning than the heated lust from before.

The ache from Elle's ire was still there, but I tried to keep it at bay. I tried, but still, I felt the sting of it in my bones.

"Want to talk about it?" Sarah whispered in my ear as her cuddle deepened.

I sighed, remembering what Sarah had said last night. "Last night, why did you call me a good man? You barely know me."

"You are. You make us feel safe," Sarah insisted as she moved her head to get more comfortable on my shoulder.

Vicky peered into my eyes. "You talk to yourself. All your inner thoughts are broadcast to the world. Well... to us anyway. Last night, you were tight-lipped. Maybe it's just us that you let in."

"Yeah. And the resolve you have, how you reason with yourself, is powerful," Sarah groggily said as her grip on me tightened.

"So that makes me a good man? Because my thoughts come pouring out of my mouth?" I shook my head slightly.

"No, you misunderstand. When you speak out loud, it gives us a window to your soul. Everything is laid bare to us; we see who you really are underneath it all." Vicky's motherly tone pushed through.

Sarah yawned before speaking in a mumble. "And who you are is exactly what we need. A good man. A strong man. A man with principles." She lovingly rubbed her face on my shoulder.

I sighed. "Right now, I don't feel like a good man."

"After you heard what Stephen did, you wanted to kill him. I could see it in your eyes. That's why I stopped you," Vicky said.

"You wanted to protect your sister. That's noble. But we can't have you beating up the world," Sarah whispered, her nose nuzzling into my neck.

I shook my head. "You just emphasized my point. Good men would find a peaceful solution."

Vicky sighed before speaking in a motherly tone. "Sometimes, violence is necessary. It keeps the real monsters at bay." Vicky's words shocked me. I had never known anyone other than soldiers who thought like that.

"Sometimes you gotta smack the baddies down," Sarah said.

Vicky took my face gently in her hands and met my eyes. "Being dangerous doesn't make you a monster. It makes you formidable. What you do with that power—how you use it—is the difference."

"Protection: that is a righteous reason to use violence, Master," Sarah said softly. I felt the heat of her breath against my neck.

I contemplated what they were saying. Yet, for some reason, I still felt bad, like I had done something wrong. Vicky stared at me for a moment. Then she hopped up and twirled around, pirouetting across the floor. Reaching out, she grabbed a hold of Sarah's arm and tugged her up, chuckling as she helped Sarah to her feet. "We have a mission."

Sarah lazily stood up, gently tugging back in a sleepy state. "I just want to cuddle with Master. What mission?"

"To make Master feel better by washing away his doubts," Vicky explained as she looked into Sarah's heavy eyes.

"Okay..." Sarah gave in with a yawn.

Both of them grabbed a hand and tugged me off the couch. They led me to the bathroom. Vicky turned on the shower; she held her hand under the water as she adjusted it to the perfect temperature. She turned to Sarah, and I watched as they slowly and sensually peeled the clothes off of each other. I stood there in awe and amazement. I was too dumbstruck to do anything as this dreamy spectacle unfolded before me.

They stepped out of their panties. Then, with a lusty gaze, they turned to me, fully nude. The sight of all of this made my member press against the fly of my pants. I had forgotten that they didn't let me have underwear yesterday.

Sarah hungrily unbuttoned my shirt as Vicky aggressively undid my belt. They seemed like feral animals, as if carnal sensuality had been channeled into them.

Sarah's emeralds held my gaze as she undid my shirt and opened it wide. Instinctively, I grabbed Sarah by the back of the neck. I pulled her face down to mine, and her mouth instantly claimed my lips. My devilish side was drawn to her angelic bliss. She took from me the fires of hell as our tongues danced. I kissed her, trying to calm all the dark emotions that had built up inside of me. She was more than happy to soothe my soul with our kiss.

Vicky roughly undid my pants and yanked them to the floor. I could feel her warm breath on my thigh, my manhood throbbing and fully extended. She playfully bit my inner thigh, suckling for a moment. Her mouth released me, and she kissed the spot before standing. She gently nudged Sarah out of the way. Sarah broke our kiss; my hand automatically released her.

Vicky's mouth replaced Sarah's. I kissed Vicky with even more fire. She attacked me with as much vigor as I was dishing out. As I was in a passionate melee with Vicky's mouth, each one took a side of my shirt. They slid it off until it fell between our feet.

Oh, God. I needed them, to be inside them, to feel them wrapped around me, around my manhood. Vicky pulled her mouth from mine.

They slowly planted kisses down my neck and kissed and licked a trail down to my chest. My hands tenderly played in their hair. Being worshipped by them drove me to a state of ecstasy.

Their breasts pressed against me and slid down my sides, so soft, so full. They nipped at my nipples. I fisted their manes tightly as I let out a soft whimper of delight. They slowly licked their way back up. I could feel the heat of their bodies.

With their hair tightly interlaced in my fingers, I pulled their faces close to mine. Their tongues whipped out as they knew what I desired. Our tongues tangled in a wild battle of control as we kissed. Sarah gave in and allowed me to take dominion almost immediately. Vicky battled me for a while until my tongue dominated hers. As our kiss settled, I released my grip on them.

My eyes danced between them as they gave me a wanton look. I hungered for them, my body nearing a supernova of sensuality, burning to have the pleasures I knew they could inflict.

They graciously guided me into the shower as they stepped in with me. The touch of their hands warmed my body. The shower rained down upon us as their fingers roamed over every inch of me as if I were a living god, divinity itself offered to them.

With the soap lathered in their palms, they washed away my fears, my doubts. They explored my body with their eyes. Every scar they paid special homage to. They didn't say anything, but I knew they honored my sacrifices. Each scar was from a different battle. A different time when my life was placed in peril. I didn't have to tell them; they simply seemed to know.

My fingers danced along their flesh. Each hand explored their bodies independently as the water cascaded over us. The flames of desire burned hot, not snuffed out by the cooling water. My index fingers rolled down their lips, down their necks. I traced every curve, every place their bodies needed my touch, craved my touch.

I took the soap in my fists, lathering my hands until the foam spilled out of my fingers. I turned to Vicky first while Sarah continued to wash me. My expedition of Vicky was underway. As I ran my strong hands over her toned body, soft whimpers escaped her lips. My fingers spread around her breast as I gave her nipple a light pinch.

I tracked further with my touch. My hand over her chiseled core made her shiver. I moved further down. The water dripped from her dark bush as my hand grazed past. I made my way to her cave; my fingers slammed in hard as my thumb rubbed harsh grinding circles on her love button.

My hand continued to work Vicky as my attention turned to Sarah. I tenderly ran my other hand over her soft body. I gently kneaded her ample breast, then trailed down Sarah's cute, zaftig stomach. My fingertips circled around her naval with a caring touch. I moved down over her wet thicket and into her soft folds, which felt like a treasure as I pressed gently inside. My thumb delicately massaged her bud. My fingers worked a soft rhythm on her.

My beauties moaned as I worked them between my fingers. Sarah leaned down; I could feel her shallow breaths on me. Vicky's mouth shot out, clamping her teeth on my throat.

"Aah," I shouted out with a painfully erotic groan as I felt her teeth sink into my flesh.

My hands steeled into them. My longing to have them was building them into a frenzy. I yearned to have them finish on my hands. I wanted them to be engulfed in a sea of ecstasy, into the depths of how I cherished them. I was lost in myself. At that moment, I knew only their pleasure. Vicky's teeth bit down harder. Sarah's breaths on me became erratic.

It wasn't long until they both reached an explosive climax. Their celestial essence of love mixed with the rain of the shower. They steadied themselves as they recovered. Vicky's bite released me as her head fell back. Sarah lovingly caressed my body as the deity they had made me feel I was.

Without warning, Vicky grabbed my shaft and squeezed it with such power. I felt the chains of restraint break from me. She started to stroke me vigorously. Like a lioness to her prey, I was taken hard and fast. Her hand was a pulsing chamber of carnal aggression. Sarah's hands ran up and down my chest in amorous fervor.

"This time, it's mine," Vicky told Sarah as she kneeled before me. Vicky looked up at me with those deep blue gems, begging me to release all of my frustrations. Her hand worked with a stride that I had never felt before. She opened her mouth wide as she waited with anticipation. A hunger deep inside her came to the surface. She yearned to taste my seed. To feel it hit the back of her maw.

I could see she wanted to give me relief from this world. Relief from my worries. I felt it building. My body tensed as I neared the edge of bliss. I fisted her hair, drawing her face closer. Her lips rimmed my tip. I could feel the heat of her breath as she pummeled my prick rapidly. Then I erupted, a volcano full of my seed blasted out. With her mouth wide, she caught every drop... as they had promised. I watched as the warm white ejaculate showered her tongue. Without a second thought, she closed her mouth, devouring it. So damn hot. A wonderful delight. My girls, my good girls.

I slumped into Sarah's caress as I was spent. But my body ached for more... I looked down at Vicky. She stared straight ahead in a daze. Her body was stiff as a board. She stayed like this momentarily before standing and turning the shower off.

"Time to dry off and get Master ready for our date," Vicky said with an evil grin.

Dammit, not again. Goddamn teasing bitches. I only had myself to blame. My soldier begged for more, but I couldn't argue with their logic. It was my rule.

As they got the towel, I watched them. The glistening wetness dripping from them held my gaze. Their bodies shined with a unique and individual feminine radiance. I was so enchanted, so captivated by them. Taking in the variety of their needs and the differences in their affections.

Sarah's soft milky skin was tender with an angelic, innocent glow. Her body mirrored her coy and tender personality.

Vicky's toned, tanned skin was rough with a devilishly ravishing dominion, imposing in the way her body displayed a feisty yet endearing effect.

They dried me off. Their eyes watched mine, staring deep into my soul. A look of deep yearning built up in Sarah's eyes. A fierce challenge swelled behind Vicky's. Their hands rubbed me with such care. With such admiration. Both their touches told me that they still regarded me as their deity. After every inch of me was dry, they handed me the towel.

I took special care to dry each one, giving them the unique treatment that their individual bodies ached for. Sarah, I dried her soft and gentle. My attentive caresses inspired loving gazes from her. For Vicky, I ran the towel over her hard and rough. Her face was a pout craving to be handled rougher, and her eyes begged for my beastly treatment. After I finished, my beauties scurried out of the shower.

The ladies gathered up the clothes. I watched their naked bodies as we walked to the bedroom. I still craved them, unsated despite our recent adventures. But I followed the rule I put in place even though my body hungered to have them. To find myself lost in them, in the depths of their bodies... their souls. To have them feel every inch of my appreciation deep inside of them. But I found my resolve. I bridled my passion in the recesses for the time being. At that moment, I was just happy to know they were mine.

We entered the bedroom in a stride. They each had an overnight bag that I hadn't noticed yesterday. They dressed as I scoured my closet for something to wear. Blue tactical pants and a T-shirt with Cloud Strife on it. He was my favorite video game character. This time, I made sure to get some boxers.

I glanced over at them. Damn. Like always, something enticing. Sarah was in blue jeans so tight they looked painted on. A tight black shirt strained across her large bosom. A picture of a blue heart in the center ruffled between the curved cove of her breasts. Vicky was in black bellbottoms. They were snug around the hips and thighs, flaring out around the calves. A tight pink shirt contoured her chest and belly. Sarah slid her elegant feet into western-style boots as Vicky laced up her combat boots.

Each one unique and enchanting. A pair of women that spoke to all of my tastes. They accepted me for who I was. My beauties. My ladies. And hopefully, one day, I could make them both my brides.

"Brides, huh?" Vicky side-eyed me as her lips formed a sly grin.

"We have a surprise for you, Master," Sarah said as her red hair whipped backward while her luscious body jolted up.

"Okay, is this about our third date?" I questioned.

"Yes, Master! Since you took us to a place that was special to you, today we will do the same," Vicky explained.

"Aren't we moving fast? I mean... we only met a week ago, and we are on date three." I tried to understand my situation. I tried to reason myself into slowing things down. I know that I was just thinking about them being my brides. That was wishful thinking, right?

It had only been a week and I was already on date three. And we'd enjoyed a few sexual encounters. Was this normal in the dating realm? This must have been what Mrs. Helderman had told me about. This type of relationship often moves much quicker than normal ones. Was that due to there being three of us involved? Was it because they had heard a lot of my inner thoughts? Or was it because of something else?

"Maybe it is moving fast. Maybe our relationship has been streamlined by hearing your inner thoughts, the ones you unknowingly broadcast," Sarah looked away quickly. Then her gaze snapped back at me, longing to say something else.

"Yeah, we peek into how you think, what you feel," Vicky said. "Those first couple of nights, you showed us a deep resolve. Most men, when faced with two random women throwing sexual advances at them, would take advantage of it. But you didn't. Instead, you reasoned with yourself to remain a moral man. An honorable man." Vicky's eyes peered deep into my soul.

82

"Besides, we love you, Master," Sarah gushed. "Yesterday, in the back seat, we decided that we had fallen in love with you."

"It's true, Master. We love you. Did you not catch that when I told your sister last night?" Vicky reminded me of her words to Elle. At the time I thought it was just something to say. But they loved me. They really did. They stared at me with deep longing, as if they wanted me to say it back.

Did I love them? I wasn't sure. How does love feel? I have never really felt it. I thought I loved Miss Dependa, but that... didn't go so well. All my recent thoughts have been centered around Vicky and Sarah. And they weren't all sexual. So, it had to be more than lust.

This past week I had thought about having children with them. Buying them a house. Making a life for the three of us. Yes, maybe I did love them. They had consumed my every thought. Every fiber of my being wanted to be with them every second of the day. It almost destroyed me when I thought I had lost them. I was ready to propose last night. So yes. Oddly enough, yes, I did love them.

"I love you two as well." My voice was low, almost a whisper.

"Really! See, I told you he did." Sarah eyed Vicky with a victory glance.

"Good. Now that's all settled. We have a surprise for you, Master." Vicky took my hand.

My mind eased. I loved two women, and they loved me. They were my beauties, my girlfriends, mine—I could call them mine.

I walked tall as we were exiting the apartment. Elle's disapproval did not cloud my mind and heart. I was no longer feeling the sting of her berating me. I knew that with Sarah and Vicky by my side, I could mend the broken relationship.

That power I had felt yesterday was returning. No longer a soldier, I was now the man. The man who was about to have it all. Two beautiful women who someday would be my brides. A business that I could call my own. And a life worth living.

Chapter 8: Untamed Menagerie

As we left the apartment, I felt a renewed sense of motivation. I had found love. Twenty-four years and I found them. Well, they sort of found me. But they were mine, all mine. I was wrapped in their armor of affection. My eyes watched as they walked. Their strides were as powerful as mine. They were in a state of elation, just as I was. I felt powerful. Like Superman, I was bulletproof. The dreads of my soul were starting to fall away with every second that I bathed in their radiance.

We made our way down the stairs. With each step, my feet beat a rhythm of joy as I descended from this spire that had trapped me in the ache of loneliness. I had never really noticed how much pain my soul was in, not until I felt what they had given me over this past week. Life was lonely without them. Love was shallow without them.

"Today, Master, we take my car. And I'm driving," Vicky said with excitement as we neared the security door of the building.

"Plus, if you drove, Master, it would spoil the surprise." Sarah grinned at me in a playful way.

When we exited the building, I felt the kiss of the sky on my face. The sun had never seemed so bright. Some dark clouds were to the north, but the sky was mostly bright. The warmth showered down upon us as if my life was just beginning. My life with them. Our life together. I admired their conviction to show me something that meant so much to them. I was okay with letting Vicky take the lead on this excursion.

As we walked through the parking lot, Sarah grabbed my hand and walked beside me. The heat of her palm on mine reinforced this feeling that had taken me over. Her long legs met my shorter strides as we walked in step. Vicky briskly walked ahead of us; her combat boots clacked the pavement excitedly. This feeling was in all of us.

We approached a black Dodge Journey. It was a much nicer vehicle than mine. But I didn't mind. They had told me before that they hadn't chosen me for what I could provide. They chose me for who I was. And in that moment, I became more than happy. My heart exploded with the one thing I had never really known. Love.

I hastily opened the driver's door for Vicky. She eased in as she started the vehicle. Upon opening the passenger door for Sarah, she gave me a pouty look.

"But Master, I wanted to sit in the backseat with you." Sarah's sad green puppy eyes had torn into me.

"Okay," I said, smiling as I closed the passenger door.

My hand opened the door to the back seat. Sarah immediately jumped in, sliding over behind Vicky. She patted the seat next to her. I sat beside her, closing the door. I was no sooner in the car before I felt Sarah's hands on me. She pulled me close to her as her fingers started to roam my body. I slid my left arm behind her, rooting around her waist. She grinned devilishly. I looked up to the front seat. Vicky was adjusting the rearview mirror so she could see us. I could see a wicked smirk crawl across her face. Damn, I was in trouble. What did they have planned? We took off down the road.

Sarah's right hand started to caress my thigh. She looked at me with a wanton gaze. I watched her green emeralds peer deep into me. Her hand undid my fly with such grace. She pulled my pole free; the warmth of her hand made it stand up. It was only at half-mast. What was she going to do? We were in public... well, sort of. We were in the car. But still. Oh, God, this was so arousing. Not knowing what she was going to do. And not knowing if we would get pulled over by some cop. Or if a bus full of nuns pulled up beside us.

"Tut tut... this won't do, Master. But I can fix that." Her fingers wrapped around the girth as she gripped me lovingly. Her hand started slow, gentle strokes. The pressure was tight yet tender. The blood pulsed to my manhood as it grew in her soft hand. I reached over with my fingertips, gingerly caressing her cheek. Our eyes locked as she worked up and down the length of my shaft. Her wrist twisted to fill my girth with a sensation of her power. She held me in her fist, and she had complete control over me. Her eyes echoed a kindled passion reaping a burning hunger. A hunger to have my hot cream. Amazed at her courage, at her fierce assault, my shaft ached for her touch. She gave me a coy look of innocence, yet she was far from innocent at this moment. I relinquished control. All control of my body was now hers.

"That's it, Master, let her work you. Let her work that seed from you," Vicky said with her dark vixen tone as I felt her eyes on us.

85

"Yes, let me milk you, Master," Sarah whispered to me as her hand slightly increased the rhythm.

Mmm... okay... take it... take all you want. My mind was in a frenzy with this sensation. My eyes stayed locked to Sarah's as I felt the vehemence of her caress. The muscles in my legs started to strain as she worked me. I began to build to orgasm.

"Hold out, Master. We aren't there yet," Sarah whispered softly, her warm breath on my cheek.

I held back, not wanting to disappoint my beauties. But that maneuver Sarah was doing made it hard to hold on for very long. My tongue whipped out, lapping across her upper lip. She playfully nipped back at me, then smiled. Squeezing around me harder, she breathed in a slight chuckle.

We hit a few turns here and there, my mind concerned that we would be caught. That around the next corner there would be someone who would see what was happening in the back seat. This worry only made me crave this treatment more. With each turn, Sarah ever so slightly hastened her pace. Our eyes peered into one another's. Taking in my erotic desires, she was becoming aroused herself. Yet she focused solely on me. My arm cradled tighter around her waist.

We took another turn. Her face pressed into mine as her hand quickened just slightly more. The force of her hand pitched me further into the ecstasy of this feeling. I glanced into the rearview mirror. The spectacle of the backseat engrossed Vicky's eyes. Darting back and forth from the road to us, her eyes had a sinister smirk. Her eyes told me—no, begged me—to release myself.

"We're pulling in. Make him cum. We can't do this without his cum," Vicky said to Sarah as she made the turn into our destination.

I felt the vehicle halt as we parked. Sarah's hand started to whip faster up and down. I could feel myself almost there.

"Oh... aah." My revelry was uncontainable.

Sarah cupped her left hand over my tip. My hot spunk started to rocket out. Sarah caught every drop in her palm. She gave me a wicked grin before kissing my cheek. With a graceful movement she maneuvered her hand over the center console in between the front seats. Vicky reached out to gather half of my creamy fluids. Sarah took her hand back after Vicky got her rationing. I watched as they both slid it in the front of their pants. So... damn... hot!

"It feels so good inside me," Sarah moaned as her fingers worked deep inside her vulva.

"Yes... so warm." Vicky's voice was a low whimper as she wriggled in her seat.

I sat for a moment in my spent state. Damn, how I wanted more. Craved more. Needed more. I wished that this was a secluded area. I looked around to figure out where we were. I saw a sign: the zoo. Damn... not secluded.

They got my seed. Shared it and put it in their pants. Never mind that that was goddamn hot. Why did they do that?

As I sunk deep into my thoughts, Sarah and Vicky sat up straight, stiffening into what looked like dolls. They seemed to go into that trance-like state that they did yesterday. It was odd and unsettling to see them like that. I waved my hand in front of Sarah's face with no response.

Then they both said in unison, "Genetic material received. DNA processing. RNA processing. Genome map acquired. Reproductive adaptation processing. Accessing configuration. Rejection of further genome maps granted. Reproductive modules calibrating. Permanent and sole ownership of reproductive access is granted to admin Kyle Forester, alias Master. Bonding complete."

"Okay, what just happened? What is happening?"

"We are taking you to the zoo, Master," Sarah said as she recovered from the trance state that they had been in.

I scratched my head in wonder. "No, what are you two doing with the jizz? And what was all that stuff you guys said?"

"Um, Master, we wanted to walk around with you inside us on our date." Vicky eyed me through the rearview mirror. "Hot, right?"

"Huh..." Though confused... holy hell was that hot. Walk around with me inside them.

"The bonding process is complete, Master. You wouldn't understand. It's a woman thing." A soft tone escaped from Sarah's lips as she slid my flaccid member back into my pants.

"Yeah, a woman thing. Now, no one can steal us away from you, Master." Vicky sinisterly tittered.

I didn't question any further. I just accepted the fact that now, on our date, they would have me inside them. They wanted to walk around with my essence deep inside their cunts. I looked at them as they both gave me sultry looks.

87

Still, what was all that jargon they had said? Was that normal? Maybe it was a weird game. Or a fetish? A joke? Yeah, it had to be some kind of joke similar to the one they had made yesterday. Probably an inside joke since they were like sisters. Maybe a game they had continued into adulthood? I didn't know.

But damn, I can't wait to plunge deep inside them. And that was a sly way to skirt my rule. They have found many loopholes in that rule. I didn't know if I should be angry or happy. They were schemers, that's for sure. Teasing schemers. My beauties, my teasing beauties. How I loved them.

"Let's go," Vicky said as she opened her door.

"I am so excited to see the birds," Sarah said as she jumped out of the car in a bubbly eruption of happiness.

I foggily exited the vehicle. Damn, how was I going to do this? My seed inside them. This was definitely going to be an interesting zoo visit. It was their favorite place. I wonder why? They must both be animal lovers. Animals, like the animalistic desires that they awaken inside of me. You dirty women. *My* dirty women.

Gently, I pushed my way between them. Sarah on my right and Vicky on my left. We walked toward the entrance gate. I slid my hands into each of theirs as my fingers interlaced with theirs. As we strode forward, I walked high above the world, my beauties by my sides. I couldn't stop thinking about touching them, kissing them, tasting them. And soon I'd feel them around me, fusing into them with passion and love.

"How many tickets?" The lady at the ticket booth asked.

"Three, please," Sarah said as she paid before I could reach for my wallet.

We walked in with a sense of joy. They broke from my hands as we passed through the gate. They both started skipping toward the first habitat. I hastened my pace. We proceeded to the reptile house. As we walked, Sarah explained that she was scared of snakes. Vicky expressed an interest in the lizards. She explained that she hoped to have an iguana one day. I was just happy that my girlfriends were enjoying themselves. As we passed by the snakes, Sarah clung to me with a deep fright. Vicky made a few snake jokes to poke at Sarah.

"Ssss..." Vicky wiggled her head.

"That's not funny," Sarah cried out in a cute, annoyed voice.

Vicky chuckled. "It is to me."

"Play nice, girls." My voice smoothed into that dominant NCO tone.

"Yes, Master," they said in unison with a smitten chime.

I looked around for a moment to make sure no one was around. That no one had heard them call me "Master." I didn't want a public repeat of last night. I didn't know if other people would react the same way Elle had. This was new to me. Was it okay for them to call me that in public? I loved hearing that from their lips. It was more than a sexual turn-on. It felt like an honorary title, much like the title husband. Was that wrong that it made me feel responsible for them, accountable to them?

We moved to the cat habitats. Vicky and Sarah both loved this one. I was relieved to find a spot they could both feel great about. We watched the lions for a while. The alpha male roared at his pride. They obeyed him. Seeing this made me think that maybe what I was doing with Sarah and Vicky was natural. There were too many stigmas around dominant-submissive relationships these days. In the pride was an alpha male with his lionesses. His wives—plural. As in more than one. Maybe this entire relationship was completely normal; it was the rest of the world that had it backward.

We made our way to the tigers. Vicky wanted to stay a while. She seemed at ease around them, expressing deep fascination as she studied them. Sarah sat on the bench, watching from afar as Vicky got closer.

"Tigers are my favorite animals." Vicky looked up at me with a tender look.

"I can see that," I said as my hand held her lower back.

"Such majestic creatures, their coats so beautiful. Their power imposing yet comforting." Vicky sighed with glee as she looked back to the enclosure.

I stood next to her in silence for several minutes as we enjoyed watching the tigers. She rested her head on my shoulder. Her dark veil was so warm against me. Leaning my face over, I kissed her on the top of her scalp. So, Vicky loved tigers. It definitely fit her personality: beautiful, strong, yet comforting. The more I knew about them, the more I fell in love.

"No, before you ask, we are not getting a tiger," I joked as my hand slid up from her back to give her a side hug.

"But Master, they are so cute." Vicky gave a playful pout.

"Okay, fine, as long as you promise only to feed it our enemies' corpses." That dark Army humor had accidentally escaped my lips.

Vicky snickered as she turned her head up to look me in the eye. Those deep oceans were filled with love and a bit of lust. She didn't mind my dark humor. That was a relief. All soldiers develop a very dark and often sick sense of humor in the Army. But she was okay with it. Not really a surprise, I guess. Her personality had a bit of resolve, a bit of darkness.

"Mmm... I am so happy being here with you, Master." She smiled. "Having your seed inside me, here in public, feels so hot."

Damn, she said it. She really did. Geeze, I had almost forgotten; I was just enjoying the zoo with them. But they had a piece of me inside them. My semen. Such dirty women. *My* dirty women. I smirked to myself. We soon rejoined Sarah and continued on.

As we walked toward the aviary, we passed by a group of people. Sarah and Vicky were close to me, lovingly cuddling around me as we traversed forward.

"Look, mama! He has two girlfriends." A little boy from the passing crowd pointed at us.

"Disgusting! He should be ashamed of himself." The woman holding his hand let out a disdainful snarl.

Maybe society will never accept this—accept us. I felt the weight of reality. No. You are a lion. This is your pride. Vicky and Sarah are your lionesses.

"But, mama..." The boy's voice faded as the crowd passed us.

As we neared the bird sanctuary's entrance, Sarah broke from me. Her feet started skipping inside. Vicky rolled her eyes; she seemed bored before we had even entered. But she drudgingly walked forward.

As we walked through, Sarah explained all the different species of birds. Her voice was filled with joy as she gave details on each.

Vicky hurried past everything and waited at the exit. She leaned against the exit with one leg propped against the wall.

"That's a swallowtail! They fly without much effort," Sarah excitedly explained.

She pointed out several other birds and gave detailed explanations, much like an encyclopedia. This was really impressive. She knew all that off the top of her head.

Sarah sat on a bench; I sat beside her with my arms wrapped around her. Her eyes were fixed on a certain spot. I looked over to see a bird with a long neck perched on a rock. I wasn't sure what type it was, but it was beautiful.

"You see that one, Master? That's a crane. My favorite," Sarah stated as she pointed to the long-necked bird.

"Very beautiful bird." As my embrace tightened, I could feel the heat of her body on mine.

"In Japan, it is said that they were messengers of the gods. They represent hope, strength, and beauty," Sarah ecstatically explained. She paused for a moment as she watched the crane in awe. "There is a myth that says if you fold one thousand origami cranes, you will be granted a wish."

It was amazing how much she knew. She looked so innocent, so youthful. I was surprised at her knowledge of these creatures. Hope, strength, and beauty: those were definitely descriptions I would use to describe her. I couldn't help it. They made me want to be with them more, to love them more—for now and always.

"Well, my wish has already been granted," I said as she turned to me.

"Really, Master? What was your wish?" Sarah's green eyes grew big.

"To be with two beautiful women. Now and always," I whispered in her ear.

"Oh, Master." Sarah swooned.

I sat silently with Sarah for a while as we watched the crane. The magical way its wings spread was majestic. The crane made a strange but beautiful sound. A reverberating call, as if it was calling out to its mate that it had been apart from for far too long. I glanced over at Vicky; she was impatiently waiting at the exit. I pulled my arms off of Sarah and motioned her on.

We walked for a while longer before making our way to the food court. It was bustling with people, and I felt a tad uneasy around that many people. But I endured because my beauties were hungry.

We found the vendor. He was a rude man to us, almost unbearable. I couldn't understand why... until he made a remark. "A street pimp out here on a Sunday? Brought his hoes with him."

"Sir, can we order?" I asked, trying to ignore his rudeness.

"This is a public place. People bring their kids here, for Christ's sake." His eyes burned ire upon me from his food truck.

"Can we order or what, mister?" Sarah seemed more agitated by the man than I was. I hadn't seen her so... aggressive before.

"Yeah... yeah. What do ya want?" He softened long enough for us to place our order.

They each wanted to pay, but I insisted on paying. We sat at one of the empty tables. We were too busy stuffing our faces, so no one talked. All I heard was crunching and munching noises. As we sat, my mind wandered. I hadn't really given them commands. I mean, sure, they called me "Master," but I hadn't commanded them.

I thought back. Nope. Not really. Nor had I actually initiated anything sexual. The sex had been them; they had started it each time. I only undressed them that first day. Then... nothing else.

I hadn't commanded them. I hadn't done anything worthy of the title "Master." I started feeling like an imposter again. A ruse. Was I really their Master? Did I deserve the title?

"Why do y'all still call me Master?" I asked.

"What do you mean, Master?" Vicky had a befuddled look on her face.

"Because you're our Master... duh," Sarah said mockingly.

"I mean... I haven't really been dominant. Not since the first day we met." I started to feel inadequate.

Vicky eyed me up and down for a minute, trying to understand where all of this was coming from. Her shimmering sapphires rang with a bit of confusion and a twinge of intuition.

"Is this because we have initiated the sexual play, Master?" Vicky eyed me with a cold stare.

"Sort of." I thought back to all of our encounters. "That and I really haven't given you guys commands."

"Yes, you have Master. No sex until three dates. That's a command," Sarah said with a mouthful of chicken.

"Master, dominance is not always about giving commands or initiating sex," Vicky sternly said before softening into a loving tone. "Most often, it is about the presence of the person, their convictions, and how they care for others."

"Yes, besides, you have a very intimidating command presence. Sometimes scary, Master, but a sexy kind of scary," Sarah said as she discarded a chicken bone.

"So, what is it that we have been doing? I mean, since I am not giving commands or initiating sex?" I questioned.

"Well, we have been dating, like boyfriend and girlfriends. And sometimes we push the boundaries of the three-dates rule. So far, you haven't complained, Master," Sarah said as she scooped mashed potatoes into her mouth.

"We know that you are inexperienced with sex. So, we initiate it until you feel comfortable doing it on your own, taking us when you please." Vicky's voice smoothed into that seductive tone as she winked at me. "We know you will, Master. And I don't think it will be long before you do."

I suddenly felt embarrassed. My experience, or lack thereof, was brought into the open. I felt the heat on my cheeks burn. I wished to be the suave lover that they truly needed. I hoped I was.

"Besides, you chose the date yesterday, Master. You decided to take us to that beautiful spot. That was your decision. You made a command decision," Sarah said as she wiped her lips with a napkin.

"We once heard you say that you thought you were a ruse. You are not a ruse, Master. You're our Master because that man, what you thought was a ruse, is you. The real you," Vicky said before she finished her plate.

"Yes, you are that man. We know that you are, Master. When you talk to yourself, we know how you feel. Unknowingly, you let us in." Sarah's words felt heavy as she smiled in that innocent way.

"We love you, Master," Vicky stated in her vixen voice.

"Yes, Master, we love you." Sarah's voice had a tender baby tone.

"I love you both as well." My voice cracked a pitch higher than normal. I smiled, feeling better.

We finished our food and discarded our trash in the waste basket. As I walked between them, they began to move gracefully. They giggled at each other and then looked at me. Their feet started moving in a rhythm, and their hips gyrated. They were dancing, yet there was no music. Dancing as they walked beside me.

I joined in as my feet hit the sidewalk. We were dancing to a rhythm that only we could hear—the rhythm of love. I pranced around them, spinning them as if in a ballroom. I picked Vicky up; her legs straddled my hips like we were swing dancing. A few moments later, I was doing the robot with Sarah.

We had so much fun. Some of the other people stared at us. Some of them made snide comments. But I didn't care. The only people that were on my mind were my beauties. They were all that mattered.

We saw the signs for the aquarium up ahead, so the dancing started to slow. When we finally began to walk normally, still laughing, we walked intertwined with our arms locked together. A throuple. A real relationship. We were all in love, and nothing—not even God himself—could pull us apart.

Even as the sky darkened with clouds, I still felt their warmth around me. I didn't need the sun to feel any warmth. All I needed was them.

As we entered the aquarium, I felt a soothing ease. We walked through the entrance together. The hallway was a glass dome that allowed us to view all the marine life. My eyes followed all the different creatures.

Then a shark swam by, and my eyes locked onto it. I tracked the shark's movements. In the few months I was a civilian, I often felt like a shark, circling those around me with a taste for blood. I hadn't forgotten the sounds of battle. Less than a year ago, I was in the heat of the fight, the rapids of war.

I guess I did have another love affair before my beauties. Her name was Lady Death. Her seduction was a deadly game. The feeling of adrenaline rushing through your veins as you became something... different. An animal. A beast. A monster. I watched the shark further.

Death. She was, at times, very tempting when the gunfire was raining down. That IED that had torn through the HUMVEE... I knew Death smirked that day, thinking that she had me. But I wasn't going to make it easy for her. I fought through all of it. Calm, Sergeant. Look at the other fish.

Before my mind could rein in, I felt something warm on my shoulders. I looked down. Sarah to my right and Vicky to my left held their hands on me, comforting me.

"Beautiful, isn't it?" My voice was a hoarse rasp.

"Are you okay, Master?" Sarah asked with concern.

"I think he will be." Vicky looked over to Sarah with an awkward grin.

"Let's hit the gift shop," I suggested as I took their arms. I forced a smile, knowing that this feeling of battle was just a fading thought. They had taken over my mind once more. My beauties.

Our strides galloped back toward the zoo's entrance. There was a doting feeling as we walked. Our feet moved in tandem with that rhythm that we danced to before. The aura of love christened us as the sky began to open. Small droplets of rain pelted down.

I glanced between my beauties; their bodies glistened in the aura. A sultry glow radiated from them, yet it was lovingly warm. Anchored deep within was a renewed sense of prowess, as if I could conquer the world. As they stood beside me, I felt that there was no obstacle that I couldn't defeat.

Our pace hastened briskly as the need to find shelter increased. We rushed into the souvenir shop. Water dripped from their curvaceous bodies. I stood in the doorway momentarily, admiring the ample way that the rain had sealed their clothes to them.

The barren avenue to their feral design, their figures met with the hunger inside. Those tight shirts were pierced with their erect nipples. The divine outline of their theurgical groins was the meddle of ecstasy. I was taken in by their raw femininity.

A sense of leaning downward came over me. An impulse to inhale with all my olfactory receptors to catch the aroma of those sweet morsels that once had been on my tongue.

Yet I digressed from such a notion in public. Stop. Not in public. You can't smell women's crotches in public. Even if they are your girlfriends, calm down, soldier. I felt the little guy jump with joy at the very thought of smelling them.

My beauties disbursed in different directions as they browsed around the shop. I took that as my chance to venture off alone. That way, I could find unique things for each one.

I perused the many selections: hats, shirts, mugs. None of it seemed to be what I wanted to get them. I wanted it to be something special to each one. Something that they would save to remember our special third date.

I was about to give up when I found the stuffed animals section. I saw the tiger first and, with haste, snatched it up. I dug around for a while and found a bird that looked very much like a crane. Both stuffed animals seemed so cute and would be perfect. Vicky, the stuffed tiger, and Sarah, the stuffed crane. Yes. Perfect. I knew that they would love these. I hurried to the register, purchased the presents, and bagged them before they could see.

I stood at the counter waiting. I thought about how rude some of the people were today, but I quickly pushed those thoughts aside. I had a fun day with my girlfriends; that's what mattered.

Before long, Vicky and Sarah approached me, ready to go. After we headed out, the rain picked up. As we made our way out of the zoo and were heading back to the car...

BOOM! BOOM! BOOM!

"Incoming!" I screamed as I threw myself to the ground. The mortar fire was raining down. I grabbed my weapon and ran to my position. Where the hell was I? Fuck! Our FOB had been overrun. The mortars were launching in with such fervor. Those fucking ragheads thought they were going to kill us. Not the fuck today. This fucking shit position in a valley was so fucking dumb to put an FOB. The bullets whizzed by; one had almost got me. Fuck this! I raised my weapon; I looked over the wall. Those bastards were right there. Shit! My finger rapidly squeezed the trigger of my M4. My magazine was black in no time.

I could hear the platoon C.O. on the radio. With all the gunfire, I couldn't make out a word. I just started yelling commands out to my soldiers. Fan fire here. Move there. I didn't think; I just reacted. All the fury of my weapon was being released upon the enemy. Those goddamn man-dress-wearing fucks. DIE, MOTHERFUCKERS! DIE!

A rage, a hatred that I had never known, consumed me. I saw Horton get hit. Fuck!

"HORTON! MEDIC! HORTON!" My voice screamed out as I peered back down the sights of my weapon. A mortar landed, exploding just a few feet behind me. A ringing in my ears deafened the battle.

Fuck these mountains, fuck Coin. Win the hearts and minds, my ass. Just waste the motherfuckers. All of them. Shit! I was down to my last mag. I hated this fucking shit box of a country. As soon as I saw one pop up, I let into my weapon. I got excited when they fell. Fuck 'em. Damned shitbags.

Then I heard it. Whistling in the sky, I knew it was close. The mortar smashed into the ground right behind me. The concussion of the blast knocked me into the air; I fell flat on my stomach. The force was so strong it almost knocked me unconscious. Unable to move. I lay there screaming.

I saw two Valkyries hovering over me. Shit, had I died? In this goddamned country? Elle, I'm sorry.

The Valkyries began speaking to each other.

"Master! Master!"

"Is he okay?"

"I am not sure."

"What happened?"

"We made it to the parking lot then... this."

Both Valkyries leaned down. They kissed me one by one. Slow, passionate kisses. The kiss of death? Were they here to take me from the battlefield? Till Valhalla, my brothers.

"Here, help me pick him up."

I felt their embrace as I was being carried away. Away from my troops. No, not yet. I promised to get them home. I can't die yet. Everyone, all of them, I promised. I swore to them. Sarge would make sure that they were honored. That they were home.

"Master, you're safe."

"I'm starting the car. He in all the way?"

"Yes, but he's still out of it."

I could feel my body floating. Drifting to somewhere else.

"We're almost to his apartment. Has he come out of it yet?"

"I don't think so."

"Damn, he is heavy."

"Get the door. We'll put him on the couch."

Then... darkness... nothing. I was gone.

My eyes opened to the angelic sight of Sarah's beautiful face; my head was in her lap. What happened? Why are we back in my apartment?

"Master is waking up." Sarah looked down upon me.

"Good." I heard Vicky sigh out from the kitchen.

"What happened?"

"There was thunder. Then you started acting strangely. Screaming out weird things." Sarah's eyes had a loving and concerned look.

"You screamed out 'Horton,' Master. I assume one of your soldiers?" Vicky came back into the living room. Her hand held a mug; I figured she had been drinking coffee.

"He was one of my troops in Afghanistan. He died in a firefight." My voice was full of remorse.

"As I suspected, you had a flashback." Vicky leaned down, stroking my hair.

"Will he be okay?" Sarah looked at Vicky with tears in her eyes.

"Yes. Unfortunately, this is the price he paid to protect us." Vicky sighed before taking a sip from her mug.

"Girls, I am fine," I said trying to comfort them. I forced another smile to make my declaration more convincing.

"You scared us, Master." Sarah's worried gaze fell upon me again. I felt her hand caress my chest.

"Yes, we were worried." Vicky took another sip; I could see her hand was shaking. I could tell that underneath that cool, calm exterior, she was just as concerned as Sarah.

"I'm sorry... sorry for worrying you." I sighed, ashamed of the episode invading our date.

"It's okay, Master. You couldn't help it." Sarah ran her hand across my chest.

"We understand. You have been scarred by war. I'm just happy that you are safe," Vicky softly said.

We sat for a few moments in silence. Did I have a flashback? I had only experienced that once before. Thunder had triggered this one. I needed to be careful. I didn't want that—me—to hurt them.

I carefully looked over them. They didn't seem to be hurt. Good. Thank God I hadn't done something outrageous. Something that would have hurt them. I loved them so much.

"Do you want to talk about it? You don't have to if it's..." Vicky trailed off before she sipped on her coffee.

"My second deployment. We were stationed at an FOB, forward operating base, in the Kaspisa province." I sighed, thinking about that hellish place.

"It's okay, Master. We are here for you." Sarah stroked my hair as she gazed at me with loving eyes.

"We are listening. Anything you need. Anything that will help you." Vicky's voice had a sympathetic tone.

"The base was located in a valley with mountains all around. It was a dumb place to put us. But we were there to win the hearts and minds of the locals." I felt the anger of my words directed at the powers over the troops. Directed at our superiors.

"That wasn't very smart. So much for military intelligence." Vicky let out a slight chuckle. Her jest seemed to ease my mood.

"Yeah, our thoughts exactly. Terrorists took advantage of our position. We constantly took fire from those mountains." I turned my head to meet Vicky's eyes. Her blue gems seemed to comfort me.

"So scary. You are brave, Master. Thank you for having that kind of courage." Sarah's voice was low and comforting; her fingers caressed my face.

"One morning, real early, we got bombarded with mortars." I started to tell the story of that morning but got choked up. Yet, looking at my girlfriends made me feel at ease. I found the courage to continue. "As the mortars kept being lobbed in, I didn't think. I just reacted. All my soldiers were on the wall, manning their posts."

"Is that when Horton met... met his end?" Sarah reluctantly asked.

"Mm-hm. We were hit pretty hard by ground forces that day. They were coming down the mountains, spraying bullets everywhere. Horton caught one of those bullets. Right in his face." I paused for a moment. I could feel my tears start to flow.

"It's okay; we can stop if you need to," Vicky said with remorse. She seemed to be thinking while holding the mug at her lips. Then, she broke from her thoughts by taking another sip.

"Anyway, I was his Sergeant; he was a good soldier. Another month and he would have been up for his stripes. I put his name in for the NCO board." My voice was shallow and full of remorse. I turned to look into Sarah's eyes. Her emeralds had tears dripping down onto me.

"How did you feel? About Horton?" Vicky asked as she pulled her mug down.

"He was a good man. I felt like I had lost a brother. I guess..." I trailed off.

"How was he? As a person?" Sarah asked.

"He was a business-as-usual kind of guy. Serious most of the time. But he would do anything for anyone. That's why I put him up for promotion." It felt good to talk about him. To share this with them, share the parts of myself I didn't let anyone else see.

"Thank you for sharing. Do you feel better?" Vicky kissed my cheek. I felt her love in each word.

99

"You are safe, Master. Safe with us. We are here for you."
Sarah's soft voice was comforting. She wiped the tears from her
eyes.

"Yes, I feel better. Thank you for comforting me. Thank you for
being here for me." I started to feel better about the experience.

They both understood. They saw my vulnerabilities and simply
comforted me. There was no judgment, just soothing words and
caring worry. Why did I feel ashamed to share this before? They
made me feel that I could share anything with them. I wanted to
love them in the same way. I wanted to share everything with them.
I wanted to be there for them when they needed me. Adorn them
with things...

Presents. Where were the presents? Did I lose them? Tear them
up in my fit?

I shot up, looking around. "My bag?"

"By the door, Master." Vicky pointed with her mug.

I rushed over to the bag and untied it. The stuffed animals were
safe. My episode and the rain did not damage them.

"I have a surprise for you both," I said, my voice filled with
affection. I pulled them out of the bag. I gave Sarah the crane, then
Vicky the tiger.

"This is so cute, Master," Sarah said in that baby voice.

"Oh, Master, you shouldn't have." Vicky's dark vixen tenor
growled like a tiger.

"I wanted to get my girlfriends something," I said, thrilled to
see the looks on their faces. They smiled wide. Those beautiful
smiles warmed my heart.

I sat on the couch as they cuddled me close for a while, my arms
wrapped around them tightly. We sat like this for several minutes
before Sarah broke the silence.

"We got to dance with you. That was awesome." Sarah's
excitement couldn't be contained.

"Yeah, we did get to dance. I liked it too." I beamed, thinking
about dancing through the zoo with them.

"Dancing... pft. I was the only one dancing. I have no idea what
you two were doing." Vicky laughed, her face nuzzled into my side.

"Yeah. Master looked like someone had electrocuted a dying
bug. All jittery." Sarah joked as she rapidly shook her hand.

"Hey! I looked like Fred Astaire dancing next to two zombies." I chuckled as I raised my arms, mocking zombie movements.

"Zombies... huh." Vicky started to tickle me.

"Better be zombie brides." Sarah joined in by tickling my other side.

"Okay... okay... Not zombies. Frankensteins." I wiggled around, laughing.

"Hear that, sis? Frankenstein?" Sarah tittered, throwing a small pillow at me.

"Yeah. I would say we are sexy vampires, at the least." Vicky's hand grabbed my cheeks.

"Okay, graceful ballerina vampires." I shook my head. Vicky released my face, then gave my cheek a playful slap.

"Better!" Vicky exclaimed with a playfully mocking tone.

"Before long, we will have to go," Sarah said in a somber tone as she looked at the clock in despair.

Vicky glanced at the time. "Yeah, we need to work tomorrow. And so does Master."

"You didn't care about time last week," I said in confusion.

"We do now," Sarah stated matter-of-factly.

After spending another hour together, it was time for them to leave. They stayed long enough to ensure I would be okay by myself. As they exited the apartment, they clung to their stuffed animals. I was overjoyed that they loved their presents.

"Good night, Master. We love you." Their farewell was that sexy unison that they had often done.

"Good night, my beauties. I love you both, too." My words trailed off as the door closed behind them.

As I was preparing for my week, I started getting tired. All the while, I remembered how Vicky and Sarah had comforted me. They made me feel better about the flashback. They seemed to pull my pain away from me. It was so encouraging.

I lay in bed thinking about what the future had in store for me. What it had in store for us. Marriage? Could I find a way to marry them both? What would life be like, married to both? I trailed off into my dreams.

Chapter 9: A Brother's Sympathy

Aunt Claira had told me that Elle was staying in a hotel. A Hamilton Suites. There were a total of three Hamilton's in town. I knew Stephen's company had ties to the Golden Rose and Sentinel, both huge companies. The Golden Rose owned the chain of Hamiltons. If Elle was hiding from him, she wasn't doing such a great job.

I was going to try to catch up with her after work and attempt to talk to her. That was if she would talk to me. Or would she berate me again? "A disgusting piece of shit." Those words still tore into my soul. I would much rather walk naked through a pit of vipers than have her hate me over whom I loved and how they referred to me. As for "she didn't know me anymore," sure, war had affected me, but I think I was still mostly me. Or was I? Had I become something different? All I knew was that my big sis was hurting and needed me. I just didn't know what to do if she didn't want my help.

Work was exhausting but short today. I had only one call—a commercial installation—but it was exhausting work. My body was sore from lifting so much, and the hot sun had melted my insides. By day's end, I felt puny, but I had to try helping Elle. The clock showed fifteen hundred hours when I made my way to the car. Before I pulled off, I texted my girlfriends. I had been sending them cute morning texts, a few memes throughout the day, thoughtful messages here and there, and goodnight messages. We had a group text together. They both responded to every text. I took the "no secrets" thing to heart.

> [Master] Tuesday 15:03
> *I will be going to find Elle. May not be able to text for a while.*

> [Sarah] Tuesday 15:04
> *Okay, Master. Send her our apologies.* ☹

> [Vicky] Tuesday 15:04
> *Be safe, Master. We are here for you.* ☺

After the texts of encouragement, I set off in my beater, pushing the engine once I got on the highway. "Come on, car. Go. Don't you dare have a flat or breakdown on me." Which Hamilton to try first? One that would be near a park and easy access to food. Possibly close to Jenny's school. There was only one that was close to a park and about ten blocks away from Jenny's school, but it didn't have much for eateries around it. Hold on, Elle, little bro is coming.

As my beater pulled into the parking lot of the one that seemed to be the right fit, I quickly spotted Elle's SUV. I parked on the other side of the parking lot in case she needed to get away from me. I could go a different way and she could feel safe. This was it. Now the hard part: talking.

If she slammed the door in my face, then what? Leave? Let her handle this on her own? I might not like it, but if that is what she wished, then yes. As I approached the building, my heart started beating rapidly. Fear rushed over me. The same kind of fear I felt right before a mission.

I took up the rifle because I wanted to be powerful enough to be of some use. I wanted to help, to protect others. That was all I wanted to do. Protect her. Shield her from Stephen. Be a shoulder for her to cry on. But my anger had stopped me from being there for her on Saturday. Then... then my beauties called me Master. Was I truly as disgusting as she believed?

"Ahem..." I cleared my throat as I approached the front desk.

Behind the counter, a cute blonde with a very crooked grin seemed to jump straight up as I approached. Her breasts jiggled in her uniform from the sudden movement. She wore a white blouse with a black vest over it. She had large pretty brown eyes. Those doe eyes watched me with suspicion as if I were a thief there to steal.

"Ma'am, what room is Elle Dolion in?" I asked with conviction ringing in my voice.

She glanced down at her computer and then back up to me. "Sorry, sir. We don't have any guests registered under that name."

Her voice had a familiar tone, like that seductive tone Vicky used... maybe... nah. Being this close, I could see something in her eyes. At first, I thought that she was suspicious of me, but she had that same look Sarah and Vicky gave me right before we played. Hmm... cute, but she wasn't them. Besides, I was here for Elle.

Elle must have used her maiden name. Maybe that was how she hid from Stephen. Yes, that had to be it.

"Ma'am, can you try Elle Forester?" I asked with hope. She looked down at her computer screen again. The sound of keys being pressed hard echoed across the lobby.

"Now that name is here—a lot. Room 303, sir." She looked up at me. The grin on her face seemed like an invite. But I brushed it off.

I hastily made my way to the elevator. Third floor. Roger. Saddle up, soldier. This can go all kinds of jacked. Be prepared, Sergeant. I breathed in deeply as the doors opened. I almost stumbled inside. Still yourself. Still your mind.

But my heart... my heart couldn't be calmed. I was pulverized by the fear that my actions might completely lose me the only people who were blood. Do it. Be safe. And if you can't be safe, be deadly. Hoo-ah. I reached up and hit the button for the third floor.

It didn't take long before the doors opened to the third level. I rushed down the hall and arrived at her door. Room 303. I knocked the rhythm she would knock when she would sneak her boyfriends in after our parents went to sleep. It was our code for "all clear."

I stood in the hallway for what seemed like a lifetime before I heard the locks start to be undone. As the door cracked open, Elle leaned her face out to look down the hallway. When she saw me, our eyes locked. Those abysmal oceans of hers held an immortal hate. A hatred so powerful, so raw... But that ire was solely for Stephen. Beyond the hatred was a sorrow the depths of which were nearing the deepest pits of purgatory.

"Hello, Sis," I croaked.

"Come in before someone sees you." Elle pulled me through the door and quickly closed it, locking every lock. As I entered, I noticed that Jenny was not in the room.

"Where's Jenny?"

"She is with Stephen. He picked her up from school before I could get there." Elle's eyes were welling up.

I didn't say anything. My arms just cradled her in a hug. She sobbed into my chest as I held her tightly for several minutes. It had pissed me off that Stephen had taken Jenny. But legally, he had all the rights to do so. He was her father, even if he didn't deserve to be. The soldier in me wanted to kill him. But that wasn't going to solve anything. It would have made it worse. There was nothing I could do but console Elle. I kissed the top of her head as she cried.

"Have you called the police?" I broke the silence.

"No, we can't. I would go to ja— we just can't." Elle looked up at me briefly before returning to her lamenting cries.

After many minutes of embracing, Elle let go and turned toward the mini fridge. She pulled out four small bottles of alcohol. She opened one and downed it fast. Her hand held out two toward me. I reluctantly took them as she passed by me. She sat on the couch near the window, peering down on the parking lot.

"Why are you here, Kyle?" Her voice was strong, but the shallowness of her power was showing.

"I came to help." I wondered about the bottles in my hand.

"I am beyond help." Elle's voice started to falter as she sniffled.

"No, you are not." My heart filled with sorrow for her.

"He has won. He has Jenny." Elle turned to me with such pain in her eyes.

"Okay, so fight back. In the divorce. Fight for her."

"Divorce? At this rate, I might end up face down in a ditch." Elle's defeated face broke me further.

"No... screw that bullshit. Listen, you have documented his abuse. You can win." The soldier in me crept in, but only enough to inspire a fight inside Elle.

"Damn, Bro, the Army made you... stronger," Elle said, then paused for a moment. "But you don't understand. The company he works for, Integrated Technological Industries, is pretty powerful." Her eyes looked down in shame.

"So, what if it looks like we won't win? Try anyway. Don't quit. Not now, not when Jenny needs you the most." I leaned over, tilting her chin up. "Besides, I am here. I can help. Remember."

My eyes burned with the fight as I gazed deep into hers. I could see that no matter what, defeat was already written in her mind.

"But... he has a wall of lawyers. I have nothing."

"To hell with that corporate bullshit. Embrace the pain and fight. Fight until you win or there is nothing left of you." I had to find a way to get her back to the fight.

Elle didn't respond; she just sat there in a stupor. I didn't know what to say. If Vicky or Sarah were here, they might. But I didn't. I was good at inspiring troops to fight. But Elle... I just... had nothing.

"I may not know what to say, but I won't leave you like this. I won't let you quit on yourself. Do you hear me?" My voice eased into that cool NCO vibe.

"Wow, your voice when you talk like that. You're so confident." Elle's voice slightly changed in pitch. Was that hope?

"Stop deflecting. We're talking about Jenny. Your daughter."

"I know." The peak of defeat seared in her voice.

"Then fight. We can do this. Together." That smoothness of the NCO rippled through my voice.

"You're right." She gazed up at me as she opened the second bottle. "To the long fight ahead... together." And guzzled it down.

"To winning." I opened one of the bottles in my hand and drank it. I set the other one on the table next to the couch.

Elle and I called several lawyers. Many turned us down once they knew what company Stephen worked for. It was disheartening how many cowards were in the civilian world. Were these the people that our bullets had protected? That we had sacrificed for? Some wimpy lame asses? To think they call themselves Americans. I felt disgusted with society. Betrayed by it. Why were soldiers laying their lives on the lines for dumbasses like these? Another reason why I had few friends. I couldn't relate to that kind of cowardice.

I had called half the lawyers in the phone book—all denied Elle—and she was working on the other half. But I could see that she was becoming more demotivated with each denial. Going through this parade of lawyers was demoralizing just to be told no. But then Elle found one that was up to the challenge.

"Okay, so you will meet with me tomorrow to discuss everything. Sure. What time?" Elle motioned me for a pen. I pulled the one off my collar and handed it to her. She scribbled down "9:00 a.m. 1846 Midway Drive."

Elle hung up the phone, then sat on the couch in silence. I didn't dare say a word; I just let her collect herself while I thought about Jenny. I missed taking her to the park. She loved to swing. She would beg me to swing beside her. We would race to see who could get higher. Somehow, she always won. Those times were filled with lots of laughter. Being an uncle was so much fun. Then, the thought of how Sarah was with Jenny the other night in my apartment came into focus. So loving, so caring. They had so much fun for that brief time.

My eyes studied Elle as she sat in silence. I wanted to say something uplifting, but I wasn't great at it. Vicky could have Elle smiling in no time if she were here. If it hadn't been for the "Master" incident, maybe they would already be friends, smiling and laughing together. But I hadn't seen Elle smile since she opened the door.

"Thank you, Bro," Elle said as she stood up.

"You're welcome." My voice was a whisper.

I embraced her again. She locked her arms around me tightly. I could feel her tension starting to slip away. Then she left my embrace and picked up her phone.

"Want takeout? The Chinese restaurant down the street does deliveries." She started to dial.

"Sure." I sat back on the bed.

I didn't have to tell her what I wanted; she already knew. Sweet & sour chicken with noodles. She ordered pork fried rice for herself. This was pretty typical of us. When we were growing up, Mom and Dad would go on dates most Friday nights. By the time I was eight or so, Elle could babysit me. She'd often use her allowance to order Chinese takeout. We'd sit in the living room on the couch, watching movies together, mostly horror movies. If Mom and Dad knew that we ate on the sofa, our hides would have been tanned. Elle would have been in even more trouble if they had known she would let me watch R-rated movies.

I sat up on the bed, glancing around the room for the remote—on the bedside table. My hand moved with haste to snatch it up. I was surfing through the channels in no time to find something like an old horror film. I found John Carpenter's *Vampires*. It was right at the opening credits.

"Hey, Sis, they have a vamp movie on. Wanna watch it?" I asked as I kicked off my shoes.

"Sure," she said with a dull voice. However, her eyes looked at me with a sense of hope.

We sat on the bed with our backs against the headboard. I gave her a comforting side hug as we watched the movie. In the opening scene, we both gasped when the vampire slayers pulled the vampires out into the sunlight. As we watched the movie, she seemed like the same teenager who had babysat her little brother all those years ago. She was enjoying herself and the movie. So was I.

107

The movie was at the part where the vampire slayers had gotten a new preacher when we heard a knock at the door. I got up and walked to it. In the peephole, I saw the delivery guy from the restaurant. I opened the door and got the food. Elle had already paid with her card over the phone, but I didn't want the delivery guy to go empty-handed, so I tipped him. He gave a gracious nod and left. I quickly locked the door so that Elle would feel safe.

I handed her the pork fried rice and took my place beside her as the action of the movie heated up again. The chopsticks felt foreign in my hands since the last time I ate with them was right before Elle went off to college. We ate while watching the film.

When the vampire girl bit the slayer and walked back to the master vampire... "Man, she looks so hot. Vampire women... mmm..." I jokingly said. I reminisced about joking with the girls, that Vicky wanted to be a vampire instead of a zombie.

"I knew your pervy ass liked those blood-sucking bitches." Elle laughed. When I glanced over, she was smiling. I was so happy.

After the movie and Chinese food, she looked at me. Her eyes filled with an apologetic look. She didn't have to say it. But I knew.

"I'm sorry, Bro," Elle whispered.

"It's okay, Sis." My hand patted her head.

"You don't understand." Elle looked away.

"Okay, enlighten me."

"When Stephen would get drunk, he... he would make me call him 'master.' Then... he'd beat me." She looked at me with tears in her eyes.

I felt angry at the idea of this. I would never do that to Vicky or Sarah. Never. I would never use that title for anything so fucked up. That was disgusting to me. But I pushed through my anger. I settled myself back down.

"I didn't know. I am sorry, Sis." I hugged her again.

"Hearing your girlfriends call you master... it brought back all the pain... all the abuse." Elle sighed.

"It's okay. I'm sorry you had to go through that." I kissed her forehead.

"Do your girlfriends hate me?" Elle's voice was filled with worry.

I thought about how Sarah and Vicky acted. They didn't seem too fazed by Elle's outburst. This was another reason I thought these women could be the ones. Maybe... if I could figure out how to marry them.

"No. Confused, yes, but they don't hate you."

"Okay... so explain this two-girlfriend thing to me anyway." Elle took that big-sis tone with me. She eyed me with concern before continuing. "Look, I am not fully on board with you dating two women. But I will try to be understanding. Besides, I see all kinds of screwed-up relationships at my job."

Crap, I was in trouble. I should explain it to her. Maybe she can help me understand it. She did work with couples for a living.

"So... they were delivering pizza to a neighbor," I said, "but they mistakenly knocked on my door. We sort of hit it off."

"Pizza? Like a porn scene or something?" Elle eyed me.

"Sorta... um... not really. They came back after they got off work. We sat discussing things for a while. Then they asked me which one I wanted to date."

"And?" Elle eyed me with anticipation.

"I said both. Surprisingly, they actually agreed."

"So, now you are dating pizza girls?" Elle asked with a slight chuckle.

"Not exactly. Vicky is getting her masseuse license soon. Sarah was working in HR until a sexual harassment issue. Pizza delivery is temporary for them."

"Cool, they sound like smart women. So why both?" Elle seemed more intrigued.

"I said it as a joke at first. I felt intimidated and thought it would get rid of them, but they took it seriously. In fact, they were more confident about the idea than I was. And now, I like different things about each of them."

"What do you like about them? Other than how ridiculously gorgeous they are?" Elle asked, really leaning into the conversation.

"Vicky is challenging, even motherly at times. She has an edginess about her, like she can cut through all red tape. Sarah is very gentle and sweet. She is encouraging and soft. They both have different things that attract me to them." I sighed. This was all surface stuff. I couldn't fully explain it.

"So, have you taken them on any dates?"

"We have had a few dates. Mostly, we hung out at my apartment, though." I shrugged, trying to keep myself tight-lipped. I didn't want to give her too many details.

"Tell me about the dates." Elle seemed awed and shocked by the relationship.

I described the dates, leaving out the sex stuff. I didn't tell her about my flashback. That kind of thing got a bad rap, so best not to let my psychologist sister know that her brother was a nutcase.

"Okay, so do you love them?" she asked, concern in her voice.

"I have only known them for a short time, but I think I do. I do love them both."

"Both." She laughed. "You love both. Silly perv. I love you, Bro."

"I love you too, Sis. And yeah, both." My words reaffirmed to myself my affection for them. I really did love them both.

"Well, your love life seems more complicated than mine. Good luck." Elle laughed more.

"Oh, you have no idea. These ladies are incorrigible and insatiable." I laughed so hard I snorted.

"Insatiable?" she questioned as she continued to laugh.

"Yeah, um... very much so." I let loose a coy smile hoping to distract from my flushed cheeks.

"Eww... still pervy as ever." She rustled my hair.

"Yep. But now I have girlfriends to be pervy with." I grinned as I remembered those encounters.

"Whatever floats your boat. So, are you dating for fun? Or is the idea of marrying both of them on the table?" Elle threw her hands up, trying to make sense of my intentions.

"I don't date for sport. So, marriage, I... I hope," I admitted.

"How the hell is that going to work?" Elle looked at me, puzzled.

"Hell if I know. I am still trying to figure all this out." I tried to mask my very real concerns about that question with a blasé wave of my hands.

"Just don't get in over your head," Elle implored. "Take things naturally as they come."

"I will. Try to, anyway, because, in reality, I barely understand it myself."

"It's getting late," Elle said through a yawn. I could see her eyes droop down. I hadn't noticed before, but she probably hadn't slept in days.

"Good night, Sis. I love you. And good luck tomorrow," I said as I put on my boots.

"Good night, Bro, I love you too," Elle said as she unlocked the door.

As soon as I stepped over the threshold, the door closed and the locks re-engaged. Smart, sis. Keep it locked. Be safe. I walked down to the elevator. I was tired myself. But to feel like I had when I was a kid—to hang out with my sister, see her smile, make up with her—it was worth it.

When I got to the lobby, the blonde behind the counter stared at me with that same look from earlier. I ignored it and walked on. I made my way out to the parking lot, relieved that Elle was okay.

As I entered my beater, my mind fixated on Stephen. That sick twisted asshole had perverted what it meant to be a Master. It's not a title to be used when you abuse people. At least not me. It was a title no less sacred than husband. You scumbag. How could you do that to Elle? And now he had Jenny...

Calm Sergeant. Keep calm. Breathe. You got this. No killing. You are a civilian now. This scumbag deserved death; he was begging for it. No! Calm! Stay calm. I thought about the look Jenny would have if she saw me slay Stephen. How would she feel if Uncle Kyle murdered her Daddy? No, we do this thing the right way. The legal way. Elle is going in the morning to set it up. Just stay the course. Don't do it, Sergeant. Just go home. Go home and sleep. Go home and get ready for your workday tomorrow.

Chapter 10: Wise Guidance

I sat on the couch and looked over to the chair. I still hadn't figured out how to fix the arm. I chuckled to myself, the memory of how Sarah fell still vivid. The way she laughed, lying on the floor. How messy she was after I had made her orgasm. How messy they both were. They had such a fun sexiness about them.

I was going to prove them right. That I was a man worthy of them. I was going to be the man that they needed. That they desired to grant the gift of submission to. They were my beauties. Genies that I had found in the cave of wonders. They fulfilled my every wish, and now was the time for me to be worthy of that.

I had been planning Vicky's birthday party with Sarah. We had a pretty good plan: a nice dinner, then a trip to her favorite ice cream shop, and last but not least, a late-night show. However, I was still trying to figure out the present part—something that she would like. I had no idea what to get her, but Sarah said she'd help.

I started missing my girlfriends. I wanted to mess with them, so I pulled my phone out. The screen had a warm glow as I texted.

[Master] Wednesday 18:23
Licky... licky... 😊

[Vicky] Wednesday 18:23
Dirty boy, we might have to spank him. 😉

[Sarah] Wednesday 18:25
Or wash his dirty mind :P

[Master] Wednesday 18:25
Me dirty minded...nah

[Vicky] Wednesday 18:26
Don't act all innocent now

[Sarah] Wednesday 18:26
Yeah, I'm supposed to be the innocent one ☹️

[Vicky] Wednesday 18:27

Miss Pushover innocent, yeah my ass

[Sarah] Wednesday 18:28
Miss Pushover?

[Vicky] Wednesday 18:32
Break any chairs lately? LOL

[Sarah] Wednesday 18:36
Not fair, I don't have a silly name for you ☹

[Master] Wednesday 18:43
Gotta go. Dinner with Mrs. Helderman. See ya later. I would say behave, but we all know that is not an option for you 2

[Sarah] Wednesday 18:44
I am always good for you, Master 😊

[Vicky] Wednesday 18:44
Good...yeah, maybe... if ur lucky. :P

As I got off the couch, I slid my phone into my pocket. Wednesday night's meal, but Mrs. Helderman didn't want me to bring anything this time. She said that she was cooking a meal that I would love. No potluck tonight. I was excited to hang out with her. Our talks were always fun. And the topic I was dying to explore was the three-way relationship. She had years of experience with that.

I walked into the hallway and strafed just one door over. I knocked, ready to see what she had cooked.

"Come in, Kyle." Her voice was filled with joy.

When I opened the door, the aroma filled the room with a heavenly delight. I wasn't sure what it was, but it smelled so good.

Her apartment had the same layout as mine, but portraits were on almost every wall. In the living room, she had a massive sectional. I was always confused about how they set it up in such a small apartment. It fit so tightly along the wall. There was no room for a coffee table due to the sheer size of the sectional. But it was comfy. Her dining table was small, like mine. A four-seater. Moving into this from where she had raised her five children must have been an adjustment.

"How has your day been, Mrs. Helderman?" I asked as I sat on the sectional.

Our routine was traditional in a sense. We would have tea or coffee, chat for a bit, then eat. She was old-fashioned that way. Which was fine, I didn't much like the modern idea of eating and running. My body slid onto the cushiony couch as it enveloped me. God, this thing was so comfy. Probably was expensive too. My mind wandered off for a moment. I thought about what kind of things I could do with Sarah and Vicky on a couch like this. Yeah...

"Fine. I went to visit Jimmy again." Her voice seemed serene. I took it that her visit was a good one.

"No more pigeons?"

"Not this week; he was still clean," she said, the sound of her voice getting closer. She winked at me as she came out with two mugs. Was it coffee or tea? I took the mug she handed me.

"Thank you," I said before blowing on the steaming mug.

She glanced at me as she peered over her mug. "You're welcome. How was your day?" She sat on the far side of the large couch.

"Good, I guess. Work is pushing me like a slave. But..." I trailed off. I soon took a sip. It was coffee. I felt relieved; tea wasn't my favorite.

"But the girls have your spirits up." She said knowingly, then took a sip of her coffee.

I grinned just thinking about it. They had boosted my spirits tremendously. I hadn't said anything about them yet, but she knew.

"Yes, how did you know?" Confusion settled into my words.

"Boy, it's written all over your face." She laughed before taking another sip.

Those frail hands must have done a lot. Behind those weary eyes must be a font of knowledge and wisdom. Even though Elle was my sister, I didn't feel as comfortable around her as I did around Mrs. Helderman. Definitely not in the state she was in yesterday. I couldn't just explain that my heart was bursting with joy.

"I had a great laugh with Jimmy today. I told him how you had become smitten, following those girls around like a lost puppy." She chuckled as she took another sip.

"I'm not a lost puppy; I'm more like a ferocious lion," I said jokingly, recalling my thoughts about lions at the zoo.

"Sure, you are," she said sarcastically before taking a serious tone. "How has the bonding experience been going?"

"Good, I guess. We have had a few dates." I smiled in remembrance. Then I remembered what they had said at the zoo. What was it? *Bonding complete.* Was that normal? I had to ask.

"They said something like bonding complete or something like that. Is that normal or were they joking around? Or something?"

"Probably a joke. You kids are always joking about something." She tittered, almost sinister in tone. "But all seriousness, what are you going to do?"

"I was thinking that I could marry them both." Words that I hadn't spoken aloud blurted out before I could stop myself.

Mrs. Helderman choked, almost spitting up her coffee. I could see the concern on her face. She didn't say anything at first. She simply sat there looking off into space as if she were deep in thought. Had I said something wrong? Was she going to berate me for wanting to marry two women? A greedy bastard... that was what she probably thought. Just a horny, greedy kid.

"Slow down, boy! Why don't you live with them first?" Her voice was loud; it felt like she was scolding me. However, she soon regained her composure.

"Like have them move in?" The question was more for me than it was for her.

"Yes, live with them. See how things work before jumping into marriage," she said with concern before another sip hit her lips.

"So, you don't think it's weird that I want to marry both of them?" I inquired, then gulped in fear of her answer.

She looked me in the eyes. "Why would I? Both are very beautiful and smart. I would be surprised if you didn't." Her tone had softened again.

"How was it with Jimmy and the other?"

"Great, really. We did everything together. We loved each other," Mrs. Helderman said as she sat in remembrance.

"I think it took all of two weeks before Jimmy had told us both that he loved us," she said, giving a brief nod. Then, the corners of her lips tugged upward with happiness. Her smile was happy but revealed a hollow ache.

"Helda was my best friend. We had always done everything together." Her voice seemed ecstatic. I didn't interrupt. Her story started to sound very familiar. "We were visiting Camp Peary, at a USO show for troops before they shipped out. That's when we spotted him. He looked so handsome in his uniform." Her voice started to crack.

I sat as she explained the beginnings of their three-way love affair. Jimmy had deployed to Vietnam. He wrote letters back home to both of them. The main rule was no secrets. They both wrote back to him. Often, they would read each other's letters giggling about the things that he had written. Sometimes, he would write one letter addressed to them both.

I could imagine how different my deployments would have been if I had someone other than Elle to communicate back home with. And the lucky son of a bitch had two. I sighed, thinking about those lonely nights. The other guys wrote home. Got care packages. Went to the recreation tent to make calls back to their spouses or kids. But I stayed in my tent in my free time. I was there unless I was on a mission, or the enemy had decided to come play with us. I would come out to speak with my soldiers. To train them. To be an ear for them. But I really didn't have that for myself.

"That must have been a great feeling to get a letter," I said eagerly, thinking about the other side of the fence.

"Yes, you boys go out there fighting. Us girls stay home, not knowing what was happening. Not knowing if those letters would stop. If..." She trailed off. The smile on her face faded for a moment.

That look, I saw it on the wives when we came home. Horton's wife... the same look she had when I visited her. I couldn't understand the pain or anxiety at home. But I knew what it was like when we were there. The fear, the anxiety, the hatred, and the rage. If only I had then what I do now, maybe I wouldn't be so screwed up. Maybe the flashbacks would have already gone away.

"What happened when Jimmy made it back?" I asked, trying to change the topic from war.

"That's when things got interesting." She chuckled. "But first, time to set the table, my boy."

I knew where everything was in her kitchen. I got the plates and silverware and set the table the way she liked it. She was very particular about the placement of each item. She had scolded me for placing the forks on the wrong side before. I didn't mind at the time. I was just happy not to eat alone. Ever since, I have always placed things just right—the way she liked it.

I sat down as she pulled the dinner from the oven. Lasagna: it smelled so good. Man, just a half-century younger, and I might have fallen for Mrs. Helderman if for nothing else than her cooking. I gave a happy nod as she set the platter on the table.

I bowed my head. She always wanted me to lead prayer. I didn't feel right about it. But to appease her I would lead a prayer. She said that the man of the house led prayer. I wasn't the man of the house, not of her house. And religion, well… religion and I didn't have a great relationship. Kind of hard to be religious when you fight religious fanatics overseas. Leaves a bad taste in your mouth for it.

"Our Father, who art in heaven, hallowed be Thy name; Thy kingdom come; Thy will be done; on earth as it is in heaven. Give us this day our daily bread. And forgive us our trespasses, as we forgive those who trespass against us. And lead us not into temptation; but deliver us from evil. For Thine is the kingdom, the power and the glory, for ever and ever. Amen." I said the words but felt no divine spark. No grace of God.

I remembered the morning and evening prayers the Muslims would do. Their voices sounded like a beautiful chant. They praised God in all aspects of life. That was interesting. Maybe I would have been more concerned with the grace of religion, but when someone wants to bleed you dry for their religious beliefs… I wish I could feel the way you do, Mrs. Helderman, but I don't think I can. I don't think I ever will.

After the prayer, Mrs. Helderman slid a large piece of lasagna onto my plate. In true military fashion, I didn't take a bite until after she had. Rank eats last. And civilians eat first. It was just how I felt about eating. Civilians, then lower ranks… finally, myself. I was responsible for those people. And yes, in a way, I felt responsible for Mrs. Helderman.

"So, how did things get along after Jimmy got back?" I questioned as I scooped up more lasagna.

She explained that she and Helda had dated him separately for a while. Both were vying for his affections. It had become a competition for them. They were turning on each other. It had actually gotten so bad, the rivalry had erupted into a fistfight. Jimmy didn't like seeing them fight... seeing them hurt. So, he came up with a solution and made a proposal. He would date both at the same time. The no secrets rule was actually his. This was the era of "free love," so oddly enough, this was more acceptable at the time. To think that being a throuple was more accepted over half a century ago than now...

"Did you guys, um... experiment?" I was embarrassed to ask but I needed to know. Was it okay? To have sex with both? To impregnate them both.

"You mean sex?" She asked with intrigue as she shook her head. "Just as perverted as Jimmy. But yes, if that is what you mean."

"How did you, uh... not get jealous?" My embarrassment started to shine through. I was a red beacon. If I were at the top of a tower, ships would be guided to shore by my crimson glow.

"Jimmy was an attentive lover. He never left either of us out, " she said swooningly, then paused for a moment. Memories seemed to briefly wash over her. She lifted her hand, pointing her finger at me as she continued. "Besides, that no secrets rule helped a lot. Constant communication."

I looked at her with ease as we finished our plates. I stood up and collected the dishes. I normally did the dishes since she put up the food. As the water filled the sink, I started to envision the water as love. The sink was my heart. Daily, I was being filled with love more and more. A slight difference from what war had made me feel. In the war, I felt empty. I felt hatred instead of love. But now, I was swimming in love. And not just my girlies. Mrs. Helderman, like that dirty old grandma. Elegant but still dirty.

As I washed the dishes, I remembered that I had finally made a guy friend. I might want to call him tomorrow. His abrasiveness was different but gave me the sense of camaraderie I felt in the Army.

After we cleaned up, she filled a Tupperware with lasagna. Then we sat on that comfy couch and talked for a while longer.

She had confessed that one day Helda went out for groceries but never came back. It had pained her and Jimmy equally. As if a piece of them had died that day. Sadness poured over my heart. How would I feel if one of them died? How would they feel if I died? This was a disheartening but necessary thought.

I hugged Mrs. Helderman. This was the first time that I had embraced her. She was hesitant to hug me back, but once she did, the embrace was tight, as though she might never see me again.

"Good night, Mrs. Helderman. Thank you for the lasagna," I said as I released my hug.

"You are welcome, my boy. And please call me Wanda. Just be sure to think about living with them before eloping," she said as she pulled back.

I made my way back to the apartment. I put the lasagna in the fridge and readied for bed. As I lay in bed, I sent my good-night text.

> [Master] Wednesday 20:16
> *Good night, my beauties, I love you two.*
>
> [Vicky] Wednesday 20:17
> *I love you too. Good night, Master, sweet dreams.*
>
> [Sarah] Wednesday 20:18
> *Good night, Master. I love you.* ☺

Chapter 11: Inebriated Acumen

Friday had come at last. Aah... I had had a long exhausting day. I just wanted to let loose. Howard was coming over and said he was bringing the bar with him. I was sure we were going to drink; I assumed this was the only way he knew how to socialize. He'd probably drink me under the table, but I didn't care. I had a friend to hang out with. A guy friend. This would keep me a bit more grounded. And his camaraderie gave me the sense of being in the Army without all the talk of killing. Was that male bonding? I guess. I never really had that outside the Army.

Drinking... geeze, I'm about to be a VA drunk statistic. Oh well. I picked up my phone and saw that Sarah and Vicky had texted.

[Vicky] Friday 18:23
Start my test in about 30 mins

[Sarah] Friday 18:23
Good Luck

[Vicky] Friday 18:25
thanx

[Sarah] Friday 18:26
Got the job at publisher

[Master] Friday 18:34
Vicky, you got this
Congratz, Sarah

[Vicky] Friday 18:35
Nervous but should pass

[Sarah] Friday 18:35
You got this

[Master] Friday 18:37
Good luck, Vicky. I believe in you. Gotta go.

I smiled at the phone as I put it down. Vicky was nervous, but I was sure that she would pass her test. I loved texting them. Another way that I could be with them when they weren't around.

Hmm... move them in. That is what Mrs. Helderman had said. Week two. Is that really something to ask on week two? "Hey, girlfriends, come move in with me." Like a psycho stalker. Might as well change my name to Buffalo Bill. It puts the lotion on its skin...

Yeah. Crazy. But would definitely make the apartment livelier. More exciting. Like being on a silly, sexy roller coaster that never ends. Or it could be bad. Maybe... I don't know. But to cuddle next to those warm bodies. To wake up to those beautiful faces. To see them smiling around the apartment. Meals together. Someone to come home to, to share my day with. Maybe... it wasn't so bad.

Would they go for it? It wouldn't be much of a change for them. They had lived with each other in the same apartment for six years. They grew up together. I would just be an add-on to what was already there. And if we all moved into this apartment, it was small yet cozy. I wouldn't get too caught up in one because they both would be around. I didn't want to neglect either one. I know that I can get tunnel vision. So, a bigger place would make it hard for me to share myself equally with them. At least for now, until I develop individual connections with each.

I glanced at the clock. Howard said he would be here around nineteen hundred hours. The clock showed nineteen-o-four. I walked to the kitchen for the snack: barbeque chips.

As I was enjoying my chips, I heard the door rattle with a strong knock. When I answered the door, there stood Howard, a large case of beer in his left hand, maybe a thirty-six-pack. I wasn't sure. And a brown paper bag in his right hand. The leather jacket had a spritz of water; it must have started raining.

"Damn, brah, ya looking at my pecker or what? Help me get this stuff on ice," Howard said as he handed me the case of beer.

"Sure," I said as I grabbed it and moved inside. He followed behind me.

Golden Royale six-point beer, good stuff. I put the case next to the bag of chips on the table. As I unloaded the case into the fridge, Howard started rummaging through my cabinets.

"Got any shot glasses, bro?" He asked over his shoulder as his arms were deep in a cabinet.

I pointed with the bottom of a can in my right hand. "Yeah, that one over there."

"Cool," he acknowledged as he moved over to the next cabinet.

Abrasive was starting to be a bit of an understatement for Howard. I wasn't sure what to call him. But it was nice to know that we were friends. After unpacking all the beers into the fridge, I grabbed two and sat one on the kitchen table. I popped open the other and took a swig. The smooth taste of GR was great. The commercials say that dwarves made it. What was the slogan? "Dwarven ale made deep in the mines." Or something like that. I always cracked up at that slogan; it was silly to put in a commercial. Might as well say that it was made by midgets in a cave.

"Here, drink this shit," Howard insisted as he slid a shot glass over the kitchen table to me.

I looked down, a reddish liquid was right to the rim. He really filled the shot glass full. I threw it back. The sensation of fire burned my throat as it went down. I felt a flame throughout me. Must have been with the way it burned. Good stuff. Probably 151 proof or something. Pretty strong stuff. The taste was like drinking pure sugar. The sweetest liquor I had ever tasted. But that burn...

"Damn that tasted so good but burned. What was it?" I asked, downing my beer to tamp down the burning.

"Cappin Holymight Rum 151. That shit's fifty grand a bottle." He showed me a bottle with a devil-looking pirate on the label.

Fifty grand a bottle? I drank like what... three or four thousand dollars in that one shot. Holy shit. I had heard of Captain Holymight, it was a fancy rum. But I had never tasted it. Fifty thousand. Okay, what is up with his money situation? Mansion, fifty-thousand-dollar rum. Like how much money did he have?

"Hey, man, what did you say you do for a living again?"

"Oh, yeah, fuck... I'ma day trader. Ya know, stocks and shit like that," Howard boasted as he downed a shot of clear liquid.

"Man, you must be successful. I mean like really good." I said as I was starting to feel the liquor kick in. I grabbed another beer out of the fridge.

"I'm okay, I guess. I bought my parents dat house. Sorta live with 'em, but really, they live with me." He said as he went for the beer on the table.

We sat down at the kitchen table as he poured another round of shots for us both. I swallowed mine down fast. The taste got sweeter, and the burn was lessening. Damn... this stuff was amazing. I felt like I could lift a car over my head. Or throw a bus into the ocean. So good.

"So, you bought that big house?" I asked as the room already began to spin.

Whatever this rum was, it was acting quickly to get me drunk. I had 151 before, and I never had the room spinning in two shots. Damn... Hold your ground, Sergeant.

"Yep, bought it, then started to buy a few other properties to collect rent," Howard explained. He downed his shot, then chased it with his beer.

We sat at the kitchen table for a while. He would make us shots, which we would throw back and chase with beer. Howard explained that in high school, he was really nerdy. No one really wanted to be his friend. He would sit alone at lunch. When he did try to make friends, they would tell him that he was too loud or too obnoxious. His eyes had a sad expression as he told me all of this.

I commiserated with him, explaining that my situation was similar but on the other end of the spectrum. I was too quiet, too shy, which made me awkward. Then I explained my sex life...

"I didn't even lose my virginity until I was twenty," I said as I picked up another shot and downed it. The shots were now going down smoothly. Like drinking Kool-Aid or something. The burn was completely gone. I was chasing it with the beer out of habit.

"Twenty. Fuck me. Like, really, twenty? Shit. I was sixteen when I bought my first hooker," he said, leaning in, his voice almost whispering the part about the hooker. As if he wasn't proud of it.

"Well, Miss Dependa—" Howard interrupted me before I could finish my sentence.

"Miss Dependa, whadda fuck is that?!" He yelled.

"A dependa is a woman who hangs out around military posts conning soldiers into giving them money," I explained. I sighed, agitated at the idea of dependas.

"I guess ya got conned. But did ya get ya dick wet?" Howard asked, making up the next round.

"Twice before I deployed. I gave that bitch my housing allowance while I was gone. That was like $2,500 a month. Would have been an extra 30K in my savings," I explained, then took the shot from Howard downing it quickly.

"Damn, was it at least good? I mean, that's a thirty-thousand-dollar pussay. Well, fifteen if ya divide the sex up," he said as he chased his shot with more Golden Royale.

"Not really. She wasn't that good. And she made me feel..." I trailed off as I grabbed another beer.

"Like a fucked piggy bank. Huh. Ya dick was spitting out money instead of cum. Shit," Howard said, looking off, agitated for a second. He was making the next round and almost overfilled my shot glass before snapping back.

"Yeah, something like that," I replied before taking the last swig of beer. After smashing the empty can, I went to the fridge.

"Fucking crack whore bitches, bro. These sluts don't care about anything but money these days."

"I don't know, man; my girlfriends don't care about money. They are amazing," I said, remembering that they didn't seem to want me as a "sugar daddy." I returned to the table with two beers. My hand pounded the shot back.

"Well, I am happy for ya, bro. Wish I coulda found a nice girl. One that could put up with my shit. And maybe lemme piss in her butthole from time to time," Howard joked, but I could see the loneliness in his eyes.

"If my sister, Elle, wasn't so dainty, she might be a good pick for you," I said as I briefly pushed my beer in his direction.

"Sista? Ya didn't tell me ya had a sista. Ass fuck, bro, I wouldn't fuck ya sista. Unless ya said it was cool to stuff my meat in." Howard stood up and swayed.

"Gotta piss, where's the toilet?" He slurred as he stumbled in the wrong direction.

"Other way, man. By the front door." I pointed toward the bathroom.

"Oh... cool." Howard headed toward the bathroom.

As Howard was in the bathroom, I took the liberty to make up the next round of shots. That Holymight rum was good. Like really good. The stuff that made you feel like you could fight an entire room of guys by yourself. I nursed my beer for a while. He didn't want to go after Elle unless I gave my blessing. That was interesting.

124

He said it a bit more crudely, but I understood what he meant. Howard came stumbling back into the kitchen.

"I just realized ya said ya got *girlfriends*. Brah, was it the two ya talked 'bout at da bar?" Howard asked as he sat back down.

"Yeah, those two. Vicky and Sarah. They... um... well, they are my girlfriends, now," I answered. Happiness washed over me remembering how cute they both looked. How fun they were. How their kisses tasted like heaven. And I wondered how they would be when we actually had sex.

"This mothafucka said kisses tasted like heaven. Shit bro, ya got it bad for these bitches. But no poundtown. Bro, seal the deal. Get in those guts. Beat those pussies up," Howard said as he took his shot.

Shit, I was talking out loud again. Careful Sergeant. Howard's words seemed insulting, but I was sure he was trying to encourage me in his own way.

"Tomorrow night, I have a date with them. Maybe we can get to the good stuff. *Seal the deal*, as you put it. That is if I don't have whiskey-dick from tonight." I laughed.

"Fucken-A right, fuckface. Get ya prick deep inside those hot snatches." Howard high-fived me with enthusiastic approval. It felt comforting to know that he was excited for me.

"Maybe... I can get this relationship to stick. More than sex. The sex would be nice, don't get me wrong, but I want to be in it for more." I sighed, hoping that the relationship would last.

"Brah, ya got two girls. Ya thinken of marry'en them or sumten?" Howard asked, his voice seemed to get serious.

"Thought about it, sure. But I don't even know if it's possible. I mean, bigamy is illegal, right?"

"Sure... but who cares. If ya love them then ya love them. Fuck the world, brah. Fuck all these jealous fucks. Ya got girls ya love. If they love ya too, just do it. Be with 'em." The way Howard encouraged me seemed more meaningful. I could see his softer side peeking through the cracks.

"Yeah. For now, I will just ask them to move in. See how that goes. If they accept," I said between swigs of beer.

"Hmm... If they was smart, they'd accept. Brah, ya a good dude." He shook his head as he looked at the beer in his hand.

"Maybe..." I trailed off.

Howard took another shot, then chased it with his beer. "So... what's up with ya sista, bro? I mean, I'm not tryna slap my dick in her ass or anything. Ya just seemed worried when ya mentioned her." His voice seemed sympathetic.

"Her dick of a husband. She is divorcing his bitch ass. This dickwad beats on her. Now he took Jenny, my niece," I explained as I kicked back my shot.

"What? Fuck that shit. Let's go kick that fuck's nuts deep into his asshole. Mothafucka punk ass bitch!" Howard bellowed. He was surprisingly angry at Elle's situation considering he didn't know her.

"Chill, bro. She's divorcing his ass. And with all the proof she has, she can get everything in the divorce. Including Jenny." I quickly explained to calm Howard. The feeling that Howard would beat the shit out of Stephen made me feel so happy to be his friend.

"Hell yeah, I hope she fucken takes his house, car, every penny. Fuck that piece-a-shit."

"Yeah, bro. Ya know what... fuck him. He is going to get what is coming to him." I slurred my words and started nursing my beer.

We moved into the living room. Howard had the bottles and shot glasses. I grabbed us both a few beers. We sat our drinking supplies on the coffee table. Howard snatched up the remote as he sat on the couch. He turned on the TV. I poured the next round of shots and sat on the opposite end of the couch.

"Shit, bro. How is dat business coming along? I mean do ya have plans. Or just air conditioners and shit," Howard said as he downed his shot.

"Well, I want to start out small. Just me and an apprentice. Then once things are moving, branch off. Set up several offices. Spacing them about an hour or so apart. Overlapping my coverage areas," I explained excitedly to the point of ranting. After speaking, I took another shot of Holymight. So sweet. So drunk. I was sure that I was wasted.

Sitting on the couch, I looked over and saw my phone. The message icon was flashing. I opened it.

[Vicky] Friday 18:38
Where did he go?

[Sarah] Friday 18:40

Don't know.

[Vicky] Friday 20:08
Passed

[Sarah] Friday 20:11
Congratz

[Master] Friday 21:34
Congratz I aam proudd

I was too drunk to spell. I had a few other messages, but I didn't bother with them. I just wanted to see if Vicky had passed, and she did. I closed the phone and looked at the TV. Howard had managed to find the Bloomberg channel. His eyes seemed glued to the numbers scrolling across the bottom of the screen, fixated as if he were attempting to find a stock pick while we were drinking.

"Stocks? Why are we watching the stocks channel this late at night?" I hazily asked, unsure what he was doing. The market closed around fifteen hundred hours or so. At least, I think it did.

"Brah, it's just research, always gotta be look'en for da next win," he explained as he nursed his beer.

"ITI stocks seem to be doing good." I pointed at the screen.

Howard looked over at me. "Yeah, was think'en 'bout investing. Rumor has it they got a new tech coming— if the FDA approves." His voice seemed to falter as he hiccuped while he spoke.

I turned my attention from the TV to him. "What new tech?"

"Sumten 'bout cloning human body parts for transplants. Ya know, like kidneys and shit. Will make the donor list almost extinct," Howard explained. He paused for a moment to take a sip from his beer before continuing. "Wit' some gene edits, the cloned transplants will prevent further deterioration."

I wondered if this technology could be used to clone an entire person. I knew that it was immoral and illegal. But still, if they could clone human kidneys, couldn't they clone a person entirely? What would it mean if someone like Stephen had that kind of power? I shook my mind loose of the thought. It was illegal; there was no way he could get away with shit like that. Maybe it was best not to think of the "what ifs" from a dystopian cloning future.

"No announcement yet. ITI was supposed to announce something big soon. Was think'en it would be this rumored clone thing. But nothing yet." Howard seemed to be talking to himself more than he was to me. He stayed deep in thought for a while.

He soon snapped out of his mind and went on a tangent about money. He explained that money is not the goal but a tool. He added that if you view money as a tool, you are no longer driven by the idea of making it. Instead, you will find ways to use it. Howard further explained the concept of leverage and how to use assets to leverage more assets.

Money as a tool. His words hit me differently. I had never thought about money in that sense. I guess he was right. To win, you must always be attempting to find new opportunities. And of course, be open to new ideas to make money.

Howard turned to me as he made up the last rounds of shots. "Hey, ya got a business plan, bro? I mean ya wrote that shit down somewhere, right?" He asked, handing me the shot.

My response was quick. "Yeah, on me lappy." I took the shot and downed it. The last of the Captain Holymight... so good. So drunk. I could feel my insides warm one last time with that final shot. No fire, no burn, just a comforting warmth.

"Get da shit, let's see wat we can fuck 'round widd." Howard's words were starting to become incoherent. Like the night we first met. I think mine were getting bad too... Nah... not yet.

I pulled my laptop out. I opened up the business plan, all my projections, and my business mission statement. Howard sat quietly for many minutes reading over everything. He swayed as he held the laptop. Almost like he was rocking. I was sure that he was drunk. Like too wasted to drive home. Hell, was I? Maybe, but I also felt like I could wrestle a bear... shit, like ten bears at the same time and win. His eyes studied my numbers. He seemed like he was deep in thought. Was he calculating my projections?

"Fuck, bro, ya growd rate is all fucked. An' these profit projections be shitfucked, like ya wrote 'em in crayon or some shit," he said as he cracked his knuckles. His hands went to work typing. They blazed across the board with the grace of a pianist.

Was he redoing my numbers, like really? Was I that bad at business? Nah...

"Wadup, what ya doin'?" I asked as his fingers flew across the keys.

Howard briefly smirked before focusing again. "Fixen' shit, bro. Chill. I got this." He declared. "Ya ne'er thought 'bout a partner, make all this shit easy," Howard asked... sort of.

"Nah, didn' why-ay," I replied.

"'Cause, fuck, bro, I got ya. Partna should make it flow-oh fast." His words jumbled. But he turned the laptop to me.

"See," he said as I read over the new numbers.

Shit, he was right. I could grow it almost three times as quickly with a business partner. And it would free up much of my liquidity for expansion or personnel. Damn, he was a genius when it came to numbers. Like a loud, rude, drunk Stephen Hawking or something.

"But, don't know anybody to partner widd," I said as I took the laptop and closed it.

"Fuck yeah, ya do. Me, fuckface. Whadda ya say?" His voice was filled with happiness but also a sense that he may get rejected.

"Fuckid, let's do it," I agreed. Hell yeah. That growth rate was amazing. And profits would soar if I partnered with him.

Howard spat on his palm, then held his hand out for a shake. I mirrored him, and we shook on it. Business partners. I'd made a friend and business partner. We sat on the couch, talking about the business plan. He'd buy rental houses and contract only with me. We schemed several other businesses and money-making ideas.

For being a drunk night, we actually made lots of progress toward the businesses. We spent several hours talking about different business ideas—growth rates, when to expand, how to expand—all of it. It was insanely productive. We made projections and business plans for each idea. Most of the worries I had about starting my own business were pretty much gone. The rest of the night was chatter about business.

I was starting to be happy. I may be able to be the kind of man who could support a family with Sarah and Vicky. Howard and I could go into business together. Then I could buy the girls a house, that dream house. I could support our children. I could make a life with them, our big family. Our three-way marriage could work.

I started feeling groggy and tired throughout our talk. However, business was intriguing to me, so I forced myself to stay up. But my eyes kept getting heavy, wanting to stay closed. I wasn't sure if I was that tired or if it was the alcohol.

After a while, I felt my body drift off to slumber. I just kicked back on the sofa and let sleep take over.

Chapter 12: Explosive Morning After

I felt warmth surrounding me. When I opened my eyes, I was lying in my bed. The ceiling fan was on slow speed; I watched the blades spin. I felt the heat of two bodies pressing into me.

I looked down. Red locks flowed across my left peck, a dark swirl of hair down my right. Wait... how the hell did I get here? Vicky... Sarah... my eyes strained to focus. Yep, it was them. They were naked, lying on top of me.

The soft sound of light snores filled the room. I could get used to waking up beside them. They were peaceful and serene. This felt so right, like I'd been molded perfectly to fit neatly between them.

How did they get here? Why were they here? How did we get into my bed? Did I have sex with them and don't remember? The last thing I remembered was talking to Howard about business. We had built some pretty good business models. But now I was lying in bed with my girlfriends. What happened?

The warmth of their bodies on mine... I leaned over, smelling each of their hair. So good, Sarah's like summer rain, Vicky's like jasmine flowers. Chill, Sergeant. What happened? Stop messing with them and think... think...

I slowly got out of bed and tried my best not to disturb the ladies. As I stood at the foot of the bed, my head exploded, as if two trains had collided, full speed, inside my skull. The calamity of the crash was banging inside my head. The echoes of drinking were aching to pink mist my cranium. The walls seemed to be swaying, my mouth dry. Hangover? Damn...

My bladder felt like it was about to explode. I had to go bad. This was my penance for drinking. Topped with a pounding headache, I stumbled to the bedroom door.

Vicky and Sarah were here... when... I hoped that I didn't have sex with them. I was really looking forward to making it special and something fun for them. Since I didn't remember them coming here, I was sure to have no memory of the act. I wanted our first time to be something that they would really enjoy. A way to bring our relationship further. But I may have screwed that up.

As I opened the bedroom door, my legs felt like Jell-O as I tried to walk. Dumbass, you drank yourself stupid last night. Chasing that

Holymight rum with Golden Royale was royally stupid. You had felt invincible at the time. Now you are just a hungover idiot.

I walked to the couch with my hands on the back of it to stabilize myself. My legs felt like they would give out at any time. A major contrast to how that rum made me feel last night. So strong, so virile. As if I could have fought wave after wave of the Taliban by myself for hours on end. I liked that feeling, but not this. I hated this. I felt so weak. So puny. As if a soft breeze could blow through the apartment and knock me down.

I glanced over the back of the couch. The pullout bed was open. Howard was spooning...

Elle?! What the hell? Elle is here... and Howard was cuddled around her like a snake. His massive arms covered most of her upper body. His legs intertwined with hers. You would swear that he was a python about to devour its prey whole. She seemed so small next to him, like a toy or a doll.

It was unreal how they looked together. He was so muscled and massive; she was a small, thin thing beside him. But they looked cute together. He might make a good brother-in—

Stop trying to marry your sister off! She isn't even divorced yet. But he's a kind man. Well, he would be the kind of man she needed right now. Abrasive, rude, yet kind. Kindness... yep, she definitely needed that. My feet pressed on. Gotta piss so damned bad.

I finally went to the bathroom; I threw the seat up and let it rip. I had never drunk myself into that much of a stupor before. But... business. The numbers looked good last night, like really good.

Howard was a genius, a business god. That dude could probably sell a dog turd to an aristocrat, claiming it a work of art. Business was his domain, where he seemed his best. I was glad to have made him as a friend. But drinking... it has to slow down or stop. At the very least, not so much when we do drink. My gut felt like someone had rammed a door breach into it several times. My legs were finally cooperating, but my head and my stomach... not so much.

I flushed as I shook the last drops out. I slid it back into my boxers. Shit, I only had boxers on. Did Vicky and Sarah undress me last night? Had I been so out of it that I didn't know they had pulled my clothes off? I guess so; they had been lying naked on top of me just minutes ago... and I had no recollection of that either.

As I opened the bathroom door, I met Elle standing between the couch and the kitchen. A very pissed-looking Elle. Her eyes burned with pure rage. I walked toward her as if I was heading toward the gallows—a condemned and doomed man ready to face his execution. Just put the noose around my neck now. String me up, hang me high. I was a goner.

Elle's eyes watched my every movement. Her arms crossed in front of her. As if anything I said would worsen the scolding that I was in for. I lowered my head and moved to the chair at the dining table, seating myself. Ready for the long lecture.

"What the hell, lil Bro?" Elle's voice was the stern tone she had used on me as a kid. I knew it well. When I often did something dumb as a kid, she took this tone with me.

"Do you have any idea how I felt seeing you like this? Do you care?" The volume of Elle's voice started rising. Yep, long morning. "And those poor women, they had to take care of your drunk ass." Elle chastised me as she pointed toward my bedroom.

"I'm sorry, Sis. It—" I was trying to apologize, but Elle interrupted me with her booming voice.

"What? It won't happen again? Bullshit, do you know how many times I heard that from Stephen? How many times he promised me?" Elle barked as she recrossed her arms.

Maybe it was best if I didn't talk for a while. Let her scold me. Let her have her say. I did deserve it, anyway. It was pretty stupid to get that drunk. I noticed Howard looking over the couch to see what the fuss was about. His eyes glanced at me seeming to feel sorry for me. But then I noticed the look in his eye as he watched Elle. He had a sense of growing admiration on his face while Elle lit into me.

As Elle was starting to get louder and ramble on, I thought about how those business plans could be used. I wondered if they were really that good. Or were we just too drunk to make anything really work? I wanted to open my laptop. To go over those plans. To check the math on the projections. I wanted to see if Howard was as good with business as I made myself believe. I was sure that wasn't a great idea at the moment, but then... Sarah and Vicky.

I thought that I may need a bigger bed if I were going to move them in. Could my full size work? I really did like being a cushion for those warm bodies. What furniture would I need? Or what other things would be needed? Redecorating the apartment? I wasn't sure. I remembered Vicky had passed her exam yesterday. And Sarah got that job with the publishing company. I felt so proud of them. I was excited and wanted to celebrate, but I couldn't do anything about that now.

I looked at Elle, who had a blank look on her face. Her mouth had stopped moving. I guess she was done kicking my pride in the dirt. I sighed with relief. Well, that was quicker than I thought.

"Are you even paying attention to what I am saying?" Elle interrogated. She looked at me, her face about to burst into flames from the fury, but she lowered her voice.

She had been talking—well, yelling—and my mind had wandered off. I had no clue as to what she just said, but I was sure of the gist. Comparing me to bitch-boy Stephen, how he made her feel. The endless barrage of broken promises. All of it. That most likely was what her rant was about. Time to start my apology.

"I am sorry, Sis. I never meant to remind you of him. I just wanted to let loose." My voice was soft as I spoke.

"Yeah, what the hell were you thinking? We can't babysit a drunk all the time. We didn't agree to that, Master." I looked up. Vicky was standing next to Elle in a nightgown, her skin glistening with that darkened hue.

Sarah, in a bathrobe, emerged beside them, standing on the other side of Elle. Her face had a soft glow as her milky skin bathed in the light, arms also crossed in front of her. Shit, this just got more intense. I was in trouble. The three of them were going to light into me. You really screwed up, Sergeant, but you deserve whatever is coming your way.

"Master, that was not fun coming over and seeing you passed out drunk," Sarah sadly expressed.

"Master? Ya mean dey call ya master? Fuck, bro, ya got it like that?" Howard asked as he sat up, still watching over the couch.

"Who the fuck is this, Bro?" Elle demanded; she pointed at Howard and eyed me with a deep, burning desire to slap me.

"Name's Howard. Was jus lea—"

"Oh, hell no," Elle scolded. "Keep your ass there. You two aren't going anywhere. This is on you as much as it is on him, How-ward."

His eyes never left hers as she was burning him down. I saw a slight smirk on his face. Was he enjoying this? His eyes sparkled as if he had found the missing piece of his heart. I would approve, but not until Elle got rid of dickwad Stephen. I just wondered how his abrasiveness would work with Jenny. He might get along with her well if he'd tone it down a notch or two... make that ten notches.

Elle lit into Howard about getting me drunk. About being drunk himself. About how we're being ungentlemanly. She ranted on about hobos in streets or something. I let it all go in and out quickly. She was so motherly and protective of me. Even with the distance of my military service, it was still there. I grinned to myself.

"What the fuck are you smiling about?" Vicky snarled as she grabbed my face, making me look up to meet her gaze. "Getting drunk like that is *un*Masterly. You think we want to submit to a drunkard?"

"Master gets it. Now, leave him alone." Sarah came to my rescue as she moved into the frame. "He needed a break. So, what if he got drunk? He is still our boyfriend."

I glanced over at Elle still hounding Howard. I would say poor guy, but he relished her harsh treatment. I hadn't seen Elle so passionate before. Did she like him back? She did let him cuddle up to her. Nah... her head was probably all jacked up from the divorce.

"Miss Pushover. Coming to his rescue. Want to wipe his ass next?" Vicky started in on Sarah, shoving her backward.

This was getting out of hand. Vicky and Sarah were ready to fight, I was sure of it. I remembered Mrs. Helderman's cautionary tale. I can't have them fighting over me, not like this anyway. Cute banter, yes, playfully trying to up each other to get my attention. But not real fighting. I had to do something, get control of the room.

"AT EASE!" My voice had that cool NCO command as it burst out louder than I'd intended.

The whole room went silent for a moment. Vicky and Sarah kneeled before me; legs neatly tucked under their thighs. Arms in front of them, their hands resting on their knees, palms up. It was an interesting pose—one I may have to use later. For now, I had to get this situation under control.

"Look, we are sorry. Elle. Vicky. Sarah. I am sorry." My voice lowered but still possessed that smooth NCO resonance.

"Howard came over, and we drank. Getting stupid drunk was dumb; you have every right to get onto us about that. But Vicky, you have no right to misplace your anger onto Sarah. Understood?" My finger lightly and lovingly ran across her cheek.

"Yes, Master." Vicky looked at Sarah. "I'm sorry, Sarah." Sarah didn't say a word, but she nodded, accepting Vicky's apology.

Elle just stood there; her mouth agape, her eyes trained on me, as if I were a car crash that she couldn't look away from. I wasn't sure if she was scared or in awe. One thing was for sure, she didn't know the extent of my power. She didn't know how commanding I was on the battlefield. And this had started to gravitate toward a battlefield, except the casualties would have been my girlfriends.

Howard sat back; hands interlaced behind his head. He was in a state of elation. Most likely from being chewed out by Elle. By having her care about him even though she didn't know him, did that make him a submissive male? That is what he seemed to be when Elle was ripping him a new one. It was kind of funny in a way. Hulking muscled up guy being told off by a small twig of a woman. But hey, if it works, if it makes them happy. Sure. Not my cup of tea, but who am I to judge.

"I came over around midnight to talk to you about the divorce," Elle explained in a soft tone. "You were three sheets to the wind."

"I'm sorry. How did it go?" I asked, concerned that the lawyer may have given her bad news.

"Great, I'll most likely get the house, and most importantly, I will for sure get Jenny," Elle replied. Her face shined with hope.

"Good. I am glad," I said, smiling as my heart swelled with relief. Jenny will be home soon, home with her mother.

"We weren't far behind her, Master. When we got here, she was cleaning up the apartment," Vicky said with saddened eyes.

"Yep. Then Miss Elle told us that she would take care of Howard. But she said you were our responsibility now, Master. She left your care to us," Sarah explained. Her eyes seemed to jump with joy when she said they were responsible for me.

I looked over at Howard. "Tell them you're sorry. And let's get some breakfast." That smile he had when Elle was lighting him up had now faded from his face. He seemed to look at me with a saddened expression.

"Ladies, I'm sorry. I swear that we won't drink like that again. I jus— I thought drinken' was how ya bond with ya friends." His eyes fell upon the floor in shame. "I jus wanted Kyle to accept me."

"It's cool, bro. I already do, no need to worry about that." My voice softened from my NCO tone.

136

"You really sorry?" Elle asked, eyeing Howard.

Howard glanced at Elle with a look of remorse. "Yes, ma'am. I thought it was normal for friends to drink togetha. Seen it on TV a lot." He said with shame in his tone.

Elle looked at Howard with pity. "Guess you are just like my brother: no friends, huh?"

"Sumten like that," Howard said, his macho bravado piqued due to Elle's interest.

"Okay, Casanova. Just don't get my brother drunk again, ya hear?" Elle sternly said, shaking her head.

My voice broke out with the NCO tone once more. "Breakfast, I'm buying. IHOP is in walking distance. 'Bout three blocks away."

"Don't gotta tell me twice," Howard announced loudly as he shot up; he was still mostly dressed. So was Elle for that matter.

Sarah, Vicky, and I... well, we were half a second away from being nude. I motioned for Sarah and Vicky to get up. Without a word, they got to their feet. I was amazed by them. And my pride ran deep. But I hadn't had a chance to congratulate the two of them. I hoped that life with them would always be so interesting. They followed me to the bedroom.

I chuckled to myself as I strode through the door. Damn, I just commanded a room the way I had commanded the battlefield. Was it the power my girlfriends had given me? Was I changing from the inside? Was it starting to move to the surface? I loved my girlfriends. And these subtle yet impactful changes they had on me were extremely addicting.

I picked out my clothes, tactical pants—did I own any other style of pants... nope—and my favorite Lords of Acid T-shirt. *Our Little Secret* album cover.

As I looked up, they were still in their skivvies. Why hadn't they dressed? Were they okay?

"What's going on? Why aren't you two dressed?" I asked, puzzled as to why they were just looking at me like two deer caught in headlights.

"Master, please pick out an outfit for each of us." Sarah gave me those sad puppy eyes. Damn, those emeralds could hold that saddened gaze all day. So cute, so damn cute.

"We brought our overnight bags with a few choices for you." Vicky handed me their overnight bags.

This was interesting. I liked the idea of choosing their wardrobe. Was I about to play dress-up with my girlfriends?

I figured I couldn't take too much time deciding their wardrobe. Big sis and my friend were in the other room waiting. Besides, you promised everyone breakfast. You owed them that. Your stupid drinking... you owed them all.

I looked through Vicky's overnight bag first. I found a fishnet shirt, some trip pants, and a belly top. Yes, that would look cute on her. I handed Vicky her clothes and instructed her to get dressed.

Sarah came over to me and watched intently. Her nails made small, tender circles over my scalp as I dug around her bag. I chose blue jeans and a white belly-cut button-up shirt for her. I just wished that we had a cowboy hat. She would look so cute in one. Sarah lovingly received the clothes and quickly dressed.

That was actually fun. I wanted to do that again. Pick out their clothes. Maybe I could brush their hair? Bathe them? I wanted to find different ways to take care of them—unique ways, things that only I could do for them.

Each day made me love them more. And they handled scolding me well. They called me out on my crap. At least I knew they could push me back when I screwed up. I just wished they hadn't turned on each other.

My girlfriends exited the bedroom before me, so I held the door for them. Then, I rejoined the group.

"Damn, Bro. Do you have to spend a hundred years getting dressed?" Elle asked sarcastically. Good, she had gotten over her anger, hopefully completely.

"Ya were in there so long, thought ya was fucken," Howard blurted out. Elle slapped him in the gut quickly and roughly.

"Do you always have to be so disgusting? Or is your mouth just so filthy that you need to eat soap?" Elle eyed him with an evil skunk-eye.

"Let's go," I spoke in that smooth NCO voice once more.

No one seemed to protest. We soon exited the apartment and headed toward our destination.

Chapter 13: Satisfying Amends

The hostess eyed me with disgust as I entered with my girlfriends on each arm. She gave me a dismissive "tut" as her head shook with disapproval. Yes, lady, I had two girlfriends. No, they don't care; they welcome the idea of it. Maybe look into your own heart before judging others. I shook my head. I wasn't going to let that kill my breakfast. Hell, I'd already been through the wringer this morning.

Elle also saw the hostess's disgust. She glanced over at me, smiling wickedly. The same smile she had when Fiona Garland humiliated me in the fifth grade. When I had asked Fiona to the school sock hop, she screamed at me in the lunchroom, telling everyone I was a creepy weirdo. But big sis came to my rescue. She convinced three of her friends to escort me to the dance and be my dates. I felt like the elementary school king, dancing with three high school chicks. Maybe that was a precursor to my current love life.

Elle spoke with the hostess. Explaining that we needed a table for five. As the hostess was getting the menus, Elle lovingly leaned into Howard. She cradled his massive arm into hers, caressing his bicep. What the hell was this?

The hostess looked up; her eyes widened as she watched Elle's behavior for a moment. She had nuzzled her face into Howard. I was sure that he didn't mind the treatment, but was Elle screwing with the hostess because of how she looked at me? This must have been a Fiona-type situation.

Big sis was still in there. This morning had drawn that girl out. It was refreshing to see her playful and protective, the way I remembered her. Her loving treatment of Howard was a ruse. A game to get back at the hostess. I had almost forgotten that spunky girl existed. When I would visit on leave, go to her house, or even have her at the apartment, that girl was nowhere in sight. I guess Stephen had beaten that playful spirit out of her. But she was back, and the game was on.

"Ugh, this way." The hostess gave Elle a "go to hell" look.

As we walked, Elle stayed glued to Howard. It was neat how he walked taller. Was that the way I looked when I walked with my beauties? Poor guy, she is using you to toy with the hostess. She didn't want her little brother to be hurt by what the world thought.

We were seated at a large table. I sat so that I was facing the door. A habit, I guess. I always had to have a view of the entryways. This began during my first deployment. The fact that I didn't like big crowds, I believed that started around the same time. War made you more cautious, more suspicious of the world. As if there was an enemy combatant around every corner. But I was sure that I hadn't strayed too far into that. At least I had hoped that I hadn't.

Sarah and Vicky sat on either side of me. Both grabbed a thigh. I glared at each, giving them the "you better behave" stare. Vicky smirked and shook her head. Sarah just shot me sad puppy eyes.

Elle sat across from Vicky, one seat over from Howard. All that loving care was now washed away. She was smiling, but she didn't acknowledge him. He was seated in front of Sarah. His face had a slight disappointment hollowed through it. It was clear that he had no idea what Elle was playing at earlier. But he obviously enjoyed it.

"That was nice," Howard dotingly said. He looked over to Elle searching for more of that worship he was adorned with.

"Don't push it. I didn't do it for you. I did it because I wanted to take the attention off of Kyle. It's bad enough you two idiots got drunk last night. The last thing I want is for my brother to be judged and feel bad because of his unusual relationship," Elle explained. She then picked up the menu and reviewed the entrees.

I scanned the restaurant to avoid the awkward differences between Howard's and my situations. My girlfriends lovingly doted over me, while Howard sat opposite my sister, who was giving him the cold shoulder. I felt bad for him. But what could I do? Make Elle apologize? She rarely, if ever, apologized when it came to taking up for me. All I could do was let it ride.

There were two other tables. An elderly couple and a young family of five. Other than that, it was a ghost town. The hostess had moved back to the podium. A waitress with a decently plump rear was standing near the front entrance. She was talking to the hostess. I could see them slyly glance over at us from time to time. Most likely talking about how much of a pig I was, or how Elle seemed like a harlot. Or something like that. But I didn't care. I was happy to be in the company of the people that I cared about.

I thought about the business plans. How nice it would be to start on these ventures with Howard as a partner. How all of it would work out. Crap! I hadn't looked through my laptop before we left. I should have brought it. That way, Howard and I could go over it sober. But again, I was a dummy. I left it in the apartment. I barely remembered any of it, just how pretty those numbers looked. How fat our bank accounts would become.

"Do you think those business plans were on point?" I croaked to Howard. I already knew what I wanted to eat. I had to figure out if those numbers were right. If I could build the financial empire he proposed.

"Yeah, brah. Like last night, I already sent 'em to my business advisor," Howard explained, his eyes didn't leave the menu. He seemed embarrassed; I hoped that Elle's game didn't hurt him.

"What plans, Master?" Vicky squeezed my thigh tightly.

I felt her nails dig in through the fabric of my pants, creating unwanted arousal. You bitch. Calm yourself, Sergeant. Focus.

"Howard and I spent most of the night working on different business ideas," I stated as I was adjusting myself in my seat. I stealthily slapped both their hands; they moved away.

"Business? What would a foul-mouth drunk know about business?" Elle's tongue was a sharpened axe chopping at Howard.

"Not much. At least not 'bout what we were talking 'bout last night," Howard explained with a smile; I was pretty sure he thought Elle was flirting with her banter.

"Are you Howard Nolan?" Sarah asked. She seemed to recognize him.

It took her all this time. Talk about a delayed reaction. I guess she was too busy worrying about me earlier. Oddly enough, it didn't surprise me. It would have been her to know his last name. It reminded me of the trivia she had of birds the day we went to the zoo.

Howard looked up, excited that someone knew him. "Yep. That's me," he said with a brief nod.

"Master, he is a very successful stock trader. I read about him in Forbes," Sarah said seemingly excited—super excited—as if she had met a celebrity. Well, I guess he was a celebrity of sorts.

"Forbes? You mean steroids over here has a brain?" Elle chuckled to herself. I could see something in her eyes. She was repulsed by him yet intrigued. Maybe there was hope for a new brother-in-law after all. One that I could get along with. That I didn't want to crush the skull of.

"Ya know, meatheads like me need hobbies too." Howard laughed. I guess he had decided to play along with Elle's "banter." He was enjoying his exchanges with her.

In the words of Mrs. Helderman, he was following her around like a lost puppy. I noticed his strange accent seemed to ebb every so often. Was that him letting his real voice through? And maybe Elle was really flirting with him. I hadn't seen her flirt in years. And I was getting a split version of her. So, it was hard to read.

The waitress approached the table. "Hello, my name's Veronica. I will be your server this mornin'. What can I start y'all off with?" Her hair was messy. Her eyes had heavy bags as if she had worked the closing shift last night, then opened this morning.

"Good morning, dear." Vicky greeted the woman compassionately.

We ordered drinks first. It didn't take long before she came back, passing out the glasses. I was amazed. Anyone could see that she was dog-tired, yet she moved with a purpose. She flipped open her tablet, pen at the ready.

"Now, what would you darlin's like?" Her voice was tender.

Our orders were taken. Of course, I ordered French toast with a side of eggs and bacon. Elle mirrored my order. Vicky and Sarah both got a giant stack of pancakes and sausage. Howard had a simple egg and sausage breakfast.

"Jus' got a text from my business advisor. He wants to sit down with us to discuss the plans further," Howard said as he put his phone away.

"That's awesome!" Sarah's words were an excited cheer, she jumped in her seat. Her glass almost fell to the floor, but I caught it just in time. Not a drop spilled.

Vicky gave me a dangerous skunk-eye. "Don't think this means you get a free pass to drink, Master." Ouch... a freezing chill ran down my spine. Scary... but sexy.

"That's cool. You can set up the meeting anytime, but I would prefer evenings if possible," I said to Howard, my new friend and business partner.

"Well, guess this means that I should apologize for earlier," Elle said as she slouched in her chair.

"No, Sis. Like I said before we left, we deserved the tongue-lashing. You were right, we can't be drinking ourselves stupid." My foot kicked Howard. He looked up.

Howard turned to Elle, seemingly understanding my kick. "Yeah, sweet mama. We were in the wrong. You got nothing to be sorry for," he said, a hint of that macho bravado glazed his tone.

"Sweet mama...geeze. At least you're talking like a normal person now." Elle rolled her eyes and shook her head. But she had a slight grin.

Elle's eyes seemed endearing as she looked at Howard. Damn, maybe she had been flirting with him the whole time. Some twisted bantered flirting. I guess it makes sense. She needed to hold the power over Howard. She had seven years of feeling powerless with Stephen. Toying with a colossus like Howard, bending him to her will, made her feel powerful. I snickered under my breath.

"How about you, me, and a bottle of honey. Letting me lick it out of that sweet ass." Howard lifted his chin to Elle.

Dammit dude, you had her. You just killed your chances. Oh well. I tried.

"Try it and I will hang you by your balls, Romeo." Elle motioned toward his crotch with her fork.

"Hey, Elle, what kind of work do you do? Mass— I mean Kyle never told us." Sarah butted in. I was sure she was trying to ease the conversation away from balls and asses.

"I am a counselor, mostly working with couples." Elle shrugged as she focused on Sarah.

"Counselor... couples?" Sarah looked dumbstruck. I knew that she was far more intelligent than she was acting. She must be trying to push Elle into a conversation about work or something.

Elle pepped up. "A therapist. Relationship therapy to be exact."

"Why didn't you fix *his* broken ass?" Vicky laughed as she poked me in the rib.

"*Pft.* You see what I'm working with. I was shocked last week to learn not only had his pervy ass got a girl but bagged two. And both hotties, if you don't mind me saying. It was quite a shock," Elle said.

"Yeah, Mass— Kyle is something else. So damned pervy. But in a cute way." Sarah chuckled as she picked up her glass for a sip.

"You know, it really doesn't bother me if you call him master. Besides, I am sure his royal perviness eats it up," Elle said as she tried to mend the damage from her outburst last week.

I sat silent for many minutes as Vicky and Sarah conversed with Elle. They talked about me and took some joking jabs at me, which I chuckled at. Their conversation circled back to careers.

Vicky expressed her excitement about passing her test. She already had clients lined up to follow her, and some of them had booked massages for next week.

Sarah explained that she had gotten the HR job at the publishing company downtown. She gleefully told Elle how delighted she was to start, and that her favorite perk was the access to books before they were published.

Elle explained that she was moving her practice to another office building two blocks from the publishing company.

Vicky had two different morning clients around those offices. The three of them talked about going out together on their lunch breaks to hang out. Knowing that Elle was getting along so well with my girlfriends felt nice.

I watched Howard as the ladies chatted. His spirit seemed to be lagging. Was it the way Elle was warm and cold with him? I didn't like seeing him so down. When he talked about business, he was strong and confident, but with Elle—and I was sure with most women—he seemed helpless. Was that me just a few weeks ago? Had I been as down as he is now? I kicked Howard, and he looked up at me. His eyes seemed sad. I gave him a look and nodded my head toward Elle.

"Hey, Elle... sorry... for... for the way I am," Howard softly said, averting his glance away from Elle.

Elle stopped mid-sentence and looked at Howard. Her eyes drooped as she spotted the depressed look on Howard's face. She reached her hand out and placed it on his shoulder.

Elle looked him in the eyes. "Thank you for the apology. Just be a good boy from now on. No more potty mouth. Got it?"

"Yes, ma'am. But that booty, though." Howard's words seemed more vibrant as he joked with her.

"Damn, you don't know when to quit. But yeah, I got a nice ass. Not like your mitts will ever touch it." Elle laughed as she joked back with him. Her hand gave him a light, playful slap on his cheek.

Howard looked at me with a huge grin. Yep, submissive male all the way. I smiled back, giving an approving nod. I wasn't sure if they would end up together. But their banter was fun to watch.

The food arrived soon after. The table was filled with laughter and munching sounds. Howard broke open again, jumping into the conversation. I started to talk as well.

We went from careers to business. Howard explained more about how he could predict stock prices with seventy-eight percent accuracy. Which was pretty good, to be honest. He explained that he had to go before the Federal Trades Commission board to exonerate himself from being deemed an insider trader. He had to show them his equation and methods to prove his stock picks were legitimate.

Howard was a bit ashamed when he explained his living situation with his parents, but Elle told him it was sweet that he bought a house for them. He invited all of us over for a barbeque and swim sometime. Sarah and Vicky jumped at the offer before I could get a word in edgewise.

Somehow the topic got onto guns. I started explaining that I had a few guns and that I needed to clean them soon. I haven't been to a range since I moved here.

"You have guns, Master?" Sarah inquired in that baby voice.

"Yep, an AR, a shotty, an M9, and a bolt action." As my words spilled out, I dreamed of buying more, adding to my small collection. I wanted so many. I wished to have my own personal arsenal, like the size of a warehouse or something. That would be so kickass.

"What the shit, brah? A warehouse arsenal. Ya readying for zombies or some shit?" Howard was surprised.

Damn, I did it again. I said that out loud. Careful Sergeant. Don't want anything else to slip. Keep it cool. Just... chill.

"Never can have enough weapons, Master." Vicky sighed, swooning before giving me a wicked grin.

"Just be careful, Master. Guns are dangerous." Sarah giggled as she pointed down toward my crotch.

"Can't say I'm surprised. You always did like blowing shit up when we were kids," Elle said as she shook her head.

"Where do you keep them, Master?" Sarah asked.

"In the back of the closet for now. I really need a gun safe. But haven't been able to budget for one yet." I suddenly felt awkward as I was reminded of my wallet size.

"Well, that shouldn't be a problem soon," Howard said as he took another bite.

"Why is that?" I asked, intrigued.

"'Cause we are business partners, now, bro," Howard explained as he tipped his glass to me.

"You sure can pick 'em, little Bro. Business partners with the not-so-incredible Hulk. Just make sure you wash his mouth out twice a week." Elle giggled as she poked at Howard.

"Maybe it should be you to wash it for me. And while ya at it, go further south... to my sugar pole." Howard winked at Elle.

"Eww... not in your wildest dreams, loverboy." Elle shook her head, as she scooped up some eggs. She seemed to be having fun with the banter she shared with Howard. Was she encouraging him or trying to deter him. Head games were never my expertise.

"So, marriage... I remember you talking about marriage the other day," Elle probed.

Shut the hell up, sis. Damn. Marriage was an option. But I wasn't ready to talk about it yet. Not with Vicky and Sarah. And I sure was not going to explore it in public.

"Just talk, nothing else." I eyed Elle with an evil gaze.

"Brah, jus' tie the knot. Ya was gushing 'bout it last night." Howard shook his head.

"We sort of, you know, overheard him talking to himself about being his brides," Vicky said as a wicked grin flashed on her face.

"Who could resist marrying hotties like us?" Sarah chuckled as her hand planted itself on my thigh, right on my dick. Teasing bitch.

For the rest of the meal, everyone talked—doted—over the idea of a three-way marriage. There were a ton of jabs at me. About moving fast, about being a smitten little boy. I tried a few times to defend myself, but I was outgunned. Elle, Sarah, Vicky, and Howard all roasted me. Every word I said was turned immediately into some sort of wedding cliché. Damn.

"Yep, you know what. I am going to marry these bitches."

"Aw, he looks so cute! Getting embarrassed the way he does." Elle cackled like a witch.

"Bitches, huh, Master? We can be." Vicky pinched my cheek, shaking my head slightly rough.

"I don't mind being his bitch." Sarah said with a bubbly tone as her grip on me tightened.

"Look at Miss Pushover. She's all smitten being called a bitch." Vicky laughed at Sarah.

"Shee-ot, marry both bitches. Tag 'em with a brand on that ass." Howard laughed.

Elle laughed, cringing. "And that is why you get no poon-tang."

"Will get yours," he said playfully, making a slapping motion.

"Might reverse it on you. How do you feel about pegging?" Elle laughed with an evil and ominous tone.

"Now, who's the perv, Sis?" I winked at her, then popped the last of the French toast in my mouth.

"I get a free pass. I'm the older, much wiser sister. Besides, women aren't pervy, they're seductive." Elle raised her eyebrows.

"Seductive. Yeah... seductive. Not pervy," Vicky said as her index finger poked me in the rib.

We carried on for several more minutes. The waitress came by with the check. I paid without hesitation. I left her a very generous tip. She didn't have to be squared away with her tired state, yet she was. I admired her efforts; she would have made a fine soldier.

I left with my beauties on each arm, the same way we'd entered. Elle and Howard were still playfully bantering as we exited.

As we passed the hostess, I kissed each of my beauties—slow, passionate kisses. Sarah moaned on my tongue; her hands ran along my chest. Vicky grabbed the back of my head. She pulled me in rough, forcing my kiss deeper. Have a great day, Miss Hostess.

"Master, can we go to the mall?" Sarah asked.

"Sure. I wanted to do something to celebrate your new job and Vicky acing her test. Does that sound like a good victory treat?"

"Sounds like a great treat," Vicky said as she leaned into me.

On our way back to the apartment, I walked on the outside edge beside my girlfriends. I was the closest to the street. I wanted to position myself to ensure that I could protect Sarah and Vicky. Elle briskly walked ahead of us as if she were in a hurry. Howard was behind us and seemed to be lazily moving along.

When our feet touched the parking lot, Elle scurried to her SUV. She seemed distracted as she waved at us.

"Bye, Bro." Elle looked at me with a smile. Then she looked at Vicky and Sarah. "Nice seeing you girls again. Call me. We can roast my pervy brother more," Elle said as she jumped in her vehicle.

Sarah and Vicky laughed and waved back. Great! Now the three of them would be making all kinds of strange jokes—at my expense, no less. Oh well. I was happy that they were finally getting along.

Howard gloomily walked over to me. A weary and saddened look etched on his face. This tugged at my heart. I wanted to reach out to hug him. But I stilled myself. I didn't know if it was appropriate. Or if he would even want me to.

"Brah, sorry about the drinken'. I honestly thought ya wouldn't like me if we didn't drink." His eyes filled with remorse.

"Like I said, it's cool. Besides, I had a great time hanging with you." I opened my arms, inviting him in for a hug. He leaned in for a moment and gave me a brief hug with a pat on the back.

"Wanna hang out 'gain?" he asked with hope in his eyes.

"Sure, bro. Anytime," I said with approval.

"Just leave the booze at home next time," Vicky interjected with her stern motherly voice.

"Yes, ma'am." Howard hung his head. Then he got in his car and drove off.

"Mall?" I turned to my girlfriends.

"Yeah. You said you wanted to treat us for our achievements," Sarah said. She skipped as she started toward my beater.

"And he owes us big for that drinking crap," Vicky said with lighthearted sternness. "Carrying his drunk ass wasn't easy."

"I get shotgun this time!" Sarah jumped in the front seat before Vicky could react.

"Miss Pushover thinks she's won." Vicky jumped in the back with an exaggerated, playful huff.

Well, they seemed to be in good spirits. And I was so proud of them. Their accomplishments were no small feats. They were very interesting women. Sex crazed one minute, then endearing, then comforting, then achieving. It was like a spectrum of something I had never known. They were a unique and complete package.

I felt bad that I had put them through that. Having to take care of me in a drunken state. And that I had put Elle through that as well. Like she didn't have enough on her plate with the divorce and

Stephen's crap. I promised myself at that moment that I would never get that drunk again, for all of their sake.

I eased into the vehicle and started it. We made our way onto the road, which seemed oddly deserted for a Saturday. The car was filled with laughter as Vicky and Sarah talked about how fun Elle was to be around.

"Do you think she'd be our Maid of honor?" Sarah asked Vicky.

Here we go again: marriage talk. I guess I did this to myself. But the idea wasn't a bad one. I mean, they are both beautiful and smart. And I do love them. But Mrs. Helderman said to move them in before the marriage talk. See how it goes living together first.

"I am sure she will be. But she would be Matron of honor. She has been married, the title changes with that." Vicky leaned forward over the center console.

"Oh, I didn't know that. Hmm, Jenny can be our flower girl." Sarah jumped with joy in her seat.

"Howard as the best man... and that is why we can't have an open bar." Vicky laughed as she threw her hands in the air.

I sat quietly as they planned an extravagant wedding, complete with a three-tiered cake, seating arrangements, and, of course, talk about the wedding night. I was happy that they were filled with so much excitement. It was fun listening to them plan our wedding.

"I wonder how he will carry us both over the threshold at the same time?" Sarah asked.

"Hogtied, one on each shoulder." Vicky chuckled with mirth.

I wondered what type of dress would make each happy, and what kind of engagement rings they'd want. Matching? Or different ones for each? Would they want matching wedding bands for the three of us? What would make them happiest? I had seen a set that I could probably order an extra engagement ring and wedding band, but I would have to dig into my savings to buy it.

Wait... Howard was my business partner now, and the business wouldn't require as much of my savings. Yes, I could get the set and stash it somewhere until I wanted to propose. I just need to get their ring sizes without them knowing.

"You seem quiet over there, Master." Sarah turned to look at me. My eyes darted to her, then back to the road.

"Just thinking," I mumbled as I watched the street.

"About?" Vicky leaned toward me, her face close to mine.

"Things. And stuff." I smirked awkwardly as I tried to avoid telling them about the rings I considered purchasing.

"Things and stuff...huh. Bet he was thinking about what kind of lingerie would be under our wedding dresses." Vicky giggled as she turned to Sarah.

"Nuh-uh. I say he's thinking about what we'll do to him once he is completely ours." Sarah snickered as she leaned back in her seat.

I chuckled. "Or what I would use to spank the two of you. Such naughty girls, you both are."

"Naughty girls. Not your good girls today, Master?" Vicky kissed my cheek.

"I am always good. Can't say the same for Bratty-pants over here." Sarah laughed as she pointed at Vicky.

"Bratty-pants... Wow. Miss Pushover grew a pair." Vicky chuckled as she leaned back.

"You know it." Sarah cheered with a sense of victory.

Approaching the mall, I could see why the roads seemed deserted. The mall parking lot was filled to the max with very few open spaces. I guess one of the stores was having a fire sale or something. Or maybe everyone just woke up and decided to bum-rush the mall.

"You girls ready?" I asked as we pulled into a parking spot.

They didn't say anything as they exited the car and were quiet as we walked to the front entrance hand in hand. Sarah was on my left, and Vicky was on my right. Our feet stayed in step as we walked through the crowded mall.

"Let's go," Sarah said as she tugged Vicky and me along. She pulled us toward the western store.

"Ugh, really? Okay." Vicky's lips curled in disgust as we entered.

The store smelled of fresh leather and a soft scent of perfume. It was a refreshing smell from the crowded walkways throughout the mall. Vicky broke free from my hand and stayed by the door. She was obviously not impressed with the store. I guess it clashed with her "goth-rocker" vibes.

Sarah dashed about to different corners of the shop in wild excitement, almost as if she had never been in a store before. I was having a hard time trying to follow her. Boots section one second, then poof to clothes. I felt like a pinball being bounced from one area to another. Then she finally stopped at the hats section.

Her eyes were fixed on a black hat. Just above the brim was a brown band adorned with sapphire-like stones. I walked up beside her, taking her hand.

"That's a pretty hat." Her eyes widened as she continued to admire it.

"Try it on."

"Nah, I can't, Master. Look at the price." She looked at me, her eyes drooped with disappointment.

"Just try it on. If it looks good on you, I will buy it." I smiled at her as my hand gave her a slight squeeze.

"Really!" She perked up with excitement.

Her hands reached out delicately as she pulled the hat off the shelf. With one sly motion, she flipped the hat on her head. It looked so good on her—really good. The way her red locks flowed from underneath the hat looked like a crimson river. It reminded me of our day at the lake.

"See, you look beautiful in it," I said as I pointed toward a mirror on the wall.

"Wow, it does look good, Master. And the stones, my favorite color." She smiled at me in the mirror.

"I sort of figured blue was your color," I admitted. She was so happy. It felt nice seeing her elated.

We made our way to the register, and I bought the hat. We met back up with Vicky at the entrance. Vicky's eyes were bright as she saw Sarah wearing the hat. Her face filled with joy.

"Whoa, cowgirl. Yeh-haw." Vicky laughed, but it was obvious she was excited for Sarah.

"Looks great, right?" Sarah spun around, exhilarated.

"Yes, awesome on you." Vicky approved of Sarah's gleeful behavior.

We chatted a bit more about the hat before moving on. Sarah skipped ahead of Vicky and me for a while. Watching her prance around was fun, and I had done that. I had made her happy. My heart felt so warm. Vicky held my hand as we kept pace together.

Sarah came running back to us in an erratic flash. Her face broke into a long grin. She pointed toward the alternative store. There was a mannequin in the window dressed in black goth-looking clothes. Vicky immediately pulled my arm in the direction of the store. Wow, she was strong. Really strong.

151

"We have to go inside! They might have the boots I've been dying to get." Vicky's tone was a strange mix of her dark vixen and motherly tones. It was odd. But strangely, it sounded nice to hear.

"Okay," I agreed as I followed.

Even though it didn't seem to be her cup of tea, Sarah still went inside with us. Sarah perused the store by herself.

Vicky pulled me straight to the shoe shelves. There were a ton of different boots, Converse-style shoes, and even high heels with spikes. This definitely seemed like a store that would be up Vicky's alley. I felt delighted and couldn't keep from beaming. They were different, yet somehow, their uniqueness was always fascinating.

"This is it. The pair I've wanted for a long time." Vicky raved as her lips curled with that beautiful bright smile. Her hand reached out, grabbing the boots from the shelf.

The black leather had a dull shine to it. The heel was long. Six inches, maybe? I couldn't tell for sure, I just knew it was long. Spikes protruded along the lace eyelets and around the top of the boot. Yeah. Definitely her.

"Try them on, walk around in them. See how they feel," I encouraged her.

She sat on the bench at the end of the aisle. She slid her boots off and put on the new boots. Her fingers laced them with feminine grace. I watched like a voyeur as she put them on her feet. As she stood, she was taller. Her eyes met mine at my level. I glanced at her with a loving gaze as our eyes peered into each other's.

"They feel great." Vicky beamed as she walked around in them.

"Good, they're yours for acing your test," I said with an uncontainable grin as I took her hand.

"You sure?" Vicky asked with a slightly puzzled look.

"Yes. I'm buying them for you." My voice smoothed into that NCO voice.

"Oh, thank you. Thank you so much, Master." Vicky leaned in and kissed me on the cheek.

I purchased the boots, and Vicky continued wearing them. We put her old boots in the box. The clerk thought it was odd, but she seemed okay with it. Sarah met us at the entrance.

"Like my boots?" Vicky asked Sarah, excited.

"Hell yeah! Makes you taller too." Sarah moved her hand out in comparison to Vicky's new height.

"Yep. But still nowhere near your six-foot-three." Vicky laughed as she looked up at Sarah.

"So. You are as tall as Master, now. What around five-eight or so?" Sarah said sarcastically as she pointed over to me.

"Hey, I'm a solid five-foot-eight *and a half*." I joked back.

"Got the half right." Vicky chuckled as she looked down at my crotch.

"Oh really? See what you say later." I arched my brow. My thoughts turned to the things I had planned for them later tonight.

We continued to joke about heights for a few minutes. It was getting close to noon, so naturally, we were all getting hungry. I took them to the food court. I paid for the meals as we continued to joke. The rest of the afternoon was spent going through various stores, chatting about different things, and laughing.

I managed to get their ring sizes when we went to a jewelry store. I used the excuse of getting birthstone rings for them as birthday presents. But when they were distracted looking at other jewelry, I ordered the engagement sets that I had been thinking about earlier.

I knew they were the women for me. My mind was made up: I was going to marry them—at least, I hoped that I would. That was if they would accept my proposal.

But the wedding. How? I was pretty sure bigamy was still illegal. And what preacher would preside over a three-way wedding?

Chapter 14: Trinity of Desire Unleashed

The room was dimly lit by candlelight. The flames danced provocatively, casting an aura of sensuality. Smooth jazz played softly in the background. I made sure the selection had sexy sax tones to infuse the mood. Jasmine-rose incense filled the room with exotic aromas. I had carefully orchestrated this sensual, romantic ambiance.

The candlelight danced wildly against Vicky's and Sarah's skin, lambent as it swayed softly against them. Their bodies oozed with carnal hunger, roaring to devour me. Their radiance purred to have me inside them. It was my pleasure to give in to my beauties. I was going to give them release. But first, they were going to earn it. Earn those orgasms. Earn to have me deep inside them.

I was comfortably seated on the couch, not a single stitch of clothes on my body. My hands were together in front of my face as I pondered what command I should give first.

They assumed the same kneeling pose they took this morning—but nude. The pose showed how much they desired to submit. Eyes to the ground, their hair draped over their faces. I sat on the couch, taking in the sight. I was in awe of the beauty that their submission held. The way their bodies seemed to glow under the candlelight had a desideratum appeal, which set the beast inside me roaring, clawing to the surface to have them. To touch. To taste. To feel myself completely inside of them.

I smiled. This was what I had desired my entire life. Luscious consorts, ready for any command my lips would utter. All their thoughts, all their desires, mine. A simple word from my lips cast into the air would be their desires made real. Each syllable spoken would make their bodies jump into any debauchery I fancied. My fingers snapped to garner their attention. Their heads shot up, eyes on me. The power... the thought that they were mine. Giving them commands. So exhilarating.

"All fours... crawl to me... slowly," I ordered. My voice let them know they were mine.

They got on all fours without hesitation and slowly crawled to me. My words had compelled them to do my will. The knowledge of them slowly inching toward me stirred a wavering feeling, their passion for me. I admired how their bodies moved. I knew that my commands were steel to their ears, that they would obey without a struggle. What a turn-on to hold such power over them. I felt my member grow thick, rigid and strong.

"Good girls." The timbre of my voice encouraged them.

Their hair bounced over those beautiful faces with each four-legged step. Those large bosoms slapped together with each stride. I knew they were excited. Their nipples became hardened pebbles putting those breasts on alert. They kept the roundness of their rears high in the air, on display for me to view. The movements of those bodies as they slid forward captured my attention. I watched, admiring the contours move with such feline grace.

They were close to me. The heat of their breaths on my thighs made my self-control waver. Both of their faces began to nuzzle into my thighs. The aroma of their fragrances hit my nostrils; I closed my eyes, inhaling their scents. I smelled their willingness, their eagerness for pleasure. I knew they were both dripping with fire between their legs. Vicky playfully bit my inner thigh as Sarah tenderly kissed the one that she had claimed.

They were waiting for permission, trapped in their own lust. They were my obedient beauties... my wanton lovers. I knew what they wanted; it was what I needed. I leaned down, my index fingers tilted their faces up to gaze at mine.

"You want to please me? To have me in those pretty mouths?" My voice was cold and stern.

They didn't say a word, but their eyes yearned for it. They were distressed by not having me. I watched as their lips quivered; they ached to taste me. I lightly traced my fingers along their lips. A slight nod was all the two of them could muster through those desiring eyes: Vicky's cerulean glistening with viciousness; Sarah's virid showing a loving need.

"You may taste me." The soft whisper of my command fueled the flames burning inside them.

Their hands moved with haste to touch me, to hold me. But they were in no rush. I watched as their gazes stayed on me. They never took their eyes off mine. As if there was no concern at this moment for any of us. We were here together. And they were mine. All mine. They knew what they needed to do. They knew what I needed, exactly what I liked.

155

Vicky pulled my member toward her lips; the warmth of her breath on my tip sent shivers down my spine. I could have exploded right at that moment. But my body stilled as my hand propelled outward, fisting her mane. I had much more in store for them— later. Vicky's lips puckered, kissing the tip of my rod. Sarah watched, enthralled by the sight.

I knew that Vicky wanted to tease me, to make me want her that much more. With my fingers interlaced into her locks, I roughly pulled her face forward. The soft skin of her cheek rubbed against the stem of my rod as I drew her face closer. Her tongue lashed out, slithering from my sac to the slit at the tip. Fuck! Lapping slowly and fiercely, she took in the taste of my essence from my head. She watched my face, curious of my entertainment of her tease. Before I knew what was happening, she wickedly gazed at me as her mouth opened wide. I felt the warmth of her close in around me. She took me in inch by inch.

Shockwaves tore through me; her saliva was a slick lubricant on me. My eyes closed, indulging in her service. I felt her tongue swirl as Vicky worked me in her wet maw. The sounds of her working me filled my body with torturous delight. I groaned when her lips hit the base of my member. I was completely in her mouth. She gagged slightly, forcing her throat to convulse around me. My legs tensed as her throat vortexed, taking me in deep.

I felt a moist heat across my chin. My eyes opened. Sarah stood on the couch, her legs bowed to straddle my face. I smelled that intoxicating aroma permeating from her. The tender flesh of her labia less than an inch from my lips. The candlelit room made her silky skin seem so enticing. My face moved forward; my tongue danced along her lips. The taste... so delicious. I whipped my tongue deep inside her. She moaned out as I probed further.

"Ah... Master... lick... me..." Sarah huffed between breaths.

The sounds of Vicky's sloppy slurps and gagging sent me reeling. Each time she moved her head, I could feel the sloshing of her salivated trail. She had lathered me with her affections, worshipping me as the deity that their bodies responded to.

Hands reached down, grabbing me behind my ears, pulling me closer, deeper into Sarah. Her thighs tightened as I lapped rapidly. Working between the inside of her to the soft tendril of her bud. She was pulsing with fire. My eyes glanced up, the way her large breasts were squeezed together as her arms crossed to the back of my scalp. So full, so gorgeous from this angle. I reached my free hand up, crawling along her thigh lightly. Wrapping it around her cheeks, I grabbed her, pulling her pelvis tight against my face.

I lapped and suckled at Sarah. Her hips rocked, gyrating in circles as her hands held me tighter, closer. I loved making her body react to me. She got up on her toes, her thighs straining. She was the instrument that my mouth played. The lyrical moans from her lips were the music that I was composing. I felt her rapids shower me as she screamed out.

"Fah... fah... fuuuuuck!" Sarah's hands held my face in place as her love flowed onto me. I drank in the juices of her love.

I could feel Vicky's mouth pull from my erection as Sarah moved off of me. When I gazed down, she was admiring the mess I had made of Sarah. Her eyes showed a twinge of jealousy and vexation. As Sarah was clear, Vicky pummeled me. She threw me to the side, forcing me to lay flat on the couch. Her rear jumped into me as she moved her body to take her seat on my face.

"My turn," she said as she lowered that tight body on me.

The aroma of her sex mixed with the feral nature of her lust intoxicated me. My tongue darted out. Lashing her anus, working around the rim. I lapped further to her taint. Her cheeks wriggled as I danced my way to her lips. I kissed them roughly as my tongue punched deep into her.

My rod was warm and wet again. Sarah started to thank me for her release. Her mouth collapsed around my shaft. She took me deeper into her throat than Vicky could. Recoils of pleasure throbbed through me as her mouth swallowed me whole, taking my sac in with the shaft. I moaned into Vicky.

My hands pulled Vicky's hips down harder onto my face. My nose dug into her bottom; she whimpered as she felt my muzzle poke in slightly. My tongue fought her love button, beating her sex into submission to my will. I wanted to taste her... to taste that saccharine cream. Her hands planted on my chest; her nails pierced my pecs. The vibrations of my moans reverberated on her; her body responded. Her back arched forward as I attacked her fiercely, bombarding her bud with sensations.

"Eat... oh God... eat that fuck-hole... so good..." Vicky mumbled through shallow breaths.

I felt the warm mist of her start to spritz me with her love. Her nails dug in deeper as I forced her body to orgasm. Then the floodgates opened as she rained down her nectar upon me. Her body spasmed. I felt her knees go weak, her body spent. She slumped over, her nails releasing me, and laid on top of me.

The sensation of Sarah taking my entire manhood down her throat brought me to the edge. My thighs tensed. My body ached to release. I tried to make this feeling last forever—I needed to—but I was powerless. I detonated deep into the back of her throat. I felt her esophagus swallow every drop. Every. Drop.

Vicky crawled off me. My face was soaked with the honey from both of my beauties. I was lying there for a second, gathering myself. I made both of them orgasm again—what a feeling to know that I could control their bodies in such a way. To feel the heat of them explode upon me. I was their Master, their sex god. They had proven their praises... their worship.

I grabbed Vicky and slung her over my shoulder, my left arm folded over her legs. My free hand darted to Sarah's, clasped her hand, and gave her a gentle tug. I lumbered to the bedroom and kicked the door open. They were mine. And I was going to take from them what I owned.

As I reached the foot of the bed, I released Sarah's hand. I gave Vicky a spank before throwing her on the bed, her body bouncing twice before settling. Her breasts moved with each bounce. The look in her eyes as she crashed into the mattress invited me to ravage her. They told me she wanted me to use her as roughly as possible. My eyes soaked in the sight of her for a moment. That messy yet sexy look. God, how I needed to take her.

I grabbed her leg with one hand, the other on her hip. I roughly twisted her body around, flinging her to her stomach. My hands groped her hips, pulling her bubble butt up to me. Her face was buried deep into the mattress. Yes... say it... say it.

"That body is mine. Mine to use. Mine to fuck." The cool NCO tones from my lips hit the core of her ecstasy.

"Y-yes, Master. All... yours," Vicky whimpered between pants.

Manhandling her and seeing her like this—vulnerably bent over—my manhood swelled. I forcibly slammed deep into her love furnace. The warmth of her around me... the softness. So good, like I had entered the gates of a fiery abyss. A sinner in the flames of passion. She was mine. I was going to take her. To make her beg to have me climax deep inside her. My hands tightly gripped her waist right where her body bent. Thrusting in fast and hard, she began to whimper and moan.

I looked over to Sarah. She was in shock at my rough treatment of Vicky. Yet she was excited. Her hand worked her love button as she watched us. I turned my attention back to Vicky. My hips rocked into her ample rear; I felt her body move at each thrust. The slapping sounds as our bodies met coaxed me to pound her harder.

"Ahh... I... I love fucking you, my dirty brat..." I growled with ecstasy, feeling the vehemence of being inside my vixen.

"Use me... fuck me... oh God, fuck me..." Vicky screamed out.

My hand reached out, fisting that dark raven hair. I pulled upward harshly. Her upper body lifted; her back arched in the middle. She moaned out with a painful, erotic cry. I hastened my pace. I was in control; my manhood was savagely taking her. With each merciless thrust, I reminded her that I was Master. I was her god. To always obey me. Submit to my will. She was my brat.

"Please... Master... please..." Vicky cried out between breaths.

"Please what, my sweet?" I knew what she wanted, what she craved. But I wanted her to say it. To beg for it.

"Please... cum... cum in... me..." Vicky sobbed breathlessly.

Her body began bucking back to meet my thrusts. I felt her tighten around me. Then she jetted her juices on me. I made her orgasm again. The heat of her honey hit my pelvis. I felt her warm sap. Damn. With this, I held her rougher, plunging with such acceleration. In no time, my climax shot deep inside her. I thrust one last deep thrust as all of my essence was spewed into her. I pulled out of her pink—and now gaping—opening.

Sarah moved under Vicky, and she lapped up all my seed that had leaked out. Vicky looked at me, her eyes filled with joy as if her god had blessed her with a miracle.

"Master, let me get you back up," Vicky begged. "Sarah needs you... needs your cum." Vicky held out her hand as Sarah began lapping at my essence that had leaked down Vicky's thigh.

I moved over to Vicky's hand; she reached out, gripping me. She started with slow strokes. Her eyes looked up at me as she worked me faster and harder.

"Look at her, Master. She needs you, needs to feel your love," Vicky whispered as her hand was starting to make me hard.

It didn't take long before Vicky had my phallus stiff and solid again. Vicky released me and rolled off the bed. My eyes fixed on Sarah's. She was still kneeling at the foot of the bed. I ran my hand through her hair, then down her cheek. My finger tilted her head up.

"Do you want me inside you, my beauty?" The NCO smoothness sent shivers across her body.

"Yes... yes I do, Master." Her green eyes sparkled in the light.

"Lay down on the bed, my sweet." I gestured to the mattress.

Without a word, she laid on the bed, legs spread wide; the silk of her sex was now a rose color. She was on her elbows; her face looked at her delicate flower. I slowly slid inside her; those emeralds watched as she devoured each inch deep inside her pinkness. This felt different, like the nirvana of heaven. She rested her feet over my shoulders as I worked slow gyrations into her. She moaned as she watched our dance.

"That's it, my beauty, feel my love. Feel it inside you." My voice steeled her desires. She loved the way I spoke to her.

"I feel it, Master, every inch of your love." Her eyes met mine and stared into my soul.

My hands grabbed her thighs as I slowly quickened the pace of my gyrations. I felt the fever of her body in exultation; blissful was the feeling of making love to her. Her body was so obedient to my touch. The soft mewls from her lips urged me to grind into her. Our eyes locked, she felt all of my love, all my affection inside of her. She was the crowning jewel. Softly submissive, so obedient.

"My tenderness... is yours," I spoke softly as my fingers traced up and down her legs.

"Oh... yes... Master..." Sarah swooned as she felt my thrusts hasten ever so slightly.

I watched as her milky breasts bounced with each drive. The thrusts made my hips hit deep into her pelvic bone. The warmth of her hairy patch hit my stomach as I pestled inside her.

I pressed my body weight onto her, crushing down upon her. Her legs stretched as I folded her. Her knees rubbed her breasts. I felt myself fall deeper into the depths of her altar. My mind was in the throes of passion. Elated by the bliss of her beatific body, I was at one with a cosmic reverence for her.

I leaned in, kissing her as I hastened my revolving thrusts. Our tongues played in the loving caress of each other's. We danced our kiss with veneration. She worshipped me, yet I was the one in prayer for having such an empyreal woman.

She squealed out as a tremendous wave of her holy tsunami shot upward onto me. Her body was mine. I hastened my circular thrusts, her body heat under me. I was close. I felt the throbbing of my scepter deep inside her. I slammed in deep as I blasted my devout love far into the reaches of her soft body. She gazed at me, her heavenly eyes aglow with exaltation. Serenity ascended in her spirit as if her living deity had blessed her.

Slowly, I lifted my body off of hers. Sliding out, a bit of my fluids streamed down from her. Vicky rushed in to lap up the excess that flowed from Sarah's vulva. I watched as they both had fulfilled the promise: every drop. Not a single drop was wasted. All of my seed was owned by them. They were the only ones worthy of it.

After they ensured every drop wasn't wasted, they lay on their sides, waiting for me to slide in the middle. Vicky patted her hand between them, motioning for me to take my place. I turned the light out before maneuvering myself in the center.

"That was amazing, Master," Sarah whispered in my ear as she wrapped herself around me.

"Fucking hot, Master," Vicky whispered in my other ear as her body snuggled in close.

"Good girls. I had such a great time." I rejoiced as my arms cradled them both.

I lay there spent, yet happy. We had finally made love. The three of us had fallen into our carnal pleasures, our need to have each other. Yet, I doubt this need would ever fade. They were mine, and I was theirs. Somehow, at this moment, I felt comfortable talking about serious things. Was it that we had just shared a passionate encounter? Or that they were so open to me... in sync?

"Was it worth taking us to the mall earlier, Master?" Sarah snickered.

"Sure was," I responded. Uncontrollably, a smile grew wide across my face. I thought about the rings that I'd purchased. The proposal seemed imminent now.

Vicky kissed my cheek. "You know we are always worth it, Master."

"True." I kissed the top of each of their heads.

"I feel like I have accomplished something," Vicky blurted out.

"What is that, sis?" Sarah asked with curiosity.

"To feel Master's love inside me. How he touched us, each of us, differently. How we needed to be sexually loved. He gave it to us," Vicky admitted.

"Yes, it was different. I watched him with you; he was so harsh. So animalistic. Then with me, tender, more loving." Sarah trailed off into a whisper.

"I simply responded to what I felt your individual sexual needs were. Loving each of you with the unique treatment that felt right," I confessed.

Vicky held me harder. "It worked. It made us love you more," she said with elation.

"Yes, how you responded to each of our needs... so romantic." Sarah sighed with a swoon.

"How did it feel for you, Master?" Vicky asked.

I reminisced about the encounter, attempting to find the words to express how it made me feel.

"I felt at one with you as we made love. A warmth surrounded me; I could feel you both. As if, at that moment, we became a single entity," I explained affectionately.

Vicky sighed with love. "I think the dominant-submissive play enhances our relationship. It unifies the individual connections of our love. Showcasing how we fit together, the three of us."

Sarah leaned up, gazing into my eyes. "True. The sexual submission allowed me to feel empowered. I didn't have to say a word; Master just responded to me in every way I needed." Sarah paused to glance at Vicky. "Then, to watch him make love to you, he was just as attentive to your needs. The entire time, I felt connected to us, all three."

"I could feel the love coursing through me. With Vicky, I was raw and rough. With Sarah, I was refined and gentle. And yet, I felt love for both of you simultaneously. I think Vicky said it best that we were unified. However, I can't describe it completely." I said, still not able to find the words.

I started to understand how I loved each of them differently. Vicky was a challenge, which created a sort of competitiveness in my love for her. Sarah was more easygoing, which gave me a sense that our love was always plentiful. Strangely, a wild night like this made me fall deeper in love with them both.

"Yeah, can't be put into words," Vicky whispered.

"Wish this could be us every night," Sarah whispered into the ether.

"What if it was?" I asked, trying to stir this conversation.

"You mean living together?" Vicky seemed surprised by the idea.

"Yeah. How would it go? Let's fantasize for a minute," I suggested, trying to figure out how this conversation would go.

"Well, I would read my books in the living room, maybe in the nude..." Sarah giggled playfully.

"It would depend on which place we go. Our apartment is smaller than yours. But we have two bedrooms instead of one." Vicky said. Her voice reflected a deep contemplation of it.

"Could you set up your painting stuff in the kitchen?" I asked, trying to explore more.

"Could work... for a while." Vicky seemed deep in thought.

"But we'll need a house once we are pregnant," Sarah interjected, her tone seeming to alternate between seriousness and giggles.

"Okay. So... how long before we needed to find a house?" I inquired.

"Depends on when things go our way financially. And when you marry us," Vicky said coolly.

"Books... where can we put them?" I asked, trying to figure out Sarah's angle.

"The bottom of your shelves should do for now. I don't own many. At the moment." Sarah giggled ominously. I was sure that she was planning to expand her personal library.

"Anything we would need to negotiate?" I asked.

"Who gets the remote, and at what time." Sarah giggled; I felt her squeeze me for a moment, then release me.

"Nothing that I can foresee at the moment," Vicky said, her voice rising to a higher pitch at the end of her sentence.

"Okay, then let me ask something." My voice was slightly shaky.

"Anything, Master," Sarah said with love in her voice.

"What is it, Master?" Vicky seemed to have that motherly concern.

163

"How would you two feel about moving in… with me. Here." I started to stumble over my words but regained my courage.

"You mean it?" Sarah asked, elated as she rocked into me tightly.

"Of course, Master. When?" Vicky rejoiced.

"Well, when would you like to move in? I cleared it with the landlord already." I felt the spring of joy jumping inside me.

"NOW! Right now, Master," Sarah bubbly exclaimed.

"We can be packed and moved in within the next week or two, Master," Vicky said, slightly laughing at Sarah.

"Your lease?" I asked, concerned they might mess up their credit or something.

"We are month to month," Vicky assured me.

"Good, I can help you pack and move." I let out a sigh of relief. The thought of helping them move made me jump with joy inside.

"It's going to be so fun living with Master." Sarah drifted off into her fantasies.

I cuddled them deeper. Mine. All mine. They were going to live here with me. My beauties, here all the time. No waiting to see them. No lonely nights by myself. They would be here. Meals. Watching them walk around the apartment. Talking about our days. A real relationship.

"We love you, Master. Good night," they said in unison.

"Good night, my beauties. I love you both, too," I answered.

I lay in bed, my eyes closing to the night. The women that I wanted to marry would soon be living with me. Next week, we will start packing up their apartment. Shifting them here with me. They had agreed. Living with them. Seeing them daily. Loving them. Happiness filled my soul as I faded into sleep.

Chapter 15: Moving Day

The boxes felt heavy as I loaded them into my beater. This was the first of many trips to gather their belongings. I placed the boxes neatly into the trunk. Beginning a life with them, sharing a home, filled me with excitement. Almost two weeks ago, they had agreed to move in. Now, it was a reality. This was all new to me. I hadn't lived with anyone other than my family. I had a roommate in the barracks, but that wasn't the same. They were my girlfriends. My beauties. My loves. I had never lived with a woman in this capacity.

I had met them almost a month ago, yet this still seemed like a dream. If it was a dream, I hoped I'd never wake up. I wanted to stay in this state of happiness forever. And they were going to be with me every second. I loved them, and they loved me. They were mine, and I was theirs.

Excitement and fear coursed through me. I wanted to be with them, yet a bit of darkness crept in. Was I adequate to be a live-in boyfriend? I knew it wasn't going to be a nonstop sexcapade. Responsibility was key; I was responsible for them. They were mine to cherish and take care of. Mine to protect and provide for in our life together. Mine to love with all that I was. Was I up to the task? Yes... yes, I was.

Thinking about them filled my heart with a deep passion for life. I wanted to share this life with them in our happiness. Our life together... our trinity of love. I wanted to caress them with my love. I wanted to give them the world and so much more.

The rings that I'd ordered had come in yesterday. My heart urged me to propose to them immediately. My ears longed to hear that "yes" come from their pretty lips. The wedding vows that would be spoken from our souls—for better or worse; for richer or poorer; in sickness and in health; to love and to cherish—kept playing in my head. To hear them repeat those vows, to say that they loved me the same as I loved them, would be the ultimate experience.

I was now their first choice. The first one that woke up to those bright smiles. The first to hear about their days. The first choice to feel their kisses. I was the first in their hearts. The last one to see them before they retired to slumber in the night. The last lover they would need. I was him, their husband. At least one day, I would be.

The road felt like a wild rush of gaiety as my foot pumped the accelerator. I was in no hurry but ecstatic as the wind blew through the open windows. Blaring through the radio was Rhianna's hit "S&M." I bobbed my head, jamming to the beat. Hearing this a few times in Afghan gave me a sense that my secret desires weren't so bad, like I wasn't a freak for wanting a woman to submit to me.

I belted out the words of the songs as I drove. My singing voice was horrid, but I didn't care. I was just enthralled by the lyrics and the feeling I was under. This was the best feeling I'd ever felt. Mine... they were mine. Marriage.

"'Cause I may be bad, but I'm perfectly good at it! Sex in the air, I don't care, I love the smell of it! Sticks and stones may break my bones, but chains and whips excite me!" I screamed out the lyrics as I was stopped at a red light. An elderly couple pulled up beside me and gave me funny looks, but the girl in the back seat hungrily eyed me.

Nope... she wasn't them.

To me, there were only two women on the planet: Sarah and Vicky. That was it. At least the women that I wanted to give my life to, my desires, my entire being. They deserved so much, and it was my mission to give it all to them.

I pulled into the parking spot and killed the engine. The sun was dazzling as it showered down upon me. I could feel the warmth hit my face as I pulled the boxes from the trunk. Stacking them neatly in my arms, I walked toward the security door. The door shuffled open quickly as I approached. The frail arm that held it open was familiar.

"Mrs.— I mean Wanda, how are you?" I asked, remembering that she wanted me to call her Wanda instead of being so formal. That was going to be hard to get used to.

"Good afternoon, Kyle." She said as she held the door for me.

"I took your advice," I said.

"I can see that. Are they moving in today?" She had a strange look on her face.

"Yep, got a few trips to make. Took off early to help them." I kept smiling, trying to understand her look. She walked beside me toward the stairs.

"Oh my... silly boy. You do move fast." She shook her head, the smile resurfaced on her face as the concerned look faded.

166

I laughed at her seemingly joking disapproval. "It was your suggestion."

"I know, the man you are becoming... so unpredictable. Unpredictable and intriguing." She nodded with slight approval. She followed me up the stairs.

"Are you free tonight?" I asked. "Sarah is cooking dinner, and they both wanted to invite you."

"Unfortunately, I can't tonight. My son is bringing my grandbabies over." Her face curled into a disdainful look, almost as if she was dreading the encounter with her son.

"Oh... maybe some other time then," I said as we made our way to our doors.

"Yes, that would be great. Besides, I haven't heard from the girls in a while. Would be nice to catch up. Girl talk and all." She winked at me before hurriedly exiting the conversation and entering her apartment.

I set the boxes down so that I could unlock the love palace. Why was she in such a rush to end our conversation? Must have had a dinner planned for her grandchildren. Or preparing for his wife to cause a scene again. I would check on her later, just to make sure that she was okay.

As the apartment door swung open, I grabbed the boxes, all labeled "*living room*," and made my way in. As I approached the couch, I stumbled over the coffee table. The top box slid off the stack and fell to the ground. Papers flew everywhere. Crap.

I set the remaining boxes on the carpet next to the entertainment center. My hands moved quickly to gather up the documents. One of them was a memorandum. Integrated Technological Industries was the header. Stephen's company? What was a memo from ITI doing in the girls' stuff? I picked it up to read.

Integrated Technological Industries

Memorandum March 16, 2012

Phase 3 of project L.O.V.

A subject has been acquired for the two bioengineered prototypes. Both prototypes have been accessing the A.I. integration node to gather

167

information on the subject. Implementation in the subject's daily life is imminent. Sourced from personal accounts, both prototypes will be launched simultaneously to ensure full immersion of the subject. Prototypes will not intervene until the optimal opportunity presents itself. The agent assigned to the subject advised proceeding with O.I. implementation cautiously. The application must be a slow immersion. The subject is prone to violent disdain, which may cause possible failure with prototype bonding. The predictive success probability for the subject to bond with one of the prototypes is approximately 49%. Prepare to design more neural-emotional algorithms to mitigate risks.

CEO Stephen Dolion

Why did they have a document from Stephen about project L.O.V.? This sounded like some kind of artificial intelligence update from four months ago. March sixteenth. That was about a month after I moved here. What was he up to? Bioengineering. In the Army there was a story about a unit called Red Dragons. A lot of mystery surrounded them, bioengineering among those rumors. Sentinel was a great contributor of technology and weapons. ITI was a subsidiary of Sentinel. Could the rumors be true... I shook off my thoughts of the military fables.

Sarah had worked in human resources at a company. Had it been ITI? I'd never asked or thought about it. Maybe that pig of a boss was Stephen. It would fit his MO. I felt the anger starting to boil inside me. Stephen had wronged not only my sister, but now I was sure he had wronged one of my wives. Calm, Sergeant. Your girlfriends are moving in. Just ask Sarah about ITI. Confirm who it was before you break Stephen's legs. Just chill.

I finished cleaning up the mess. Neatly, I placed the papers back into the box. I would ask about ITI over dinner, but for now, another load. I was sure they had packed more than a few boxes for this go-round.

Surprisingly, they had very little in the apartment. A few electronics, some clothes, what-nots, and a few pieces of furniture. Since I didn't possess nightstands, they wanted to take them home with us. Two stand-up style dressers to put their clothes in. And they were going to put their TV in the bedroom. Something about Netflix and chill. I knew it was code for watching movies while playing sexy time. Interesting. I could imagine the fun, chill things we could do... Mmm...

Get back to it, Sergeant. I made my way back downstairs. Time to pick up another load. Or shoot a load inside them. Chill. Plenty of time for that once they are moved in. Besides, Howard was going to come by later tonight. Bring his pickup so we can take the furniture in the back of it. The man had like a dozen vehicles. Almost one for every occasion.

Howard and I had moved forward on our partnership. We signed the paperwork. He had put up almost seventy percent of the capital I needed. But he only asked for a third of the business. I maintained sixty-six percent ownership. I tried to argue with him to at least take half. But he wasn't having it. I had majority control over Forester Heat & Air. He was my silent business partner. Things were shaping up.

As I approached the car, I felt eyes on me. I looked around. Who would be watching me? My eyes scanned the parking lot.

There he stood; his suit neatly pressed. If I didn't know him—know the atrocities he had committed—I might have seen him as a friend. But he was no friend of mine. He was nothing. No, he was less than nothing. He was scum. Just a mess under my boots. I calmed myself as I closed my eyes. Don't do it, Sergeant, he is not worth it. You are honorable. Don't kill him. Just remember he is not worth it.

"Kyle, how is Elle these days?" The wicked grin on his face made me want to break his jaw.

"I have to go, Stephen." My eyes glared at him. My hands balled up into fists. Calm... stay calm.

"Can't chat a bit with your brother?" Stephen approached me.

"I don't have a brother. If I did, he wouldn't be you." My eyes followed his movements, focusing on his hands. Just give me an excuse, one wrong move. Please do it, Stephen. Just one reason for me to unleash all this rage.

"Jenny is doing fine. She started piano lessons last week."
Stephen was talking to me as if nothing was wrong. As if he wasn't
the monster that I knew he was. But he underestimated the beast
that lingered inside me. Chill, Sergeant. Stay peaceful.

"What do you want?" Rearing inside was a hatred that burned
within me down to the bone.

"To talk with my brother. That's all." Stephen's smile widened.

"Like I said, I don't have a brother." Watching him with intent
and a dangerous fury, my knuckles ached to break his bones.

"Well, Elle has been naughty lately. Lawyers... it isn't too late
for her to come home. I can still forgive her." Arrogance reigned in
his eyes as he shook his head.

"*Si vis pacem para bellum.*" I mumbled under my breath,
remembering the old saying: if you want peace, prepare for war.
And with this man, it wasn't simply a divorce. My sister was at war
with him. Elle the Allies, Stephen the Axis. D-day was coming, and
it would be an awakening for him. Just remember not to do
something stupid, nothing to jeopardize her case.

"Well, if you still need a job. The maintenance position in my
office is open. I would make your pay more than generous for the
work." Pointing at my beater, he made an obvious suggestion about
my financial insufficiencies.

"I'm doing fine just the way I am." If my eyes could shoot
lasers, he would have been vaporized.

"Anyway, good luck with your new girlfriends. Sarah and Vicky
can come with a lot of maintenance." Stephen walked off twirling
his key ring on his index finger.

He knew both of their names. He knew that they were mine.
How? I haven't talked with him since Jenny's birthday more than
three months ago. Had he been watching me to get information on
Elle? Sarah most likely had worked for ITI, was it possible that
Vicky had visited her at work? Could she have mentioned her in
passing? They were best friends, sisters even. It wasn't a stretch for
him to at least know about Vicky if Sarah had worked for ITI. The
two of them were practically inseparable.

As he jumped in some fancy-looking car, he waved at me. The
car looked like a spaceship or something out of a sci-fi movie.
Sentinel was the manufacturer. Probably a perk of the job. A perk
awarded to senior executives. Pen II was the model. A pen, huh.

That was all we needed from him. His signature on those divorce papers. Then I wouldn't have to look at his face—at least I wouldn't feel the need to rearrange it. My fists twinged, ached even, to pummel him.

Bink!

The metallic sound rang in the silent parking lot as my fist crashed into the top of my beater. Damn! He was standing right there. I could have killed him. He was right there. Taunting me. I should have beaten him. No Sergeant. What would that have solved? Jenny would have stayed in his custody. He would have proven that she would be endangered by being in Elle's care. That I was too violent to even see my niece.

Standing at the car, I sighed. I closed my eyes. Calm... calm down, Sergeant. What was it that Vicky told me? I didn't have to be a soldier anymore. I could live without the remorse of inflicting pain on others. But he so needed it, deserved it.

No! Focus on Vicky and Sarah. I needed to move them in.

I made one more trip to the girls' apartment to gather the last of the boxes. The ladies had loaded up their vehicles. Of course, Vicky had the black Dodge Journey, and Sarah had a red Chevy Cobalt stuffed with clothes. Vicky had a more practical vehicle for family planning. Sarah had a souped-up compact vehicle. Their vehicle choices contrasted with their personalities. It was odd.

I didn't tell Sarah and Vicky about my encounter with that scum. I just wanted to forget that he had even made an appearance. Simply thinking about it made my hands twitch, to want to fight him. Destroy him. But he wasn't worth my time; I had other things to focus on.

As we pulled up to the parking lot together. We wasted no time hauling the contents of their old place into our new love haven. I gathered up several boxes before heading off to the building.

"Master, be careful, you might hurt yourself," Sarah hollered with a deep concern from the trunk of her car.

"I'm fine; I got this," I responded, but then I felt an elbow poke my side. I looked to see Vicky carrying a couple of boxes.

"You're always fine, Master." Vicky winked at me. I playfully shook my head, knowing that there was no sleep for me tonight.

171

"The sky, it's so beautiful this evening," Sarah pointed out as she joined us with a box.

I glanced up, peering into the dark night sky. Even with the city lights saturating the sky, the stars still glowed with elegance. This gave me an idea. I could take them to the roof of the building. The super had given me a key to the roof since I had helped him a few times with the air conditioners. Yes, grab the spare blanket and some hot chocolate. It would be a great night to cuddle with them under the stars.

"After we get everything in the apartment and have dinner, I have a surprise. It will make up for me working on the fourth." I explained as we trampled up the stairs.

"A surprise, Master? That's so awesome. And don't worry, there will be other Independence Days we can celebrate together." Sarah beamed with excitement.

"Surprise, huh? Better not be something dirty this early on, Master." Vicky laughed with sarcasm.

"Dirty? You mean fun. I don't think I would mind." Sarah giggled as we continued up the stairs.

Damn, they had such dirty minds. Only just moving in and already talking sexiness. I hadn't really had dirty thoughts today. I was just happy to move them in. But they were now readily available to me. And their promise: every drop in every hole. They were mine. Shake it off, Sergeant.

We got to the door. Sarah reached into my pocket to retrieve the keys. She fumbled for a second in my pants as she searched for them. The warmth of her hand on my thigh felt so sensual. I looked at her with a desirous stare. Sarah smiled a wicked grin.

Vicky groaned. "Miss Pushover gets to play with Master while I hold a thousand pounds of our crap? I don't think so. Hurry up."

"Got 'em," Sarah announced as she pulled the keys out. Then she briefly turned, blowing a raspberry at Vickey as she jingled them. With ease, she opened the door, even while holding the box.

We no sooner got inside and placed the boxes down than my phone made a text message *ding*. I pulled it out of my pocket. I had been waiting for Howard to contact me. Sure enough, it was him.

[Howard] Friday 20:03
Sorry bro, can't come tonight. Mom is sick ☹

[Kyle] Friday 20:04
Its kewl bro. Take care of mom. Be safe. 😦

[Howard] Friday 20:05
Thanx bro be deadly 😊

I felt bad for Howard's mother. My heart ached for her. I hadn't met her yet, but she was the mother of my brot— Wait. Brother. Yes, He was now my brother. I guess in a short time, I felt like we had bonded so well. Just like my guys on my first deployment, an instant chemistry to brotherhood. I smiled.

Turning to my girlfriends, my smile widened. I had started my own tribe. Sarah was in the kitchen starting dinner. Her curvaceous body moved with a determination to prepare the meal that would feed us all. Vicky seemed ready to go back down to gather more boxes. Her arms crossed as her foot tapped the floor in anticipation.

"Howard can't come tonight; his mom is sick. I will try to get him some other time to go after the furniture." I told them with the feeling that I had failed them.

"Okay, no problem, Master. I will start dinner." Sarah didn't look up as she started chopping ingredients.

"Let's go get the rest, Master." Vicky didn't seem too concerned either.

We made several more trips as Sarah diligently worked to make the food. With each trip, the apartment smelled more and more delicious. I wasn't sure what Sarah was making, but it smelled so good. We continued to stack most of the boxes in the living room. The bags that had their clothes were stowed in the bedroom.

As we finished the last load for the night, I carried their TV. I made my way into the bedroom and sat it on my dresser. I started hooking it up but didn't have cable in that room. However, they had a Roku connected to the TV. We could stream Netflix movies while lying in bed. Netflix and chill. I would become one of those guys who was lucky enough to "chill." Sexy fun while watching a movie. Cool off, Sergeant. It should be about time to eat.

As I exited the bedroom, Sarah was starting to set the table. Vicky was rummaging through the boxes to place things around the apartment. I didn't say a word as I watched them from the bedroom door. They hadn't noticed that I was standing there. Watching those

173

graceful movements that they both had. How determined they each were in their actions. I felt happy.

This was my life now. Being able to watch them *be...* to share life with them. Even mundane activities like these made them look so stunning. My beauties. It was no wonder that I had a marriage scheme in play. Rings. I hid them well.

"Beautiful. Both of you. So beautiful," I stated as I walked into the kitchen. "What are we having?"

Sarah dotingly gazed at me as she shook her head in elation. Vicky stared at me with a deep love twinkling in her blue eyes. I walked toward the silverware drawer to help set the table.

"No, Master. I got this. Please go help, Vicky." Sarah's soft hand caressed mine as I reached out to open the drawer.

"Okay, my sweet." I looked up at those green eyes. They held me in a trance for a moment before I moved toward Vicky.

"What are we do'in, darling?" I asked as I slumped over a box.

Vicky smiled at me. "Placing the what-nots next to your dragon guys." I looked over to the shelf.

A cute teddy bear figurine was beside my beholder, and a few other eclectic mismatches to my D&D figures. She was incorporating their cutesy figurines with my hardcore monsters, much like our life together. They were the cute elegance. I was the hardened monster to their softness. As we worked, we laughed about what cute figure would go best beside each creature. From the kitchen, I could hear Sarah laugh every now and then as she listened to our banter.

"You can't put a cherub next to the owlbear. The poor guy will be ripped to pieces," I exclaimed, concerned for the little figurine.

"Um... okay. But, he still looks cute next to this owl thingy." Vicky laughed as she seemed to relish my concern for the figurine.

Sarah laughed from the kitchen and called out to us. "Put one of your knight guys next to him, Master. You know, for protection."

"Fine. I'll put my barbarian between them." I gave in to appease my beauties, moving my barbarian figure to protect the cherub.

"See, compromise. We got this." Vicky chuckled as she leaned into me. I could smell the intoxicating aroma of her perfume.

It was fun being able to joke and play with them. Even though the interactions were not sexual in nature, you could feel the sexual tension. All the reciprocity of banter now seemed to be a dance of constant admiration and seduction. As if sensuality and love were now harrowing manifestations of our need for each other. Aching to be fulfilled by one another. Was this what it was like to be in a relationship? A constant melee of love and lust? I wondered if the heaviness of this would continue to define our playful banter for years... for decades to come.

"Dinner is ready," Sarah announced from the kitchen.

Vicky and I wasted no time sitting at the table. Sarah moved the platter over; it was shepherd's pie. It smelled so good; I couldn't wait to grab a forkful of the deliciousness. I watched as the ladies put it on their plates. I took my turn spooning a large bundle onto my plate. I waited for them to take the first bite. After I was satisfied that they had started to eat, I plunged the first scoop into my mouth. I wasted no time gobbling my plate down.

"Why do you do that?" Vicky looked at me with concern.

"Yeah, are you afraid we would poison you, Master?" Sarah laughed as she moved a scoop to her mouth.

"What do you mean?" I asked, confused. I was eating as I normally did. What was I doing?

"You wait for us to eat first, always. It's just odd." Vicky explained. Her motherly tone stepped to the forefront.

"Oh, it's a military thing. Rank eats last. You see, those that we are responsible for, they eat first." I shrugged, hoping that my explanation cleared up any misunderstandings.

"He feels responsible for us." Sarah rejoiced as she turned smiling to Vicky.

"Well, he should. He is our boyfriend... Our Master, after all." Vicky nodded as she smiled back with just as much joy.

"Husband soon, too." Sarah giggled.

I almost spat up the bite I had in my mouth. Husband... soon... I planned to propose to them soon, even against Mrs. Helderman's advice. I felt like being their fiancé was a move in the right direction. Right? And that should appease the topic of marriage for a while. Until I could get things in a better place before we started a family.

Then, my mind wandered back to their previous talks about babies. I'd come in them, and they'd walked around with ejaculate inside them at the zoo. Pregnant... crap. Was I ready to be a father right now? Are they on birth control? I hadn't even asked.

"Are you two on birth control? I mean, for the time being." I croaked. My fork dropped on my plate, afraid of the answer, afraid that I had done something dumb.

"Of course." The unison of their words eased my mind.

"Okay... okay... good. Not until we get married. Is that okay?" I stammered.

"To have babies, Master?" Sarah asked, puzzled, as her fork hovered over her plate.

"We don't want to get pregnant until we are married. No worries, Master." Vicky comforted me before taking another bite of shepherd's pie.

"Good... good. I just don't want to be one of those baby-daddy types. I want to have kids with my wives," I explained. My words were more of a reassurance for myself. I picked up my fork, shoveling down another bite.

"Wives. Did you hear, sis? Wives!" Sarah beamed as she bounced with joy, turning to Vicky.

"Yeah, I heard. But that's not a proposal, just a statement. Calm down," Vicky said, trying to act cool, but I could see the excitement in her face as well.

I called them my wives. I needed to ease up on that. I hadn't even proposed yet. I needed to slow down until the proposal. Yeah, slow down... sure... right. They live here now. Slow didn't seem to be in our vocabulary. I needed to move the conversation away from marriage to... ITI... yes. I needed to talk to them about ITI. Subtly find out how Stephen knew them. And that memo...

"Oh, by the way. Some paperwork fell out of a box. ITI. Did either of you work for ITI?" I asked.

They stared at me blankly, falling quiet for a moment. They looked confused and a bit concerned. They froze. Did I have a blue dick on my forehead? Was I turning colors? What's wrong?

Vicky finally broke the silence. "No, neither of us have. My mother works there. She has for several years."

"Oh, okay," I said with the feeling that there was more to it. Why the big pause if it was no big deal? Could it be because they didn't want to upset me? They knew that Stephen was my brother-in-law. Well, soon to be nothing.

"Mama Naomi! I hope she visits us in our new home," Sarah said excitedly.

"She said that she would after she got back from overseas. Hopefully, in time for my birthday this week," Vicky said. She seemed drab and smiled awkwardly.

Crap. Meeting the parents, already. I didn't know what I would say to them. Oh, of course, I intend to marry your daughter and her best friend, Mrs. Schein. Children? Yep. Impregnating both of them. Yeah, this was going to be an interesting meeting.

"Master looks like he just swallowed his heart." Sarah laughed.

"Don't worry, Master. My mother approves of this relationship," Vicky reassured me.

"Yeah, I hope so." I exhaled.

"What was this surprise you had for us, Master?" Sarah asked as she was starting to clear the table.

"I will make some hot chocolate and show you," I responded. The thought of showing them the stars eased my mind away from what Vicky's mother would say about their situation.

"Okay, Master. We will clean up the dinner mess," Vicky stated softly, then started helping Sarah.

I made hot chocolate the way my mother had shown me. I spent some time as a child learning various things in the kitchen. I was not the best at cooking, but my hot chocolate was something that I was proud of. I heated milk in a pot and brought it to a slight boil. I got the packets of hot chocolate and mixed them in slowly. This allowed the flavor to be richer. I stirred it slowly and let it simmer for a little while.

My beauties had all the dishes done and all the food put away. They also swept and mopped the kitchen. As I was making the nectar, I watched them clean.

It was amazing to feast my eyes on them. Just watching them move, work, and laugh. It was nice. I made the right choice by moving them in. I knew it, right at that moment.

The apartment was no longer a quiet tangle of my loneliness. It was bustling with them playfully making fun of each other cleaning.

"You slut." Vicky laughed.

"What? If Master wants it, he gets it." Sarah laughed back.

"What are you two bickering about?" I asked sternly as I poured the hot chocolate into three mugs.

"Nothing for you to concern yourself with, Master." Vicky smiled a devilish grin.

"About *mmhhm—*" Vicky quickly covered Sarah's mouth with her hand.

"Nothing, right," Vicky said looking at Sarah as she removed her hand.

They both broke into laughter, their bosoms bouncing as they punctuated the air with hysterics. I shook my head with a big smile on my face. I was sure it was dirty. Something about sex. My brides, my dirty brides. Yep, the right choice. As long as they were here, the loneliness would never surface. They were my companions upon this journey we call life.

"Welp, Vicky, can you please grab the spare blanket out of the closet?" I asked as I handed their mugs to Sarah.

"Yes, Master," Vicky said. She went to the closet. It wasn't long before she had the blanket.

"Follow me," I said in that cool NCO tone as we exited the apartment.

We walked past Mrs. Helderman's place to the "Maintenance only" doorway. I took them up the maintenance stairwell, which echoed with our footfalls as we made our way up. Each stride forward felt taboo, yet I knew that it was worth it.

"Are we supposed to be here, Master?" Sarah warily asked as she tried to keep the mugs from spilling.

"Aren't you excited? He is showing off his bad boy side." Vicky snickered; her face glowing as she continued to smile with the blanket slung over her shoulder.

"It's cool; I have the key," I said as we reached the top. The key turned with ease, and I sprung the door open.

"Lay the blanket out over there, please." I pointed to a clear spot on the roof.

"Okay," Vicky answered and quickly sprawled the blanket out.

Soon, I sat in the middle of the blanket, taking a sip. The heat of the drink blazed with sweet cocoa. It was like drinking down the ambrosia of life.

"Come sit," I instructed them.

They both got their mugs and sat on either side of me. The smoothness of their bodies gave an erotic sense of wonder. We sat in silence for a while as we drank our hot chocolates. I wondered what their minds were thinking of. Was the future in there?

Fantasies of what life would be like in the coming years? I shook my mind loose for a moment. I brought them here to show them.

"Look up, my beauties," I said as my hand set my mug down on the side of the blanket.

My back crashed softly as I laid back. My fingers interlaced over the back of my head as I stared up into the sky. Vicky and Sarah followed me, both lying beside me. The stars twinkled with the luminescence of dancing angels. The city lights tried to wash away the radiance of the night sky, but we could still see its beauty. The night glowed from each star, and the moon christened the twilight sky with its lunar aura. I was so happy to show them this. And this was the beginning of everything I wanted to share with them.

"Beginning. That sounds nice," Vicky whispered.

"Yes, the beginning of our shared life," Sarah echoed.

The cool breeze of the night wind fell upon me. But the warmth of my girlfriends was like a hearth of love. The fires of heavenly light lay on either side of me. Emblazed by my passion to be with them, to love them, I was also warming their souls. Despite the day's downfalls, it still turned out to be wonderful.

Sarah and Vicky were everything that felt like home to me. They were my home now. As Vicky said when we first met, home is around the people you care about the most. That was them, my girlfriends. I cared about them the most.

"The stars look so gorgeous tonight, Master," Vicky whispered, she turned to look me in the eyes.

"Lovely, Master. Thank you," Sarah said as she turned to me, mirroring Vicky.

Vicky leaned down, biting my lower lip. Sarah's nose nuzzled into my cheek. My tongue shot out, hitting Vicky's upper lip. She released her nibble as she moved her mouth over mine. She slammed her lips into mine with fierce force. Our lips blazed with passion as our tongues were locked into a hostile war. Her hand fisted my hair, tugging at the turf. Twisting into each other, our faces battled for supremacy. I thought she would rip my head off with our kiss. Ascending into the dreamscape of this savage kiss, I was reeling with ecstasy.

We fought with vehemence through the kiss until Sarah's face moved Vicky to the side. Sarah's lips were a gentle caress as our tongues danced in sync, tongues swaying from her mouth to mine, like dancers on a dance floor. We tangoed into the sip of each other's lips. A slow and loving kiss. Hollowed into the bliss of her, I was entranced. I felt as though the wings of angelic bliss had been bestowed upon me. Divinity reigned from the heavens as her submission could be felt in her lips. Sarah broke from our kiss, leaving me longing for them both.

"Such a romantic night," Sarah stated as she took her place lying beside me.

"Yes, romantic with so much love," Vicky echoed.

They both cuddled into me deeply as we lay watching the stars. My heart throbbed in my chest, pounding to a rhythm of passion, a rhythm of love. They were my beauties. Each was unique yet the same. The same because they were equally loved by me. As we lay on the blanket, I pointed out Orion.

"That's the hunter, Orion. He is always on a quest to pursue his game." My eyes stayed on the constellation as I explained.

"You two are the wild game, my loves, that I promise to always pursue. To always desire. To never stop finding new ways to love you both." My words continued as I watched the sky. "Always my center. My focus. I would fight the world for you two if I had to." An oath in my words as I lay on the blanket cuddling them close.

"So sweet, Master." Sarah swooned as her grip on me tightened.

"Our warrior... our man... our Master," Vicky softly purred.

I pointed out a few other constellations that I could remember, and they showed me a few that I didn't know about. The night trailed on but was filled with happiness and laughs. We lay in this state of elation and romance for most of the night.

If this was my life with them, then I would have no regrets moving them in. Yes, things had moved fast. But there was no denying that we were meant to be together. Our souls were tied—no, chained—to each other. They were the missing parts of my soul. The pieces that completed the complexity of me. I hoped that I was the same to them, the missing piece of their souls. There was no other explanation for all of this, for them being with me. We completed each other.

Chapter 16: Night Terror

We had stayed on the roof for a long while before tiredness settled in. We headed back to the apartment to retire for the night. As soon as we got in, Vicky and Sarah stripped nude to sleep. I wasted no time following suit. I usually slept in my boxers, but with them moving in, I was sure this needed to change.

Vicky erratically moved to her side, pulling the covers over her. Sarah lazily slid into her place. They both eyed me as I stood there in silence for a moment. My mind rang with the notion that they were now living with me, sleeping beside me every night.

"Your spot is ready, Master." Sarah coyishly smiled as she patted the middle of the bed.

"Come lay down, sweetheart." Vicky smiled at me through her tired eyes.

"I had a great time stargazing with you two. I love you, both," I said as I slid in between them.

"Yeah, it was fun. I love you too, Master," Sarah said as she cuddled into me snuggly.

"Thank you again, Master. I enjoyed watching the stars with you. I love you too," Vicky said as she flung herself over me, cradling my side.

"Good night, my beauties," I whispered into the air.

"Good night, Master," they whispered in unison.

Vicky and Sarah were out in no time. However, I was a bit uneasy. My mind reeled over the encounter with Stephen for a time. I wanted to rip him apart. Treat him like we did terrorists overseas. Waterboarding him—hell, any form of torture would do. No, I'm not that man anymore. I quickly pushed those warrior thoughts aside.

What was I worried about? I had peace. I live a peaceful life now, at least in comparison to war. And I had finally found a friend, a brother, like I had on my first deployment. Women who are far better than Regina ever thought to be. I hadn't thought about Miss Dependa's real name in years. Maybe things were turning around.

Yeah, things were. I now had a brother in Howard and two beautiful women I loved. I focused on the ceiling fan spinning at low speed. I thought about all the positive things in my current life. My body started to relax. I lay there listening to my ladies' soft snores.

I focused on the soothing beauties next to me. The tender feeling of their chests rising and falling on me with their every breath. The heat of their bodies comforted me. I turned, inhaling a whiff of their essence. Sarah smelled like summer rain, and Vicky had the aroma of jasmine flowers.

They always had a calming fragrance encompassing them. How did they always have those scents? It didn't matter; all that mattered was that it was tranquil. I started to drift off to sleep with ease next to my beauties. Just the thought of them beside me allowed my slumber to come quickly.

I woke up to the roar of an engine. I was seated in a vehicle traveling somewhere. The vehicle was moving roughly; it felt like it would rattle my bones out of my body. Crap, had I fallen asleep? Where was I?

Sand blasted across the windshield. The wipers did their best to push the sand away, clearing my view for a moment. Sand dunes... was this Iraq? I hated driving through the desert. Hot as hell during the day, cold as shit at night.

I looked around the vehicle. I was in a Humvee. All fifty-five miles of Uncle Sam Hyper Drive seemed to be at top speed. I remembered the A/C in these trucks was for shit. I was sitting in the truck commander's seat. That's right, I had just been ranked up. I guess this was what rank gets you. A new seat in the truck. Specialist, my new rank... Not yet an NCO, but no longer a Private.

I felt like I was already missing being in the gunner seat. My hands on that 50 caliber was always an awesome feeling. However, I hated the bugs and the sand in your face. But now Donovan took my place in the truck. Yeah, Donovan was the new Private assigned to the truck. He had replaced me as the gunner.

I looked around. Wier was driving, Donovan was strapped into the gunner turret, and Gordon was holding his rifle in the back. I turned my eyes forward. We had been in the country for several months, almost close to the end of our deployment.

We had a mission... what was it? A bomb maker: Ahmad Kareem Abdul, code-named Roadside Mawt. We had to apprehend a suspected bomb maker and take him in for interrogation. He had been buddies with some of the higher-up guys. Chemical Ali, along with many others, was on his dance card. He would be a high-value asset for intel—at least once we get him safely into custody.

"What ya think, Forester?" Gordan tapped my shoulder, jarring me from my thoughts.

"Of what?" The engine whining muffled my voice.

"Ya think Donovan really gonna fuck dat girl with the big titties?" Gordan asked as he tapped Donovan's leg.

"No way, man. Not a chance in Hell." I chuckled over the roar of the engine.

"Hey, fuck ya. Fuck the two of ya. Right up the ass," Donovan yelled down from the gunner's turret.

"About the only fucken he's getting. Sure ain't getting none of that sweet pussy." Weir laughed, his eyes still on the road, if you call sand dunes a road.

"Shit. Show ya fucks the pics she sent, now ya gotta bust my balls. Cum stains, the lot of ya," Donovan yelled down. So much for keeping this mission quiet.

"Brah, ya dick 'bout the size of a baby carrot. You ain't tappen dat ass. We get home, she gonna be with some suave muddafucka." Gordan laughed trying to keep the truck cheery in his own way.

"Baby carrot? Shit. More like a fucken grain-o-rice," Weir piped in.

"Shut the fuck up, Weir, ya dick ain't no bigger," Donovan growled loudly, pulling his hand down from the gunner's turret shooting a bird to all of us.

"Aww… we love ya too." Gordan laughed.

"I'ma 'bout to cry, there is just so much love in this truck. Makes my heart swell," I chimed in.

"Swell, huh… heart or dick?" Weir chuckled.

"Like he'd know. Forester's still pretty much a virgin." Donovan took a hit at me.

"Got more pussy than you. Least mine was real." I laughed.

We drove a while longer, roasting Donovan all the while. New Privates were fun to mess with. He got himself an internet girlfriend and spent a lot of time with that Haji air card. Lately, he had been constantly on his laptop. Talking dirty to her. We could all hear him whack it in the tent. About five or six times a night. Just the sounds of "fap, fap, fap" well into the morning. I had to wear my headphones all night just to sleep. Like dude, really? How much can your dick shoot out… fucking crazy.

Most of the guys in the truck were from up north. They all had odd accents, but the accents made their jokes that much goofier. We all joked, all the time. About sex, about life, about death, and most often about the war. We were a bunch of dumbasses. It was fun being with these guys.

My brothers. I wouldn't be here if it weren't for them. They had saved my life more times than I can count. Goofy but damn loyal. Damn good soldiers. I couldn't imagine going through this desert with anyone else. No matter what dumb shit we got into, they were there. We had become brothers. A bunch of silly-ass brothers, but brothers nonetheless.

Iraq was a shitty place with shitty people. They would smile at us, then inform the enemy of our movements. I fucking hated this country. I hoped to blow the whole place up one day.

Maybe this was God's promised land at one time. But now, it was just another fucking wasteland. It often felt like we were in the wild west or some post-apocalyptic movie. Like a surreal version of war set in a desert wasteland. Like The Postman or Mad Max or whatever. If Mad Max were real, Iraq would be where that Pursuit Special was driving around. Gunslingers, that's what we were. The new sheriffs in town. The bad guy in the black hat, us with a quick gun hand. Yeah, it was more like a Western.

"Da fuck are we?" Weir asked, driving with his night vision on.

"Blue Force says about twenty clicks from the mission. Just go straight. Until we hit something," I said as some sand was kicked down on me from the turret.

"Fucken love da Army. Stupid ass shit," Gordan said. His anger was directed at good old Uncle Sam.

Gordan was already unhappy before this mission. I had to talk with him before we headed out. Right before the train model, he was in the MWR tent. He'd called his wife, who informed him that she'd filed for divorce. Some lame-ass excuses about the distance, the war, and other bullshit. This had happened to plenty of our guys in the past few months. I didn't understand why these women couldn't be faithful, why they couldn't wait. Most knew what they'd signed up for: the military lifestyle. My Regina knew. She had three kids with other soldiers. She knew our lifestyle.

I hadn't heard from Regina this entire time. All my letters were returned, my emails weren't going through. And I could only get her voicemail when I called. She's been the only woman who gave me the time of day. The only one who wanted me. Had I become one of those "Dear John" types? Had a Jody swooped in while I was busy getting shot at? Maybe it was just that things had gotten bad for her back home. But I was sending her money. I had been for months. Maybe it wasn't enough; she did have three kids. And life can't be easy as a single mom with three kids.

"Wat's dat?" Donovan yelled out from the turret.

"I see it too," Gordon confirmed.

"Looks like fire in the distance," Weir said as my eyes focused on the distant glow.

"I'ma call it in. Maybe some shit." My hand reached for the hand mic. I started to comm up when I felt it.

The truck flew up in the air; the boom was so loud that every fiber of my being vibrated. Flames flashed across the windshield. I felt weightless. My arms were thrown about. Fuck, was this it? Were we going to die? Regina. Elle. Jenny, my niece. I hadn't seen her in person yet. Fuck! Then it all went dark.

I awoke, something warm running across my face. My hand traveled up; I tapped the fluid to bring it to my eyes. Blood. Fuck. I unbuckled my seat belt. Ouch. I fell on my head, my helmet crashing against the roof of the truck. We were inverted. Dammit.

The truck was dark, I couldn't see shit. I heard faint sounds of Arabic from outside the truck. Goddammit, those raghead fucks were right outside. They must have used an IED. Those fucks. I had to kill them, but first, my guys.

"Wier... Donovan... Gordan..." I kept my voice to a whisper, but got no response.

"Wier... Donovan... Gordan..." I repeated. Again, nothing.

In the pitch dark, I started crawling through the truck. My hands felt around as if I were a blind man. I reached for the driver's seat. My hands felt Weir's chest.

"Weir, wake up." I shook him as I whispered. "Wake up, fuck nuts." I shook him again.

I reached down to where his face would have been. But there was nothing there. Just warm liquid dripping into my hand. Fuck. No. Damn it. My heart raced. Dead. Weir was dead.

I moved to the middle of the truck. Donovan. My hands reached out. I felt his feet and moved up to his waist. That was it, there was nothing else of him. Just his hips and his legs. He must have gotten bisected when we rolled.

My heart sank. No... Gordan. He had to be alive. Someone had to be.

I moved to Gordan; my hand reached up to his chest. A large hole was at the center. No, fuck this. No. They can't die. They can't. Fuck. This was a fucking dream, right? A nightmare? My guys weren't dead. They couldn't be. We were... just laughing. Just fucking with Donovan. Now... now I was alone. My weapon...

I fumbled around and found my weapon. I kicked the door open. Without a single word or thought I started firing rounds at the silhouettes. I saw the muzzle flashes as they fired back at me. Before I knew it, I was fully engaged in a firefight.

At that moment I didn't care. I felt fearless... in a scary way. I enjoyed the fighting. My eyes glowed with joy when I knew that I had made a kill. Was this the monster that I had become? A beast that basked in the glory of what his inhuman side could do? I knew that the monster had awoken inside me at that time. They had murdered my friends, my brothers. They were going to pay.

The rounds of my weapon tore through the flesh of my enemies. My thirst for death and destruction was unleashed. And those that dared cross me felt the full extent of my wrath. The joy of murder grew inside me. I wanted them all dead.

"FUCKING RAGHEAD FUCKS! DIE! DIE! FUCKING DIE!" I screamed into the night air as I fired shot after shot. Once a mag was spent, I would reload without thought. With a movement so fast and graceful, I don't think I had ever moved that way.

I roared with a fury I had never shown to this world. I felt the fires of war inside my heart. I clenched my teeth as my soul became the monster. I was murder incarnate, claiming all those lost to carnage. If I was ever a warrior, it was at that moment. I lost all of myself, emerging as the beast of the painful souls. The souls of my brothers. They had died so violently, and these cowards had done it. The evil of my foes was nothing compared to the darkness within. I had become a horror to destroy them all.

The other trucks in the convoy showed up. They finished the fight. I felt the adrenaline leaving my body. Pain set in. Falling to my knees, I huffed out. I looked down. I was covered in blood.

Mine? My brothers? The enemies? I didn't know. But the pain was sharp. Then, my eyes went dark.

Lady Death knew I was merely sleeping through the valley of life. She was reaping the soul of this undead creature that I had become. With the precision of a necromantic hearth, her fingers danced along my flesh. I shall never escape her grip, her seductive caress. The cool feeling of her breath was always beating down upon me with a sensual fire. And now... I was hers. My secret lover... a sick twisted love. I was no more.

"FUCK!" I screamed as I woke up. My body was covered in sweat, tears cooling on my cheeks. I saw darkness. Nothing but darkness as I sat up. Where was I? Iraq? Hospital? Lady Death's bedroom? Where...

"Do you think he is okay?" A soft woman's voice came from the darkness.

"Maybe... not sure." A raspier woman's voice on the other side of the darkness.

"Who's there? I got a gun. Stay back." My voice was hoarse.

"Master... are you okay?" the soft voice asked.

"Show yourselves!" I yelled, demanding to know who my captors were.

My eyes were hit with a blazing light. Fuck. Was I captured? Had the Haji got me before the other trucks could? Name... Rank... Serial Number... That was all they were getting from me.

"Wait, don't touch him yet. I don't think he is back completely," The raspy voice said; my eyes started to focus.

I looked around, ready for anything. I was in a small, simple room with white walls. I was lying on a bed. Just a few feet from the foot of the bed stood a wooden dresser. A TV sat on the dresser.

What was this place? I looked to where the voices came from. At the side of the room where the raspy voice came from, a fully nude dark-haired woman stood. Wait... Vicky. Her name was Vicky.

My eyes darted to where the other voice had come from. A redhead, of course fully nude, seemed scared standing next to the door. Sarah... she was Sarah. They were my girlfriends... my beauties. What happened? What did I do? I had another episode, a nightmare, this time.

"My sweets, are you okay?" I asked, slouching down as I pulled the cover off my torso. My eyes were still adjusting to the light.

I slid to the foot of the bed and sat on the edge. I felt the plush carpet between my toes. I sighed, relieved. My mind raced for a moment.

What could have caused this dream... this nightmare? Stephen... it had to be my encounter with him earlier today. And I had thought about my men when thinking about my brotherhood to Howard. Could my anger toward Stephen and my fond thoughts of my friends have triggered this?

"Yes, Master. We're fine. Are you?" Sarah responded. She came over and leaned in. Her hand gently caressed my cheek.

"We're okay, Master. Nightmare?" Vicky asked. She sat on the bed beside me, and her arm gave me a side hug.

"Sorta, I guess. More like a memory." I explained, my eyes looked at the floor. Embarrassment and shame hit me with a seasoning of remorse.

"Want to talk about it?" Sarah asked while she took her place at my other side. Her hand still caressed my cheek.

"Iraq... on my first deployment. I had made friends with the guys assigned to my truck. We were..." My voice trailed off. I could feel the soft wind of the ceiling fan cooling my body.

"On a mission?" Vicky asked. She tilted her head as she watched my expressions.

"Yes, a simple snatch and grab of a bomb maker," I explained, my gaze focused on a spot in the carpet. It was stained from when I had spilled a drink the first day in the apartment.

"Then what, Master?" Sarah asked. Her hand stopped caressing my cheek; she leaned her head into my shoulder.

"We took an IED. Flipped the truck," I said as I felt a tear roll down my cheek.

"You had been laughing... about big titties... or something," Vicky said, her eyes continuing to watch me.

"Donovan had a girl that he had been talking to on the internet. We were fucking with him. Joking about how he wouldn't bang her," I said, my eyes glanced at them before returning to that spot.

"Then the bomb?" Sarah whispered, her voice sorrowful.

"Yes. The three of them died. We were supposed to have another with us. But he was cut from the mission... Hairline fracture on his leg or something. He was lucky. I was luckier, I guess." The tears started to flow, but my voice stayed strong.

"Wier, Donovan, Gordon. You kept repeating that. I guess those were the men who died?" Her face nestled onto my bicep.

"Yes. We were always goofing off. We got in so much trouble. All the joking, all the pranks. Silly goofy assholes." I smirked through the pain.

"It sounds like you had some good friends," Vicky said. I felt her hand caress my thigh.

I sighed. "Yeah, I guess they were my first friends ever."

"What happened? I mean, the explosion must have banged you up?" Sarah sheepishly asked.

"Um... I got banged up pretty good. I had broken ribs, a twisted ankle, and hairline fractures in several discs in my back. Traumatic brain injury. Some other stuff..." I trailed off, thinking about being exiled to Germany for recovery.

"What happened to your buddies?" Vicky asked; I could feel the warmth in her voice.

"Flag draped coffins. Each one sent home with honors." I felt the sting of it in my soul, yet Vicky and Sarah seemed to bring me back with their warmth.

Sarah's arm reached out and hugged my waist. "It sounded like you made the ones that did it pay. Did you, Master?"

"Uh huh... got a silver star for it. But I would trade that medal for just one more day with those goofy idiots." Tears soaked my cheeks. The pain inside swelled like a black hole in my heart.

"It's okay, Master. We are here for you." Sarah encouraged me before she kissed my cheek. I felt myself start to ease.

"If you ever need to talk about the war, we will listen. We will help," Vicky said as her hand ran through my hair. I felt all the pain flush from my soul. Their light brought me back to our life together.

"Thank you, my beauties," I said graciously as the pain started to fall away.

"We love you, Master." That unison thing they do never got old.

"I love you both as well." I leaned down, kissing Vicky's lips. I sipped in the fire that she held, more tender than she usually kissed me. I turned to Sarah; her lips took my pain as I probed her.

I felt paralyzed by how much love we had together. They were more than just my lusty girlfriends; they were the women that I wanted to spend my life with. To give all of myself to. They saw the weaker side of me, and they just comforted me. No insults, no

189

degrading remarks. They just wanted to be with me. To be my strength in the moments when I was no longer strong. Such women. I had never thought that this would be real, yet it was.

The scars of war were on my body, but the hidden scars that I had tried to bury deep, they had seen twice now. First, the flashback at the zoo, now this. But they eased me back to reality. They had soothed the pain, soothed the monster that dwelled within me.

Soulmates? Were they my soulmates? I felt complete with them. Marriage started to seem right. I just moved them in, yet they seemed to have been here my whole life. I felt the joy, the happiness of our relationship washing over me. Cleansing my sorrows. Moving them in was the right choice; I just knew it. They were my strength. And with them by my side, I would become a better man. I just hoped that I was a good man... a good husband for them.

"I'm sorry. This is the second time that you two have had to endure my broken mind. My combat trauma." I shifted my gaze between them.

"It's okay. The trust you place in us, Master, sets us ablaze with love. You allow us to see you so vulnerable. Yet we know you are so strong. Your vulnerabilities are only for us. They are ours." Sarah whispered as she looked me in the eyes.

"Vulnerable Kyle is my favorite version of you," Vicky said, her voice assuming her motherly tone. "It means that you love us enough to take your armor off. To let us into the places of your soul that you close off from the world. But the other versions of you are just as loved."

"Thank you both for understanding. For being here for me. I'm glad that you're my girlfriends. I was afraid to share this with anyone. Afraid of being judged." My words were a wave of my appreciation for them. I kissed each of them on the forehead.

"We love you, Master. And we are just happy that you can share this with us." Sarah purred as she nuzzled her head into my neck.

"Besides, ain't no big titty bitches getting in our way." Vicky chuckled before giving me a playful bite on my neck.

"Huh?" I asked, chuckling.

"Yeah, no more dreaming about big titties. Unless those titties belong to us." Sarah laughed as she poked her chest out.

"Well, if they are a good pair, who can blame me." I chuckled. My hands reached out, grabbing an imaginary pair in the air, giving two quick squeezes. My hands fell to my sides.

"Shame on you. We might have to punish you for being a bad boy." Vicky laughed as she poked me in the rib.

"I say we pour cold water on his thingy until it shrivels up." Sarah laughed. Her hand reached down, gripping my member roughly, then released it.

"Damn, that's a bit rough." I gasped with a slight chuckle.

"Rough, huh? You haven't seen rough. Better only be dreaming about us from now on." Vicky laughed. Her fingers gave my nipple a light pinch.

"Uh-huh. Let's get some sleep." I feigned a playful, hurt tone before my voice eased. I moved us up further on the bed.

"Sleep...yeah." Vicky playfully hissed as we all laid back down.

"Good night, Master," Sarah said as she fell on me, cuddling around my right side.

"Good night, my beauties," I said, folding my arms around them.

"We'll keep you warm and safe tonight, Master," Sarah reassured me as she nuzzled into me.

"Sweet dreams, Master. When you wake up, we will make sure you feel completely loved and cherished," Vicky said, her body cuddled in close to me on the left.

"I love you both," I said with elation.

"We love you, Master," they whispered in unison.

"The light..." Sarah said but was soon interrupted by Vicky.

"Leave it, we can sleep like this," Vicky explained as she eased into me further.

I closed my arms around them. I was happy that it was only a nightmare. My life with Sarah and Vicky was peaceful... more loving than what I had endured at war. I kissed their foreheads one by one. My beauties, I loved them more than I knew how to say. Relaxing back into the serenity of my girlfriends, I drifted back asleep.

Chapter 17: A Terrible Monday

When I woke up that morning, I didn't want to leave. It was the first workday after moving them in. I just wanted to stay with them in the blissful state that I experienced with them. Sarah had left for her corporate office before I'd opened my eyes. Vicky was cuddled deeply around me; she didn't have a client until around nine.

This was the first time I was alone with one of them. I couldn't help but want to explore how things were one-on-one. My fingers traced along her skin. As she lay there in a slumber, the toned flesh felt so wonderfully enticing under my fingertips. I cupped her breast, kneading it softly. My thumb drew harsh circles around her nipple, then my hand traveled further down. I passed her navel, and my fingers were about to find her soft paradise. My hand was abruptly halted before I could reach the cave for exploration.

"Master, you have work. We can play later." Vicky's hand gripped my wrist. I was frustrated, but she was right. Reluctantly, I removed my hand.

As I peered deep into her ocean pools, a charged, yet loving look fell upon me. She smiled at me as she shook her head. Her disheveled morning hair still garnered the mystique of a dark veil.

"I know. You are curious to see what it's like with each of us. One-on-one. And if you didn't have to be at work in less than thirty minutes, I would... But you gotta go. Now get your ass to work, dirty boy." Vicky giggled before dozing off to sleep.

I begrudgingly rolled off the bed and made my way to the shower. The water rained down upon me. A warm feeling coursed through my heart, as if they had consumed all of my darkness.

I spent most of the last two days learning about their habits. Vicky cutely pursed her lips when she brushed her hair. Sarah would bob her head side to side, like a child, when she ate sweets.

Vicky had set up her easel in the kitchen. I had fun watching her dance around the canvas with her headphones on. She was wild and free, jamming out as she painted a mountain scene.

Sarah's eyebrows stayed raised the entire time she read her book. She seemed to hang on the edge of each sentence. I had spent some of the time learning how to braid Sarah's hair. She loved the treatment, and so did I.

The cute noises, strange faces. All of it. Those small details about them made me fall further in love with them. I was now getting to see more of their daily routines. And sex was not a scarcity anymore. Tiredness racked my body, but satisfaction tethered to my smile.

I shook my mind back to reality. I needed to be responsible. I needed to provide for them. Besides, it wasn't much longer before I would work with my own business. The capital had been acquired, as had the licenses and partner agreement. It was all legal. Howard and I would be getting together next week to pick up a work truck. I wanted to be dependable for them.

I dressed, clearing my head for work. A moment later, I was out the door. Hastily, I scurried into work. On my way in, I couldn't help but feel that I was without... a longing that I couldn't place. I always felt this when I wasn't around Sarah and Vicky. I walked in the door of the company holding my head higher than I ever had.

"Wow, Kyle. You look different. More..." Myra smiled at me as she trailed off.

I smiled back at her. "Thank you. You look lovely as always." Each word was a product of the high I was on from Vicky and Sarah.

All the time I had worked here, she'd never once smiled at me. Not once. Every time I passed her desk to punch in, she had a very stern face. Almost like she was a "strictly business" person, though there was that time when she saw me come in late and didn't rat me out. She had complimented me that day. I walked past her, smiling.

I thought of Vicky's birthday party as I walked toward the meeting room for the morning briefing and my assignments.

Focus, Sergeant. Time to get serious. You have work today. Mr. McKellen had mentioned something about a big job planned for this week. I walked into the briefing room. Most of the apprentices looked up to me since I always cared for them. And I wasn't afraid to get my hands dirty by doing the work beside them. I had hoped to get the chance to work with them, maybe on this project.

The morning briefing was about the big job. We were putting in four twenty-ton rooftop units, and several smaller ones. The contract was for the new research facility. Of course, it had to be an ITI building. I couldn't escape Stephen, not even for one week. I was annoyed that the job was for ITI, but I bit my tongue.

During the meeting, Mr. McKellen was so excited about the job. The contract would guarantee more commercial work with even bigger companies. I had hoped he would've put one of the other journeymen on it, but instead, he announced that I would oversee this project. I was agitated by the very thought.

I tried to get out of it but to no avail. Mr. McKellen just winked at me and said that no one else was qualified. I was sure he was talking about my connection to CEO Stephen Dolion. Such a glorious title for such a massive douche.

I didn't argue. I knew he wasn't going to let me off the hook. I couldn't blame him; I was his client's brother-in-law, after all. Well, soon *not* to be. Mr. McKellen most likely thought that some form of nepotism would gain him further high-yielding contracts. I didn't protest any further. I just got in my van and went to the work site.

The crane operator was already there. I immediately got out and started directing him. The system was chained up to the arm.

I started thinking about chains. The old ball and chain. My proposal. And Vicky's birthday was this week. Would that be a great time to propose? She said that her mother might be there. And Sarah's parents were in Florida. Maybe wait until I meet their parents. I knew next to nothing about my in-laws. Is that the right word? The crane pulled up the unit with a booming sound. This shook me from my thoughts.

I watched the crane move the machine up. The arm extended over the building. I began directing him to the place where the system needed to go.

"Over to the left just a bit!" I yelled out to the crane operator waving my arms. "Good, right there, let it down!"

I watched my crew guide the massive machine into place. As the crane lowered it onto the building, I felt relieved. The first one was set, so all the other work could begin: electrical, economizers, ductwork, heat strips, all the fun. I hoped that Stephen did not show up while I was working on this project. I really couldn't be bothered by his gloating or taunting, or whatever his stupid face would do.

The day moved along well. The install crew that McKellen had hired for this job was skilled. I was amazed at how quickly they were getting things done. I had only worked with these guys once before, on another install job, but they were quite impressive.

"Kyle, can you help me?" David asked as I walked past him. He seemed to be having trouble with the thermostat wires.

David was a part of the install crew; his short dark hair was always messy. I had often seen him in and out of the office. His uniform was always dirty as if he had rolled in the mud all day. But I knew that he was a hard worker. And most likely his clothes stayed dirty due to him doing more than his share of the work. I could see a young Private in David's face. He would have made a fine soldier.

"Sure, what's up?" I asked.

"These wires... I'm colorblind." He seemed discouraged.

I could see the feeling of hopelessness in his eyes. In the Army, this was common; a good portion of soldiers were colorblind. Someone was always asking for help with colors. It was hard to believe that lifestyle. That person was no longer me. Service members from the GWOT generation were the first soldiers... the first war that was an entirely volunteer force, at least since 1776. I felt a dire need to help him.

"No problem. Let me see what we have." I quickly identified each wire and marked them for him.

"Anything else?" I asked. My mind was half on the ductwork.,

"No sir, thank you," he said as he hastily returned to his work.

Making my way to the scissor lift, I rode it up to the ceiling. There was another crew member on the lift with me. As the guys below raised the duct lift with our first run of the square duct, we were readying to mount it. We screwed it in place and moved down to the next area. Even though I was the journeyman, I didn't like to just watch. I helped where I could.

Two hours went by as we continued to hang the square ducts. I looked along the row of metal boxes that were meticulously connected. It looked like a three-dimensional puzzle being constructed. Like large Legos that had been suspended from the ceiling. Seeing progress in real time gave me a sense that our efforts were accomplishing something big. An achievement to be proud of. That's one of the reasons I liked this career: I could build the world with my hands. Well, maybe not the world, but at least someone's air conditioning.

As I was admiring the work, my crew readied the next run of ductwork. They started hoisting it up to us on the duct lift. Anxiously waiting, the crew member and I were ready to connect it and strap it to the beams. Then I heard it. A voice I knew all too well echoed in the empty building. Oh crap.

"I'm looking for the boss man. Do you know where I can find him?" Stephen leaned down to David. Without looking up from his work, David pointed in my direction.

I watched Stephen's head shoot up; his eyes tracked to me. That crisp suit looked wildly out of place with all these rugged blue-collar workers. I shook my head. This was the exact thing that I wanted to avoid, but here he was, all buck-fifty of his thin frame. My brows furrowed as my hand moved the controls. The lift descended. The feeling... the rage of a fight was festering deep inside me.

"I've got to talk with the client," I said to the duct crew. I motioned one of them to take my place on the lift. As the lift collapsed back completely, I stepped off. My replacement quickly moved past me and mounted the scissor lift.

"Mr. Dolion, what can I do for you?" My voice was smooth and cold. My eyes stayed on him, and my jaw clenched.

"That's no way to greet your brother, Kyle." Stephen looked disappointed and even a bit hurt by my coldness.

I glanced over at the crew; they seemed taken aback by him calling me brother. I fixed my gaze back to Stephen. He wasn't going to provoke me; I wouldn't let him. Not on the job. Calm it down, Sergeant. Just breathe. Remaining silent, my demeanor and stance tensed. I squared off with him. My shoulders were much larger than his puny frame. Seeing that I wasn't going to respond to his last comment, he continued.

"Can you go over the blueprints with me? I don't quite understand the area around the server room." He moved his hand out to place it on my shoulder.

Without thinking, my arm blocked his hand, shoving it back. I heard a gasp from several of the crew members. I didn't look back at them, but I knew that they were in shock by this encounter. Most likely they did not understand the undertones of this interaction. How could they? They didn't know my connection to Stephen. Mr. McKellen only knew because it was Stephen who had introduced me to him. As much as I hated to admit it, Stephen got me this job.

"Whoa, brother. Are you okay? You seem tense?" The look in Stephen's eyes as he said that was of deep concern.

Why was he playing? We both knew this was a charade. You just want to get close to me, again. A lazy attempt to make Elle come back to you. It wasn't enough that you beat my sister. Destroyed her self-esteem. Took my niece. Now you have to harass me at my job. I felt like bashing his skull open just to see what was inside it. No, Sergeant. Remain professional. Deep in the recesses, I pushed all of my anger, all of my hatred, back. I feigned the fakest smile I could.

"I'm fine. Sorry about that. Reflexes." My voice kept its chilly tone.

"Okay. So, can we discuss this server room?" He started walking away from the crew. I followed him with deep regret. I didn't want to be around him. But I also didn't want his antics to be in front of my crew. I needed to stay professional.

We approached the area where I had laid out the blueprints. I had built a makeshift table out of plywood and sawhorses. I moved over to the plans, and my hand shuffled to the server room. I placed it on the top of the stack and slammed my hand down, startling Stephen. Fuming, my eyes peered over at him in anticipation of his professional concerns.

"So, this server room needs to maintain a constant sixty-eight degrees year-round. We are moving in the organoid intelli— I mean the most advanced and state-of-the-art systems." Stephen pointed to the blueprint.

"Yeah... I know how a server room works." I huffed, not needing him to explain my job to me.

We stood in silence. His eyes studied mine for a moment. I couldn't tell if he was sizing me up for a fight or trying to beckon me for a kiss. Was he going to hit on me? Or hit me? I shook my head in disgust. Either way, I really didn't care. I just wanted to be done with this. I wanted to go back to work, back to my crew. He looked up from the blueprints and pursed his lips, as if he were in deep thought for a moment. Then his voice broke the silent standoff.

"How are you getting along with Vicky and Sarah?" Stephen surprisingly asked. Hearing their names from his lips felt dirty... disgusting even.

"How is Naomi?" I retorted in a sarcastic voice.

"Wouldn't know. She has been abroad for a while." He seemed shocked that I had finally figured out his connection to my lovelies.

"Is she the one you're having an affair with?" He stared at me for a moment. Hurt and confusion filled his eyes.

"Kyle, you don't understand. You don't understand my situation with Elle." He looked at me, pleading for my concern.

"I don't understand what? That you beat on your wife, my sister? That you took her only child away from her?" My eyes were seared with an overwhelming disdain for this man.

He took a few steps back. A single tear fell down his cheek. Looking at me with a sense that he no longer held my grace, he sighed. Hanging his head low, he sniffled before returning to a stern posture. As the tear faded from his chin, he smiled again.

"Anyway, the board wanted me to take a hands-on approach to this server room." He eyed me, and I could tell he was attempting to maintain a professional composure, similar to how I was trying to keep my professional bearing. "I just wanted to clear up some things about the construction. Some details that may have been overlooked. Maybe I was too late." The smile on Stephen's face seemed forced. Without another word, he turned to walk away.

My mind wandered off. I figured his last statement wasn't about the server room. He most likely wanted me to feel sorry for him. He seemed so broken. So pitiful. How was he broken? He did this. He chose to get drunk. Chose to hit Elle. Went after Jenny. Then he took Jenny. That was him, all him. He had no right to feel broken. No goddamned right at all.

My fists balled; I wanted to dole out a heavy dose to him for trying to pull at my heartstrings. At this moment, waterboarding started to not seem like a war crime. I needed to focus.

Fazed by this situation, I briefly turned my attention to the pedestrians across the street. My thoughts merged with life after service. I watched as those people trampled on.

Hurry off, civilians. You will never know what it took, what sacrifices were made for you. The screams of all those yielded for your freedoms. The pain of those that shielded you. The nameless that had died for you. We were pathetic savages. But when you needed us most, we were there. When the monsters were at the door, we became your sheepdogs. We had slain for you, vanquishing your woes. And now... now I couldn't even end Stephen.

I couldn't believe the thoughts I was having. It wasn't their fault that I signed on the dotted line. That I chose to join. And the fight wasn't on them. That was on those man-dress-wearing psychopaths. My inaction to Stephen wasn't their fault either.

Wallowing in my sorrow for Elle, my heart... my soul felt disgraced. Why couldn't I just thrash him? He had been such a monster to my family. But now, he seemed to need redemption. Sorry, Stephen, I am all out of redemption. It seemed I was all out of punishment as well. You would get no peace, either way, from me.

As I glanced over the crowd on the street one last time, I saw Howard. He was briskly walking into the coffee shop on the corner. Coffee sounded nice. And I needed a break. I moved without thinking. Before I knew it, I'd crossed the busy street, and my hand had pulled open the door. I held it for a young lady before finally entering. Howard spotted me the second I stepped inside.

"Bro, what ya doin' here?" Howard's voice was a soothing relief. And his smile was a stark contrast to the emotions inside.

"Getting coffee. What else, fuckface?" I laughed.

"Shit, thought ya was a groupie stalker for a second." He said as he held up his cup.

I smiled; this smile was genuine. In the few minutes I'd spent with Stephen, I'd almost forgotten that I could smile for real.

"Be there in a minute. Lemme get an espresso." As I stood in line, I took out my phone and texted the group chat. I needed a pick-me-up.

[Master] Monday 11:38
Was thinking about you 2 earlier
Wanted to aggravate you

[Sarah] Monday 11:39
Never an aggravation, Master ☺

[Vicky] Monday 11:40
Trying to tie us up, huh ☺

[Master] Monday 11:40
You would bite through the rope

[Vicky] Monday 11:41
Tru but would be fun ☺

199

[Sarah] Monday 11:41
Dirty… both of you

[Master] Monday 11:42
Me? Never

[Vicky] Monday 11:42
Huh 😊

When I glanced up from the blue glow, I was next up. I ordered my drink without incident. The girl behind the counter grinned, but I could see the pain it masked. Her mousy brown hair was pulled back into a ponytail. Her face seemed to be lamenting something. I dared not comment or ask about what was bothering her. Adding a twenty to the tip jar, her face sparkled. My smile widened, knowing that I had made her day better.

I seated my tired ass across from Howard. After placing my hot coffee on the table, my index finger pulled my collar down over my left pec. "Autograph my tiddy, oh, great and powerful Howard." I laughed as I released my shirt collar.

"Fucken' knew ya was a groupie." He chuckled with a boom.

"What are you doing here, anyway?" This didn't seem like his normal type of hangout.

"Shit, was about to ask ya the same. But me, thinking 'bout buying this place." He motioned around us. "Wanted to check it out for myself."

"See that mess over there." I pointed across the street to the construction site. "Installing some units on it."

Howard looked out the window for a moment. He seemed to be in awe of the construction site across the road. Then his gaze fell back on me.

"Have you heard any rumors of organ… um… organoid something or other?" My words stumbled, trying to remember what Stephen had slipped up saying.

"Nah. Don't sound familiar. Is that some kind of comic or sumten else nerdy?" Howard replied with sarcasm.

I blew on my espresso to cool it. "Just something I overheard. Thought the investor rumor mill might have something on it." I shrugged.

Howard took a sip of his coffee. "Hey, was thinking of askin' ya if ya wanted to be partners on this place. Guess I didn't have to drag ya ass here."

I looked around at the establishment. The shop was small, but I had noticed traffic in and out all day. There were five four-seat tables on the floor space, most of which were empty. But the line at the counter never seemed to dissipate. Could be a good investment. I sipped on my espresso, thinking about the possibility.

Maybe I should talk this over with Sarah and Vicky. I didn't want to jump into big decisions without their counsel. What a great way to start a relationship. "Honeys, I'm home. Oh, I bought a coffee shop with all of our savings." Yeah, smooth. At least get the information so that they can help make an informed decision.

"How much to buy in?"

"Lemme get the contract out." He reached under the table, pulling up a briefcase. It was older; the leather on the exterior had seen better days. Cracks had formed throughout the dark brown hide. Light danced along the metallic clasp. The initials "L.J.N." shimmered. I assumed this case had some sentimental value to him.

He ruffled through several papers that had been stowed in the case. I could see that he read the headers of each before placing them in a neat stack upside down on the table. Then he pulled out one near the middle of the stack. His finger flicked it, as if in victory.

"This one, bro. Half of what's on the contract." He said with a victory in his voice as he handed me the paperwork.

Silence pierced the air between us as I read over the document. I scanned every line so that I could fully understand the complete deal. We would get this shop and another one in a county about an hour or so away.

The price, even if my part was half, was nearly the rest of what I had in my savings. Did I want to take the chance? Take a risk with the rest of what I had spent my entire adult life saving? I definitely had to talk with my girlfriends about this. I looked up at Howard, he seemed distracted. His eyes were on his phone, his fingers blazing with texts.

"Let me think about it, bro. I really want to go in halfsies with you, but I need to think about it for a day or two." I said as I returned the contract to him.

He looked up from his phone, his eyes sparkling with joy.

"Okay, bro. But will have da suits make a new contract. Just in case." He nodded at me, taking the contract back.

"By the way, fucker, you still gotta help me get the girls furniture." I laughed.

"Yeah, yeah. Be by later with da truck."

"How is your mom doing?" I asked, my hand swirled my cup.

"Mom is doin' betta, still sick though." He said in a low voice. His lips curled into a coy smile as he glanced down at his phone.

"That's good, bro. I hope she gets well soon."

"Hey, has Elle said anything?" He seemed nervous to ask. I knew he was fishing for information about her.

"Just that the divorce was on track." I shrugged. My face uncontrollably smirked an evil grin. I quickly forced my grin down before it gave something away.

Elle confessed to me last week that she had been flirting with Howard at our breakfast, but I didn't want him to blow it up into something more. At least not for now. She needed to heal from Stephen. I wasn't trying to block him. I just wanted things to be more concrete, more stable for them. She might treat him like a rebound, and I couldn't see either one hurt by that.

His eyes stared deep into mine for a moment. I was pretty sure that he could read that I was hiding something. But he didn't say anything. He just smiled to himself.

"Well, gotta go." Howard stood after he placed all the paperwork back into his briefcase.

"Me too." I looked back at the construction site with contempt.

As we made our way out of the shop, we gave each other a fist bump. Our farewell was short-lived as he hurried off. I was sure he wanted to check on his mom.

Walking back across the busy road, I saw that fancy sci-fi car still parked next to the work trucks. I couldn't go back there, not right now. I had just briefly forgotten about Stephen's awkwardness. The overwhelming feeling—need—that I had to wreck his body with as much pain as I could. I lazily made my way to my van.

It was too early to attempt to clock out for the day. Instead, I drove around for a while. I needed to avoid that place. To avoid Stephen. If I had stayed, I might've had some new jewelry in the form of handcuffs, with a red-and-blue light show escorting me to my new abode: a cold jail cell.

I found a park on the edge of the city. I needed to take a walk. With some form of exercise, I might feel better. I started down the pathway. My thoughts were still on kicking Stephen into oblivion.

As I walked by the park benches, I heard a man's withered voice. I looked over. "Anything will help. I am so hungry."

The man seemed to be middle-aged; age lines had formed on his face and hands. His ratty clothes were tattered and torn. He had a weary and downtrodden look in his eyes. I felt bad for him. I wanted to help. I pulled out my wallet. All I had left in cash was a hundred-dollar bill. Without another thought, I held it out to him.

"Here you are, sir. Please get a meal and a warm place for the night." I attempted to console him as I smiled at him.

"Thank you, son, thank you. Name's Jerry." His voice filled with a hopeful tone. He smiled oddly at me as he stood.

"Well, have a great day, Jerry. I hope things get better." I nodded at him.

He reached out, grabbing my palm and gripping it tightly. His other hand clasped on the outside of my hand, and I was caught between both of his strong grips. I felt powerless as I tried to pull my hand free. But struggling with him was pointless. He had me in a good lock, I couldn't break free. I watched him, my left hand ready to strike if needed.

"You know, they cloned sheep a while back. The sheep died. I don't think it was from a defective clone. Maybe those scientists were just heartless. Creating life, you have to love it. Love is just as essential for life as food or water. Without love, all things die. So, be sure to love those in your life, son." He gave me a slight smile as he released my hand, stepping away with the hundred in his fingers.

That was so bizarre. I shook my head. He was strong, way stronger than me. And that crap he said. Sheep... Clones... The only thing that I agreed with was his sentiment about love. Love was just as essential as food and water. I did love Sarah and Vicky. With all my heart, my being. I returned to the van. I didn't want to encounter another crazy person, so I decided to drive around again.

After a while, my temperament had completely calmed. My thoughts fell back to my lovelies. Mrs. Helderman would come over for dinner later. And I was sure that my girlfriends would make something really delicious. Vicky had yet to cook, so I wondered what her food would taste like.

When I made it to the office to turn in the van, Mr. McKellen wasn't there; only Myra was in the office. She didn't question me. She just beamed.

"Have a good night, Kyle. And like I have always said, if you need anything, don't hesitate to call me," she said in a soft tone.

Her skin radiated a glow that I had never noticed. She had lipstick on, which she never wore. At least I hadn't seen her wear any before. Come to think of it, she didn't have any on this morning. Why did she doll herself up? Did she have a date?

"Thank you, Myra. Have a great night." I nodded and smiled back at her before turning on my heels.

I moved quickly to escape Myra's stare. This was the first time I had seen her smile in that office. I didn't want to spoil her good mood with my angst against Stephen. I surely didn't want to explain that I had left the job site early. I would let her have a happy day.

I drove home, relieved of my encounter with Stephen. As the streets passed by, I could feel my soul starting to balance again. My powerful love for my girlfriends replaced those powerful and hateful emotions against Mr. Dolion.

As I parked, I saw Howard's truck in a spot next to mine. A newer Chevy Silverado. He was standing beside it, motioning me to get in. Without a word, I locked my beater and jumped in the passenger's seat.

We rushed off in his pickup before Vicky or Sarah could get home. I wanted to surprise them by having the dressers and nightstands ready for them. I needed to see their faces when they came home, finding the pieces they wanted from their old apartment here. As we drove to get the furniture, we talked.

The conversation was mainly about that coffee shop. He was excited to buy it. I found out that he wanted that shop because his mother once worked there. She was a barista when his father met her. His father had stopped in right after court, on his way back to the office. He was a junior legal aid, not quite a lawyer yet.

I was right about the briefcase; it was his father's. The same one he was carrying the day he met Mrs. Nolan. Knowing why he wanted it gave me second thoughts about the investment.

"I feel a little awkward about going in on the shop. I mean, it holds more than monetary value for you." I looked over at him from the passenger seat.

"Nah, bro. It's all good. I know that ya will treat it with respect and care." He glanced at me before returning his eyes to the road.

"Why bring me in on this? You have more than enough money to buy it a million times over."

"'Cause we're bros. Gets lonely maken' money with no one to share it with." He choked up; I wasn't sure if he was going to cry.

I understood that lonely feeling. This coffee shop would be another concrete connection between us. A way for us to work together, to have a commonality besides loneliness. Business was his superpower. His way of sharing the strongest part of himself with me. A bonding experience that he knew and was comfortable with. Maybe it's why he helped fund my HVAC business.

My mind bent to my own loneliness. It had recently been smoldered out. But his loneliness was still there. He still had a piece of himself missing.

"I can see that. I have been lonely most of my life." I said, attempting to reassure him.

"Yep, that's why we're bros. Two peas 'n a carrot... all that." He chuckled. I was pretty sure he messed up that comparison, but I just chuckled back.

We pulled up to Vicky and Sarah's old apartment. I had the key in my pocket; they didn't have to turn it in until Friday. But I wanted to finish the move for them. It felt nice to finalize the previous chapter and start the rest of our happily ever after.

Wow. That thought was a far cry from those days in battle. I thought my end would be at the wrong side of a weapon. Now I wanted to die an old man. An old man in the arms of my beloved wives. Did these fairy tales truly exist? Was I in one? My heart only hoped that I was. Yes, a sexy kinky fairy tale.

"Ya okay, bro? Ya got that thousand-yard stare 'gain." Howard looked at me with deep concern.

"Do you believe in fairy tales? Sexy fairy tales?"

"Da fuck? Ya mean like love or sumten?" A knowing look crossed his face as he stared at me.

"Yeah. Like some kind of happily ever after." I couldn't contain my grin.

"For ya... yes. The way those girls look at ya. Any fool can tell they love ya. For me... well... don't know if it's in the cards." He looked down at the dashboard. His eyes seemed to water up for a moment.

"Maybe it is. Your hand is not played out. Besides, cards have a way of changing." I patted his shoulder, trying to comfort him.

"We'll see." His head shot up. "For now, let's get ya girls' stuff."

It didn't take long to get the dressers and nightstands. They had a downstairs apartment, so there were no cumbersome areas to navigate. We grabbed the dressers first, tilting them over. Howard grabbed the top and me at the bottom. We lugged them onto the bed of the truck. Then the nightstands. In the back of the truck, they fit neatly. We strapped them down to secure them in place.

I looked around the empty apartment. This was where my beauties had called home for most of the past half-decade. I wondered how they felt leaving it behind. Now our homes were with each other. I double-checked that I had locked the door. In no time, we were back in the truck, off to deliver the furniture.

"Shit, bro, I am so excited for ya." Howard had a broad smile on his face as he started the truck.

"Thanks, bro. I would be lying if I said I wasn't a bit scared." The road ahead seemed long, yet I knew that the destination was home. Home to them.

"Bro, ya just moved ya girls in. 'Course ya scared. But I know things will be a'ight." He chuckled. I could sense he was happy for me, and maybe a bit jealous. I decided to throw him a bone.

"I will give you Elle's number. But…" I trailed off. How could I tell him that he needed to wait a while, that it might be too soon without causing him more pain? "But you have to promise that, for now, you will just be her friend." I looked over at him, his smile didn't falter. It seemed to grow wider.

"I can be her friend. Told ya before, I won't do anything without ya blessing." Howard kept his eyes on the road. He really was a good man. Awkward and obnoxious but a good man.

We were pulling into the parking lot when I spotted the strange sci-fi car passing us. Stephen. Why was he here at my building? It wasn't as if anything needed to be said between us. I thought our confrontation earlier was enough. The jaded feeling started to rise inside me again when Howard broke the awkwardness.

"Bro, time to get this up there." He said as he patted my shoulder. I didn't say a word; I just nodded.

Even though the dressers were cumbersome up the stairs, we quickly got everything in the apartment. Not long after, Howard and I said our goodbyes. I typed Elle's number in his phone. He smiled and took his leave.

I went into the bedroom, moving the dressers in place. I slid the nightstands by each side of the bed. That's when I noticed them. They had neatly placed them on the pillows. The stuffed tiger was on the pillow that Vicky had claimed. And the stuffed crane was on the side that Sarah had cozied to. I smiled; they had placed their cherished gifts on the bed. I guess it was their way to always have a piece of me to sleep beside.

I began looking around the apartment. They'd finished unpacking everything. When did they do this? I took out my phone.

[Vicky] Monday 16:49
One more client
Will be home in a bit

[Sarah] Monday 16:49
Okay on my way home to start unpacking
Get us settled in

[Sarah] Monday 17:23
Master, where are you? Car is here but no
Master.
Halfway through unpacking

[Vicky] Monday 17:42
Leaving last client

[Sarah] Monday 17:45
Got us unpacked but Master is still gone

[Master] Monday 18:12
I am in the apartment, where are you 2

Just as I had pressed send on the last message, the door burst open. Sarah rushed in, her face paler than normal. Vicky, behind her, had a stern look on her face. Mrs. Helderman trailed in last.

"Good evening girls. Evening Wanda." I bowed to them.

"Good evening? Where were you?" Vicky questioned in a scolding tone.

"Oh, Master, you are okay." Sarah's tone was relieved, and as the worry on her face dissolved, she smiled.

"Hmm..." Mrs. Helderman looked at me with a sense of disdain.

"I went with Howard, to get a surprise for you," I tried to explain while my face gave a self-deprecating smile.

Vicky came over to me, sniffing in harshly. Her nose made a slight whistling sound as she smelled me. I was sure she was trying to find a scent of alcohol. Yet to her surprise, there was no alcohol on my breath.

"Surprise, Master?" Vicky eyed me with challenge in her voice.

I watched all three ladies for a moment. Sarah seemed shaken, Vicky pissed, and Mrs. Helderman had a disappointed look. Vicky and Sarah's faces made me ache in my heart. I wanted to say something to defend myself. But I dared not make the situation worse. Instead, my voice smoothed into that dominant tone.

"In the bedroom. You can look for yourselves." Coolly, my voice was low, but that NCO tone was distinct.

Mrs. Helderman looked at me with a beguiled look. That was the first time she had heard that tone from me. It was funny, her expression was that of a giddy schoolgirl. But she held her elderly composure, though the shock was pinned to her face.

The three of them rushed past me. I watched as they entered the bedroom. They both started chuckling with elation when they saw the dressers and nightstands. However, Mrs. Helderman seemed unmoved. Instead, she let out a disappointed sigh. I wasn't sure what I had done to upset her.

"Thank you, Master," I heard Sarah and Vicky say in unison.

"You're welcome, my lovelies," I said as I walked toward the kitchen. It seemed that the meal had not yet been prepared. Was it that they were too worried about me? Had I caused them that much trouble? I sighed to myself. I was trying to do something nice for them, yet it turned out that I had only worried them. As I was deep in thought, I felt a soft frail hand on my shoulder.

"Boy, we need to talk." I turned to see Mrs. Helderman peering at me with a concerned look. "I told you to be honest with them, yet..." She trailed off as her wise eyes looked away.

I was confused. I hadn't lied to them. I just finished moving them in. What was she talking about? Why did she assume I had lied? Sure, I should have called or texted them. But I hadn't lied.

"I didn't lie to them." My voice cracked with confusion.

"You foolish boy. Honesty isn't always about lies. You didn't tell them where you were going." Mrs. Helderman held a stern gaze.

"No, because it was a surprise." I felt a dull slap across my face from that brittle hand. It didn't hurt, but I was shocked by it.

"They were worried about you, dumb kid." Mrs. Helderman quickly pulled her hand away. She seemed to regret slapping me.

"I didn't mean to worry them." I looked at her with remorse.

"They really love you, you silly boy." Her tone softened. She smiled as her hand returned to my cheek. She tenderly rubbed my face, as if she were trying to lessen the sting from her previous assault. "You are in a completely committed relationship with those two. You are responsible for them. And accountable to them." Mrs. Helderman's voice was low as she stared into my eyes.

Damn, she was right. I was in a committed relationship. And I had failed to communicate my whereabouts. This worried them and caused them pain. I didn't want to cause them any pain.

"What do I do now?" I asked.

"Be a good man. A good 'Master,' as you have them call you." That wrinkled face curled into a smile.

"Master, sorry that the meal wasn't prepared." Sarah's soft voice had that cute baby tone.

"Don't be sorry. It's his own damned fault. Making us worry like that." Vicky sneered, looking at Sarah.

"How about we order Chinese takeout? My treat," I said. I looked at them with a pitiful face, hoping this would make things right. It was a good thing I remembered that place Elle had called a few weeks ago.

"Sure," Vicky said with that dark tone.

"Yes, Master," Sarah said as she bounced. She smiled at me after blowing a kiss to me.

"Chinese sounds... okay." Mrs. Helderman shrugged in agreement before she smiled at me.

I ordered each dish that everyone wanted. As we sat around the living room talking, my mind swirled around the idea of already being responsible. Accountable. How could I have been so dumb not to realize that my absence would cause them pain?

And if I were to propose sometime soon, I would have to do better. My heart smiled through my chest. Propose. The rings, how they would look on those fingers. Those beatific smiles brightly across their beautiful faces. Yes. Propose.

How could I propose? I left my job early today and didn't tell them. What was I worried about? Why didn't I tell them? I felt so comforted by being with them that it erased the day. I had to tell them about my encounter with Stephen. I had to. But not now. For now, we have Vicky's birthday party tomorrow night. I didn't want to muddle that with my personal issues.

Sarah and Howard helped me find a nice restaurant. Then the Italian ice cream shop after. Sarah had told Naomi, so she planned to meet us at the restaurant as a surprise for Vicky. I smiled. The silver necklace I got her would fit her dark goth style well.

Chapter 18: Divine Birthday

Tuesday: Vicky's birthday. Rather than go to work, I avoided it. Last night, I had omitted yesterday's incident from the conversation. I thought it would be best to wait until I could figure out a solution. There was no need to worry them until I had a solid plan.

After Vicky and Sarah left for work, I jumped in my beater. I thought about going to work but instead drove around aimlessly. I felt like a nomad, but this reprieve couldn't keep my mind still.

I worried about how my girlfriends would feel about me avoiding work. Would they be disappointed? It felt as though I was letting them down. If I avoided my job for too long, I could be fired. How would that make Sarah and Vicky feel? To have a jobless bum for a boyfriend. Yeah, what every woman wants, right? Some lazy man mooching off them. I didn't want to think about the realities of being a man. For now, I just wanted to enjoy my relationship.

I started thinking about the real problem: Stephen. I wasn't afraid of him; rather, I was scared of myself. I was frightened that I could not cage the beast inside me, the monster that wanted to rip him limb from limb. I needed to learn to control that side of myself. I would have to confront that part at some point.

After a while, I returned to the apartment and sat on the couch playing a tactical game on my Xbox. I played for a few hours to clear my head of Stephen and the job. Once I'd purged all of that, my mind was focused on the night that we had planned for Vicky.

Howard helped me get reservations at the five-star restaurant downtown on Turtle Creek Boulevard. It wasn't easy to get a table in that place. He had said the French food was exquisite and the dining experience was like a genuine Parisian restaurant. It had better be a great experience. A three-course meal was like a hundred bucks. And the wine pairing, whatever that is, was another hundred bucks. So, each meal would hit my wallet for around two or three hundred dollars. But it was worth treating Vicky to something nice.

After eating, we would hit a gelato cafe for Italian ice cream. Sarah said that gelato was Vicky's favorite type of ice cream. I had never had it, so I wasn't sure how it tasted. But if it was Vicky's favorite, I was willing to try it.

And finally, catch a Viva Dallas burlesque show, which Sarah insisted on. I wasn't sure if a striptease show was a great choice for a birthday, but Sarah was adamant about going. Sarah had an idea that would pique Vicky's more sensual interests. The show would set the mood for what she had schemed up for the nightcap.

The guest list was easy. Birthday girl Vicky, Sarah, myself, Elle, and the surprise guest, Naomi. Howard was hesitant to come, even though he got me the reservation. He told me he feared his crudeness would ruin Vicky's birthday. I sensed shame in his voice. I knew what he meant because I'd experienced that feeling in the past. I thanked him for the reservation and tried to console him. I repeatedly invited him for a week, but he insisted that he sit this one out and to enjoy. I respected his wishes and left the topic alone.

I told Sarah that I would come home early to prepare things for the night. After I had eaten lunch, I set up the bedroom with rose petals on the bed. I pulled out the dresses that I had purchased for Vicky and Sarah. I laid them at opposite corners of the bed. A black cocktail dress for Vicky with black high heels. A blue evening gown for Sarah with blue open-toed heels. And, of course, a three-piece suit and tie for myself. This wardrobe was well worth the cost. My beauties would be adorned in nice dresses. I wanted to treat them like the queens they were.

After setting up for the party, I cleaned the apartment to ensure the night went smoothly. During my cleaning, I received a text.

[Elle] Tuesday 13:23
Will be running late tonight

[Kyle] Tuesday 13:23
Is everything okay

[Elle] Tuesday 13:25
Yeah got new clients that can only meet late

[Kyle] Tuesday 13:26
Kewl, want us to wait for you

[Elle] Tuesday 13:34
No just go ahead to the restaurant
I shouldn't be too late

don't want to delay the birthday girl

[Kyle] Tuesday 13:35
Okay, love you sis

[Elle] Tuesday 13:35
Love ya bro, see you tonight

It took me most of the afternoon to tidy things up for them. Sweeping, mopping, dusting, and laundry were all done in no time. Finally, I took a shower to be fresh and clean for the night.

As I was drying off, I heard the front door. I finished with the towel and poked my head out. Sarah had made it home before Vicky. I strode out nude.

"Master, you are home earlier than I thought," Sarah said as she saw me emerge from the bathroom.

"Yeah, I pulled away around noon today." I felt awkward about the lie but pushed on.

"Well, Master, it looks like you already have everything under control," Sarah said with elated surprise. She was happy that our plan for Vicky's birthday seemed to be going well.

"Your dress and shoes are in the room. And do you know when Vicky will be done with her last client?" I took Sarah's hand, leading her to the bedroom. As we walked, she was giddy, almost skipping.

"Shouldn't be much longer, Master. She said that her schedule was mostly clear this afternoon." Sarah looked at me with that bright smile. We crossed the threshold into the bedroom.

"I hope you like the dress." I let go of Sarah's hand as I motioned to her evening gown.

"Blue! Oh yes! It's lovely. Thank you, Master." Sarah's voice was filled with a loving tone as she picked up the dress.

"Good, I'm glad you like it." I could see the sparkle in her eyes as she admired the dress. "Since Vicky can be here any moment, let's get ready."

We both got dressed quickly in our evening garments. I helped her zip the back of the blue dress. I put on my suit, ensuring my gig line was sharply aligned. I slipped the jewelry box into my coat pocket. Vicky would get the present at the restaurant.

Sarah sat on the bed and handed me her hairbrush. I knew what she wanted. She sat still as I took the brush. The soft scent of her perfume was intoxicating as I started to sweep through her mane. I enjoyed caring for her in this way, and there was something sensual about running the bristles through her fiery locks.

My care of Sarah's hair enthralled us. We both seemed to enjoy our roles in the treatment. I found it strangely intimate to care for them like this. I hadn't bathed them yet, but that was on my list.

"It feels so nice to be pampered, Master." Sarah's voice was a low, soft mewl.

"I love brushing your hair, my sweet," I admitted as I continued to work the brush through her scalp.

Vicky walked into the bedroom. We hadn't heard the front door, I guess because we were both enjoying the brushing. I turned to be met with her smiling face.

"Is that my dress?" Vicky, with a beamish smile, eyed the cocktail dress.

"Yes. Let me finish with Sarah's hair, and I will zip you up." I said as I gave Vicky an adoring look. She hurried over to pick up the dress. She held it up, admiring how it looked against her body.

"Happy birthday, sis," Sarah said as I finished with her hair.

Vickey swooned. "Looks beautiful... and feels soft against my skin. Thank you, Master."

"I'm thrilled that you like it. Happy birthday. Please put it on. We have a night planned for you." I coaxed Vicky. Her eyes swelled with tears of joy. Seeing her so happy filled my heart with love. Without hesitation, she started to pull off her work clothes.

Sarah, satisfied with her hair, planted a kiss on my cheek.

"I always love it when you brush my hair, Master." Sarah's words filled me with a sense of accomplishment. I stared at her momentarily, my eyes peering deep into those green pools of longing. Then I shook my daze.

I stood and moved over to Vicky. She was struggling with the zipper. I smirked. Without hesitation, I zipped up the back of the black dress. "Told you I would get it for you," I said, smiling at her independent spirit.

"I know, Master, but I had to try." Vicky turned to stare into my eyes with love. "So, what are you two planning for me?"

214

"Surprises!" Sarah rejoiced with pleasure as she slid her feet into the open-toed heels. Her cheeks seemed to turn red. I was sure she was thinking about the end of what we had planned.

"Surprises... huh. Okay." Vicky chuckled, shaking her head.

"Yep, surprises. Sarah is driving. You sit in the front seat. Think of us as your personal butler and maid for the night." I chimed in with a playful tone.

"That's weird, but okay," Vicky said as she slipped her heels on.

"Want me to do your hair?" I picked up Vicky's brush.

"Yes, please, Master. Can you braid it?" Vicky looked back at me with a smile.

"Absolutely." It was good that I had been practicing braids on Sarah over the weekend.

I brushed Vicky's dark veil; she moaned softly as I ran the brush through her hair. As soon as it smoothed out, I started a French braid. It felt right to do their hair. Another way that I could care for them. Caressing them with an intimate touch as I ran my fingers through their manes. The braids were loose but still looked good. After I was done, I draped it over her right shoulder.

"What do you think?" I asked, running my hand down Vicky's neck.

"Looks so cute, Master." Sarah squealed with excitement as she admired my braid on Vicky's hair.

"It will do," Vicky said, feigning ambivalence. Then she gazed at me with the look she usually gave me when she was ready to attack me sexually. Later, my sweet. Later.

I looked at the clock: it read sixteen twenty-four hours. "Are we ready? The reservation is in about thirty minutes."

"Going now," they said in unison as their high heels started clacking against the floor.

We hurried to the parking lot. When we got in the Chevy, we took our assigned seats. I was excited as we made our way to the restaurant.

"So, why are we hurrying to a reservation? Where are we going?" Vicky asked.

Sarah briefly looked over at Vicky before returning to the road. "You know that French place you have always wanted to eat at?"

"Yeah... wait, no way! Really!" Vicky smiled at Sarah.

215

"Yes way! I got us a reservation with my connections." I beamed; it was fun watching her get excited.

"Connections, huh…" Vicky side-eyed me with a chuckle.

"Just be sure to keep some room for gelato afterward," I advised as I leaned forward in the backseat.

"Five-star dinner… gelato… Anything else I need to know about?" Her question was filled with enthusiasm.

"Maybe…" Sarah darkly chuckled as she focused on the road.

"A late-night show for a finale. It should be a fun night," I said as I patted the necklace case in my pocket.

"Thank you. Both of you. Thank you." Vicky said softly. I saw in her face that she felt so loved.

"Oh, Elle will be running late. She got new clients," I explained; I had almost forgotten about Elle's texts from earlier.

"No worries. As long as she makes it, I'll be fine." Vicky said, her hand turned the dial on the radio, blaring rock music.

In no time, we had pulled up to what looked like a castle. The building was creamy white. The accents looked like Gothic architecture. There was a covered walkway with a red carpet. It was a fairy-tale restaurant, the kind of place that only the elite or movie stars might frequent.

The valet approached the car. We exited the vehicle and started toward the entrance. I held out my arms, and they both locked their elbows into mine. I felt like Prince Charming, escorting his lovely princesses to the ball.

The sharp-dressed man at the front desk looked at me. "Good evening. Reservation?" He seemed a bit puzzled. I was pretty sure it was the Chevy that we'd just valeted.

"Yes. Forester. Kyle Forester," I said, as I watched him. He looked down at his book; his finger traced down the page, then looked up at me with a smile.

"Right this way, sir." He motioned us in.

As he escorted us into the restaurant, Sarah giggled. Vicky was scanning the room, her face bright with a large smile. Yes, my loves, you are my queens who deserve this and so much more.

I looked around. The room seemed simple yet had large arched windows on one side. The stained glass of each window broke the sunshine into a colorful spectrum across the room. Paintings adorned the walls. The coffered ceiling had beautiful and ornate trim. An artisanal marble fireplace with carved cherubs sat at the end of the room. Smooth jazz softly played throughout the dining area. This place felt sophisticated and elegant. A place worthy of my beauties.

We were seated at a table near the fireplace. I looked over at Vicky and Sarah. Both seemed to enjoy the atmosphere. The light of the fire danced along their faces, making them seem like goddesses. The host motioned for the waiter. The waiter approached from the left side, his black suit tailored to fit his thin frame. The nice suit contrasted his pale complexion.

"How are we starting the night off, sir? Wine?" The waiter looked at me; his light blue eyes had a knowing look.

"Yes, what would you suggest?" I did my best to hide my embarrassment from inexperience. I didn't know what to expect. This was the first time I had been to a place like this. And I didn't want to seem like a putz in front of Sarah and Vicky.

"Château Margaux. A 1980 vintage. A white wine, sir," he suggested as he nodded at me; his kindness told me that no matter what, I was tipping him well tonight.

I nodded. "Sounds great. Thank you." He had just saved me from trying to figure out wines, which I knew nothing about.

"Good choice, sir. I'll have it right out," he said and walked off.

"Wine? Wow, fancy birthday party." I heard a woman's voice coming from the side of the table. I looked over. A shapely young woman who seemed taller than me stood beside us. She was wearing a green dress. Her ginger hair was in two long braids that rested on each shoulder.

"Hi, Mom. This is my boyfriend, Kyle." Vicky introduced me to her mother. She stood to hug the woman briefly, then sat down.

This was Naomi? Vicky's mother? She didn't look a day over thirty. Like she had found the fountain of youth or something. It was amazing that she had a daughter who was turning twenty-four.

"Mama Naomi! Happy to see you; this is also my boyfriend, Kyle." Sarah jumped from her seat as she hugged Naomi tightly.

"So, you are dating both my daughters? Interesting." Naomi chuckled a bit as she smirked at me. I stood and shook her hand.

"Yes, ma'am. Both. Nice to meet you." Stammering, I simpered shyly. She must've thought I was a horndog.

"Well, sit down. No need to be formal." Naomi nodded at the table as she released my hand. She sat opposite me. I was sure she did so to gauge what kind of man I was.

"How was your trip abroad?" I asked, nervously trying to move the subject away from me dating my two girlfriends.

"Fine. Germany is a bore at times, but my work keeps me interested," Naomi said with a sigh in her voice.

"Germany? I thought you had a shareholders meeting?" Vicky asked; she seemed agitated.

"Not really a shareholders meeting. I was researching some new tech. May need to go back sometime soon." Naomi shrugged, ignoring Vicky's agitation. She was hiding something, but I wasn't sure what it was. An affair... with Stephen, maybe?

"So cool. Mama Naomi, you are awesome." Sarah's excitement rang out.

"Sir, your wine." The waiter politely interrupted as he held out the bottle.

"Yes, thank you," I said, trying to ignore the growing tensions between Vicky and her mother. The waiter started pouring glasses. Once he had filled everyone's glass, he placed the bottle on ice in the middle of the table. He then turned to me.

"We are waiting on one more. Can you give us a few minutes until she shows up?" I looked up at him, not knowing the proper etiquette.

"Yes, sir. I will give your guest some time. If you need anything, call me." His voice was low and subservient, yet somehow, it held an air of command.

"Thank you, Albert. We will call when our last guest arrives," Naomi said in a soft tone. Her lavender eyes revealed a sense of familiarity with the waiter. She then picked up her wine glass and looked over at me.

After nodding to Naomi, the waiter walked off.

"So, Kyle, tell me about yourself." Naomi's voice was soft with a sarcastic undertone. I eyed her, grabbing my glass. I swallowed a big gulp of wine. Crap. What do I say?

"Not much to say really. I am a veteran. Work in HVAC now. Mostly a shut-in," I stammered nervously.

"There has to be more to you than that. You are dating both my daughters." Naomi eyed me with intrigue.

218

"He is building a business. An investor picked him up." Vicky jumped into the conversation, saving me.

"Investor?" Naomi looked at Vicky with a puzzled look.

"Yeah, Howard Nolan. He is best friends with Kyle." Sarah clapped excitedly.

"Nolan... wow. That's surprising. He's an oaf but rich. You have an interesting life, son." Naomi looked at me, her eyes staring into my soul. She seemed to be searching for more about me. But tonight was about Vicky.

"Ahem, Vicky, I got you this." I pulled the case from my pocket. My fingers opened it, turning the box toward Vicky. Her eyes lit up as she took the necklace from the case. The silver chain shimmered in the light, and the tiger pendant dangled at the bottom.

"Sarah, can you put it on me? Please." She turned her back to Sarah and handed her the necklace.

"Sure." Sarah quickly grabbed the necklace and placed it on Vicky. Vicky turned around, looking down at the necklace. The corners of my lips raised with elation. I knew the silver would complement the black dress well. Her face was filled with joy.

"Looks good on you," Naomi said before taking a sip of wine.

"Thank you. It looks so pretty." Vicky looked up at me, her face bright with a large smile.

"And it complements your style. The tiger shows your ferocious nature. Since tigers are your favorite animals, it just seemed to make sense," I explained, happy with how it looked on her. And the roaring tiger head seemed to showcase her more dangerous side.

"You remembered. Tigers are my favorite." Vicky blushed, looking down at the table with tears on her cheek. Her finger traced the tiger pendant.

"I remember everything about my beauties." I sighed with a sense of love as I looked between Vicky and Sarah.

"He does love them; bonding seems complete," Naomi whispered to herself. She seemed pleased with the display before her. I felt relieved that she was pleased. At least she hadn't berated me for dating both.

"Wait for your other present... later." Sarah giggled at her own words. She took a sip of the wine. I shook my head, such an innocent dirtiness about her.

"Well, you kids seem to be getting along. Are you planning to marry my lovely daughters?" Naomi asked. Her purple eyes gave me an odd look.

I gulped hard. I picked up my glass again, taking in another swig. Damn, what do I say? How do I respond?

"He hasn't proposed yet. But we sometimes catch him calling us his brides." Vicky chuckled; her eyes sparkled at me.

"He said he was going to marry us. Told his sister at breakfast awhile back," Sarah chimed in, her voice filled with happiness.

I sat quietly, watching Naomi's expressions. She seemed to smile at the idea of marriage and was more than happy to accept the notion of a three-way marriage. Was this normal?

"Hmm... good. Just take care of my girls. You hear?" Naomi pushed her arm toward me, shaking her glass.

"Yes, Miss Schein." I nodded slowly. I saw the waiter out of the corner of my eye.

"Call me Mom. Someday, you're going to be my son-in-law twice over." She chuckled as she brought the glass to her lips, waiting for a moment before taking a sip.

"Yes, ma'am." My voice cracked as I stammered. "I mean Mom."

At that moment, I felt two warm arms wrap around me in a hug.

"Hey, little Bro. Hmm... Happy birthday, Vicky." Elle's voice filled my ears. I saw a disdainful look on Naomi's face as she glared at the person behind me.

"Thank you, Elle." Vicky looked at Elle with a smile.

Elle glanced at Sarah. "And how have you been?"

"Miss Elle! I have been great. Lunch together yesterday was awesome." Sarah bounced gleefully in her seat. Her arm landed on the table, almost knocking her glass to the floor.

"Guess they let any trollop in here these days." Naomi snidely remarked, her eyes burning a hole through Elle.

"Oh, hello, Naomi. Didn't see you there. A five-star place like this and trash at the table. Tsk. Such a pity." Elle sat beside me; her eyes glared back at my future mother-in-law.

"Trash... Hmm. At least I can keep my legs crossed." Naomi let the daggers fly.

"Ahem! Yeah. Um…" I interrupted whatever this was. I didn't want their rivalry to ruin Vicky's special night. "So, Vicky's birthday. We… um… Yeah."

"How is my husband anyway?" Elle took the menu from the waiter as he slid it beside her.

"Enough," I said. "This is Vicky's night." I'd had it with the snark between them. The smooth NCO voice slipped out just enough to calm this down. "Whatever is going on, it can wait for another time."

"Now that… is a manly tone. No wonder my daughters fell for you." Naomi seemed flustered at the sound of my voice. Maybe that NCO voice carried a lot of merit.

I heard the waiter clear his throat. He seemed to want this night to go smoothly, too.

"Your orders, sir?" the waiter asked slyly as he pointed to something on the menu. I looked; it was Entrecôte a steak—a man of good taste.

"Oh, Albert. Prompt service, as always." Naomi cheered as her hands clasped together briefly.

I ordered the house special. I looked over at Vicky and Sarah. Vicky ordered the waiter's recommendation as well, and Sarah, Langouste which was the lobster.

Elle looked at the waiter; she also seemed familiar with him. "I will have Mr. Dolion's usual."

"Miss Schein, would you care for your usual as well?" The waiter asked as he looked at Naomi.

"Please do, Albert. Thank you," Naomi said coquettishly. Her eyelashes fluttered for a moment.

I didn't think about the rivalry anymore. I put it out of my mind. Tonight was Vicky's special night, her birthday. And I was determined to make it a good night for her. Still, I felt a chill in the air. The table seemed awkwardly quiet; it was that way for many minutes. I needed to bring life back to it.

"So, you have new clients?" I asked Elle, who had just finished drinking some wine.

"Eh…" Elle coughed slightly. "Another marriage on the rocks, needing a mediator. That's all I can really say."

"It's so admirable that you help couples find their way back to love," Sarah said. Her finger playfully ran over her wine glass's top as she watched Elle. Her face seemed excited, as if she idolized Elle's profession.

"Sometimes. But mostly, I'm love's Reaper, confirming, for their lawyers, what they'd already decided: to end the relationship," Elle somberly replied. She paused to take a sip of her wine. "Divorce is usually their escape. For every ten couples, I help one reconnect." Her words seemed to reflect her own marital discord.

"But for that one couple, you are the savior of love. Not the Reaper." Sarah beamed, tilting her wine glass to Elle before taking a sip. Elle glanced at her but said nothing.

"Love's Reaper, hmm. No one can kill Love. She is in all living creatures, all that possess a heart," Naomi said, every word spoken slowly and with purpose as she glared at Elle.

Elle looked at her glass for a moment. "It's just the facts of my job..." She trailed off as a saddened expression washed over her face. She released a soft sigh. "I often wonder if people actually know what love is... Or if they are just under an illusion of its allure. From my expertise, love, real, true love is unjustly scarce." She side-eyed me with a look of envy on her face.

Naomi sat quietly, disdainfully watching Elle's expressions. She obviously wanted to say something to Elle, but she held her tongue.

Vicky tilted her head. "That seems to be a calloused way of thinking about it."

Naomi's gaze fell back to me. "Darling, do you view love as jadedly as your sister?" she asked.

"Uh. No, I guess not. This is... uh... my first actual relationship. So..." I stammered nervously before pausing. Being put on the spot after Elle's depressing rambling jarred me. I wondered how to respond properly, express what I truly felt.

The sentiment from that man in the park yesterday came to the forefront. I agreed with him: love is essential to life. I sighed with elation, regaining my composure.

"To me, love is as essential as food and water," I replied with that NCO confidence in my voice.

Naomi seemed happily taken aback as my words came through. She was about to speak, but the waiter interrupted her.

"Sir, your entre." He looked at me with a smile as he placed my plate in front of me.

"Thank you." I nodded at him. I was sure he had just saved me from answering another question.

The waiter continued to serve the dishes. His hands moved with an unworldly grace. He refilled everyone's glasses with wines that seemed to complement their food. I watched as everyone started diving into their meals. After everyone had begun eating, I took a bite of my steak. Wow, it was amazing.

Since everyone was distracted by the first savory bites of their food, this would be a good time to change subjects. I wanted to change it before Elle sullied Vicky's special night further. Besides, this was an excellent opportunity to bring up the coffee shop to my girlfriends.

"Howard wants me to partner with him on buying a coffee shop. Well, I guess two is what the contract is for," I said, steering the conversation to a brighter discussion.

Vicky eyed me with concern. "Coffee shops? Aren't you spreading yourself too thin?"

"Kyle can handle it. Can't you, little Bro?" Elle exclaimed; her hand slapped me on the back.

"Yeah, maybe think about it, Master. Do we have enough to buy it?" Sarah asked, putting a fork full of lobster into her mouth.

"Listen to your brides, darling." Naomi looked at Elle. Her eyes filled with flames as she shot a grim and ominous glare at Elle.

"I'm not sure, but I don't think we will run the shops. And yes, we have just enough to buy in, at least for half." I explained as I shoved a spoonful of mashed potatoes into my mouth.

"I'll give you this, darling; you don't seem scared of risks. A good pick, girls. A keeper." Naomi approved of my brash thinking. She looked at me, and then her face turned sour. "Oh, and darling, this is not the gruel from the barracks. You're a civilized man now. Use the fork." Naomi said sarcastically as she winked at me.

"Uh... yeah. Thanks, Mom." Embarrassment filled my voice as I put the spoon down, replacing it with a fork.

"Ahem." Naomi cleared her throat, then said. "The other fork, darling."

I changed forks, smiling like an idiot as I nodded my head. Everyone around the table seemed uncomfortable. I became leery of eating, wondering what else she would criticize.

Vicky started to chuckle, trying to divert attention from my culinary mishap. "Risks... you don't know the half of it. I have to tell you about how he met Howard."

She began explaining my adventure of becoming friends with Howard. Sarah chimed in, of course, making sure to mention the Harley Quinn bust. The table roared with laughter.

"You mean my pervy brother got a sexy-looking toy... wow." Elle's laughter rang loudly in my ear.

"Hey, at least I know he has what it takes to give me grandchildren. Even if he eats like a barbarian," Naomi chimed in with her soft chuckle and winked at me.

"Whoa, no kids just yet," I said nervously, trying to slow down the talk about children. Yet my mind was reeling at the idea. I looked at Sarah and Vicky. They both would make great mothers.

The somberness and embarrassment that we felt earlier started to fade. The table became filled with stories about my relationship with Vicky and Sarah. They explained more about our dates, how they felt about them, and about moving in with me.

"My heart pounds out of my chest around him," Vicky explained as her sultry eyes fell upon me.

"He is always encouraging us. Always supportive of our dreams. Sometimes, he doesn't say it right. But we know." Sarah chuckled as she winked at me.

"When he asked us to move in, I felt like I had won the lottery," Vicky said before looking down coyishly.

"I wanted to move in that night!" Sarah bubbly beamed with a smile tugging at the side of her lips.

"A month isn't so bad. I once moved in with a guy after two days." Naomi sighed in a swoon as she nodded at me. "Besides, a man like Kyle is a great pick. That waterfall date sounded wonderful."

"Well, it's been nice. Thank you for inviting me. Happy birthday again, Vicky. Enjoy your night." Elle said as she finished her plate.

"Leaving? Already?" Naomi tilted her head as she eyed Elle. That hateful look returned.

"Yeah. Good night, little Bro. Take care of my friends. No pervy stuff." Elle stood up; she poked my nose before giving me a brief hug. Then, without another word, she left.

"Guess I should be going too. Happy birthday, daughter. And Kyle, treat my girls right. Got it, darling?" Naomi said as she stood. Her eyes stayed fixed on Elle as she walked off. I thought I heard her mumble something about LOV, but I wasn't sure. Maybe it was just my imagination.

Once they were both out of earshot, Sarah shook her head. "What was with those two?" She asked in a soft voice.

"Who cares. We have a birthday girl to celebrate," I said, turning the attention away from Naomi's and Elle's odd behaviors.

"Yeah, someone promised me gelato," Vicky said with a smile as she pushed her plate away.

It wasn't long before I had paid. I made sure to leave a large tip for the waiter. The dinner was over fifteen hundred dollars, but it was well worth it. We walked out, each locked into my elbows on either side. Making our way to the front, Sarah handed the valet her vehicle ticket. The vehicle was ready in moments. We piled into the car and started toward the gelato cafe.

"Why coffee shops?" Vicky asked as she fastened her seatbelt.

"Howard told me how his parents met at the coffee shop here in town. The one that he asked me to go in on," I explained.

"That's romantic. He is buying it for his parents to memorialize their love," Sarah said with a tender voice as she took a left.

"Yeah, I thought so too," I said, happy at the idea of buying something like that for my girls. Something that they could always own as a reminder that I loved them.

"Why let us buy in? It seems he wants it for sentimental reasons." Vicky's motherly tone was weighing in.

"Making money leaves him lonely. He wants someone to share in his triumphs. I sort of understand. Like him, I had no one to share things like that with for a long time," I explained. My mind drifted off into my feelings before I met Sarah and Vicky. Then, the feeling of being with my girlfriends broke through the darkness. "But now, I do. With my beauties."

"You will always have us, Master," Sarah whispered as the dashboard lights cast a glow on her face.

"We are bonded for all time," Vicky whispered as she looked out the passenger window.

The Cobalt stopped at the parking lot in front of the cafe. We walked toward the entrance. The girls locked into my arms again.

They both leaned into me with a caring caress. We walked happily toward our ice cream treat.

"What a sick world we live in," someone said loudly. It came from a group of ladies who had exited the gelato shop. They watched us in disgust.

"Sick indeed. Look at that," the second one said, pointing at us.

"Damn, what an asshole! How can they stand to be played like that?" The third one piped in.

The snide remarks made me feel embarrassed and a bit angered. I knew that society would not accept this relationship, but it was sometimes hard to hear.

"Evening, ladies," Sarah said as her arm gripped me tighter. "Nice night to hold your boyfriend close, huh."

"Why yes, a great night to cuddle with our boyfriend," Vicky said mockingly as we passed the group.

"Eww... disgusting," the group muttered as they passed by us.

I guess I should get used to these kinds of encounters. This seemed to be an ongoing trend. But it has been mostly judgmental women who didn't seem to like my relationship. The men we passed barely acknowledged us. If they did, they just grinned. Why are women so judgmental? I shook my head. Vicky's night. It was her birthday. Fun night. Yes.

We walked into the shop. It looked simple. Not much for décor, but the place smelled amazing. The aroma of flavors beckoned your nose in a way that felt like you had already tasted the entire store before a single spoonful hit your mouth.

Vicky knew what she wanted right away. She ordered *cioccolato*... I had no idea what that was. Sarah took her time and then ordered *al cocco*. I looked at the menu, confused by what I was reading. *Alla* this, *mandorle* that. I honestly didn't know what to order.

"*Vaniglia* is vanilla. You should start there since vanilla ice cream is your favorite," Sarah whispered to me. I looked over; she smirked, knowing I had no clue what I was looking at. I mouthed a thank-you to her, then I turned to order what she had suggested.

We got our gelato and sat in a booth along the wall. I sat on the side facing the entrance while Vicky and Sarah sat opposite me.

"Why are you so nervous to talk about children?" Vicky lit into me as she stabbed her spoon into the dark ice cream.

"Um... I don't know," I stammered. I pulled a spoonful up. The ice cream was the richest and sweetest vanilla I had ever had.

"Yeah, are you scared to have babies with us? Every time it is mentioned, you seem shaken. Like you had seen the boogeyman or something." Sarah wondered.

I wasn't afraid. The idea of fatherhood left me with a great feeling. Taking them to parks. The first day of school. Teaching them to ride bikes. Playing video games. Sports... or cheerleading. Or hearing them play an instrument. All the odd and cute things the kids would say. Flashes of being there for my children. Of running around in a big yard playing games we make on the spot. Showing them the beauty of the world. Guiding them to fight against its dangers. All of it. All that it means to be a father. But...

The thoughts of the monster within. Would he destroy them? Scare them? Torment them? Was a beast like me fit to be a father?

"I'm not scared. I... I just don't know. Like I said before, I want to be married before kids. I don't want to be an absent father." I licked up another spoonful.

"Don't worry, Master. You would make a great father." Sarah comforted me as she ate her gelato.

"Marriage... seems to be where all of this is heading. Wouldn't you say?" Vicky eyed me as she seductively licked her spoon clean.

"Yeah... I bought... I mean, yes. Seems to be." Damn, I almost told them about the rings. Chill, Sergeant. It's not the right time— Vicky's birthday. Get things back on track for that.

Vicky smirked devilishly. Sarah eyed me in surprise. I wasn't sure if I had let it slip or not. Maybe I had broadcast it... like I had done in the past? No, they would have said something if I did. Surely, they would have...

"Anyway," I said, "as delicious as this is, let's not take too long with our gelato. We have a show to go to."

The talk of children and marriage died off. They sat whispering and giggling to each other. I tried to listen, but they just whispered softer, like they knew I was trying to hear them. I playfully shook my head.

"This has been a fun night so far." Vicky suddenly said.

"That's good. I'm happy you're enjoying yourself. I was so excited to plan your birthday." I took another scoop of my ice cream.

"He always makes us feel like we are the only women in the world." Sarah tapped her spoon against Vicky's in a toast.

"Yes... yes, he does. And you two have done a great job of making my birthday feel special. The most special one I ever had. You made me feel like royalty." Vicky squealed with joy.

We bantered for a few more minutes before finishing our treats. After we left, they giggled together the entire walk back to the car.

The ride to the Burlesque show was quiet. I looked up at the front; both were smiling. They seemed to be fantasizing about something. I was pretty sure it had to do with kids... or the wedding day... or something like that.

I relaxed in the back seat, thinking about how and when to propose. Dinner with everyone? Or alone with the three of us? In public? Or make it more private and intimate? I knew that I wanted to spend the rest of my life with them. So sooner? Or let it ride for a while? Give it another week or two? Or months? How many months? One year? I didn't know.

Before I knew it, we had parked again. I looked out the window. The building was a simple brick building. The sign "*Viva*" hung over the door. Before we knew it, we were at the double doors.

The doorman ushered us in quickly. As I entered with my girlfriends, he nodded at me knowingly. I gave him a slight nod.

There were rows of seats; we had tickets for the back, nearest the door. The stage was large; it looked more like a concert than a theater show. Once at our seats, I sat on the outside. I cantered my body to watch over Vicky and Sarah.

The curtain opened, and the show began. However, my eyes couldn't help but watch my future brides. Sarah seemed to be completely involved in the show's theatrics. Vicky seemed to be... well... more interested in the undressing. Her eyes roamed over the actresses on stage with a hunger... a sexual hunger.

I would periodically watch the show; however, I enjoyed watching my girlfriends more. Each was obviously getting aroused by the show. Sarah's hands gripped the armrests as the show continued. Her fingers seemed to have a need to feel the heat of flesh under them. Vicky just caressed her own cheek as the nudity began. She seemed flushed at the scene before her. She pulled her braid out as she became more aroused. Her hands ran through her hair, straightening it.

My member stayed stiff throughout the show. However, the hunger inside me was only for them—my beauties, my queens, my goddesses. After the show ended, we walked back to the car, the night air cool and calming.

"That was an interesting show. You two didn't tell me we were going to a burlesque." Vicky seemed to still be flustered.

"Hehe. Yeah, it was my idea." Sarah giggled as she covered her mouth.

"Um, I was a bit leery of the idea at first, but gave in." I looked over to Vicky.

"Besides, it sets us up for your last gift." Sarah let out a girlish giggle.

"Last gift? Now I am scared," Vicky said as we hopped in the Chevy.

"Once we're home, you'll get it." Sarah was about to burst with laughter as she started the engine.

"Ooh-kaaay." Vicky chuckled as she shook her head.

The ride home was silent again. My thoughts were reeling about the night we had set up for Vicky. She seemed to enjoy it, and I just hoped she would enjoy Sarah's gift. Even with our bumps, it turned out to be a great night. A night filled with love.

I rolled down the window; the night air flowed in with a cooling breeze. The city's lights felt like we were passing by the world as passengers on our own path. It was a destination of love... a destination for only the three of us.

Once home, I looked at the apartment. It was time to fulfill Vicky's last birthday present. We hastily made our way in.

As we stepped inside the apartment, Vicky was ahead of Sarah and me. As soon as I entered, my hand gave Vicky's shoulder a light shove. I relished how her body fell back against the wall. I quickly grappled her throat; I held her in place as my free hand explored her curves, blazing along her dress with merely the tips of my fingers. My eyes dug into her soul as we were locked in a war of who had control. We never lost sight of one another. I heard Sarah close the front door behind us.

I released my grip around Vicky's neck, only to move to her darkened mane. I quickly laced my digits deep within her locks as I fisted her hair, pulling back harshly. I watched as she pretended to struggle against me. Her body rubbed against mine, causing friction on my thigh. She knew exactly what she was doing, but tonight wasn't about me.

I leaned my face close to hers, cheek to cheek, my breath on her ear. She smirked devilishly as I felt her nails dig into my collarbone. I studied her lips in dire desperation.

"What are you doing, Master?" Vicky erotically said.

"Worshipping you as a goddess." My soft, dominant tone whispered into her ear.

She pulled her face down even under the pressure of my hand as I held her hair tightly in my grasp. She eyed me with a predatory glare as she challenged me. That look set my soul on fire as my need for her burned through me.

I couldn't resist any longer. My lips clashed into hers with a hearth of passion, melting us both to the searing kindle of unbridled desire. As our tongues battled for control, I parried her assault for a while. But I let my guard down. I let her win. Her kiss fiercely claimed me. Her mouth had conquered mine. She broke from my lips with a deep sense of victory.

"You are worshipping me tonight?" Vicky said with that deep, vixen tone.

I leaned forward again, my lips close to her ear. I let her feel the heat of my breath on her cheek. "Not just me," I whispered with that dominant tone.

My hand released her as I stepped aside. Sarah moved into place, running her hands along Vicky's hard body. I watched as their eyes never left each other's. Sarah leaned down, kissing Vicky passionately. I watched as Sarah's hands moved under Vicky's dress. When Vicky whimpered, I knew Sarah's fingers had entered the warmth of her hot pinkness. Her fingers worked Vicky into a frenzy. Their kisses became wild.

I enjoyed the show. Stepping forward, I took my place beside Sarah. My mouth slightly clamped down onto Vicky's neck. My teeth playfully bit into her flesh. I ran my hand from her thigh up the curves of her body. She seared with passion, her body aflame with desire. The vehemence of our love for her enthralled her.

Sarah and I soon pulled away from Vicky. We both grabbed a hand, lightly tugging her toward the bedroom. As we entered, Sarah pushed Vicky against the bed. She fell back, softly crashing on the mattress. Without hesitation, Sarah pushed Vicky's legs apart. I leaned over, ripping the goddess's panties at the crotch. The fabric tore easily under the strength of my hand.

"Tonight, Vicky, you are our goddess. Tell me what you want, mistress." Sarah's soft voice filled the air with a seductive tone I had never heard from her.

"Lick me. Show me how much you worship me. How much I'm loved," Vicky said, her vixen tone sent shivers through my member. I enjoyed the sight for a moment; it was beautiful to see our goddess's divine wings spread.

Without another word, Sarah kneeled. Her face moved into Vicky's sex. I watched as Sarah's tongue darted out and started to sing praise to our goddess. Vicky's left hand shot out, pulling Sarah closer... deeper into her. She let out a moan as she felt Sarah's tongue push further.

Vicky eyed me with a deep need; her free hand motioned me to her. I peeled off my shirt, moving to the side of the bed. I kneeled on the mattress at Vicky's side. Leaning down, my face was close to hers. Her eyes studied me for a moment before her hand grabbed a tuft of my hair. She roughly pulled me closer; my lips took in the fire of her passion. Our tongues battled once again.

My hand made its way to her side, roughly stroking along her curves. The soft silk of her dress felt smooth on my fingers. As my hand traveled against her feminine divinity, I felt her moan into our kiss. My fingertips lightly danced against her chiseled stomach.

Our kiss became a fray of rage. She was wild and feral as Sarah worked her, worshipped her. Sarah became a devout acolyte in this new religion. A priestess in this feeling of heavenly love.

My hand roamed over her, venerating my dark goddess. Vicky broke our kiss as she began to whimper; she was close. Her body tensed, her grip on my hair tightened as she pulled my face to hers.

"Fuck! Worship me. Eat me. Show your goddess... oh shit... show her your love," Vicky screamed out. Her body tensed; I peered down. Sarah was covered in hot fluids. I smirked wickedly.

"Ah... let me taste your kiss. And you, manservant. Your turn to worship your goddess," Vicky commanded as she roughly pulled my head up. Her eyes glared into mine before she released my hair, flinging my head to the side.

I moved into place between her legs. Sarah took her place on the other side of the bed. She leaned down, tenderly kissing Vicky. Without hesitation, I started my prayer to my goddess.

My tongue lapped at the sweet ambrosia of her sex. My kiss passionately praised the folds of her divinity, the tender flesh under my praise as I worked circles around her bud. I slid two fingers inside her pink furnace, rubbing roughly against the upper wall of her cave. I felt her pelvic bone with the pressure I was applying. She moaned with pleasure.

My mouth moved over her bud. I gave it a light nibble before suckling her sensitive button with a powerful vortex. Her hands wrapped around my head. With great force, she shoved me into her with all of her strength. My goddess was pleased by my praise... my worship of her body. Gripping her hips, my free hand wrapped around her.

"Ahh! I'm... I'm cumming again!" Vicky screamed out as Sarah's face pulled away from their kiss.

Her thighs tensed harshly. I felt the pressure around my head. All the sounds were muffled by the thick, muscular legs clamping me tightly. I suckled harder on her bud; my fingers worked her inner walls faster. My face was soaked with her nectar. I drank in all that I could. After my faith was rewarded, she relaxed. I felt her body retreat; her thighs fell limp.

"Use your cock to worship me, to fuck your goddess," Vicky commanded. "Fill me with your hot sticky faith. And you, my reverend minx," she said to Sarah, "let me taste you. Sit on your goddess's face. Let me taste the essence of you."

Without a word, I moved into place. I undid my pants. Letting them hit the floor as I stepped out of them. My member was throbbing, aching to be inside her. I slid in slowly; the feeling of her heat on me drove my senses into the depths of spirituality. My newfound religion, the religion of love.

I watched as Sarah moved to lower herself onto Vicky. Her dress draped over Vicky's face. Even though I couldn't see, I knew what was happening. Sarah let out a squeal, alerting me that Vicky's tongue had begun to taste her.

"Thank you, my goddess! Thank you for— ah fuck... for this miracle!" Sarah's head rolled backward; her hair dangled into a crimson feathering that touched Vicky's core.

I thrust with gyrations into Vicky's warmth. My hands grabbed her at the waist, using her body as a stabilizer to increase my pace. As my thrusts became faster and more powerful, Vicky started to tremble. Her body was nearing her third climax.

"I worship you, my goddess. Fucking you with all my faith." I groaned as my body teetered on its own release.

"Aah! Fuck her. Fuck our goddess! I can— I can feel her divine presence! Aah... in... in my pussy!" Sarah screamed out as her body slumped forward. She howled a loud final scream before collapsing.

I felt the celestial fountain of life deluge toward my hips. Vicky twitched as her body expelled her divinity onto me. The heat of her nectar sent my body into a frenzy. My own orgasm was on the brink. I forced one last thrust of my bishop deep within her as my sexual mana erupted. I slowly pulled out of Vicky.

Sarah lazily moved off Vicky; she rolled off the bed. Her weakened body crawled to lap up all of my leaked seminal fluids. In no time, she had made sure their promise was kept.

"Wow. Fucking... fucking wow. That was... yeah... that was something different." Vicky huffed out as she propped up on her elbows. A crooked grin laced her face as Sarah's juices dripped down her chin.

"You really liked it?" Sarah asked in her normal baby voice.

"Liked? Hell, I loved it! Maybe not all the time. But yeah, that was exhilarating." Vicky sat up on the bed.

"So, how was your birthday?" I chuckled as I started to pick up the shoes and clothes that had been scattered around.

"Five-star dinner. A pretty necklace. Gelato. Burlesque. And sex that I dominated in. Best birthday ever!" Vicky was dreamily elated; she started to get off the bed. Some of the rose petals were stuck to her wet body.

"Good," I said with elation as I helped Sarah with her zipper. I felt accomplished having made Vicky's birthday a good one.

Sarah blew a kiss at Vicky. "So happy you had a great birthday."

"Can we go back to you being dominant, Master? It's good to be in control, once in a while, but I absolutely love it when you take the reins," Vicky said as she approached me, turning her back so I could unzip her dress.

"Sure. I figured you would only want this occasionally." I pulled the zipper down her back. Vicky turned around, hugging me tightly.

"Thank you for a fun birthday," Vicky whispered in my ear.

"It wasn't all me. But you are welcome," I said as my arms engulfed her. We held our hug for a moment before she broke away.

"Thank you, sis. This was an awesome birthday." Vicky said as she made her way to Sarah, embracing her tightly.

"You're welcome, sis. Master and I made sure that it would be fun for you." Sarah hugged Vicky back.

"You just going to stand there gawking? Come cuddle with us." Vicky took her goddess tone once more.

"Maybe... or maybe I just stand here all night watching my beauties." I chuckled.

"Like you did at the burlesque?" Sarah giggled as she hugged Vicky tighter.

"He thinks we didn't notice. We saw you; you didn't watch the show for a second." Vicky laughed as she gazed into Sarah's eyes.

"Me? Nah. I was totally involved in the show."

"Liar. You couldn't keep your eyes off your hotties." Sarah tittered, turning her head to me.

"I think he's embarrassed to admit that he liked watching us more than the other women." Vicky let loose a wicked grin.

"Let's get some sleep." I took my place in the middle of the bed.

"Avoid it all you want, but we know." Vicky sighed with a titter.

"Know what?" I questioned.

"That you love us. You only have eyes for us, Master." Sarah giggled.

"Yeah, eyes only for us," Vicky smirked mischievously.

"Maybe I like ya. Maybe I like ya a lot." I playfully said as they made their way onto the bed. Each took their place and wrapped themselves around me.

"Just like, Master?" Sarah asked in her cute baby voice.

"Maybe I love ya," I said as my arms closed around them tightly.

"Just maybe?" Vicky whispered into my neck.

"Hmm... maybe," I said playfully.

"Good night, Master Maybe. I love you," Sarah whispered, cuddling deeper into my side.

"I love you, Master. Now, get your 'maybe' ass to sleep. Before you may be in trouble." Vicky softly laughed.

"Good night, my beauties. I love you both." I finally gave them the words they wanted. I felt so happy to cuddle with them. I lay there as they started to doze off. Thinking about how fun tonight was. About the crazy wild night that we had.

Sarah was right; this was the perfect birthday celebration for Vicky. Both of my future brides felt loved tonight. And I had made one of their birthday celebrations a special one.

Indescribable feelings always engulfed me by simply being in the orbit of my beauties. Every time I see Vicky and Sarah happy, it fills my heart to the brim. How they had become everything to me. And how I couldn't help but love them, each of them, more every day. I must marry these women. I have to. They are too wonderful for me not to make them my brides.

Chapter 19: All Doves Cry

Wednesday morning, geez. What was I going to do about Stephen? How could I go to work? I left early on Monday and haven't been back. But Vicky's birthday last night was great, besides the odd standoff between Naomi and Elle. I wasn't sure what that was all about.

Sarah had left for the publishing office early. Vicky left about an hour later. Something about getting to the Chamber of Commerce office early. I wasn't entirely sure, but I knew it had to do with her business license. Somehow, the license was filed incorrectly for her to operate her masseuse services in the city limits.

I turned over in bed. Drive around again? But I felt bad lying to Vicky and Sarah like that. I couldn't avoid my job forever... could I? I mean, I am not being responsible. Am I failing as a boyfriend? Did I deserve to ask for their hands in marriage?

My phone sounded, alerting me to a call, interrupting my thoughts. I leaned over and saw it was Mr. McKellen. Shit! He must have noticed my absence. I answered the phone with caution.

"Hello." My voice sounded groggy, which I further exaggerated.

"Kyle, I need you here. First thing. My office." Mr. McKellen's voice was oddly low, yet I could hear the anger in his tone.

"Yes, sir. I will be there in about thirty minutes," I said into the phone; dread crept into my soul.

"Good," he said with a stern voice. I knew that voice. It was the same as my NCO voice. That quiet yet commanding voice. I hung up before I agitated him any further.

I quickly got to my feet and dressed. The feeling of being on the chopping block was twisting my stomach into knots. I trudged out of the apartment, making my way down the hall. Each step felt like I was walking to my doom.

I got into my beater and drove slowly to the shop. My mind was a worried mess. Was he going to write me up? Fire me? I'd proved myself irresponsible. So, whatever he was going to do was deserved.

If he fires me, I can't collect unemployment. But I had savings tucked away. That could hold us over for a while. What about my license? How will this affect that? And my proposal? Can I propose to them being an unemployed scrub? Would Sarah and Vicky want to marry a jobless bum? Fuck!

I calmed myself as I started to pull into the shop. As I parked, I glanced over at my work van. All my tools had been moved out of it. They were sitting neatly beside the company vehicle. Yep, fired. I just knew it. But I had to face the music like a man. Take my licks and move on.

As I entered, Myra looked sad, her eyes welled with tears. I punched my card. I knew any disciplinary action had to happen on the clock. I didn't want to cause Mr. McKellen any further trouble.

"I tried to cover for you. But... he got a call from the crew." Myra sobbed.

"It's okay, Myra. It's my fault. I should have told Mr. McKellen about all this when it started," I said in a calm voice; she seemed confused at my stoic stature.

"Kyle, I'm... I'm sorry," Myra said as her hand soothed mine. I felt the warmth of her touch on the back of my hand. Her face seemed filled with remorse... Or was it mourning?

"I know what's coming. I should, anyway. I abandoned my job." My voice stayed calm. But the calmness was a mask to hide the disappointment I had for myself.

"If you ever need anything, just call me." Myra held back her tears as she caressed my hand tenderly. This was the first time I had noticed that she may have been attracted to me.

"Thank you, Myra. I will," I said as I slowly pulled my hand away. Time to face the consequences.

"Wish he would call," Myra whispered as I started down the hallway.

I knocked on Mr. McKellen's office door. My heart sank. These were the final moments of my employment here.

"Come in, Kyle," Mr. McKellen said in a low gravelly voice. I opened the door; he was seated behind his desk. His eyes glared at me, and I knew he was trying to contain his anger. I sat on the chair in front of his desk.

"Do you know why you are here, Kyle?" Mr. McKellen placed his elbows on the desk. His hands smashed into each other as he moved them to his face.

"Yes, sir, I do. I left the job site on Monday. And I haven't been back since," I explained as I looked him in the eye, being completely honest with my actions.

"Although Stephen came here pleading your case, it's still job abandonment. You know what I have to do for job abandonment, right?" Mr. McKellen glared at me with fire in his eyes.

"Stephen was here?" I asked. This was a puzzling thing to me.

"Yes, he was. He declared that your absence for days was because of him. A personal altercation between you two that he had started. But that is no excuse to abandon your job. You should have talked to me about it. Called me." Mr. McKellen huffed as he moved his hands down to his desk.

"I'm sorry, Mr. McKellen." My eyes stayed on him as my apology came out sincerely and remorsefully.

"No, I am sorry. You are terminated effective immediately." Mr. McKellen slid an envelope over to me.

"Understood, sir." I reached over and picked up the envelope from the desk. The stationery felt heavy. "What's in here?" I asked as I peered down to the sealed document in my hand.

"Your last paycheck, a letter of recommendation for your next employer, and a severance check." Mr. McKellen eased back in his chair. He seemed to relax. Maybe he wasn't as mad at me as I had thought.

"Thank you, sir," I said as I stood up. I pushed my hand out, offering him a handshake.

"You're a good kid, Kyle. Just get your head on straight. Okay?" He reached out, shaking my hand. He shot me a semi-smirk.

"Yes, sir. Sorry about the trouble." I admired him for not taking this personally. I nodded as I broke away from the handshake.

"Now get out of here before someone finds out that I can be a softy." He waved me off.

"Thank you for the opportunity." I did an about-face and walked out of the office. That went better than I had imagined. I thought there would be yelling and maybe a few insults. But he was surprisingly cordial about the entire thing.

As I returned to the time clock, Myra held me in her gaze. I punched out on the clock for the last time. As I turned toward the exit, Myra spoke up again.

"Remember, you can call me about anything." Her voice was low, with a sorrowful tone.

"Thank you, Myra," I said as I headed to the exit.

I got to work loading my tools into my car. My trunk was filled, my backseat piled up, and even my passenger seat had tools crammed in. I hung my manifold gauges on the "oh shit" handle in the back seat. I started the ignition and pulled out for the last time.

I made my way to the bank's drive-through and deposited my checks. The severance check was for a full three months of my wages. Mr. McKellen was more than gracious to give me a severance check in the first place, but three months' worth? That was surprising.

I drove around for a while, trying to figure out how to tell my loves what happened. Honesty was my best bet. I should just come clean to them and tell them what I did to be fired.

Yeah, this will surely go over swell. Sarah might be okay, though maybe a little disappointed. Vicky will blow a gasket, which I was sure about. With her temperament, she would be pissed that I lost my job.

I pulled into the apartment parking lot. As I exited my beater, I locked the doors. Sitting in my junker were several thousand dollars in tools that I now had nowhere to store.

I trudged into the building, slowly ascending the stairs. Luckily, Mrs. Helderman was not around. She would have surely quizzed me about what was going on. And I didn't feel like explaining it to her, at least not until I had talked with my girlfriends.

After unlocking the door, I threw the envelope on the coffee table. Apprehensively, I sat on the couch. My hand reached for the remote, and I found something to distract me, at least until the girls got home. Until I had to explain my irresponsible choices, I just hoped they didn't see me as a worthless, idle bum.

I found an old horror movie to distract me and keep myself calm, to keep my mind from going into a dark place. Three movies later, Sarah and Vicky came home. I turned off the TV after they had made it inside the apartment.

Sarah was giddy, as always. Vicky still seemed to be zinging from her birthday.

"Master, home early again?" Sarah grinned at me.

"Did you even move off the couch today?" Vicky jokingly jabbed at me.

"Yeah, I have some news." I looked at them. Sarah walked to the front of the couch, peering into my eyes. Vicky moved behind the sofa; her hands reached down, massaging my shoulders.

"Me too. I got my license issue fixed. They thought my social security number was fake. But got it straightened out." Vicky said as her hands worked deeper into my tense shoulders. "What's your news, Master?"

"I lost my job." My words came out in a low mumble.

"What?" Vicky exclaimed in shock.

"I'm sorry, Master." Sarah leaned over, rubbing my cheek.

"What happened, Master?" Vicky asked in a daze.

"Stephen was at the job site Monday. I left early to avoid him and didn't go back. I stayed out of work yesterday for the same reason." I babbled in a defeated tone.

"You lied to us?" Vicky asked, her tone started to change. Her hands pulled away from me.

"Are you okay, Master?" Sarah asked with concern in her voice.

"I don't know what to do." My gaze turned to the floor. Had I failed them? Was I a failure? They must be disappointed in me.

"What the hell?" Vicky asked with scorn in her voice.

"I know, I just..." Before I could finish, Vicky cut me off.

"You really fucked up. You did well not to go to work, Kyle, but you tossed us aside like trash," Vicky growled with a fierce heat.

"Calm down, Vicky. He didn't do it on purpose." Sarah tried to de-escalate the situation.

"What do you mean 'not on purpose'? He purposefully left us in the dark. We loved him for his honesty... his loyalty. Both of which he has broken." Vicky turned her ire toward Sarah.

"No, he didn't. He may have..." Sarah attempted to explain, but Vicky cut her off mid-sentence.

"Fuck yeah, he did! In his cowardice, he treated us like trash. Like we were nobodies. I refuse to be trash. I refuse to be nobody." Vicky's voice started to rise.

"I can't stand Stephen. You know this. And I might have done something idiotic if I had stayed." My voice trembled.

"I don't give a good goddamn about Stephen. Or that you got laid off. You're supposed to be our boyfriend! Our Master! You should be honest with us! Yet you can't be. You fucking lied to us for days!" Vicky yelled, disappointment in her words.

"That's enough, Vicky! Master may have made a mistake by not talking to us. But have you considered that he may have been afraid of this? Us acting exactly how you are now?" Sarah seemed to have finished the statement she had started earlier.

"Always sticking up for him, huh, little Miss Pushover." Vicky had disdain in her voice.

"Why do you have to act like this? Every time Master doesn't act a certain way?" Sarah sobbed.

"Because he needs to be a good man. He wants to be our boyfriend, our Master; he needs to act like the man we deserve," Vicky snarled.

"This is not the way to make him see that." Sarah's whisper rang with sorrow.

"I am sorry." I sighed and hung my head down.

"Sorry for what... huh?" Vicky's words were daggers attacking the core of me.

"Don't take that harsh tone with him! No matter what, he is still our loving boyfriend, our Master." Sarah's gaze fell upon me with pity and love.

"I don't give a fuck. Right now, he is not being *masterly*." Vicky lowered her tone. But her rage was still in every word.

I had failed them. I never wanted to. I wanted—needed—to be the man that they saw. But I lost that. I had lied to them, kept them in the dark. I was now branded a loser by the very women that I loved. My heart felt shredded, torn apart, as if now I was nothing.

"Sorry that I lied to you... both of you." I looked up at both of them, my eyes bouncing between them.

Sarah kissed my cheek. "It's okay, Master. I understand."

"The hell it is," Vicky growled; her face looked at me with such scorn.

"We can forgive you. Just talk to us from now on. Right, Vicky?" Sarah said as she looked over at Vicky.

"The fuck you want me to do? We dedicate all of ourselves to him, but he can't involve us in a work disagreement. Makes me think what else Kyle is hiding from us!" Vicky stood on her toes to appear more intimidating than Sarah.

I sat silent as they continued to bicker. I wanted to stop it. But at the same time, Vicky was right. I had screwed up. I broke their trust. I should have told them from the beginning, but I was a coward. I was too ashamed to include them.

"Yes, but we know he is a good man. And we know he is sorry for all of it." Sarah glared at Vicky, searing her with an angry glare.

"Doesn't excuse him lying to us. Doesn't make it okay that he felt he shouldn't include us in a major life decision." Vicky sighed in disappointment and paused for a moment. She seemed to be working back into her rage. "This lie. Not telling us where he was. Babysitting his drunk ass twice. And we are always catering to him. He doesn't appreciate any of it."

"Stop it. He is a great man. Sure, he makes mistakes. But he is our boyfriend, so forgive him. That's what good women... good wives do. Forgive him for trivial shit. Then help him stand back up for another round in the ring." Sarah sobbed out, trying to plead my case to Vicky. I didn't feel like I was the man Sarah was describing.

"We even severed..." Vicky trailed off. Did she stop herself before she let something slip? She hurried toward the door.

Me lying? Hell, what is it with all this weird shit? When they are about to say something about it, they just stop.

"I know, but we have a better life now." Sarah rushed over to Vicky in an attempt to bring her back.

"Yeah? Where? He treats us like meat he can fuck whenever he wants. Then pulls shit like this! Lying to us for days!" Vicky's voice started to get louder.

"Don't you dare say he treats us like meat! We engaged all the sex until recently. He has never..." Sarah's fingers grasped Vicky's arm, tugging her in. However, my voice boomed before she could finish her statement.

"Then fucking leave! Yes, I lied, just once. Yet you lie, too. Or at least keep me in the dark. You won't tell me what is happening to you. All that weird crap. Servers... bonding. The fuck does all that mean?" I didn't mean for my anger to slip out, but it had. Everything that had heated up in me boiled over in a hateful tone.

Elle... Stephen... being fired... all the weird behaviors I had excused. It all bubbled up to the surface. My words were a fireball that burned their love away. I saw at that moment that I had destroyed my relationship with them.

242

"Fuck you!" Vicky yelled as she broke free of Sarah's grasp.

"Fuck me? No, fuck all this weird-ass shit. Your mother's hateful tone with Elle. That was uncalled for. Now get the fuck out of my apartment!" I spat with anger.

Vicky didn't say anything; she just trampled and flung the door open. Her boots echoed down the hallway with each heavy footfall. Sarah stood there, motionless for a moment. Her eyes teared up. I could see the pain in her face.

"You didn't..." Sarah softly said through her crying. She pivoted and followed behind Vicky.

"Vicky, wait up." Sarah's voice was shaky as she rushed out.

I walked over to the door, slamming it shut. The monster inside me had just destroyed my chance at happiness.

I guess I got my wish. The wish I had the first night I met them. When they forced their way into my apartment. Now, they had left me alone. Just as my antics the first night were trying to make them do. Yet that wish was no longer what I desired. My heart felt like it had been smashed into oblivion. What had I done?

I should have told them about my encounters with Stephen, him being at the job site, and my decision not to go back as soon as it happened. Maybe they would have supported my decision. Maybe they would have convinced me to talk with Mr. McKellen before I got fired. And maybe they would still be here, right now, with me.

But I was a fuckup. I hid it from them. Lied to them. Maybe I deserved to be alone. Maybe I wasn't worthy of them in the first place. Maybe... Damn, all the fucking maybes of the world.

The reality was that they were gone. And I had done it. I was to blame for them leaving me. It was my fault. I couldn't believe I told them to leave. Kyle, you fucking loser. You told the women that you love to leave. So damn stupid. FUCK!

I walked back to the couch and plopped down. I sat in the quietness of the lonely room. I looked over at the chair. The arm of it was still cantered out; I needed to replace that damned thing.

I turned my gaze to the dark TV screen; my reflection stared back at me. The darkness of the screen reflected more than my face. It reflected how my soul felt: dark, alone, and empty. My mind pondered my mistakes, thinking of how I messed up my relationship and how I just lost the women that I loved.

Chapter 20: Champion of Melancholy

Three days had passed since they left. The apartment had that gloominess about it again. I felt like I had ascended back up that spire of loneliness, isolated from the world. Alone. Cold. My heart felt so cold. I sat on the couch, barely moving. I hadn't eaten since they departed. I just simply stared at the blank TV, deep in thought. How could I have let them down? I screwed up.

FUCK! The pain of their absence made my body ache. My heart was gone. How could I run into a fray of bullets unfazed but be so fragile when it comes to this? When the thought of not being with them was imminent, I would rather fight a million psychopathic fanatics than know that I lost them to my own stupidity. To a lie.

I started to think that some of those politicians may be correct. That a man touched by war can't be civil any longer. Was I that far gone? Were those politicians right? Was I lost? Or could I be tamed back to society? I knew that I had lost the two things that were bringing me back to myself. Back to a world of peace. Back to life. Yet the stupidity of that creature in me had run them off.

I was a killer, a monster. How could they love such a creature? Yet they did. They loved me for who I was. Or at least for who they thought I was. Then I go and fuck it up royally by lying. By not letting them in, locking them away from what was really happening.

Vicky felt slighted, like I had treated them as trash. Had I? Had I treated them like nobodies? Had I made them feel disposable? Was that what I did?

I still can't believe I was too cowardly to tell them the truth. To confide in them about what was really going on. To explain how I felt. What I had done to stay away from Stephen.

I wanted to call them... apologize. But I didn't know if I should. If I was still wanted.

I looked at the coffee table. I got the engagement rings out yesterday. I placed them on the table with the boxes open. A reminder to myself of what I had lost. What I had pushed away. I watched the light dazzle around the diamond in the center of each ring. Yet the rings didn't seem to shine like they did when I first purchased them. Wasn't there a song like that? What were the lyrics to that song? "This diamond ring doesn't shine for me anymore..."

Yeah, those were the lyrics. But it was my fault the diamonds didn't shine anymore. Was it fucking worth it, Sergeant? To lie to your girlfriends? To lose the women you love?

From now on, I will always be honest with my significant other. I will let them in, even when I feel ashamed. I will never break their trust. Never break Vicky and Sarah's trust, if I got them back.

I looked to the other side of the table. My pistol sat to the left of the rings on the far edge. I had many thoughts over the past few days about washing my mouth out with a 9mm round. I couldn't believe it. That I might have joined the twenty-two veterans statistic. Had I really been contemplating that?

I needed to do something to help me apologize. Take a shower, get out of the apartment, eat something, and talk to Vicky and Sarah. Just do something.

I got up and moved toward the bedroom. I would start with a shower. It would wash away this stink, and maybe... it could help remove some of this dread. I walked into the bedroom; my eyes looked over to the bed. Just a few days ago, it was a warm place to sleep. Now, it was empty. Empty like how the apartment felt. But the emptiness was not restricted to this place; I felt it, too. Deep inside my soul was a hollowed shell.

I rummaged through the closet: a T-shirt and some pants. That was all I needed. No, that wasn't all I needed. I needed *them*. Vicky and Sarah. My beauties. I needed to feel their hands warming my body. To feel their happiness warming my heart. Their lips pressed against mine, warming my soul.

But you can't, Sergeant. You can't feel any of that. Not anymore. Did I even deserve to feel their warmth? I left the bedroom, my clothes draped over my forearm. I made sure to close the door. I didn't want to be reminded that my bedroom was once warm with the fires of love.

As I walked to the bathroom, this place felt like a haunted house. The silence felt eerie, as if the apartment was haunted by the ghosts of a life that could never be. The remnants of a life... a love doomed never to exist. And I... I was the assassin of this love. I had snuffed it out with my own hands. With my poor choices.

Stop it, Kyle! Shower! Get to the shower. My body moved with a will of its own against the protests of my heart. My mind shattered. Was this heartache? True heartache? I needed a plan to help me, to show them that I could change, for them. Be a better man. But what could I do?

I turned on the shower. The water splashed fiercely against the plastic curtain. I started removing the dirty clothes I had been in for days, lazily letting each piece fall to the floor. Stepping in, I tilted my head under the rain. This was the place where I made up that stupid three-date rule.

I chuckled to myself. The point of that rule seemed moot now. I lost them. There was no point to any of it. I looked over to the bar of soap and picked it up. Clean this feeling; clean it away. I lathered up my body, trying to scrub away the heartache with it. But it made no difference. I still felt them. Felt the missing pieces of my soul.

Was there anything that could heal an amputated soul? A remedy to mend an eviscerated mind? An adhesive to piece together a shattered heart? Or was I out of luck? Was there nothing?

After carefully washing my body, I turned the shower off and reached for the towel. The one that I had playfully run over their bodies. I dried off, then dressed myself. I was readying myself to take my post on the sofa.

As I exited the bathroom, I heard a knock. My heart raced. Was it them? With a pizza? To reenact how we met? Please be them. I would spend the rest of my life apologizing if it was them. Loving them exactly how they needed. Spending every day continually showing them that I loved them.

I moved to the door in haste. But as I pulled it open, disappointment rippled through my bones.

"What the hell, lil Bro? You don't answer the damn phone anymore?" Elle stared at me with a deeply concerned look.

"Yeah, bro. Ya fucken' lose the bastard or sumten?" Howard tilted his head, eyeing me with a distraught glare.

"Sis...bro... why are you two here?" I looked at them in surprise. Howard pushed past me and made his way to the living room.

"Why do you think, dummy?" Elle said, shaking her head. "Let's get inside before we do this in the hallway."

I let Elle in; she moved to the couch, sitting one seat over from Howard. I didn't want to be sandwiched between them, so I moved over to that damned chair. I sat down, avoiding the broken arm. Fuck, they were both here. Why? I wanted to be left alone. Left to the consequences of my stupid choices.

"What happened?" Elle asked, her voice filled with a professional tone. I had never heard that tone from her.

"Nothing. I'm fine." I said, trying my best to mask the pain.

"Nothing huh? What's this shit?" Howard pointed at the gun on the coffee table.

"Was doing some early spring cleaning," I quipped.

"And the rings? Polishing them up after a heist?" Elle said.

"No, I had planned to propose to Sarah and Vicky," I confessed. I felt the sting of my failed relationship in my heart.

"Fucken' hell, bro. Ya all mind-fucked, huh?" Howard sat forward on the couch.

"Mind-fucked? He's a goddamn mess!" Elle glared at Howard before returning her attention to me. "I was surprised you didn't smell like a garbage dump. I figured you would've been sitting on this couch for days, overthinking everything."

She didn't know how spot-on she really was. That would have been the case if they had arrived just a half hour earlier. Wait... what did she know? What did they both know? I hadn't told anyone about anything. I was alone on the couch for days. Sure, I got up to go to the bathroom or get a drink. And to get the gun and rings. But I had posted up on the couch.

"Any word on the divorce?" I deflected from my situation for a moment. Besides, I had been so caught up in my drama that I had forgotten about Elle's.

"I got a court date. I did get to talk to Jenny on the phone this week. I haven't spoken to her since Stephen took her." Elle frowned.

Howard stayed silent. He watched Elle with intent. He seemed to be intrigued to hear about Elle's life.

"How is she?" I leaned forward, curious about my niece.

"Doing good. She played the piano for me. It wasn't too bad. She is starting to pick up notes pretty well." Elle said, her face looked dazed for a moment. I could see that she was wrapped up in her memories of Jenny.

"Is she happy? How is her summer going?" I asked, I wanted to know all I could about my niece's circumstances.

"Oddly, she seemed happier than she was with me. Maybe it was my affa..." Elle trailed off. She seemed guilty about something.

Howard looked concerned as he watched Elle. He reached his hand over, patting her back for a moment, then pulled it away.

"Are you okay, Sis?" My concern filtered through my despair. Talking to her made me forget about my own issues for a moment.

"Yeah, all good," Elle said as a tear ran down her cheek.

"You sure?" I asked. My eyebrows raised with sympathy.

"Yep. I'm sure. Besides, we aren't here to talk about my failures. We are here to talk about yours, so stop deflecting." Elle gave me a stern look; she saw right through me. It was a deflection, but a sincere one. Deep down, I was concerned about Elle. I... I had no idea what to do with people, as evidenced by my current situation.

"Yeah, stop with ya lolligaggen'," Howard added.

"What do you mean?" I questioned.

"Do you think we don't know?" Elle wiped the tear away before she shifted her body toward me. "I'm friends with your girlfriends... Duh! At lunch yesterday, Sarah and Vicky said you guys had a fight. That they had left the apartment."

That's right; I was trying to foster friendships between them. I didn't think that it would backfire on me. I was sure Elle was here to jump on me. To reinforce everything I was already thinking, already feeling. Failures—that was a term you could use.

"Yeah, we had a fight." I sighed, then turned to Howard. Why was he here? "How did you get mixed up in all this?"

"Damn, bro. Put me on the spot like dat. Elle called, said ya needed us." Howard glanced at me before his eyes snapped to the gun on the table. "She was right. Ya need us."

"Talk to us," Elle pleaded. "Please, Kyle. Let us in."

"There's nothing to talk about. I broke up with my girlfriends." I said confidently. I tried to hide my pain once more. Those words, "broke up," hit me harshly. I held back my tears.

"I would remind you that I am a clinician. And by law, I am legally bound to report shit like this," Elle pointed to the weapon. She seemed to be getting annoyed by my evasive attitude. "So, talk to us because we aren't leaving."

"Stephen... was at the job site. The day Howard and I saw each other at the coffee shop, I left the job to avoid dealing with him." I felt a tear crawl down my cheek.

"That why ya seemed weird that day? Shit, thought it was sumten I did." Howard hung his head low. His head tilted slightly to look at me. "Bro, if I had known, I would have talked with ya then."

"Yeah, I know that part. But why did you not talk to Vicky and Sarah about it? Vicky was really torn up. She felt that you didn't trust her." Elle tilted her head back, sighing loudly.

"I don't know. I guess..." I paused for a moment. Why did I not tell them? This entire situation could have been avoided if I had. I'm a fucking loser.

"Ya not a loser, bro." Howard pulled his head up, looking at the shelf next to the entertainment center. "I'd kill to have ya kinda life, brah. Ya always so confident."

"If I had to guess, I think you were afraid, in my expert opinion." Elle moved her hand to her chin as if she had an aha moment.

Scared? Of What? There was nothing that I was afraid of. I was the big bad; the only thing that scared me was me.

"Man, ya gonna have that creepy thousand-yard stare all night?" Howard asked. He seemed freaked out by me. But he soon relaxed. "Told ya once, those girls love ya. And I know ya love them. What's wrong with ya. Can't ya see dat?"

"I do love them, but—"

"But nothing, Bro. Admit it. You were scared. Scared to tell them. Scared they may leave you. Scared that if you didn't have a job, they would—poof, up and disappear." Elle gestured with her hands as if she were conducting a magic trick.

Was that why I was hesitant to tell them? Frightened that they would leave me if I didn't save face in front of them? Maybe... But they were there for me during my flashbacks and nightmares. They didn't judge me then.

"I... Maybe. I don't know. I really don't." I tried to understand what made me not confide in them about the job issue and about Stephen.

"Bro, I never let anyone close. I'm start'en to see that all dis crudeness was a defense. Ya don't need a blanket like me. Ya stronger, bro." Howard kicked his feet up on the coffee table. "Ya girls saw that. Saw how strong ya are, most importantly how kind ya can be."

The room was silent for a moment. Howard moved his hands behind his head, making himself comfortable. Elle just watched me. Her eyes seemed glossy as if they were watering up again.

"Look, them girls love ya. I doubt money means a damn thing to 'em." Howard's feet crossed at his ankles. He took a deep breath before continuing. "I'm always afraid that women only wanna be 'round me for money. But Vicky 'n Sarah see ya for more than that. It's in their eyes. I can see it."

"Damn, Howard. When did you become so insightful? That was good." Elle smirked at him.

I knew I was afraid of myself, of what I could do to Stephen. I knew all too well what kind of damage I could inflict. But why was I scared to talk to my girlfriends about Stephen? Was it because I didn't want them to know the extent of the monster inside?

And why didn't I tell them about not going to work? I was mortified by the idea that they would leave me. I made the excuse to myself that I wanted to enjoy my relationship... But that wasn't the entire truth. If they knew that I may not be able to provide, they might have left me. Seen me as a bum... as a "beta."

"And what if you are right? That I was afraid of them leaving me over my job status? What now?" I asked.

"You are afraid of what is known as hypergamy. But your girlfriends don't seem to subscribe to that ideology. In all my talks with them, I analyzed them. They were genuine in their feelings for you. No hidden motives." Elle's professional voice returned. A head-shrinker for a sister. What was this? A therapy session?

"Ya analyze me too?" Howard asked as he looked up to the ceiling. Elle looked at him, annoyed. Then she turned back to me, seeming to ignore Howard's question.

"Anyway. Stop with that 'all hope is lost' face. They are hurt," Elle pointed at me, "but they are waiting for you. However, I would suggest you get your shit together before you face them again."

"And what does that mean?" I leaned forward in the chair.

"Means, bro, stop this depressed shit for one," Howard answered. "Then pick ya damn self up. How far are ya from ya license, huh?" He pulled his feet off the table as he sat up straight, his hands at his sides. He assumed his business posture.

"I don't know. I could call the construction board to find out." I looked at Howard. His demeanor was back to that serious businessman attitude.

"That's a start," Elle said. "I'm going to set you up with a colleague of mine. She deals with veterans all the time. It could do you some good to see a therapist. Maybe visit the VA for meds? At least until you can cope on your own."

"Whoa, Sis. I can't go to a shrink. I—"

"Stop right there!" she snapped. "You are going! Those poor girls can't shoulder your baggage on their own."

"Bro, listen to ya sista. Ya have a lot of kooky carry-on. But ya a good guy. Ya my bro 'cause ya a good dude."

"Thanks, Howard," Elle smirked. She seemed happy that Howard had her back.

"Why can't you therapize me, or whatever it's called?" I asked in recourse. I didn't want to let a stranger into my mind, kicking their feet around in areas they had no right to.

"Conflict of interest. I can't be your therapist. I have a biased view of your life. You need a third party that is not in your immediate circle," Elle calmly explained.

"Great, that's all I need. A stranger trampling around my already screwed-up mind." I shook my head.

"It's that or face it alone. And from the looks of it, you're doing a great job, huh!" Elle yelled as she pointed to my sidearm.

"Could be worse, bro. Could have them tramplen' ya balls." Howard joked, trying to bring the tensions down.

Silence momentarily filled the air. I thought about therapy during this quiet reprieve. I figured I would at least give it a try. What could it hurt? I had already lost my job... and the women I loved. There wasn't much else for me to lose.

"Okay, set it up. But the meds... The VA... It's like a circus. Doubt I get an appointment any time soon." I caved with a sigh.

"Now, discharge this gun. Or whatever you have to do to keep it from being used." Elle looked at me. I started to laugh at her comment. Discharge it?

I chuckled. "I think you meant to say disassemble it. Discharge means to shoot it."

"Ya know what she meant, bro. She ain't a gun person." Howard backed up Elle, yet his voice had a lightheartedness to it.

I leaned forward, picking up the sidearm. I dropped the magazine and cleared the round I had chambered. I pulled the slide apart, removed the bolt, and handed it to Elle. "Happy?" I asked the room as I set the remaining pieces of the gun on the coffee table.

"Is this what makes it shoot?" Elle asked, examining the bolt.

"Yes. That's the bolt. The little pokey piece sticking out the front sliding back and forth, that's the firing pin." I explained, on a basic level, the nomenclatures of the weapon to Elle.

"Good. Now, what do you want to eat? I am sure your pervy ass hasn't eaten in days." Elle put the weapon piece in her pocket.

"Food, shit, I'm down." Howard chuckled as he stood up, stretching.

"Chinese? I know they deliver here."

"Chinese it is. What do you want, Howard?" Elle looked up to Howard as she reached into her purse to retrieve her phone.

"Those noodles with chunks of beef." Howard gave Elle his food order as he walked over to the shelf with my D&D figures. He started to scan each shelf carefully.

"Beef Chow Mein, got it." Elle gave a mockingly weak salute to Howard, then she started speaking on her phone.

"Brah, is this da stuff at that geek shop?" Howard picked up my barbarian, which I had placed on the shelf to protect the girls' cherub figure. I smirked, reminded of the silly exchange about protecting their cherub from the owlbear.

"Mm-hm, they have loads of stuff like that. Most of those figures are from there," I explained.

"Even these?" Howard pointed toward several of the cute figurines the girls had placed on the shelves.

"No, those are theirs." I looked down at the floor.

The heavy feeling of missing my girlfriends hit me once more. I remembered standing in the bedroom doorway, watching them. How beautiful they were just doing things around the apartment. All the cute things we talked about. And yes, my desire to marry them. But I shook it off for the moment. I didn't want to cry again.

"Takeout should be here in about twenty or thirty minutes." Elle broke my focus as she explained the food situation.

"Cool. In the meantime, wanna play a game?" I directed my question to the entire room.

"What game? Oh! Do you have that one that I used to kick your ass on when I came home from college?" Elle asked excitedly.

"You mean Halo? Sort of... I got Halo 3," I explained, laughing at her excitement.

"Halo! Fuck yeah! I'm in! Gonna kick both ya asses." Howard moved over to the entertainment center, gathering my controllers. He soon handed them out.

We played for hours, only taking a break to eat our Chinese food. I had fun playing with them. Elle and Howard went back to their usual banter. Both of them talked all kinds of crap back and forth. I think that was the best part. Seeing them get along in their unique and eccentric way.

At one point, while the game was paused for Elle to take a bathroom break, Howard mentioned finishing up the coffee shop deal. We discussed it for a while. When Elle got back, she joined in the conversation encouraging me to go for the deal. I eventually agreed to buy half and partner in on the deal.

The gaming got intense by the climax of the night. Elle was screaming profanities. Howard was mostly laughing; I was sure he was laughing at Elle's heated gaming banter. I came out victorious, winning most of the matches we played. We simmered down from the gaming, talking for a bit longer. When they were satisfied that I was in a better state of mind, they called it a night.

After Elle and Howard left, I laid down in bed. I had a mission: Start working on the lesser parts of myself. Then, go to my beauties and apologize for my screwups. Hopefully, they'd accept my apology.

Should I propose? I couldn't decide if I should or not. I didn't know if it was warranted at this point. Or if they would still want me, but I had to try. I wanted to earn back my girlfriends. I wouldn't fail them again. This time, I would ensure I was worthy of their love.

I needed to work on many preparations for their arrival home. Home, that was what they meant to me. I loved them with all that I was, and the mission I gave myself was proof of it. I started to drift off into my rest. I was going to need it. This week was going to be high-paced, one of those "high speed, low drag" weeks.

Chapter 21: Panacea of a Triangle

I began the week on a sprint. I spent all of Sunday cleaning every inch of the apartment. I wanted to make sure everything was in top shape when Sarah and Vicky came home.

On Monday, Howard and I closed on that coffee shop deal. It had become as important to me as it was for him. It was a memorial for his parents' love, a way for him to honor their devotion to each other. And to show gratitude for their parental love of him.

His mother cried when Howard took her to the shop that they now owned. His father hugged him tightly. Howard was ecstatic about giving his parents such a gift. I enjoyed watching their reactions. It made me think about my beauties.

To me, the shop was a proclamation of my love. It meant that I had a secondary source of income. Regardless of our financial circumstances, I could always provide for Sarah and Vicky. They weren't materialistic, but I wanted to start a family with them. I wanted to prove that I would be the husband they deserved. One day, hopefully, be the father our children deserve. That's if they still wanted to have children with me.

Later that day, I called the construction board. I discovered that I had enough hours to sit for my test. While in the Army, I took some correspondence courses in HVAC, which I didn't know counted toward my time. The construction board approved all my hours, so I had more than enough for my license. My test was scheduled for next Friday. I had almost two weeks to prepare. I would spend the rest of the week and next week studying. I knew that I would pass; I felt it in my bones. Hoo-ah!

Howard and I couldn't find a commercial truck available. However, we did find an excellent commercial van. We settled on the idea and signed the purchase agreement. The van was a good choice because, at the moment, I didn't have a place of business. I could store my tools and equipment in it for now. I could also run the business out of the van until we found a location for me. I was happy that Forester Heat and Air would be my new place of employment.

Things were shaping up for me to be a self-made man. Now, all I needed to do was work on myself. Straighten up my mind.

Tuesday morning. I had my first session with my therapist. I was nervous about it, but I had to try. I had to get my mind right. I put on my boots and made my way out of the apartment. I walked down the stairs to the car.

As I exited the apartment building, I noticed the van was gone. Howard must have already picked it up. He was having it wrapped professionally, and he already had a logo for the HVAC company. He said that he had paid to have it designed the day after our drunken episode. I was surprised but knew things would turn out right in his capable hands.

I got in the beater and headed toward the shrink, driving leisurely to the address. I was in no hurry to get there. Was it hesitation? Or was it shame? I had no idea.

What was this therapist going to say? Would she think that I was a rabid dog? That I needed to be taken out back and shot? Or would she understand?

I thought about Vicky and Sarah. My mind fell upon how I had scared them with my flashbacks. Could this psych stuff work to stop those? Could it help with my anger?

I was worried that I was about to be judged harshly. Maybe a mirror reflection of how I felt over the weekend would be shoved in my face. No, Elle had said that this therapist was good at handling veterans. Maybe she knew her way around my brand of crazy.

I pulled into the parking lot. It was mostly empty, with only three other vehicles. The car slid smoothly into a spot right in front of the door. I looked at the time before turning the car off. Eight thirty-nine. Good, I made it on time. My appointment was at nine. The building was constructed of red brick. There was a large pane-glass window overlooking the parking lot.

I took a deep breath before leaving the vehicle. I shuffled toward the entrance. As I entered, I was met with light blue walls. A circular desk poked out from the far wall. Behind the desk sat an elderly man in a brown cardigan. His eyes seemed kind.

"Good morning, sir. Appointment?"

"Yes, sir. Forester. I have a nine o'clock," I said with a bit of apprehension.

"Ah, Holly's new client. Let me get the paperwork. Do you have your insurance card?" He asked warmly. He turned around and shuffled through some papers, then he turned back and neatly put them on a clipboard.

"Yes, sir, here you are." I handed him my VA card. He took the card and gave me the clipboard.

"Have a seat over there. Holly will be out in a minute." He pointed toward a row of black chairs. Then he went to the back of the office. I picked up a pen from the plethora in a cup on the desk.

I sat in the waiting area as I filled out the paperwork. It included questions like how are you feeling today?; on a scale of one to ten, how depressed are you?; how often do you feel angry?; how often do you feel overwhelmed? I answered each one honestly with as much detail as possible.

Before I knew it, there was a tap on my shoulder. I looked up. A brunette woman with sharp brown eyes leaned down. She looked at me with sympathy in her eyes.

"Kyle? I'm Holly." The woman said.

"Hello, I guess you're the therapist my sister set me up with." I looked into her eyes; they seemed empathetic.

"Yep, let's go to my office. Would you like something to drink?" Holly motioned me to follow her.

"No, ma'am. I'm fine," I answered as I got up from the chair. "The clipboard?"

"Bring it; we'll go over it." She turned and led on.

I followed behind her on the blue-gray carpet. We made it to her office. She ushered me in, taking the clipboard from me. Then, as I made my way in, she closed the door behind us.

Military paraphernalia decorated the room. I walked over to the shelf where most of it was. There was a picture on the top shelf. A bunch of Marines huddled together around a HUMVEE. On the right side was Holly in uniform.

"Marine?" I asked before turning around.

"Navy, actually. I was a Navy corpsman. A medic." She grinned as she walked behind her desk. The fact that she was a fellow veteran made me start to feel at ease.

"I was Army, eleven bang-bang in the fourth infantry division." I smirked, sitting in the chair opposite her desk.

"Ah, a grunt. I was assigned to the second Marines when I was in Iraq," she responded as she sat down.

"So... what do we do?" I asked, trying to figure out the process.

"Why don't we start with what brought you here today?" She set the clipboard on her desk after skimming it.

"My girlfriends... I lost them," I said with remorse.

Holly leaned forward, her eyes focused in on me. She looked surprised. It was a strange, funny look. I wanted to laugh at her face but held my composure.

"Girlfriends? How many do you have?" Holly leaned back in her chair, her eyebrows furrowed.

"Two. I screwed up with them."

"Did they find out about each other?" Her eyes seemed to turn cold for a second.

"I didn't cheat on them if that's what you're implying." I shook my head. "I'm in a poly relationship."

The room was momentarily silent. She seemed confused yet intrigued. I wasn't sure what she was thinking. Then she spoke up.

"Okay. So, what happened?" She was still masking a shocked expression.

"Stephen, Elle's husband, was the client of my last job. I was an HVAC tech. Well, he was at the job site where I was doing an installation. I was having a hard time... not... attacking him," I explained, leaning forward in my chair.

"Why did you want to attack him?"

"He abused Elle, hit her. She left him. Then he took Jenny, my niece." The anger in me started to surface, but I pushed it down. I wasn't sure if she knew about Stephen's abusive behavior or not.

"Okay. Sounds reasonable that you wanted to do something about it." She nodded her head knowingly.

"So, I left the job site. That was last Monday. On Tuesday, I stayed out of work; I didn't even call in. It was also Vicky's birthday." I started to feel that shame again.

"Hmm... Vicky is one of the girlfriends?" She placed her hands together on the desk.

"Yes. Sarah, my other girlfriend, and I had planned a special birthday for her. We had a great night." I felt the loss of not having them with me.

"Sounds like you were doing good with them. What happened?" Her hands pulled away from each other. She seemed intrigued.

"I didn't tell them about staying out of work. I was afraid to. I didn't want them to think less of me." I averted my eyes.

"Uh-huh. Why would they think less of you?" she asked softly.

"The anger inside me... That I couldn't handle my job. I was semi-aware that I could lose my job if I skipped out of work. I felt they wouldn't want to be with a jobless bum," I admitted. When our eyes met, tears started to form.

"I assume you did get fired." She tilted her head, looking at me with a knowing face.

"Yep, you guessed it. So, I had no choice but to tell them. Vicky was pissed. But not about me losing my job. She was mad that I lied to them and kept them in the dark. Things escalated, and I yelled at them to leave." I felt my heart getting tight as the words came out.

"Okay, and now they are gone. How did the fight make you feel?" Holly asked.

"Like shit. Like I had wronged them. Vicky was saying some harsh things. I pretty much felt she was right. Sarah, on the other hand, had stood up for me."

"What did you feel when Sarah took your side."

"I felt better, but I didn't feel like the man she was describing. I felt... felt more like what Vicky was saying about me." I started feeling the emotions inside build up again.

"Do you love them?" She looked at me with an odd face.

"Look, I know it's wild. I sometimes don't fully understand it myself. But..." I thought about Sarah and Vicky. I wanted to see their beautiful faces again, even if for only a moment. "I know the whole three-way relationship is odd, but I love them more than words can describe." I stared intensely into Holly's eyes.

How do I tell Holly about my feelings for Vicky and Sarah? I felt I couldn't live without them... almost ended things because of it.

"I remember every detail of their faces. Those beatific smiles always melted my heart. We had fun on our dates. I was overjoyed at how special we made Vicky's birthday celebration. The look on her face that night was something from a movie." I paused again, smiling in remembrance of that night. Then I snapped back.

"I want to plan more events for them. Making each one special, just to see them happy. And our banter, that cute, funny, and sexually charged banter we shared. The way we always encouraged each other. And I was always fascinated by how they said things with that creepy but cute unison." I paused, thinking about all of it.

"But most importantly, how I feel around them. The jumble of emotions they inspired simply by existing. They're worth everything. I would give them the deed to the entire universe if I could. Well, maybe not the universe, but I'd give them the deed to my heart, to my soul. I wanted to give them everything they deserved and more. So yes, I do love them." Tears fell from my eyes.

"Do you have a plan? What have you done to show them that you love them?" Holly asked, her face seemed to soften.

"I need to apologize first. Then, I will explain what I did to get my career back on track. Maybe... tell them about this. About therapy. But I don't know." I trailed off. What would they think about me going to therapy?

"Sounds like a solid plan. Look, I can see you deeply care about them. Just be honest. Open up like you are here. I am sure they love you." Holly leaned forward; her eyes peered deep into mine.

I felt a bit of the pressure ease. "Thank you. I hope they do."

"I saw on your questionnaire that you have flashbacks and nightmares." She flipped through the pages on the clipboard.

"Yeah, stuff from overseas on my deployments," I confessed.

"Okay, I suggest we meet three times a week. We need to explore your trauma from combat." She paused for a moment, looking over the paperwork. "And your anger..."

"Yeah, what can we do about it?" I asked, wiping away tears.

"Medication can help. I assume you get your meds from the VA?" Holly looked at me. I was sure she understood the VA process, so I nodded to her.

"Okay, until you can visit the VA, I want you to do something physical, like sports, working out, jogging, to relieve stress." Holly smiled at me before she started writing something on a paper.

"I know one physical activity that would be a great stress reliever. It would work to relieve stress for me and my lovelies." I quipped with a chuckle.

"Hmm... haha." She tittered as she continued to write.

"I'm a guy; sex is a constant." I chuckled.

The rest of the hour was spent digging into my military career. She asked questions about my feelings toward it and about it. She seemed to listen with care as I explained my mixed emotions.

"Okay, Casanova, take this to the VA. Well, whenever you have an appointment. And I will see you on Friday. Starting next week, we will do Mondays, Wednesdays, and Fridays." She folded the paper and put it in an envelope.

"Okay, thank you. See you Friday." I smiled and grabbed the envelope.

"On Friday, we will start getting into your service's bad stuff. Be prepared. It can get emotional from here on." Her words were encouraging.

"Yes, ma'am. Wilco," I said before exiting.

I left her office and walked down the hallway back to the lobby. The receptionist waved me over as I walked by.

"Here's your insurance card. I already have you down for Friday. Have a great day, Kyle." He smiled at me as he handed me my insurance card.

"What's your name? Sorry, I didn't ask earlier."

"John." His smile widened, ironing out some of the age lines.

"Have a good day, John," I said before turning and exiting.

I got in the car, feeling better about the situation. Not much was said to me, but I somehow felt better. I drove home with the sense that this would be achievable, to win back the hearts of my loves.

Traffic seemed clear as I moved forward. I made it back to the apartment. I looked over; the van was still gone. I was sure that Howard still had it at the body shop. I exited the car and made my way inside the apartment building.

After arriving home, I pulled out my books. I eased into the couch, getting comfortable to study. The rest of the day was mostly spent studying my HVAC books. I wanted to ace the test. When it got around seventeen hundred hours, I stopped studying.

I had dinner planned with Elle, just the two of us. She wanted to discuss my therapy session and my love life. Elle picked a diner on the outskirts of town. I was sure she chose this place because of its remote location. Probably to avoid areas she frequented with Stephen. She said they served southern homestyle cuisine.

I went downstairs to my vehicle and started my beater again. I headed toward the directions Elle had given me.

With the traffic, it took almost forty-five minutes to get there. I pulled into the parking lot and killed the engine. I peered over the dashboard at the restaurant. It appeared to be a simple mom-and-pop place. The building was made of aged red brick. The paint on the sign was faded, with cracks along the surface. I got out of my beater and walked toward the entrance.

The doors were hard to pull, and as they opened, I felt a vortex of air hit me. Someone had miscalculated the air conditioning system's CFM, probably to compensate for the kitchen's heat. I stepped in, the space seemed unfinished. The tables had mismatched chairs around them, you could see the rafters, and the ductwork was exposed. But the aroma of the food smelled delicious.

Elle waved at me. "Bro, I got us a table." I started moving toward the table. Elle shifted from the seat that faced the door to the opposite side. Was she aware of my need to face the entrance?

"Hey, Sis." I sat down at the table.

"How did your session with Holly go?" Elle dived straight into her questioning.

"Good... I guess. She seemed shocked that I was dating two women." I chuckled slightly, remembering the look on Holly's face as I explained my love life.

"No surprise there. I was shocked, too, at first." Elle smirked with a funny smile.

"It's different. But—" I was interrupted by the waitress.

"Welcome. Can I take your orders?" the waitress asked. Elle and I both ordered the chicken fried steak with a side of mashed potatoes. I got fried okra, and she got mac and cheese.

"So, you were saying?" Elle encouraged me to continue as the waitress walked off.

"I am still trying to navigate the whole three-way relationship. But I do love them." I finished the thought that I had earlier.

"Are you feeling any better after talking with Holly?" Elle asked as the waitress placed our drinks on the table.

"I am still feeling off about how I treated Sarah and Vicky. Not only the lie but my outburst, too." I sighed, pausing for a moment. I reached over to take a sip of my drink before continuing. "But I'm feeling better than a few days ago."

"I haven't talked with them since the day they told me everything over lunch. So... I don't know what's going on with them." Elle seemed disappointed in herself for not getting me an update on my girlfriends.

"It's okay." I reached my hand out, patting her head.

"Hey. I'm the eldest; I'm the only one that can do stuff like that." Elle smiled, reaching over and patting my head back.

"Really? Got a monopoly on that, huh." I joked as I put my hand back on the table.

"Yeah, I do. So, how are we going to win your princesses back, oh kind, prince charming?" Elle pulled her hand back, making a slightly mocking bow as she joked.

"Start with an apology, I guess. Hope they accept my apology." My words came out with a bit of sorrow. My smile faded.

"I am sure they will. They love you, silly. Even with your goofy pervyness." Elle encouraged me with a chuckle. Her smile widened.

"I was planning on looking for them tomorrow. But... I have no idea where to start." I said in a low voice, almost whispering. A sense of hopelessness filled me.

"I think I may have an idea." Elle pulled a pen from her purse and jotted something down on a napkin. Then she slid it over to me. "This is Naomi's address. Try there first."

"Thank you. I won't ask how you have her address. But... thank you." I smiled.

There was hope. Hope that I could find them and apologize. Hope that I could win them back, win back their affection.

Then, the idea of Vicky and Sarah rejecting my marriage proposal entered my mind. This sent my thoughts into a panic. Had I broken this relationship bad enough to not be worthy of marriage? Would they say yes? Or was the answer a harsh no?

Elle looked at me with concern. "What's with that face? Why do you look like someone punched you in the stomach?"

"Was thinking about my proposal," I said as I saw the waitress out of the corner of my eye. She set our plates on the table.

"Need anything else?" The waitress asked.

"No, but thank you." Elle smiled at the waitress.

"Okay, so what about the proposal?" Elle picked up her fork and started to cut into her chicken-fried steak.

"I'm afraid they will reject the idea of marrying me." I stabbed my fork into the fried okra. "Or that they won't like the rings."

"Listen, Bro... Stop worrying. They are going to be happy with the rings. And I know they will say yes." Elle's voice got low. She pulled her fork up for a bite.

"Or maybe I screwed up too much. Maybe they'll turn me down." I looked at the mashed potatoes before gathering a scoop.

"Thick-headed as ever. They will say yes. Believe in yourself. Believe in them. Believe in the love you three have." Elle waved her fork around, exaggerating her point.

"Yeah..." I looked down at my plate.

"Start with the apology. The rest will fall into place. Let your love guide you. And just believe." Elle smiled at me before taking a sip of her drink.

"I choose to believe. I will have hope." I appreciated her encouragement.

The rest of the dinner went well. We talked about how Howard stomped us for the first half of our Halo match the other night. Then, my victorious return by the latter half. She was surprised by how much fun she had with us that night. I could tell something was growing inside her. A fondness of Howard... maybe?

After we paid, I went back to the apartment. On the drive, I thought about what I was going to say.

Apologize first, yes that was best. Then... hmm... explain the things that I had started to improve on. Should I tell them about my therapy session? Maybe. But I was definitely not leading off with that. Great way to get your girlfriends back. What would I say? "You know how crazy I am... well, now I have a shrink to explain my craziness to me." Yeah, that will go over well.

I could explain that I bought the coffee shop. I could also tell them about the HVAC business. That we have a chance to start it up earlier than we thought. What else?

I wanted to propose. But was it right to? I would bring the rings, just in case things went well. But then I started to imagine how the proposal would go. I imagined both scenarios: If they said yes, and if they said no, either decision would change my life forever. I just had to believe... have hope that it was brighter.

I turned on the radio to distract myself from bad thoughts. I didn't want them to creep in. During the rest of the ride, I jammed out to different songs. Before I knew it, I had pulled into the apartment parking lot, sliding in next to my work van.

Howard had taken it earlier to get a wrap done on it. This was the first time I had seen it. I excitedly examined the van top to bottom, admiring how the wrap looked. Large "Forester Heat and

Air" logos were printed on the sides. Forester... my name on a professional vehicle, made me feel accomplished.

"Kyle, is that yours?" I heard a familiar voice behind me.

"Yes. How are you, Wanda?" I turned to see Mrs. Helderman standing a few feet from me.

"You are intriguing indeed, my boy." She said as her head shook slightly. "I'm fine. But you didn't seem to be for a few days."

"Fought with the girls the other night. They left." I looked down at the pavement to avert my eyes for a moment.

"I know, I heard the commotion. You broke one of the golden rules: communication." Mrs. Helderman gave me a stern look.

"Yeah... I did. I hurt them." I looked at the streetlight momentarily as I felt the shame of my actions again.

"The same thing happened in my relationship." Mrs. Helderman looked distraught in her memory.

"Did Jimmy lose his job and lie about it?" Did the same thing happen. Was I stuck in a cycle of history repeating itself?

"No. Nothing like that. Helda had an affair. She kept it from us." Her face turned sour for a moment before returning.

"Oh. I'm sorry. What happened?" I felt empathy for her.

"Jimmy found out. He was furious at first. He wasn't angry at the affair. But..." She trailed off in her memories again.

"He was upset about the lie." I knew all too well what her following words were going to be. I felt it in my own situation.

"Yes... We had a sit-down. Laid all the cards out." She paused. Her face seemed to ease. "Then the truth came out. She was feeling neglected by us."

"I have tried to make sure that doesn't happen with Vicky and Sarah." I looked at her with understanding. I knew what she was talking about. I'd feared that was the case with my relationship.

"I know you have, my boy. But we didn't have someone with experience to guide us." She smiled for a moment, then continued. "We all three learned a lesson that day."

"Did things go back to normal afterward?" I could only hope.

"No, they didn't." She paused and looked at me intently. My heart sank. Things didn't go back to normal... If she couldn't get things back on track, how could I?

"Instead, they got better," she continued. "We were more open with each other. With each talk, our relationship grew stronger. The drama of it all taught us major lessons." She smiled with hope for a moment.

"I am glad." I felt the smile on my face come back.

"Did you learn your lesson? Learn always to be honest with them?" Mrs. Helderman folded her arms in front of her.

"I learned my lesson. You were right; I should always be open and honest with them." I leaned against the chilly surface of the van.

"Good, my boy. You have grown into a different kind of man," she said as her frail arms uncrossed and fell at her side. She started to walk toward me. "I thought you may have lost them for good."

"Me too. But I have started to make changes. And I plan to find them tomorrow. Apologize for being such a moron." As Mrs. Helderman approached, she held out her arms, inviting me in for a hug. I accepted it, both our arms closing around each other.

"Go to them, my boy. Rekindle that love. Bond with them again. Strengthen that love," Mrs. Helderman whispered in my ear. Seconds later, she released her hug.

"I will. Thank you," I whispered. I released her. That hug was what I needed to see this through.

"Let's get inside. Youth can handle this chilliness, but these old bones ache from it." Mrs. Helderman chuckled as she turned toward the apartment building. I escorted her inside. Before she entered her apartment, she turned to me. "Have a good night. And good luck tomorrow." Then she went into her abode.

"Good night." I smiled at her encouragement.

After getting settled in, I set out my suit. Then I showered and groomed, readying myself for the morning. Tomorrow was the day that I would go to them. Attempting to win my beauties back. When all the preparations were complete, I decided to lie down.

I lay in bed for hours as I tried to sleep. I tossed and turned, but my mind wouldn't shut off. I think the anxiety about tomorrow kept me up. About my attempt to win them back. Damn!

If they said yes, we could move back in together. I'd propose. Give them the rings. Then figure out some way to marry them, even if it wasn't a legal marriage. We could live together and in our hearts be married, right? Society doesn't matter. Our love matters. It's all that matters. My mind dwelled on this most of the night.

I picked up my phone. I needed a failsafe if I overslept because of this. I hastily texted Howard.

[Kyle] Wednesday 03:42

Hey bro if I haven't texted by noon call me please

    I was about to give up trying to sleep. Just see if I could stay up. As I placed my phone on the nightstand, my eyes saw them. The stuffed animals I bought for Vicky and Sarah on our zoo date were lying on it. Maybe they will help me sleep.

    Instinctively, my arms reached out, pulling them to my chest. I cuddled around the stuffed animals, feeling the essence of Vicky and Sarah nearby. Soon after, I started to feel my eyes get heavy. The tiger and crane pulled me into dreamland. Into dreams of them... my wives...

Chapter 22: Souls Found

Bah-ring! Bah-ring! Bah-ring!

I was startled awake by my phone ringing. Aah! The sun broke into the window, blinding my eyes. But I opened them anyway. My vision seemed foggy. I answered the phone in haste, just to stop it from ringing. I put it to my ear.

"Brah, ya up?" The voice on the other end said loudly... Howard, it was Howard.

"I am, now." My voice bellowed groggily. I tried to get my orientation.

"Ya said if ya hadn't texted by noon to call." His voice sounded like he was yelling into the mouthpiece.

"Thanks, bro... Wait... It's noon... crap." I looked over at the alarm clock. Twelve thirty-three hours. How long had I slept? How long was I tossing and turning before falling asleep?

"Ya gonna be okay?" Howard's voice softened.

"Yes. Thanks again, bro. I'm getting up now." My free hand placed the stuffed animals back on the nightstand.

"Welcome, bro. Ya gonna look for ya girls?" His voice seemed sympathetic.

"Yeah, after I'm up and around. Oh... Saw the van; looks sweet as hell." I yawned as I was starting to wake up fully.

"Knew ya'd like it. Hey... gotta go, bro. See ya tonight. Tell me how it goes with ya girls," Howard said. He seemed distracted by something.

"See you later, bro," I said before the call ended.

Wednesday... noon. The girls would be at work until fifteen-hundred hours or so. I had time to kill, so I laid in bed for a while longer. I looked at the stuffed animals. They helped me fall asleep. They gave me the feeling that Sarah and Vicky were next to me.

I lay on the bed for a while, my thoughts being nothing but them. I finally got motivated to put some finishing touches on the apartment. I cleaned up the final areas that needed it. Music jammed throughout the apartment.

Around fourteen forty-five hours, I got dressed. I put on my suit, aligning my gig line. I wanted to look sharp for them. I slipped the ring boxes in my coat pocket.

I went to the mirror and stared at the man on the other side. Gazing into my own eyes, I started to gather my courage. Apologize to them. Explain to them how much I loved them. Then... propose. Yeah, the proposal. It didn't matter what their answer was. I just needed to let them know how I felt. I pivoted from the mirror.

When I left the lonely apartment, I hoped to bring its life, its heart, back with me. Hastily, I descended the stairs and made a beeline for my car. I was on a mission. Love was your objective, Sergeant. Retreat was not an option. It was do or die, now or never.

My foot felt heavy on the accelerator. I pulled out of the parking lot and headed across the city toward the address Elle had provided. I was looking for 721 Venus Drive.

The traffic was thick, but my tactical driving skills enabled me to navigate it. I switched lanes often, trying to pass by the slower vehicles. I focused on my mission. Get there. Just... get there.

I drove for what felt like forever. Then I finally turned down the street written on the napkin. The neighborhood was upper middle class. Large two-story homes on both sides of the street. Most of the houses had gray bricks that looked like granite. The trim was painted in a light blue to accent the bricks. These houses weren't mansions, like Howard's place, but they were still nice.

I slowed down to read the addresses: 715...717...719... I saw it just a few houses down. I pulled into the driveway and parked. I'd finally made it. This was it, Sergeant. You can do this. I hurried to the door. My knuckles rapped loudly on the dark oak door.

I waited for what felt like a lifetime. My heart was in my throat, and I felt the full force of my anxiety. I knocked once more. Then it started to open. Standing in the doorway was Naomi, dressed in business attire. Her eyes widened when she saw it was me.

Naomi smirked. "You don't have to kick the door off its hinges."

"Can I speak with Vicky and Sarah?" I stammered, my courage waning a bit.

"They're not here, darling." Naomi slanted her body to rest on the door frame.

"Okay, sorry to bother you, Mrs. Schein." I looked down, disappointment slicing through me.

Naomi chuckled and shook her head. "Son, I told you to call me Mom."

"I know, but... I don't know if that future, me being your son-in-law, will happen," I said somberly, looking up into her eyes.

"So naïve. Tell you what... if my daughters take you back, invite me to dinner at least once a month." She moved forward as her hand reached out and caressed my cheek. "And make sure my ungrateful progenies remember me on Mother's Day."

"I will, Mom... if they take me back."

"Good boy. And have faith, darling," Naomi said as she gave me a light, playful slap. "Love is a powerful thing. It can change the very essence of the universe. Remember that, Son?" Naomi smiled knowingly, as if she knew something but wanted to keep it hidden.

"Yeah, it is very powerful." I smiled. Whatever she was hiding had to be positive—hopeful even.

"Well, darling, I have a business meeting soon. Let me know how it goes. I'll be waiting for my dinner invite." Naomi winked.

"Goodbye, Mom," I said, feeling renewed. It was strange that being in her presence made me feel at ease.

"Bye, Son," Naomi said before she closed the door.

I turned and walked back to my beater. As I was opening the car door, I heard an excited squeal from down the street. I looked to see where it came from. Vicky and Sarah were on the sidewalk less than half a block away rushing toward the house.

"Master! It's Master!" Sarah excitedly shrieked.

Vicky huffed with agitation. "Quiet down. I have eyes, you know."

I closed the car door and walked to the end of the driveway. In less than a moment, they had made their way to me.

"Yeah, what do you want, Kyle?" Vicky snarled; her tone felt like ice shards attacking my heart. She aggressively crossed her arms in front of her.

"Master, I knew you would come!" Sarah bounced with gleeful giddiness.

"I wanted to apologize. I'm sorry for lying to you about my job." The remorse in my words could be felt by anyone listening.

"And?" Vicky eyed me; the look on her face said that she wanted to rip my head off.

"And I am sorry I yelled at you... both of you. Sorry that I got angry." My eyes darted between them, seeking some sign of what they were thinking.

"*Pft*. That it?" Vicky tilted her head; she huffed out a low sigh. Her eyes studied me with a chilly stare. "That all you got to say?"

"Vicky, lay off him. He's here. Apologizing." Sarah turned to Vicky. Her fiery locks flowed around her body as she turned. The sun hitting the crimson hue of her hair made it seem like flames were engulfing her.

"That's not all... Not in the least." Courageously, my words came out with that NCO tone. This surprised me. Had that tone become instinctive to use around them?

There was a brief silence as both looked at me. They had that look, reminiscent of their glow the first time I called them good girls. Maybe there was hope for this. Hope for us. But that look quickly faded from Vicky's eyes.

Sarah broke the silence as she turned to me with confusion. "It's strange. You don't talk out loud as much as you used to... You don't unknowingly let us in anymore..." She leaned forward for a moment. Her eyes squinted as if she were a doctor examining me.

"Okay. So, you came here to apologize. And you did. You can leave now." Vicky gave me a brief mock smile as her hand feigned a quick wave.

The way Vicky dismissed me hurt. The pain of her rejection started to make me rethink this. Creeping in was a dreadful feeling I was failing. It washed over me. My courage started to falter. Maybe I should leave. It's not like they were interested in what I had to say.

"That's not all I came for. I came... I..." My words were barely there. Dammit, Sergeant, say it. Just... fucking say it.

"Sarah, we don't have time for this. Let's go inside." Vicky briefly glanced at Sarah. Uncrossing her arms, she grabbed Sarah by the wrist, giving Sarah a light tug.

I had lost; they hated me. I was nothing to them. Nothing at all.

"But... I... Please, can we hear him out?" Sarah stammered. Vicky turned to walk away, still tugging Sarah's arm.

No, goddamn it. I came here with a mission. To tell them everything. To tell them how I felt. Sarah was still interested in hearing what I had to say. I must give it one last shot. I couldn't just give up. Get your courage up. Remember, you are a soldier. You can do this.

"I started therapy yesterday. And I will be seeking help from the VA, too." I timidly admitted.

"That's wonderful... Vicky, he is doing it. He is seeking help. That should count for something, right?" Sarah said as she broke away from Vicky's grasp.

"Yeah... I guess." Vicky sighed in disgust as she turned back to me. I could see her eyes had a slight warmth to them.

Okay... I got their attention again. I can... I can do this. Even if they say no. Even if they never want to see me again. I have to be honest with them. I have to speak my mind... speak my heart.

"I am studying for my license. I found out I can take the test now. Also, Howard and I got a van instead of a truck," I explained. As I talked, Vicky just sighed.

"Congratulations, Master. I know you will pass the test. I just know it!" Sarah burst out with elation.

I watched Vicky. Her body seemed tense; nothing I said seemed to break through her wall of ice.

"Who cares? You were going to do that anyway." Vicky huffed with annoyance. It seemed that I was starting to bore her again.

"I went ahead with that coffee shop deal. And I know—before you say it, I know—you think it's a mistake. But I bought it for a reason." I shifted my weight. I thought about the real reason I bought it. It was for them.

"You bought it? Cool. Now I can get a lifetime supply of free coffee." Sarah chuckled with happiness. Excited, she bounced in a sort of dance on the sidewalk.

"Reason, yeah. Let me guess, to make money." Vicky waved her hand in a circling motion to coldly mock me.

"Not exactly to make money. Not entirely, anyway. My true reason for buying it was you two. I bought it for you." I paused for a second, feeling drowsy; the almost sleepless night still weighed on me.

"So sweet! Vicky! Did you hear? For us... He bought it for us." Sarah's excitement was boiling over.

I looked at them, trying to guess what they were thinking. I glanced over at Sarah, whose face was nothing but a smile. Vicky looked intrigued as if she was watching me with anticipation.

"Regardless of our financial circumstances, I want to always provide for you. I know that money doesn't matter to either of you. But... I want to start a family with you both. And to do that. I need secure ways to bring income into our home."

271

My gaze fell back on Vicky. I could see a slight smile on her face. Her eyes showed that warmth again. Maybe I was starting to melt through Vicky's glacier. Seeing that smile made my heart race.

"Makes sense." Vicky's smile grew a little more.

Both of their beautiful smiles were tugging at me to keep going. And the thought of seeing those smiles every day for the rest of my life, that would be heaven. Keep going, Sergeant.

"And from now on, no matter what, I will always come to you, both of you." With deep remorse, I continued. "I will never lie to you… never again. I will tell you what is happening when it happens." My NCO tone surfaced once more.

"See, Vicky…" Sarah's face glowed as she side-eyed Vicky.

"More… I'm still listening," Vicky said as she eyed me with a lighthearted gaze. Her words were reminiscent of the talk we had early in the relationship, the conversation we had about how this three-way relationship could work.

My mind lingered on that day for a moment. I had convinced myself that they were dreams. Fantasies that I had made up. How wrong I was… Or was it that I was right? They were and still are dreams… my dreams. My living dreams. Dreams that I loved. That I wanted to marry.

"Earth to space cadet… we are in the middle of a conversation here." Vicky snapped her fingers at me.

"Ahem… yeah. I was thinking about the first days of us. Of our relationship." I smiled, honestly telling them what was on my mind.

"Mmm… I've been thinking about those days, too." Sarah purred with a playful coquettish tone.

"Hmm…" Vicky slanted her body toward me as she bit her lower lip. She seemed to be caught in memories of that time too.

"I want to prove that I am the husband you both deserve. And hopefully, one day, be the father our children deserve. Truth is… I love you both. I can't… can't live in a world without my beauties." My voice was soft in that dominant tone as I confessed.

"Aw, Master. We love you too." Sarah leaned over, placing her hand on my shoulder.

"So, you don't hate me?" I questioned; my eyes started to joyfully tear up.

"We don't like you… right now…" Vicky's face scrunched into a mean look, but her eyes still seemed warm.

I couldn't tell if I should accept defeat or what. Was I getting through to Vicky or not? That face was sending me mixed signals. I think I should leave, for now. There seemed to be an opening for reconciling. So, maybe try again later at another time. Let things cool off a little while longer, Sergeant.

"I see; I will take my leave. I will try—"

"Shut up, you fool! We forgave you days ago." Vicky shook her head before she smiled brightly at me.

I looked at her, stunned at what she had said. She continued before I could get a word in edgewise.

"We had decided together that we wanted you to come here. Come to us on your own. Apologize like a mature adult. Prove that the man we fell in love with was still in there." Vicky said in that dark vixen voice; the smile on her face seemed wicked.

"But... you just said... that you both didn't like me." I was puzzled at what was happening.

"Like and dislike are temporary emotions. Love and hate are permanent commitments. We don't have to like you in the moment to love you." Vicky's voice softened to a low, vulnerable tone.

"What Vicky is so rudely saying, Master, is that you never lost us. We were always yours." Sarah's emeralds stared into my soul. She pulled her hand down from my shoulder.

"Okay... so now what?" I asked, elation ringing in my voice. They were always my girlfriends. I hadn't screwed up nearly as badly as I had thought.

"Now, you be a good man. As you said, be the husband we deserve." Vicky's body relaxed, and her demeanor became endearing. Her sapphires gazed into my eyes with admiration.

"In that case. I have something I need to do." My NCO voice rang through the street. I decided that this was the proper time. I smiled as I took a knee.

Vicky's eyes widened as her head followed my movements. Sarah gasped before placing her hand over her mouth. My smile widened; they were the women for me. And I was going to love them... love them as they deserved to be loved.

"You have both been in my heart since I met you. Sarah the tender and Vicky the harsh. Light and dark, you both complete me." My hand pulled the ring boxes from my coat pocket. Holding them both in one hand was hard, but I managed to do it.

273

"I love you both with all that I am. So…" My free hand pulled the tops of the ring boxes open. I could see the sparkle of the diamonds reflected in their eyes. I felt relieved that the shine of those gems had returned.

"Will you—both of you—marry me?" I peered up at them, my eyes roaming over them. My heart waited with anticipation at their response. Excitement, joy, and even fear coursed through me. A beamish trepidation of sorts. Were they going to say "yes"?

I watched as tears started running down their cheeks. An uncontainable merriment filled both of their faces. They looked so beautiful at that moment. The glow of their happiness radiantly shattered into a spectrum of blissful nirvana. The world felt the warmth of their elation. And I was humbled by the very stature of this divine warmth.

Vicky wiped the tears from her eyes. Sarah's hand fell from her face. Smiles… they both were smiling. Smiles so beatific that they melted into the core of my being.

"Yes!" In unison, they shouted with glee.

My heart was filled to the brim with love. I began to place the rings on their fingers. Sarah, first, her face filled with the softness of an angel. Vicky, second, smirked at me; a bit of the devilish brat inside her was pushing through the happiness.

"I'm not calling you Master. Not for a while, anyway. Not until you earn it back. Prove to me that the honorable and loyal man is still there." Vicky sighed, almost as if it had disappointed her to strip me of the title.

"Yes, ma'am," I said, my eyes filled with joy. I was okay with her not calling me Master… so long as she called me hers.

"You will always be my Master." Sarah beamed at me. "Always Master, always."

The Sun's warm glow on my skin felt like a new beginning. I stood promptly, my eyes studying my fiancés. The burning feeling of love seared into my soul. They had said yes. I felt my heart return; I loved them so much. They were mine, and I was theirs. I didn't care about all the weird things that surrounded them. I would figure that out in time. For now, we were together… happily together.

"I love you both, my beauties." In my dominant tone, my words were ethereally written into the air around Vicky and Sarah, surrounding them with my affection.

"I love you too, Master," Sarah said. She tackled my left side, crashing into an embrace. Her soothing tenderness tranquilly wrapped around me.

"I love you too, Kyle," Vicky whispered. She passionately leaned against my right side, cuddling into me. Her serene harshness enveloped me in an elevated enlightenment.

I leaned further into them, my arms folded around them in a loving embrace. My body was neatly between them, a testament to how we fit together in tendresse. My devotion to them reverently caressed my fiancées. Pulling both nearer to me, I locked them in with my lips. Sipping in their individual and unique essences, I kissed my beauties one after the other.

First, I felt the tenderness of my angel, Sarah. Our mouths danced to the hymns of a seraphim blessing, forever blissful in each other's caress.

Then I turned to my infernal devil, Vicky, feeding from her flames. Our tongues skirmished in our eternal war, never to retreat from each other.

After our kisses broke, I stared at them. I felt complete with them. I gazed with awe into their eyes. Vicky's sapphires and Sarah's emeralds both captured my soul. Each had a piece of it. And I knew that I had a piece of theirs as well.

We once were three separate souls lost in the abyssal realm. But now we are something else. Three souls who found one another. Three souls traversing our shared destiny, starting a life together. Daring, against all odds, to love one another as an unconventional trio.

They were happy, and so was I. We were in love; nothing could break that. And we were finally engaged to be married. My mind contemplated what fate had in store for our love.

What new adventures would our relationship traverse? What would the future reveal for the trinity of our souls?

For now, these questions were just the beginning.

www.ingramcontent.com/pod-product-compliance
Lightning Source LLC
Chambersburg PA
CBHW052032240626
47153CB00006B/2054